THE POWER OF FIVE: BOOK FOUR

NECROPOLIS

Anthony Horowitz

GALAXY

PLUS

First published in 2008 by Walker Books Ltd
This Large Print edition published by
BBC Audiobooks by arrangement with
Walker Books Ltd 2010
Based on an idea first published in 1989 as
The Day of the Dragon

ISBN: 978 1405 664097

British Library Cataloguing in Publication Data available

Printed and bound in Great Britain by
CPI Antony Rowe, Chippenham and Eastbourne

For Nicholas

CONTENTS

NIGHTRISE CORPORATION

STRICTLY CONFIDENTIAL
Memorandum from the Chairman's Office:
October 15

We are about to take power.

Four months ago, on June 25, the gate built into the Nazca Desert opened and the Old Ones finally returned to the world that once they ruled. They are with us now, waiting for the command to reveal themselves and to begin a war which, this time, they cannot lose.

Why has that command not been given?

The triumph of Nazca was tainted by the presence of two children, teenaged boys. One has already become familiar to us . . . indeed, we had been watching him for much of his life. His name, or the name by which he is now known, is Matthew Freeman. He is fifteen and English. The other was a Peruvian street urchin who calls himself Pedro and who grew up in the slums of Lima. Between them, they were responsible for the death of our friend and colleague, Diego Salamanda. Incredibly, too, they wounded the King of the Old Ones even at the moment of his victory.

These are not ordinary children. They are two of the so-called Gatekeepers who were part of the great battle, more than ten thousand years ago, when the Old Ones were defeated and banished. It is absolutely crucial this time, if our plans are to succeed and a new world is to be created, that we understand the nature of the Five.

1. Ten thousand years ago, five children led the last survivors of humanity against the Old Ones. The battle took place in Great Britain, but at a time when the country was not yet an island, before the ice sheets had melted in the north.

2. By cunning, by a trick, the children won and the Old Ones were banished. Two gates were constructed to keep them out: one in Yorkshire, in the north of England, the other in Peru. One gate held. The other we managed to smash.

3. The Five existed then. The Five are here now. It is as if they have been reborn on the other side of time . . . but it is not quite as simple as that. They are the *same* children, somehow living in two different ages.

4. Kill one of the children now and he or she will be 'replaced' by one of the children from the past. This is the single, crucial fact that makes them so dangerous an enemy. Killing them is almost no use at all. If we want to control them, they have to be taken alive.

5. Alone, these children are weak and can be beaten. Their powers are unpredictable and not fully in their control. But when they come together, they become stronger. This is the great danger for us. If all five of

them join forces at any time, anywhere in the world, they may be able to create a third gate and everything we have worked for will be lost.

The fifth of the Five

So far only four of the children have been identified. The English boy and the Peruvian boy have now been joined by American twin brothers, Scott and Jamie Tyler, who were revealed to us by our Psi project. At the time, they were working in a theatre in Nevada.

Note that Scott Tyler was thoroughly programmed whilst held captive by our agents in Nevada, USA. Although he was subsequently reunited with his twin brother, it is still possible that he can be turned against his friends. A psychological report (appendix 1) is attached.

We know very little about the fifth of the Five. She is a girl. Like the others, she will be fifteen years old. We expect her to be of Chinese heritage, quite probably still living in the East. In the old world, her name was Scar. It is certain that the other four will be searching for her and we have to face the fact that they may succeed.

We must therefore find her first.

We have agents in every country searching for her. Many politicians and police forces are now working actively for us. The Psi project continues throughout Europe and Asia and we are still investigating teenagers with possible psychic/paranormal abilities. There is every chance that the girl will reveal herself to us. It is likely that she still has no idea who and what she really is.

Once we have the girl in our hands, we can use her to draw the rest of them into a trap. One at a time, we will bring them to The Necropolis. And once we have all five of them, we can hold them separately, imprison them, torture them and keep them alive until the end of time.

Everything is now set. The Gatekeepers have no idea how strong we are, how far we have advanced. Our eyes are everywhere, all around the world, and very soon the battle will begin.

We just have to find the girl.

Ia sakkath. Iak sakkakh. Ia sha xul.

ROAD SENSE

The girl didn't look before crossing the road.

That was what the driver said later. She didn't look left or right. She'd seen a friend on the opposite pavement and she simply walked across to join him, not noticing that the lights had turned green, forgetting that this was always a busy junction and that this was four o'clock in the afternoon when people were trying to get their work finished, hurrying on their way home. The girl just set off without thinking. She didn't so much as glimpse the white van heading towards her at fifty miles an hour.

But that was typical of Scarlett Adams. She always was a bit of a dreamer, the sort of person who'd act first and then think about what she'd done only when it was far too late. The hockey ball that she had tried to thwack over the school roof, but which had instead gone straight through the headmistress's window. The groundsman she had pushed, fully clothed, into the swimming pool. It might have been a good idea to check first that he could swim. The twenty-metre tree she'd climbed up, only to realize that there was no possible way back down.

Fortunately, her school made allowances. It helped that Scarlett was generally popular, was liked by most of the teachers and even if she was never top of the class, managed to be never too near the bottom. Where she really excelled was at sports. She was captain of the hockey team (despite the occasional misfires), a strong tennis

5

player and an all-round winner when it came to summer athletics. No school will give too much trouble to someone who brings home the trophies and Scarlett was responsible for a whole clutch of them.

The school was called St Genevieve's and from the outside it could have been a stately home or perhaps a private hospital for the very rich. It stood in its own grounds, set back from the road, with ivy growing up the walls, sash windows and a bell tower perched on top of the roof. The uniform, it was generally agreed, was the most hideous in England: a mauve dress, a yellow jersey and, in summer months, a straw hat. Everyone hated the straw hats. In fact it was a tradition for every girl to set the wretched thing on fire on their last day.

St Genevieve's was a private school, one of many that were clustered together in the centre of Dulwich, in South London. It was a strange part of the world and everyone who lived there knew it. To the west there was Streatham and to the east Sydenham, both areas with high-rise flats, drugs and knife crime. But in Dulwich, everything was green. There were old-fashioned tea shops, the sort that spelled themselves 'shoppes', and flower baskets hanging off the lampposts. Most of the cars seemed to be four-by-fours and the mothers who drove them were all on first-name terms. Dulwich College, Dulwich Preparatory School, Alleyn's, St Genevieve's . . . they were only a stone's throw away from each other, but of course nobody threw stones at each other. Not in this part of town.

It was obvious from her appearance that

Scarlett hadn't been born in England. Her parents might be Mr and Mrs Typical-Dulwich—her mother tall, blonde and elegant, her father looking like the lawyer he always had been, with greying hair, a round face and glasses—but she looked nothing like them. Scarlett had long black hair, strange hazel-green eyes and the soft brown skin of a girl born in China, Hong Kong or some other part of Central Asia. She was slim and small with a dazzling smile that had got her out of trouble on many occasions. She wasn't their real daughter. Everyone knew that. She had known it herself from the earliest age.

She had been adopted. Paul and Vanessa Adams were unable to have children of their own and they had found her in an orphanage in Jakarta. Nobody knew how she had got there. The identity of her birth mother was a mystery. Scarlett tried not to think about her past, where she had come from, but she often wondered what would have happened if the couple who had come all the way from London had chosen the baby in cot seven or nine rather than cot eight. Might she have ended up planting rice somewhere in Indonesia or sewing Nike trainers in some city sweatshop? It was enough to make her shudder . . . the thought alone.

Instead of which, she found herself living with her parents in a quiet street, just round the corner from North Dulwich station which was in turn about a fifteen-minute walk from her school. Her father, Paul Adams, specialized in international business law. Her mother, Vanessa, ran a holiday company that put together packages in China and the Far East. The two of them were so busy that

7

they seldom had time for Scarlett—or indeed, for each other. From the time Scarlett had been five, they had employed a full-time housekeeper to look after all of them. Christina Murdoch was short, dark-haired and seemed to have no sense of humour at all. She had come to London from Glasgow and her father was a vicar. Apart from that, Scarlett knew little about her. The two of them got on well enough, but they had both agreed without actually saying it that they were never going to be friends.

One of the good things about living in Dulwich was that Scarlett did have plenty of friends and they all lived very nearby. There were two girls from her class in the same street and there was also a boy—Aidan Ravitch—just five minutes away. It was Aidan who had prompted her to cross the road.

Aidan was in his second year at The Hall, yet another local private school, and had come to London from Los Angeles. He was tall for his age and good-looking in a relaxed, awkward sort of way, with shaggy hair and slightly crumpled features. There was no uniform at his school and he wore the same hoodie, jeans and trainers day in day out. Aidan didn't understand the English. He claimed to be completely mystified by such things as football, tea and *Dr Who*. English policemen in particular baffled him. 'Why do they have to wear those stupid hats?' He was Scarlett's closest friend, although both of them knew that Aidan's father worked for an American bank and could be transferred back home any day. Meanwhile, they spent as much time together as they could.

The accident happened on a warm, summer

afternoon. Scarlett was thirteen at the time.

It was a little after four and Scarlett was on her way home from school. The very fact that she was allowed to walk home on her own meant a lot to her. It was only on her last birthday that her parents had finally relented . . . until then, they had insisted that Mrs Murdoch should meet her at the school gates every day, even though there were far younger girls who were allowed to face the perils of Dulwich High Street without an armed escort. She had never been quite sure what they were so worried about. There was no chance of her getting lost. Her route took her past a flower shop, an organic grocer's and a pub—The Crown and Greyhound—where she might spot a few old men, sitting in the sun with their lemonade shandies. There were no drug dealers, no child snatchers or crazed killers in the immediate area. And she was hardly on her own anyway. From half past three onwards, the streets were crowded with boys and girls streaming in every direction, on their way home.

She had reached the traffic lights on the other side of the village—where five roads met with shops on one side, a primary school on the other— when she noticed him. Aidan was on his own, listening to music. She could see the familiar white wires trailing down from his ears. He saw her, smiled, and called out her name. Without thinking, she began to walk towards him.

The van was being driven by a twenty-five-year-old delivery man called Michael Logue. He would have to give all his details to the police later on. He was delivering spare parts to a sewing machine factory in Bickley and, thanks to the London traffic, he was late. He was almost certainly speeding as he approached the junction. But on the other hand, the lights were definitely green.

Scarlett was about half-way across when she saw him and by that time it was far too late. She saw Aidan's eyes widen in shock and that made her turn her head, wanting to know what it was that he had seen. She froze. The van was almost on top of her. She could see the driver, staring at her from behind the wheel, his face filled with horror, knowing what was about to happen, unable to do anything about it. The van seemed to be getting bigger and bigger as it drew closer. Even as she watched, it completely filled her vision.

And then everything happened at once.

Aidan shouted out. The driver frantically spun the wheel. The van tilted. And Scarlett found herself being thrown forward, out of the way, as something—or someone—smashed into her back with incredible force. She wanted to cry out but her breath caught in her throat and her knees buckled underneath her. Somewhere in her mind she was aware that a passer-by had leapt off the pavement and that he was trying to save her. His arm was around her waist, his shoulder and head pressed into the small of her back. But how had he managed to get to her so fast? Even if he had seen the van coming and sprinted towards her immediately, he surely wouldn't have reached her in time. He seemed to know what was going to happen almost before it did.

The van shot past, missing her by inches. She actually felt the warm breeze slap her face and smelled the petrol fumes. There had been two books in her hand: a French dictionary and a maths exercise book . . . an hour and a half's homework for the evening ahead. As she was carried forward, her hand and arm jerked, out of control, and the books were hurled into the air, landing on the road and sliding across the tarmac as if she had deliberately thrown them away. Scarlett followed them. With the man still grabbing hold of her, she came crashing down. There was a moment of sharp pain as she hit the ground and all the skin was taken off one knee. Behind her, there was the screech of tyres, a blast of a horn and then the ominous sound of metal hitting metal. A car alarm went off. Scarlett lay still.

For what felt like a whole minute, nobody did anything. It was as if someone had taken a photograph and framed it with a sign reading ACCIDENT IN DULWICH. Then Scarlett sat up and twisted round. The man who had saved her was lying stretched out in the road and she was only aware that he was Chinese, in his twenties, with black hair, and that he was wearing jeans and a loose-fitting jacket. She looked past him. The white van had swerved round a traffic island, mounted the pavement and smashed into a car parked in front of the primary school. It was this car's alarm that had gone off. The driver of the van was slumped over the wheel, his head covered in broken glass.

She turned back. A crowd had already formed— perhaps it had been there from the start—and people were hurrying towards her, rushing past Aidan, who seemed to be rooted to the spot. He was shaking his head as if denying that he had been to blame. There were twenty or thirty school kids, some of them already taking photographs

11

with their mobile phones. A policeman had appeared so quickly that he could have popped out of a trapdoor in the pavement. He was the first to reach Scarlett.

'Are you all right? Don't try to move . . .'

Scarlett ignored him. She put out a hand for support and eased herself back onto her feet. Her knee was on fire and her shoulder felt as if it had been beaten with an iron club, but she was already fairly sure that she hadn't been seriously hurt.

She looked at Aidan, then at the white van. A few people were already helping the driver out, laying him on the pavement. Steam was rising out of the crumpled bonnet. Next to her, the policeman was speaking urgently into his shoulder mike, doing all the stuff with Delta Bravo Oscar Charlie, summoning help.

Finally, Aidan made it over to her. 'Scarl . . .?' That was his name for her. 'Are you OK?'

She nodded, suddenly tearful without knowing why. Maybe it was just the shock, the knowledge of what could have been. She wiped her face with the back of her hand, noticing that her nails were grimy and all her knuckles were grazed. Her dress was torn. She realized she must look a wreck.

'You were nearly killed . . .!' Why was Aidan telling her that? She had more or less worked it out for herself.

Even so, his words reminded her of the man who had saved her. She looked down and was surprised to see that he was no longer there. For a moment she thought that it was a conjuring trick, that he had simply vanished into thin air. Then she saw him, already on the far side of the road—the side that she had been heading towards—hurrying

12

past the shops. He reached a hair salon on the corner, where a woman with hair that was too blonde to be true had just come out. He pushed past her and then he was gone.

Why? He hadn't even stayed long enough to be thanked.

After that, things unravelled more slowly. An ambulance arrived and although Scarlett didn't need it, the van driver had to be put on a stretcher and carried away. Scarlett herself was examined but nothing was broken and in the end she was allowed to go home. Aidan went with her. A WPC accompanied them both. Scarlett wondered how that would go down with Mrs Murdoch. Somehow she knew it wasn't going to mean laughter and back-slapping at bedtime.

In fact, the accident had several consequences.

Paul and Vanessa Adams were told what had happened when they got home that night and as soon as they had got over the shock, the knowledge of how close they had come to losing their only child, they began to argue about whose fault it was: their own for allowing Scarlett too much freedom, Aidan for distracting her, or Scarlett for showing so little road sense, even at the age of thirteen. In the end, they decided that in future Mrs Murdoch would take up her old position at the school gates. It would be another nine months before Scarlett was allowed to walk home on her own again.

The identity of the man who had saved her remained a mystery. Where had he come from? How had he seen what was about to happen? Why had he been in such a hurry to get away? Mrs Murdoch decided that he must be an illegal

13

immigrant, that he had taken off at the sight of the approaching policeman. For her part, Scarlett was just sorry that she hadn't been able to thank him. And if he was in some sort of trouble, she would have liked to have helped him.

That was the night she had her first dream.

Scarlett had never been one for vivid dreams. Normally she got home, ate, did her homework, spent forty minutes on her PlayStation 3 and then plunged into a deep, empty sleep that would be ended all too quickly by Mrs Murdoch, shaking her awake for the start of another school day. But this dream was more than vivid. It was so realistic, so detailed that it was almost like being inside a film. And there was something else that was strange about it. As far as she could see, it had no connection to her life or to anything that had happened during the day.

She dreamed that she was in a grey-lit world that might be another planet . . . the moon perhaps. In the distance, she could see a vast ocean stretching out to the horizon and beyond— but there were no waves. The surface of the water could have been a single sheet of metal. Everything was dead. She was surrounded by sand-dunes—at least, that was what she thought they were, but they were actually made of dust. They had somehow blown there and—like the dust on the moon—it would stay the same forever. She walked forward. But she left no footprints.

There were four boys standing together, a short distance away.

The boys were searching for her. If she listened carefully, she could actually hear them calling her name. She tried to call back, but although there

14

was no wind, not even a breeze, something snatched the words away.

The boys weren't real. They couldn't be . . . Scarlett had never seen them before. And yet somehow she was sure that she knew their names.

Scott. Jamie. Pedro. And Matt.

She knew them from somewhere. They had met before.

That was the first time, but over the next two years she had the same dream again and again. And gradually, it began to change. It seemed to her that every time she saw the boys, they were a little further away until finally she had to get used to the fact that she was completely on her own. Every time she went to sleep, she found herself hoping she would see them. More than that. She needed to meet them.

She never spoke about her dreams, not even to Aidan. But somewhere in the back of her mind she knew that finding the four boys had become the single most important thing in her life.

THE DOOR

Two years later, Scarlett had turned fifteen—and she had become an orphan for a second time.

Paul and Vanessa Adams hadn't died but their marriage had, one inch at a time. In a way, it was amazing they had stayed together so long. Scarlett's father had just started a new job, working for a multi-national corporation based in Hong Kong. Meanwhile, her mother was spending more and more time with her own business, looking after customers who seemed to demand her attention twenty-four hours a day. They were seeing less and less of each other and suddenly realized that they preferred it that way. They didn't argue or shout at each other. They just decided they would be happier apart.

They told Scarlett the news at the end of the summer holidays and for her part she wasn't quite sure what to feel. But the truth was that in the short term it would make little difference to her life. Most of the time she was on her own with Mrs Murdoch anyway and although she'd always been glad to see her parents, she'd got used to the fact that they were seldom, if ever, around. The three of them had one last meeting in the kitchen, the two adults sitting with grim faces and large glasses of wine.

'Your mother is going to set up a company in Melbourne, in Australia,' Paul said. 'She has to go where the market is and Melbourne is a wonderful opportunity.' He glanced at Vanessa and in that moment Scarlett knew that he wasn't telling the whole truth. Maybe the Australians were desperate for exotic holidays. But the fact was that she had chosen somewhere as far away as possible. Maybe she had met someone else. Whatever the reason, she wanted to carve herself a whole new life. 'As for me, Nightrise have asked me to move to the Hong Kong office . . .'

The Nightrise Corporation. That was the company that employed her dad.

'I know this is very difficult for you, Scarly,' he went on. 'Two such huge changes. But we both want to look after you. You can come with either of us.'

16

In fact, it wasn't difficult for Scarlett. She had already thought about it and made up her mind. 'Why can't I stay here?' she asked.

'On your own?'

'Mrs Murdoch will look after me. You're not going to sell the house, are you? This is my home! Anyway, I don't want to leave St Genevieve's. And all my friends are here . . .'

Of course, both her parents protested. They wanted Scarlett to come with them. How could she possibly manage without them? But all of them knew that it was actually the best, the easiest solution. Mrs Murdoch had been with the family for ten years and probably knew Scarlett as well as anyone. In a way, they couldn't have been happier if they had suggested it themselves. It might not be conventional but it was clearly for the best.

And so it was agreed. A few weeks later, Vanessa left, hugging Scarlett and promising that the two of them would see each other again very soon. And yet, somehow, Scarlett wondered just how likely that would be. She had always tried to be close to Vanessa, recognizing at the same time that they had almost nothing in common. They weren't a real mother and daughter and so—as far as Scarlett was concerned—this wasn't a real divorce.

Paul Adams left for Hong Kong shortly afterwards and suddenly Scarlett found herself in a new phase of life, virtually on her own. But, as she had expected, it wasn't so very different from what she had always been used to. Mrs Murdoch was still there, cooking, cleaning and making sure she was ready for school. Her father telephoned her regularly to check up on her. Vanessa sent long e-mails. Her teachers—who had been warned what had happened—kept a close eye on her. She was surprised how quickly she got used to things.

She was happy. She had plenty of friends and Aidan was still around. The two of them saw more of each other than ever, going shopping together, listening to music, taking Aidan's dog—a black retriever—out on Dulwich Common. She was allowed to walk home from school on her own again. In fact, as if to recognize her new status, she found herself being given a whole lot more freedom. At weekends, she went into town to the cinema. She stayed overnight with other girls from her class. She had been given a big part in the Christmas play, which meant late afternoon rehearsals and hours in the evening learning her lines. It all helped to fill the time and to make her think that her life wasn't so very unusual after all.

Everything changed one day in November. That was when Miss Chaplin announced her great Blitz project—a visit to London's East End.

Joan Chaplin was the art teacher at St Genevieve's and she was famous for being younger, friendlier and more easygoing than any of the dinosaurs in the staff room. She was always finding new ways to interest the girls, organizing coach trips to exhibitions and events all over London. One class had gone to see the giant crack built into the floor of the Tate Modern. For another it had been a shark suspended in a tank, an installation by the artist, Damien Hirst. Weeks later, they had still been arguing whether it was serious art or just a dead fish.

As part of their GCSE history coursework, a lot of the girls were studying the Blitz, the bombing of

London by the Germans during the Second World War. Miss Chaplin had decided that they should take an artistic as well as a historical interest in what had happened.

'I want you to capture the spirit of the Blitz,' she explained. 'What's the point of studying it if you don't feel it too?' She paused as if waiting for someone to argue, then went on. 'You can use photography, painting, collage or even clay modelling if you like. But I want you to give me an idea of what it might have been like to live in London during the winter of 1940.'

There was a mutter of agreement around the class. Walking around London had to be more fun than reading about it in books. Scarlett was particularly pleased. History and art had become two of her favourite subjects and she saw that here was an opportunity to do them both at the same time.

'Next Monday, we're going to Shoreditch,' Miss Chaplin went on. 'It was an area of London that was very heavily bombed. We'll visit many of the streets, trying to imagine what it was like and we'll look at some of the buildings that survived.'

She glanced outside. The art room was on the ground floor, at the back of the school, with a view over the garden, sloping down with flower-beds at the bottom and three tennis courts beyond. It was Friday and it was raining. The rain was sheeting down and the grass was sodden. It had been like that for three days.

'Of course,' she went on. 'The trip won't be possible if the weather doesn't cheer up—and I have to warn you that the forecast hasn't been too promising. But maybe we'll be lucky. Either way, remember to bring a permission slip from your parents.' Then she had a sudden thought and smiled. 'What do you think, Scarlett?'

It had become a sort of joke at St Genevieve's.

Scarlett Adams always seemed to know what the weather was going to do. Nobody could remember when it had first started but everyone agreed—you could tell how the day was going to be simply by the way Scarlett dressed. If she forgot her scarf, it would be warm. If she brought in an umbrella, it would rain. After a bit, people began to ask her opinion. If there was an important tennis match or a picnic planned by the river, have a word with Scarlett. If there was any chance of a cross-country run being called off, she would know.

Of course, she wasn't always right. But it seemed she could be relied upon about ninety per cent of the time.

Now she looked out of the window. It was horrible outside. The clouds, grey and unbroken, were smothering the sky. She could see raindrops chasing each other across the glass. 'It'll be fine,' she said. 'It'll clear up after the weekend.'

Miss Chaplin nodded. 'I do hope you're right.'

She was. It rained all day Sunday and it was still drizzling on Sunday night. But Monday morning, when Scarlett woke up, the sky was blue. Even Mrs Murdoch was whistling as she put together the packed lunch requested by the school. It was as if a last burst of summer had decided to put in a surprise appearance.

The coach came to the school at midday. The lesson—combining art and history—was actually going to take place over two periods plus lunch and, allowing for the traffic, the girls wouldn't be back until the end of school. As they pulled out of St Genevieve's, Miss Chaplin talked over the intercom, explaining what they were going to do.

'We'll be stopping for lunch at St Paul's Cathedral,' she said. 'It was very much part of the spirit of the Blitz because, despite all the bombing, it was not destroyed. The coach will then take us to Shoreditch and we're going to walk around the area. It's still a bit wet underfoot so I want us to go indoors and the place I've chosen is St Meredith's, in Moore Street. It's one of the oldest churches in London. In fact there was a chapel there as long ago as the thirteenth century.'

'Why are we visiting a church?' one of the girls asked.

'Because it also played an important part in the war. A lot of local people used to hide there during the bombing. They actually believed it had the power to protect them . . . that they'd be safe there.'

She paused. The coach had reached the River Thames, crossing over Blackfriars Bridge. Scarlett looked out of the window. The water was flowing very quickly after all the rain. In the distance, she could just make out part of the London Eye, the silver framework glinting in the sunlight. The sight of it made her sad. She had ridden on it with her parents, at the end of the summer. It had been one of the last things the three of them had done while they were still a family.

'. . . actually took a direct hit on October 2, 1940.' Miss Chaplin was still talking about St Meredith's. Scarlett had allowed her thoughts to wander and she'd missed half of what the teacher had said. 'It wasn't destroyed, but it was badly damaged. Bring your sketch books with you and we can work in there. We have permission and you can go anywhere you like. See if you can feel the atmosphere. Imagine what it was like, being there with the bombs going off all around.'

Miss Chaplin flicked off the microphone and sat down again, next to the driver.

Scarlett was a few rows behind her, sitting next to a girl called Amanda, who was one of her closest friends and who lived in the same road as her. She noticed that Amanda was frowning.

'What is it?' she asked.

'St Meredith's,' Amanda said.

'What about it?'

It took Amanda a few moments to remember. 'There was a murder there. About six months ago.'

'You're not being serious.'

'I am.'

If it had been anyone else, Scarlett might not have believed them. But she knew that Amanda had a special interest in murder. She loved reading Agatha Christie and she was always watching whodunnits on TV. 'So who got murdered?' she asked.

'I can't remember,' Amanda said. 'It was some guy. A librarian, I think. He was stabbed.'

Scarlett wasn't sure it sounded very likely and when the coach stopped off at St Paul's, she went over to Miss Chaplin. To her surprise, the teacher didn't even hesitate. 'Oh yes,' she said cheerfully. 'There was an incident there this summer. A man was attacked by a down-and-out. I'm not sure the police ever caught anyone, but it all happened a long time ago. It doesn't bother you, does it, Scarlett?'

22

'No,' Scarlett said. 'Of course not.'

But that wasn't quite true. It did secretly worry her, even if she wasn't sure why. She had a sense of foreboding which only grew worse the closer they got to the church.

The art teacher had chosen this part of London for a reason. It was a patchwork of old and new, with great gaps where whole buildings and perhaps even streets had been taken out by the Germans. Most of the shops were shabby and depressing, with plastic signs and dirty windows full of products which people might need but which they couldn't possibly want: vacuum cleaners, dog food, one hundred items at less than a pound. There was an ugly car park towering high over the buildings, but it was hard to imagine anyone stopping here. The traffic rumbled past in four lanes, anxious to be on its way.

But even so there were a few clues as to what the area might once have been like. A cobbled alleyway, a gas lamp, a red telephone box, a house with pillars and iron railings. The London of seventy years ago. That was what Miss Chaplin had brought them all to find.

They turned into Moore Street. It was a dead end, narrow and full of puddles and pot-holes. A pub stood on one side, opposite a launderette that had shut down. St Meredith's was at the bottom, a solid, red-brick church that looked far too big to have been built in this part of town. The war damage was obvious at once. The steeple had been added quite recently. It wasn't even the same colour as the rest of the building and didn't quite match the huge oak doors or the windows with their heavy stone frames.

23

Scarlett felt even more uneasy once they were inside. She jumped as the door boomed shut behind her, cutting out the London traffic, much of the light—indeed, any sense that they were in a modern city at all. The interior of the church stretched into the distance to the silver cross, high up on the altar, caught in a single shaft of dusty light. Otherwise, the stained glass windows held the sun back, the different colours blurring together. Hundreds of candles flickered uselessly in iron holders. She could make out little side-chapels, built into the walls. Even without remembering the murder that had happened there, St Meredith's didn't strike her as a particularly holy place. It was simply creepy.

But nobody else seemed to share her feelings. The other girls had taken out their sketch books and were sitting in the pews, chatting to each other and drawing what they had seen outside. Miss Chaplin was examining the pulpit—a carving of an eagle. Presumably, most Londoners chose not to pray at two o'clock in the afternoon. They had the place to themselves.

Scarlett looked for Amanda, but her friend was talking to another girl on the other side of the transept so she sat down on her own and opened her pad. She needed to put the murder out of her mind. Instead, she thought about the men and women who had sheltered here during the Blitz. Had they really believed that St Meredith's had some sort of magical power to avoid being hit, that they would be safer here than in a cellar or a Tube station? She thought about them sitting there with their fingers crossed while the Luftwaffe roared overhead. Maybe that was what she would draw.

She shivered. She was wearing a coat but it was very cold inside the church. In fact it felt colder inside than out. A movement caught her eye. A line of candles had flickered, all the flames bending together, caught in a sudden breeze. Had someone just come in? No. The door was still shut. Nobody could have opened or closed it without being heard.

A boy walked past. At first, Scarlett barely registered him. He was in the shadows at the side of the church, between the columns and the side-chapels, moving towards the altar. He made absolutely no sound. Even his feet against the marble floor were silent. He could have been floating. She turned to follow him as he went and just for a second his face was illuminated by a naked bulb, hanging on a wire.

She knew him.

For a moment, she was confused as she tried to think where she had seen him before. And then suddenly she remembered. It was crazy. It couldn't be possible. But at the same time there could be no doubt.

It was the boy from her dreams, one of the four she had seen walking together in that grey desert. She even knew his name.

It was Matt.

In a normal dream, Scarlett wouldn't see people's faces—or if she did, she would forget them when she woke up. But she had experienced this dream again and again over a period of two years. She'd learned to recognize Matt and the others almost as soon as she was asleep and that was why she knew him now. Short, dark hair. Broad shoulders. Pale skin and eyes that were an

25

intense blue. He was about her age although there was something about him that seemed older. Maybe it was just the way he walked, the sense of purpose. He walked like someone in trouble.

What was he doing here? How had he even got in? Scarlett turned to a girl who was sitting close to her, drawing a major explosion from the look of the scribble on her pad.

'Did you see him?' she asked.

'Who?'

'That boy who just went past.'

The other girl looked around her. 'What boy?'

Scarlett turned back. The boy had disappeared from sight. For a moment, she was thrown. Had she imagined him? But then she saw him again, some distance away. He had stopped in front of a door. He seemed to hesitate, then turned the handle and went through. The door closed behind him.

She followed him. She had made the decision without even thinking about it. She just put down her sketch book, got up and went after him. It was when she reached the door that she asked herself what she was doing, chasing after someone she had never met, someone who might not even exist. Suppose she ran into him? What was she going to say? 'Hi, I'm Scarlett and I've been dreaming about you. Fancy a Big Mac?' He'd think she was mad.

The door he had passed through was in the outer wall underneath a stained glass window that was so dark and grimy that the picture was lost. Scarlett guessed it must lead out into the street, perhaps into the cemetery if the church had one. There was something strange about it. The door was very small, out of proportion with the rest of St Meredith's. There was a symbol carved into the wooden surface: a five-pointed star.

She hesitated. The girls weren't supposed to leave the church. On the other hand, she wouldn't exactly be going far. If there was no sign of the boy on the other side, she could simply come back in again. The door had an iron ring for a handle. She turned it and went through.

To her surprise, she didn't find herself outside in the street. Instead, she was standing in a wide, brightly lit corridor. There were flaming torches slanting out of iron brackets set in the walls, the fire leaping up towards the ceiling which was high and vaulted. The corridor had no decoration of any kind and it seemed both old and new at the same time, the plasterwork crumbling to reveal the brickwork underneath. It had to be some sort of cloister—somewhere the priests went to be on their own. But the corridor was nothing like the rest of St Meredith's. It was a different colour. It was the wrong size and shape.

It was also very cold. The temperature seemed to have fallen dramatically. As she breathed out, Scarlett saw white mist in front of her face. It was as if she were standing inside a fridge. She had to remind herself that this was the first week of November. It felt like the middle of winter. She rubbed her arms, fighting off the biting cold.

There was a man, sitting in a wooden chair opposite her, facing the door. She hadn't noticed him at first because he was in shadow, between two of the torches. He was dressed like a monk with a long, dirty brown habit that went all the way down to his bare feet. He was wearing sandals, and a hood over his head. He was slumped forward with his face towards the floor. Scarlett had already decided to turn round and go back the way she had come, but before she could move, he suddenly looked up. The hood fell back. She gasped.

He was one of the ugliest men she had ever seen. He was completely bald, the skin stretched over a skull that was utterly white and dead. His head was the wrong shape—narrow, with part of it caved in on one side, like an egg that has been hit with a spoon. His eyes were black and sunken and he had horrible teeth which revealed themselves as he smiled at her, his thin lips sliding back like a knife wound. What had he been doing, sitting there? She looked left and right but they were on their own. The boy called Matt—if it had even been him—had gone.

The man spoke. The words cracked in his throat and Scarlett didn't understand any of them. He could have been speaking Russian or Polish . . . whatever it was, it wasn't English. She backed away towards the door.

'I'm very sorry,' she said. 'I think I've come the wrong way.'

She turned round and scrambled for the handle. But she never made it. The monk had moved very quickly. She felt his hands grab hold of her shoulders and drag her backwards, away from the door. He was very strong. His fingers dug into her like steel pincers.

'Let go!' she shouted.

His arm sneaked over her shoulder and around her throat. He was holding her with incredible force. She could feel the bone, cutting into her windpipe, blocking the air supply. And he was screaming out more words that she couldn't understand, his voice high-pitched and animal. Another monk appeared at the end of the corridor. Scarlett didn't really see him. She was just aware of him rushing towards them, the long robes flapping.

Still she fought back. She reached with both hands, clawing for the monk's eyes. She kicked back with one foot, then tried to elbow him in his stomach. But she couldn't reach him. And then the second monk threw himself onto her.

The next thing she knew, she was on her back, her arms stretched out above her head. Her legs had been knocked out from underneath her. The two men had grabbed hold of her and there was nothing she could do. She twisted and writhed, her hair falling over her face. The monks just laughed.

Scarlett felt her heels bumping over the stone cold floor as the two men dragged her away.

FATHER GREGORY

The cell was tiny—less than ten metres square—and there was nothing in it at all, not even a chair or a bench. The walls were brick with a few traces of flaking paint, suggesting they might have been decorated at some time. The door had been fashioned out of three slabs of wood, fastened together with metal bands. There was a single window, barred and set high up so that even for someone taller than Scarlett, there wouldn't be any chance of a view. From where she was sitting, slumped miserably on the stone floor, she could just make out a narrow strip of sky. But even that was enough to send a shiver down her spine.

It was dark. Not quite night, but very nearly. She realized that it would be pitch black in the cell in just a couple of hours as they hadn't left her a candle or an electric light. But how was that possible? It had been around two o'clock when she had entered St Meredith's and the sun had been shining. Suddenly it was early evening. So what had happened to the time in between?

Scarlett was shivering—and not just because of the shock of what she had been through. It was freezing in the cell. There was no glass in the window and no heating. The bare brickwork only made it worse. Fortunately she had been wearing her winter coat when she set off on the school trip and she drew it around her, trying to bury herself in its folds. She had never been so cold. She could actually feel the bones in her arms and legs. They were so hard and brittle that she thought they might shatter at any time.

Desperately, she tried to work out what had happened. For no reason that she could even begin to imagine, a man she had never met had grabbed her and thrown her into a cell. Could she have strayed into a secret wing of St Meredith's, somewhere that no one was meant to go? The single strip of sky told her otherwise. That and the freezing weather. She remembered that the monk had spoken in a foreign language.

She was no longer in London.

It seemed crazy but she had to accept it. Maybe she had blacked out at the moment she had been seized. Maybe they had drugged her and she had been unconscious without even knowing it.

Everything told her that this wasn't England. Somehow she had been spirited away.

With a spurt of anger, she scrambled to her feet and went over to the door. She wasn't just going to sit here and wait for them to come back. Suppose they never did come back? She might die in this place. But she quickly saw that there was no way through the door—not unless it was unlocked from the other side. It was massive and solid, with a single keyhole built for an antique key. She tried to squint through it but there was nothing to see. She straightened up, then hammered her fists against the wood.

'Hey! Come back! Let me out of here!'

But nobody came. She wasn't even sure if her voice could be heard outside the cell.

That left the window. Could she possibly climb up, using the rough edges of the brickwork to support herself? Scarlett tried but her fingertips couldn't get enough grip, and anyway the bars at the top were too close to squeeze through, even assuming she could drop down on the other side. No. She was in a solid box with no trapdoors, no secret passages, no magic way out. She would just have to stay here until somebody came.

She sank back into a corner, trying to preserve what little body warmth she had left by curling herself into a ball. The strange thing was, she should have been terrified. She was completely helpless, a prisoner. This was an evil place. But she still couldn't accept the reality of what had happened to her and because of that it was difficult to feel scared. This was all like some bad dream. Once she had worked out how she had got here, then maybe she could start worrying about

31

what was going to happen next.

An hour passed, or maybe two. Finally there was a rattle of a key in the lock, the door swung open again and two monks came into the cell. Scarlett couldn't say if they were the ones who had grabbed her in the corridor as all these people were dressed the same way. Their hoods were up and they were skeleton-thin. Even if you stood them up against a wall, it would have been difficult to tell them apart.

One of them barked out a command in the strange, harsh language she had heard before and when he saw that she didn't understand, made a rough gesture, telling her to stand up. Scarlett did as she was instructed. Her face gave nothing away but she was already thinking. If they took her out of here, maybe she would be able to break away. She would run back down the corridor and find the nearest exit. Whatever country she was in, there would have to be a policeman or someone else around. She would make herself understood, somehow find her way home.

But right now, the two monks were watching her too closely. They led her out with one standing next to her and the other directly behind, so close that she could actually smell them. Neither man had washed, not for a long time. As they reached the corridor, Scarlett hesitated and felt a hand pushing her roughly forward. She turned left. The three of them set off together.

Where was she? The place had the feel of an old palace or a monastery, but one thing was certain— it had been abandoned long ago. Everything about it was broken down and neglected, from the peeling walls to the paved floor, which was slanting and uneven with some sort of mould growing through the cracks. Naked light bulbs hung on single wires (so at least there was electricity) but they were dull and flickering, barely able to light the way. The air was damp and there was a faint smell of sewage.

Scarlett noticed an oil painting in a gilt frame. It showed a crucifixion scene, but the colours were faded, the canvas torn. An antique cabinet with two iron candlesticks stood beneath it, one door open and papers scattered on the floor. The three of them turned a corner and for the first time she was able to see outside. A series of arches led onto a terrace with a garden beyond. Scarlett stopped dead. Her worst fears had been realized. She knew now that she definitely wasn't in England.

The garden was covered in snow. There were trees with no leaves, their branches heavy with the stuff. The ground was also buried and, in the distance, barely visible in the darkness, she could see white-topped mountains. There were no other buildings, no lights showing anywhere. The monastery was in some sort of wilderness—but how had she got here? Had she been knocked out and put on a plane? Scarlett searched back in her memory but there was nothing there . . . nothing to indicate a journey, leaving England or arriving anywhere else. Then one of the monks jabbed her in the back and she was forced to start moving again.

They came to a hallway, lit by a huge chandelier, not electric but jammed with rows of candles, at least a hundred of them, the wax dripping slowly down and congealing into a series of growths that reminded Scarlett of the sort of shapes she had once seen in a cave. Some of it had

33

splattered onto a round table beneath. An empty bottle lay on its side along with dirty plates and glasses, mouldering pieces of bread. There had been a dinner here—days, maybe weeks before. There were no rats or cockroaches. It was too cold.

Several doors led out of the hallway. The two monks led her to the nearest of them. One of them opened it. The other pushed her inside. He had hurt her and Scarlett spun round and swore at him. The monk just smiled and backed away. The other man went with him. The door closed.

She turned back and examined her new surroundings. This was the only half-way comfortable room she had seen so far. It was furnished with a rug on the floor, two armchairs, bookshelves and a desk. It was warmer too. A coal fire was burning in a grate and although the flames were low she could feel the heat it was giving out and smell it in the air. More paintings hung on the walls, also with religious subjects. There was a window, but it had become too dark to see outside.

A man was sitting behind the desk. He also wore a habit, but his was black. So far he had said nothing but his eyes were fixed on Scarlett and, with an uneasy feeling, she walked over to him. He was the oldest man she had seen—at least twenty years older than the others, with the same bald head and sunken eyes. There were tufts of white hair around his ears and he had thick white eyebrows that could have been glued in place. His nose was long and too thin for his face. His fingers, spread out across the surface of the desk, were the same. He was watching Scarlett intensely, and as she drew closer she saw that there was a growth—a sty—sitting on one of his eyes. The whole socket was red and dripping. It was as if, like the rest of the building, he was rotting away. Scarlett shuddered and felt sick.

The man still hadn't spoken. Scarlett drew level with him so that the desk was between them. Despite everything, she had decided that she wasn't going to let him intimidate her. 'Who are you?' she demanded. 'Where am I? Why have you brought me here?'

His eyes widened in surprise. At least, one of them did. The diseased eye had long since lost any movement. 'You are English?' he said.

Scarlett was taken by surprise. She hadn't expected him to speak her language. 'Yes,' she said.

'Please. Sit down . . .' He gestured at one of the chairs. 'Would you like a hot drink? Some tea should be arriving soon.'

Scarlett shook her head. 'I don't want any tea,' she snapped. 'I want to go back where I came from. Why are you keeping me here?'

'I asked you to sit down,' the monk said. 'I would suggest that you do as you are told.'

He hadn't raised his voice. He didn't even sound threatening. But somehow Scarlett knew it would be a mistake to disobey him. She could see it in his eyes. The pupils were black and dead and slightly unfocused. They were the sort of eyes that might belong to someone who was mad.

She sat down.

'That's better,' he said. 'Now, let's introduce ourselves. What is your name?'

'I'm Scarlett Adams.'

'Scarlett Adams.' He repeated it with a sort of satisfaction, as if that was what he had expected to

35

hear. 'Where are you from?'

'I live in Dulwich. In London. Please, will you tell me where I am?'

He lifted a single finger. The nail was yellow and bent out of shape. 'I will tell you everything you wish to know,' he said. His English was perfect although it was obvious that it wasn't his first language. He had an accent that Scarlett couldn't place and he strung his words together very carefully, like a craftsman making a necklace. 'But first tell me this,' he went on. 'You really have no idea how you came here?'

'No.' Scarlett shook her head. 'I was in a church.'

'In London?'

'Yes. I went through a door. One of the people here grabbed hold of me. That's all I can remember.'

He nodded slowly. His eyes had never left her and Scarlett felt a terrible urge to look away, as if somehow he was going to swallow her up.

'You are in Ukraine,' the man said, suddenly.

'Ukraine?' Everything seemed to spin for a minute. 'But that's . . .'

It was somewhere in Russia. It was on the other side of the world.

'This is the Monastery of the Cry for Mercy. I am Father Gregory.' He looked at his guest a little sadly, as if he was disappointed that she didn't understand. 'Your coming here is a great miracle,' he said. 'We have been waiting for you for almost twenty years.'

'That's not possible. What do you mean? I haven't been alive for twenty years.' Scarlett was getting tired of this. She was feeling sick with

36

exhaustion, with confusion. 'How come you speak English?' she asked. She knew it was a stupid question but she needed a simple answer. She wanted to hear something that actually made sense.

'I have travelled all over the world,' Father Gregory replied. 'I spent six years in your country, in a seminary near the city of Bath.'

'Why did you say you've been waiting for me? What do you mean?'

The door suddenly opened and one of the monks came in, carrying a bronze tray with two glasses of tea. Scarlett guessed that Father Gregory must have ordered it before she was brought in because there was no obvious method of communication in the office, no telephone or computer, nothing modern apart from a desk lamp throwing out a pool of yellow light. The monk set down the tray and left.

'Help yourself,' Father Gregory said.

Scarlett did as she was told. The liquid was boiling hot and burned her fingers as she lifted the glass. She took a sip. The tea tasted herbal and it was heavily sugared, so sweet that it stuck to her lips. She set it down again.

'I will tell you my story because it pleases me to do so,' Father Gregory said. 'Because I sometimes wondered if this day would ever come. That you are sitting here now, in this place, is more than a miracle. My whole life has been leading to this moment. It is perhaps the very reason why I was meant to live.'

Scarlett didn't interrupt him. The more he talked, the more passionate he became. She could see the coal fire reflected in his eyes, but even if the fire hadn't been there, there might still have been the same glow.

'I was born sixty-two years ago in Moscow, which was then the capital of the Soviet Union. My father was a politician, but from my earliest age, I knew that I wanted to enter the Church. Why? I did not like the world into which I had been born. Even when I was at school, I found the other children spiteful and stupid. I was small for my age and often bullied. I never found it easy to make friends. I did not much like my parents either. They didn't understand me. They didn't even try.

'I was nineteen when I told my father that I wanted to take holy orders. He was horrified. I was his only son and he had always assumed that I would go into politics, like him. He tried to talk me out of it. He arranged for me to travel around the world, hoping that if I saw all the riches that the West had to offer, it would change my mind.

'In fact, it did the exact opposite. Everything I saw in Europe and America disgusted me. Wealthy families with huge homes and expensive cars, living just a mile away from children who were dying because they could not afford medicine. Countries at war, the people killing and maiming each other because of politicians too stupid to find another way. The noise of modern life; the planes and the cars, the concrete smothering the land. The pollution and the garbage. The people, in their millions, scurrying on their way to jobs they hated . . .'

Scarlett shrugged. 'So you weren't happy,' she said. 'What's that got to do with me?'

'It has everything to do with you and if you interrupt me again I will have you whipped until the skin peels off your back.'

Father Gregory paused. Scarlett was completely shocked but didn't want to show it. She said nothing.

'I entered a seminary in England,' he continued, 'and trained to become a monk. I spent six years there, then another three in Tuscany before finally I came here. That was thirty years ago. This was a very beautiful and very restful place when I first arrived, a refuge from the rest of the world. The weather was harsh and, in the winter, the days were short. But the way of life suited me. Prayer six times a day, simple meals and silence while we ate. We cultivated all our food ourselves. I have spent many hundreds of hours hacking at the barren soil that surrounds us. When I wasn't in the fields, I was helping in the local villages, tending to the poor and the sick.

'A holy life, Scarlett. And so it might have remained. But then everything changed. And all because of a door in a wall.'

Father Gregory hadn't touched his tea, but suddenly he picked up his glass between his finger and thumb and tipped the scalding liquid back. Scarlett saw his throat bulge. It was like watching a sick man take his medicine.

'It puzzled me from the start. A door that seemed to belong to a different building with a strange device—a five-pointed star—that had nothing to do with this place. A door that went nowhere.' He lifted a hand to stop her interrupting. 'It went nowhere, child. Believe me. There was a brief corridor on the other side and then a blank wall.

'The monastery was then run by an abbot who

39

was much older than me. His name was Father Janek. And one day, walking in the cloisters, I asked him about it.

'He wouldn't tell me. A simple lie might have ended my curiosity, but Father Janek was too good a man to lie. Instead, he told me not to ask any more questions. He quickened his pace and as he walked away, I saw that he was afraid.

'From that day on, I became fascinated by the door. We had an extensive library here, Scarlett, with more than ten thousand books—although most of them have now mouldered away. Some of them were centuries old. I searched through them. It took me many years. But slowly—a sentence here, a fragment there—a story began to emerge. But in the end, it was one book, a secret copy of a diary written by a Spanish monk in 1532 that told me everything I wanted to know.'

He stopped and ran his eyes over the girl as if she were the most precious thing he had ever seen. Scarlett was revolted and didn't try to hide it. The eyes underneath the white eyebrows were devouring her. She could see saliva on the old man's lips.

'The Old Ones,' he whispered, and although Scarlett had never heard those words before, they meant something to her; some memory from the far distant past. 'The diary told me about the great battle that had taken place ten thousand years ago when the Old Ones ruled the world and mankind were their slaves. Pure evil. The Bible talks of devils . . . of Lucifer and Satan. But that's just story-telling. The Old Ones were real. They were here. And the one who ruled over them, Chaos, was more powerful than anything in the universe.'

'So what happened to them?' Scarlett asked. Her voice had almost dropped to a whisper. Apart from the flames, twisting in the hearth, everything in the room was still.

'They were defeated and cast out. There were five children . . .' he spoke the word with contempt. 'They came to be known as the Gatekeepers. Four boys and a girl.' He levelled his eyes on Scarlett and she knew what he was going to say next. 'You are the girl.'

Scarlett shook her head. 'You're wrong. That's insane. I'm not anything. I'm just a schoolgirl. I go to school in London . . .'

'How do you think you got here?' The monk pointed in the direction of the corridor with a single trembling finger. Some sort of liquid was leaking out of his damaged eye, a single tear. 'You have seen the monastery and the snow. You know you are not in London now.'

'You drugged me.'

'You came through the door! It was all there in the diary. There were twenty-five doorways built all around the world. They were there for the Gatekeepers so that when the time came, they would be able to travel great distances in seconds. Only the Gatekeepers could use them. Nobody else. When I pass through the door, I find myself in a corridor, a dead end. But it's not the same for you. It brought you here.'

Scarlett shook her head. Nothing she had heard made any sense at all. She didn't even know where to begin. 'I'm not ten thousand years old,' she said. 'Look at me! You can see for yourself. I'm fifteen!'

'You have lived twice, at two different times.' He laughed delightedly. 'It's beyond belief,' he

41

said. 'Finally to meet one of the Gatekeepers after all these years and to find that she has no idea who or what she is.'

'You mentioned there was an abbot here,' Scarlett said. 'I want to talk to him.'

'Father Janek is dead.' He sighed. 'I haven't told you the rest of my story. Maybe then you will understand.' He nodded at her glass. 'You haven't drunk your tea.'

'I don't want it.'

'I would take what you are given while you still can, child. There is much pain for you ahead.'

Scarlett's tea was right in front of her. Briefly, she thought about picking it up and flinging it in his face. But it wouldn't do much good. It was probably lukewarm by now.

'The discovery of the diary, along with all the other fragments, changed my life,' the monk continued. 'I began to think about the reasons why I had come to the monastery in the first place. Did I really think that religion—prayer and fasting— would help me change the world? Or was I just using religion to hide from it? Suddenly I knew what had brought me here. Hatred. I hated the world. I hated mankind. And praying to God to save us was ridiculous. God isn't interested! If He was, don't you think He'd have done something centuries ago?

'My whole life had been devoted to an illusion. All those prayers, the same words repeated again and again. Did they really make any sense? Of course not! The cries for mercy that would never come. Kneeling and making signs, singing hymns while, outside in the street, people were killing each other and trying to make as much money as they could to spend on themselves and to hell with everyone else. Do you never read the papers? What do you see in them except for murder and lust and greed, all day, every day? Do you not see the nature of the world in which you live?

'There is no God, Scarlett. I know that now. But there *are* the Old Ones. They are our natural masters. They deserve to rule the world because the world is evil and so are they.'

He paused for breath. Scarlett looked at him with a mixture of pity and disgust. She had already decided that this wasn't about God or about religion. It was about a man who had nothing inside him. The years had hollowed out Father Gregory until there was nothing left.

'I will finish my story and then you must be taken back to your cell,' he said. 'You will not be staying with us very long, Scarlett. You have a long journey to make. You will not return.'

Scarlett said nothing. She knew that he was trying to frighten her. She also knew that he was succeeding. A long journey . . . where? And how would they take her there? Would they force her through another door?

Father Gregory closed his eyes for a few seconds, then continued.

'When I came here, there were twenty-four brothers at the Monastery of the Cry for Mercy,' he explained. 'Some of them, I knew, felt the same as me. They were disillusioned. Their life was hard. There were no rewards. The local people, the ones they were helping, weren't even grateful. Gradually, I began to sound them out. I shared with them the knowledge I had discovered. How many of them would abandon their religion and

43

turn instead to the Old Ones? In the end, there were seven of us. Seven out of twenty-four. Ready to begin a new adventure.

'We could of course have left. But I already knew that was out of the question. We were here for a reason, and that reason was the door. It had been here long before the monastery existed. Indeed, why was the monastery built in this place at all? It was because the architects knew that the door was in some way magical even if they had forgotten what its true purpose was. Do you see, child? The monastery was built *around* the door just as you will find holy places connected to the other doors all over the world: churches, temples, burial sites, caves.

'The seven of us agreed that we would stay here and serve the Old Ones. We would guard the door and should a child ever pass through it, we would know that we had found one of the Gatekeepers and we would seize hold of them just as we have taken hold of you . . .'

'What happened to Father Janek and the other monks?' Scarlett asked, although she wasn't sure she wanted to know.

'I killed Father Janek,' the monk replied. 'I crept into his room while he slept and cut his throat. Then we continued around the monastery and did the same to all the others. Seventeen men died that night and in the morning the corridors were awash with blood. But don't mourn for them. They would have died happily. They would think they were going to Heaven, into the embrace of their God.

'We have been here ever since. Of course, with so few of us, the monastery has fallen into disrepair. Once, the villagers brought us food because they revered us. Now they give it to us because they are afraid. We have survived a very long time, always waiting, always watching the door. Because we knew that you would come. And recently we realized that our time had come. We were expecting you.'

'How?'

'Because the Old Ones have returned to the world. Even now, they are gathering strength, waiting to take back what was always theirs. Their agents have contacted us. Very soon, we will hand you over to them. And then we will have our reward.'

'What will happen to me?'

'The Old Ones will not kill you. You don't need to be afraid. But they will need to keep you close to them and you still must pay for what you did to them so many years ago.'

'I didn't do anything. I don't know what you're talking about . . .'

He nodded his head sadly. 'A great pity,' he murmured. 'I had expected more of you. A warrior or a great magician. But you really are nothing. A little girl, as you said, from school. Maybe the Old Ones will let me torture you for a while before you go. I would like that very much. To pay you for the disappointment. We will see . . .'

He stood up and went over to the door. He walked with a limp and it occurred to Scarlett that as well as the diseased eye, he might have a withered leg. It took him a while even to cross the room and she briefly wondered if she might be able to overpower him. But it wouldn't have done any good. When he opened the door, the two

45

monks who had brought her there were waiting on the other side.

'They will take you back to your cell,' he said. 'They will also bring you food and water. I imagine you will be with us a few days.'

Scarlett stood up and walked past him. There was nothing else she could do. For a brief moment, the two of them stood shoulder to shoulder in the doorway. Father Gregory reached out and stroked her hair. Scarlett shuddered. She didn't even try to hide her revulsion.

'Goodbye, Scarlett,' he said. 'You have no idea how glad I am that we have met.'

Scarlett let the two monks walk her away. She didn't look back.

DRAGON'S BREATH

They took Scarlett back to the same cell she had occupied—but they had been busy while she was away. Someone had carried in a bed, although the moment she saw it she knew she wasn't going to be allowed the privilege of a comfortable sleep. It was little more than a cot with sagging springs and a metal frame and she wouldn't even be able to stretch out without her feet going over the end. There were just two coarse blankets to protect her from the chill of the night and no pillow.

They had also supplied her with a table, a chair and a bucket which she guessed she would be expected to use as a toilet, although she didn't even want to think about that. A candle in a glass lantern now lit the room and they had provided her with a meagre dinner. A bowl of thin, vegetable soup, a hunk of bread and a mug were waiting on the table. There was a spoon to eat with—and if Scarlett had any thought of using it as a weapon, her hopes were soon dashed. It was flimsy, made of tin. They hadn't bothered with a knife or a fork.

She didn't feel like eating yet. If anything, the sight of the starvation rations brought home the full horror of her situation. These people were utterly merciless. They wanted her to live but they didn't care how miserable or painful her life became—they had made that much clear. Scarlett sat down on the bed and sank her head into her hands. She thought she was going to cry, but the tears didn't come. The Old Ones. The Gatekeepers. The twenty-five doors around the world. Everything that Father Gregory had said seemed to spin round and round her, sucking her ever further into a tunnel of misery and despair. How could this have happened to her? Could any of it really be true?

Somehow, she forced herself to go over it, to unpick the words. Much of what Father Gregory had said sounded completely insane. But at the same time, she had to admit that a lot of it was strangely familiar. There were echoes. There had been strange incidents in her life and they had taken place long before she walked through the church door.

The dreams, for one. Father Gregory had mentioned five children—four boys and a girl. Scarlett had been dreaming exactly the same thing for almost two years. And how had this all started? She had actually seen Matt, in St Meredith's. He had been the one who had led her through the door, although now she wondered if he had really been there at all. He had been silent, ghost-like. It wasn't that she had imagined him. But perhaps what she had experienced was some sort of vision. If he had really gone through the door, wouldn't he be here now?

And then there was the door itself. Scarlett had tried to persuade herself that she had been drugged and kidnapped, but the more she thought about it, the more she accepted that it hadn't happened that way. Father Gregory had told her the truth. She had gone through a door in London and ended up in Ukraine. There had been no flight, no drugs. And if she accepted that, what choice did she have but to accept the rest?

She went over to the table and examined the food. It looked far from appetizing, but she made herself swallow it, the soup cold and greasy, the bread several days old. It was all she was going to get and she needed her strength. The candle in the lamp was only an inch tall and she wondered how long it would last. When it went out, she would be left in total blackness. The thought made her shudder. There was already so much to be afraid of but being on her own, locked up in the dark was somehow worse than any of it.

It would be better if she could sleep. She didn't undress. It was far too cold to even think of taking off her coat. She climbed onto the bed and pulled the two blankets over her, burrowing into them like an animal in a cave. She lay like that for a long time and when sleep did finally come she didn't even notice it. She only knew that she was no longer awake when she realized that she had begun to dream.

She was back in the strange, airless world that she had visited many times. She recognized it and she was glad to be there. She was desperate to see Matt and the other three boys. If anyone could help her, they could. At least they might show her a way to break out.

But there was no sign of them. While part of her slept, alone in her cell, the other part was stranded here, alone on the edge of a grim and lifeless sea.

Something in the dreamworld had changed. Scarlett became aware of it very slowly, not seeing anything but sensing it, a sort of throbbing in the air that was coming from very far away, from the other side of the horizon. She heard a faint rumble of thunder and saw a tiny streak of lightning, like a hairline crack in the fabric of the world. Her head was pounding. She noticed the water, the surface of the ocean, begin to shiver. A gust of wind tugged at her hair. The sand, or the grey dust, or whatever it was, spun in eddies around her feet, then leapt up, half blinding her and stinging her cheeks. She backed away, knowing that she needed to hide. She still didn't know what she was hiding from.

And then, in a single moment, the ocean split open. It was as if it had been sliced in half by some vast, invisible knife—and the black water rushed in, millions of gallons pouring from left and right into the chasm—a mile long—that had been formed. At the same time, something rose up, twisting towards the surface. At first, she thought it was a snake, some sort of monstrous sea serpent that had been resting for centuries on the ocean bed and had only now woken up. She smelled its breath—how was that possible . . . how could you smell anything in a dream?—and cried out as it rushed towards her, its eyes blazing, flames exploding around its mouth. It was a dragon! Straight out of ancient folklore. And yet it was horribly real, howling so loudly that she thought her head would burst.

SIGNAL ONE

The two words had appeared in front of her. They were written in neon: huge red letters hanging from some sort of frame, the light so intense that they burned her eyes. Where had they come from? They must have risen out of the ground because only a moment before the landscape had been empty. The neon buzzed and flickered as some sort of electric power coursed through it. Scarlett looked down at her hands and saw that they were blood red, reflecting the light. It was as if she were on fire.

SIGNAL ONE . . . SIGNAL ONE . . .

It flashed on and off. The dragon was there one minute, then gone the next, lost in the darkness, reappearing in the light. But each time she saw it, it was a little closer. The wind was blasting her. If it got any stronger, it would throw her off her feet. She tried to run but she couldn't move. The dragon opened its mouth, showing teeth like kitchen knives.

And that was when she woke up and found herself still lying on top of the bed and covered by the two blankets, but with the first, dreary light of the morning creeping in through the window and ice cold all around.

Scarlett sat up. She was already beginning to shiver. What had that all been about? Signal One? She had never seen the two words written down before. She had no idea what they meant, even if she was certain that they must be important. They had been shown to her for a reason.

She looked up at the window and guessed that it must be about five or six o'clock in the morning. It was difficult to say without her watch. Presumably the monks would bring her some sort of breakfast. They had made it clear that they needed to keep her alive. Could she somehow overpower them when they came in, fight her way through the door and make a run for it? She doubted it. The monks were thin and malnourished but they were still a lot stronger than her. If only she had a weapon! That would make all the difference.

Sitting on the edge of the bed, she searched through her pockets. All she had was a blunt pencil, left over from art class, a comb and an Oyster card. The sight of it made her sad. It was so ordinary, a reminder of everything she had left behind. How many thousands of miles was she now from London buses and Tube trains?

There was nothing she could use. She considered taking off her coat, throwing it in the face of whoever carried in her food. But it was a stupid plan. She still didn't know there was going to be any food and anyway, it wouldn't work. They would just laugh at her before they took her away and whipped her or whatever else they planned to do.

There had to be a way out of the cell. Scarlett got up and examined the door a second time, running her hands over the hasps, pressing against it with all her weight. It was so solid it might as well have been cemented into the wall. That just left the window. There were three bars and no glass. The cell had been built to house a man, not a child—and certainly not a girl. Might it be possible to squeeze through after all?

She hadn't been able to reach the window before but maybe these monks, as clever as they might be, had made a mistake. They had supplied her with a table and a chair. Quickly, she dragged the table over to the window, put the chair on top and climbed up.

For the first time, she was able to look outside. There was a view down a hill, the ground steep and rugged, thick patches of snow piled up against black rocks. A few buildings stood in the near distance, scattered around. They looked like barns and abandoned farm houses which might belong to the monastery but which were more likely part of a village, just out of sight. A series of icicles hung above her, suspended from a guttering that ran the full length of the building. She had forgotten how cold it was but she was quickly reminded by a sudden snow flurry, blowing in off the roof. Her lips and cheeks were already numb. It had to be less than zero out there.

There was no way down. The bars were too close together and even if she had managed to slip through, she was at least twenty metres above the ground. Try to jump from this height and she would break both her legs.

She was still in the cell two hours later when the door opened and they finally brought her something to eat.

Breakfast was a bowl of cold porridge and a tin

mug of water, carried in by a monk she hadn't yet met—for his face certainly wasn't one that she would have forgotten. It was horribly burned. One whole side of it was dead and disfigured as if he had fallen asleep with his head resting on an oven. Scarlett turned her eyes away from him. Was there anyone at Cry for Mercy who hadn't rotted over the past twenty years? A second monk stood with him, guarding the door.

'You . . . eat . . . little . . . girl.' Burnt Face was proud of his English but his accent was so thick she could barely make out the words.

He set the tray down, and Scarlett moved towards him. Her hands were clasped behind her back and she was clearly on the edge of tears. 'Please,' she said. 'Please let me out . . .' Her voice was trembling.

The sight of the girl, pale and bleary-eyed after the long night, seemed to amuse him. 'Out?' He sneered at her. 'No out . . .'

'But you don't understand . . .' She was closer to him now and as he straightened up she brought her hands round and lashed out.

She was holding an icicle.

She had broken it off the guttering and she was holding it like a knife. The point was needle sharp. Using all her strength, she drove it into the flesh between his shoulder and his neck. The monk screamed. Blood gushed out. He fell to his knees, as if in prayer.

Scarlett was already moving. She knew that she had to take advantage of the surprise, that speed was all she had on her side. The second monk had frozen, completely shocked by what had just happened. Before he could react, she threw herself at him, head and shoulders down, like a bull. She hit him hard in the stomach and heard the breath explode out of him. His hands grabbed for her but then he was down, writhing on the floor. She pulled away and began to run.

According to Father Gregory, there were just seven monks in the Monastery of the Cry for Mercy and she had just taken out two of them. How long would it be before the ones that remained set off after her? Scarlett had to find the door that had brought her here. She knew where it was—a short way down the corridor, only a minute from the cell. With a bit of luck, she would be gone before they knew what had happened.

It was only when she had taken twenty paces that she knew she had gone wrong. Somehow she had managed to get lost. She was in another long corridor and it was one that she didn't recognize. There was a picture of some holy person hanging crookedly on the wall. An ornate wooden chest. Another passageway with a flight of stone steps leading down. For a moment they looked tempting. They might lead her out of the monastery. But at the same time, she knew they would take her further away from the door. The door was the fast way back to St Meredith's. She had to find it.

In the distance, a bell began to ring. Not a call to prayers. An alarm. She heard shouting. The second of the two monks—the one she had hit—must have recovered. Forcing herself not to panic, she continued forward even though she knew she was heading in the wrong direction and that the further she went, the more lost she would become. She heard flapping ahead of her, the sound of sandals hitting the stone floor and a moment later another monk appeared. He saw her and cried out. There was an opening to one side. She took it, passing between wood-panelled walls and a great tapestry, hanging in shreds, the fabric mouldering away.

The passage emerged in a second corridor and with a surge or relief she realized that she knew where she was. Somehow she had found her way back. There was the table with the candlesticks, the painting of the crucifixion. The door was just beyond. There was nobody in the way.

The noise of the sandals. If the monk had been barefooted, Scarlett might not have heard him. But even without looking round, she knew that someone had caught up with her, that he was running towards her even now. In a single movement she reached out, grabbed a heavy, iron candlestick and swung it round. She'd timed it exactly right. The end of the candlestick smashed into the side of the monk's bald head, knocking him out. Scarlett hit him a second time, just to be sure, then dropped the candlestick and made for the door.

Someone appeared at the far end of the corridor.

It was Father Gregory. He saw Scarlett and screamed something—maybe in English, maybe in his own language. The words were trapped in his throat. The door was now between the two of them, exactly half-way. Scarlett wondered if she could reach it. Father Gregory was dancing on his feet as if he had just been electrocuted. His good eye was wide and staring, making the other one look all the more diseased. Scarlett was about thirty metres away, panting, gathering all her strength for one last effort.

The two of them set off at the same moment.

In a way it was weird. Scarlett wasn't running away. She was actually hurtling towards the one man she most wanted to avoid. But she had to reach the door before he did. She had made her decision. It was the only way home.

Father Gregory was surprisingly fast. His limp had disappeared and he moved with incredible speed, his fury propelling him forward. Scarlett didn't dare look at him. She was aware of him getting closer and closer but her eyes were fixed on the door. There it was in front of her. She lunged forward and grabbed hold of the handle, but at the same moment his hands fell on her, seizing hold of the top of her coat, his fingers against her neck. She heard him cry out in triumph. His breath was against her skin.

She didn't let go of the door. She wasn't going to let him drag her back. Instead, she dropped down, twisting her shoulders so that the coat was pulled over her head. She had already undone the buttons and she felt it come loose, falling away. Father Gregory lost his balance and, still holding the coat, fell backwards. Scarlett was free. She jerked the door open and threw herself forward. For a few seconds her vision was blurred. The doorway seemed to rush past. She heard Gregory screaming at her, suddenly a long way away.

The door slammed shut behind her.

She was lying, sobbing and shaking on the floor of St Meredith's. And there was a man standing in front of her, a young policeman, dressed in blue, staring at her with a look of complete

56

bewilderment.

'Who are you?' he demanded.

'I'm . . . Scarlett Adams.' She could barely get the words out.

'Where have you been? What have you been doing?' The policeman shook his head in disbelief. 'You'd better come with me!'

FRONT PAGE NEWS

Scarlett had only been missing for eighteen hours but she was a fifteen-year-old student on a school trip in the middle of London, and her disappearance had been enough to trigger a major panic with newspaper headlines, TV bulletins and a nationwide search. Both her parents had been informed at once and Paul Adams was already on a plane, on his way back from Hong Kong. He was actually in mid-air when Scarlett was found.

Scarlett had begun to realize that she was in trouble almost from the moment she found herself back in St Meredith's, sitting opposite the policeman who had immediately launched into a series of questions.

'Where have you been?' he began.

Scarlett was still in shock, thinking about her narrow escape from Father Gregory. She pointed at the door with a trembling finger. 'There . . .'

'What do you mean?' The policeman was young and out of his depth. He had already radioed for backup and an ambulance was on the way. Even so, he was the first on the scene. There might even be a promotion in this. He took out a notebook and prepared to write down anything Scarlett said.

'The monastery.' Scarlett muttered. 'I was in the monastery.'

'And what monastery was that?'

'On the other side of the door.'

The policeman walked over to the door and opened it before Scarlett realized what he was going to do. At the last minute, she screamed at him, a single word.

'Don't!'

She had visions of Father Gregory flying in, dragging her back to her cell. She was sure the nightmare was about to begin all over again. But the policeman was just standing there, scratching his head. There was no monastery on the other side of the door, no monks—just an alleyway, a brick wall, a line of rubbish bins. It was drizzling—grey, London weather. Scarlett looked past him. She couldn't quite believe what she was seeing.

And that was when she knew that she was going to have to start lying. How could she explain where she had been and what had really happened to her? Magic doors? Psycho monks in Ukraine? People would think she was mad. Worse than that, they might decide that the whole thing had been a schoolgirl prank. She would be expelled from St Genevieve's. Her father would kill her. She had to come up with an answer that made sense.

The next forty-eight hours were a nightmare almost as bad as the one she had left behind. More policemen and paramedics arrived and suddenly the church was crowded with people all asking questions and arguing amongst themselves. Scarlett didn't seem to be hurt but even so she was wrapped in a blanket and whisked off to hospital.

Somehow, the press had already found out that she was back. The street was jammed with photographers and journalists threatening to mob her as she was bundled into the ambulance and there were more of them waiting when she was helped out on the other side. All Scarlett could do was keep her head down, ignore the flashes of the cameras and wish that this whole thing would be over soon.

Mrs Murdoch had been called to the hospital and stayed with Scarlett as she was examined by a doctor and a nurse. The housekeeper was looking shell-shocked. It was obvious that nothing like this had ever happened to her before. The doctor took Scarlett's pulse and heart rate and then asked her to strip down to her underwear.

'Where did you get these?' He had noted a series of scratches running down her back.

'I don't know . . .' Scarlett guessed that she had been hurt in her final confrontation with Father Gregory but she wasn't going to talk about that now. She was pretending that she was too dazed to explain anything.

'How about this, Scarlett?' The nurse had found blood on her school jersey. 'Is this your blood?'

'I don't think so.'

The jersey was placed in a bag to be handed over to the police for forensic examination. It occurred to Scarlett that they would be unable to find a match for it . . . not unless their database extended all the way to Ukraine.

Finally, Scarlett was allowed to take a shower and was given new clothes to wear. Two policewomen had arrived to interview her. Mrs Murdoch stayed with her and just for once Scarlett was glad to have her around. She wouldn't have wanted to go through all this on her own.

'Do you remember what happened to you from the time of your disappearance? Perhaps you'd like to start when you arrived at the church . . .'

The policewomen were both in their thirties, kind but severe. The rumour was already circulating that Scarlett had never been in any danger at all and that this whole thing was a colossal waste of police time. By now, Scarlett had worked out what she was going to say. She knew that it would sound pretty lame. But it would just have to do.

'I don't remember anything,' she said. 'I wasn't feeling well in the church. I was dizzy. So I went outside to get some fresh air—and after that, everything is blank. I think I fell over. I don't know . . .'

'You fainted?'

'I think so. I want to help you. But I just don't know . . .'

The two policewomen looked doubtful. They had been on the force long enough to know when someone was lying and it was obvious to them that Scarlett was hiding something. But there wasn't much they could do. They asked her the same questions over and over again and received exactly the same answers. She had fallen ill. She had fainted. She couldn't remember anything else. And what other explanation could there be?

The interview ended when Paul Adams appeared. A taxi had brought him straight from Heathrow Airport and he burst into the room, his suit crumpled, his face a mixture of anxiety, relief and irritation, all three of them compounded by a generous dose of jet lag.

'Scarly!' He went over and hugged his daughter.

'Hello, Dad.'

'I can't believe they've found you. Are you hurt? Where have you been?' The two policewomen exchanged a glance. Paul Adams turned to them. 'If you don't mind, I'd like to take my daughter home. Mrs Murdoch . . .'

They left the hospital by a back exit, avoiding the press pack who were still camped out at the front. By now, Scarlett was exhausted. She had been found mid-morning, but it was early evening before she was released. She was desperate to go to bed and once she got there, she slept through the entire night. Maybe that was just as well. She would need all her strength for the headlines that were waiting for her the next day.

MISSING SCHOOLGIRL FOUND AFTER JUST ONE DAY

POLICE ASK—WAS THIS A PRANK?

Mystery still surrounds the return of fifteen-year-old schoolgirl, Scarlett Adams, who was discovered by police, just one day after she went missing on a school trip. Scarlett was feared abducted after she vanished during a visit to St Meredith's church in East London, prompting a national search. She was later found unhurt inside the church itself.

Although she received hospital treatment for minor scratches, there was no indication that she had been assaulted or kept against her will.
So far, the girl—described as 'bright and sensible' by the teachers at the £15,000-a-year private school that she attends in Dulwich—has been unable to offer any explanation, claiming that she is suffering from memory loss.
Her father, Paul Adams, a corporate lawyer, angrily dismissed claims that the whole incident might have been a schoolgirl prank. 'Scarlett has obviously suffered a traumatic experience and I'm just glad to have her back,' he said.
Meanwhile, the police seem anxious to close the file. 'What matters is that Scarlett is safe,' Detective Chris Kloet said, speaking from New Scotland Yard. 'We may never know what happened to her in the eighteen hours she was gone but we are satisfied that no crime seems to have been committed.'

The report had been sent ten thousand miles by fax. It was being examined by a boy in a room in Nazca, Peru. The boy got up and went over to a desk. He held the sheet of paper under a light. There was a picture of Scarlett next to the text. She had been photographed holding a hockey stick with two more girls, one on either side. A team photo. The boy examined her carefully. She was quite good-looking, he thought. Asian, he would have said. Almost certainly the same age as him.

'When did this arrive?' he asked.

'Half an hour ago,' came the reply.

The boy's name was Matthew Freeman. He was the first of the Gatekeepers and, without quite knowing how, he had become their unelected leader. Four months ago, he had faced the Old Ones in the Nazca Desert and had tried to close the barrier, the huge gate, that for centuries had kept them at bay. He had failed. The King of the Old Ones had cut him down where he stood, leaving him for dead. The last thing he had seen was the armies of the Old Ones, spreading out and disappearing into the night.

It had taken him six weeks to recover from his injuries and since then he had been resting, trying to work out what to do next. He was staying in a Peruvian farmhouse, a *hacienda* just outside the town of Nazca itself. Richard Cole, the journalist who had travelled with him from England was still with him. Richard was his closest friend. It was he who had just come into the room.

'It's got to be her,' Matt said.

Richard nodded. 'She was in St Meredith's. She must have gone through the same door that you went through. God knows what happened to her. She was missing for eighteen hours.'

'Her name is Scarlett.'

'Scar.' Richard nodded again.

Matt thought for a moment, still clutching the article. He had spent the past four months searching for Scarlett in the only way that he could—through his dreams. Night after night he

63

had visited the strange dream world that had become so familiar to him. It had helped him in the past. He was certain that she had to be there somewhere. Perhaps it would lead him to her, helping him again.

And now, quite unexpectedly, she had turned up in the real world. There could be no doubt that this was her, the fifth of the Five. And she was in England, in London! A student at an expensive private school.

'We have to go to her,' Matt said. 'We must leave at once.'

'I'm checking out tickets now.'

Matt turned the photograph round in the light, tilting it towards himself. 'Scar,' he muttered. 'Now we know where she is.'

'That's right,' Richard said. He looked grave. 'But the Old Ones will know it too.'

MATT'S DIARY (1)

I never asked for any of this. I never wanted to be part of it. And even now, I don't understand exactly what is happening or why it had to be me.

I hoped that writing this diary might help. It was Richard's idea, to put it all down on paper. But it hasn't worked out the way I hoped. The more I think about my life, the more I write about it, the more confused it all becomes.

Sometimes I try to go back to where it all began but I'm not sure any more where that was. Was it the day my parents died? Or did it start in Ipswich, the evening I decided to break into a warehouse with my best friend . . . who was actually anything but? Maybe the decision had already been made the day I was born. Matthew Freeman. You will not go to school like other kids. You won't play football and take your A-levels and have a career. You are here for another reason. You can argue if you like, but that's just the way it's got to be.

I think a lot about my parents even though sometimes it's hard to see their faces, and their voices have long since faded out. My dad was a doctor, a GP with a practice round the corner from the house. I can just about remember a man with a beard and gold-rimmed glasses. He was very political. We were recycling stuff long before it was fashionable and he used to get annoyed about the National Health Service—too many managers, too much red tape. At the same time, he used to laugh a lot. He read to me at night . . . Roald Dahl . . . The Twits *was one of his favourites. And there was a comedy show on TV that he never missed. It was on Sunday night but I've forgotten its name.*

My mum was a lot smaller than him. She was always on a diet, although I don't think she really needed to lose weight. I suppose it didn't help that she was a great cook. She used to make her own bread and cakes and around September she'd set up a production line for Christmas puddings which she'd flog off for charity. Sometimes she talked about going back to work, but she liked to be there when I got back from school. That was one of her rules. She wouldn't let me come home to an empty house.

I was only eight years old when they died and there's so much about them I never knew. I guess they were happy together. Whenever I think back, the sun always seems to be shining which must mean something. I can still see our house and our garden with a big rose bush sprawling over the lawn. Sometimes I can even smell the flowers.

*   *   *

Mark and Kate Freeman. Those were their names. They died in a car accident on their way to a wedding and the thing is, I knew it was going to happen. I dreamed that their car was going to come off a bridge and into a river and I woke up knowing that they were both going to die. But I didn't tell them. I knew my dad would never have believed me. So I pretended I was sick. I cried and kicked my heels. I let them go but I made them leave me behind.

I could have saved them. I tell myself that over and over again. Maybe my dad wouldn't have believed me. Maybe he would have insisted on going, no matter what I said. But I could have poured paint over the car or something. I could even have set fire to it. There were all sorts of ways that I could have made it impossible for them to leave the house.

But I was too scared. I had a power and I knew that it made me different from everyone else and that was the last thing I wanted to be. Freakshow Matt . . . not me, thanks. So I said nothing. I stayed back and watched them go and since then I've seen the car pull away a thousand times and I've yelled at my eight-year-old self to do something and I've hated myself for being so stupid. If I could go back in time, that's where I would start because that's where it all went wrong.

After that, things happened very quickly. I was fostered by a woman called Gwenda Davis who was related in some way to my mother—her half-sister or something. For the next six years, I lived with her and her partner, Brian, in a terraced house in Ipswich. I hated both of them. Gwenda was shallow and self-centred but Brian was worse. They had what I think is called an abusive relationship which means that he used to beat her around. He hit me too. I was scared of him—I admit it. Sometimes I would see him looking at me in the same way and I would make sure my bedroom door was locked at night.

And yet, here's something strange. I might as well admit it. In a way, I was almost happy in Ipswich. Sometimes I thought of it as a punishment for what I'd done—or hadn't done—and part of me figured that I deserved it. I was resigned to my life there. I knew it was never going to get any better and at least I was able to create an identity for myself. I could be anyone I wanted to be.

I bunked off school. I was never going to pass any exams so what did I care? I stole stuff from local shops. I started smoking when I was twelve. My friend, Kelvin, bought me my first packet of Marlboro Lights—although of course he made me pay him back twice what they'd cost. I never took drugs. But if I'd stayed with him much longer I probably would have. I'd have ended up like one of those kids you read about in the newspapers, dead from an overdose, a body next to a railway line. Nobody would have cared, not even me. That was just the way it would have been.

But then along came Jayne Deverill and suddenly everything changed because it turned out she was a witch. I know how crazy that sounds. I can't believe I just wrote it. But she wasn't a witch like in a pantomime. I mean, she didn't have a long nose and a pointy hat or anything like that. She was the real

67

thing: evil, cruel and just a little bit mad. She and her friends had been watching me, waiting for me to fall into their hands because they needed me to help them unlock a mysterious gate hidden in a wood in Yorkshire. And it seemed that, after all, I wasn't just some loser with a criminal record who'd got his parents killed. I was one of the Five. A Gatekeeper. The hero of a story that had begun ten thousand years before I was born.

How did I feel about that? How do I feel about it now?

I have no choice. I am trapped in this and will have to stick with it until the bitter end. And I do think the end will be a hard one. The forces we're up against—the Old Ones and their allies around the world—are too huge. They are like a nightmare plague, spreading everywhere, killing everything they touch. I have powers. I've accepted that now and recently I've learned how to use them. But I am still only fifteen years old—I had my birthday out here in Nazca—and when I think about the things that are being asked of me, I am scared.

I can't run away. There's nowhere for me to hide. If I don't fight back, the Old Ones will find me. They will destroy me more surely and more painfully than even those cigarettes would have managed. After I was arrested, I never smoked again, by the way. That was one of the ways that I changed. I think I have accepted my place in all this. First of all, I have to survive. But that's not enough. I also have to win.

At least I'm no longer alone.

When this all began, I knew that I was one of five children, all the same age as me, and that one day we would meet. I knew this because I had seen them in my dreams.

Pedro was the first one I came across in real life. He has no surname. He lost it—along with his home, his possessions and his entire family when the village in Peru where he lived was hit by a flood. He was six years old. After that, he moved to the slums of Lima and managed to scratch a living there. The first time I saw him, he was begging on the street. We met when I was unconscious and he was trying to rob me. But that was the way he was brought up. For him, there was never any right or wrong—it was just a question of finding the next meal. He couldn't read. He knew nothing about the world outside the crumbling shanty town where he lived. And of course he could hardly speak a word of English.

I don't think I'd ever met anyone quite so alien to me . . . and by that I mean he could have come from another planet. For a start (and there's no pleasant way to put this) he stank. He hadn't washed or had a bath in years and the clothes he wore had been worn by at least ten people before him. Even after everything I'd been through, I was rich compared to him. At least I'd grown up with fresh tap water. I'd never starved.

Almost from the very start we became friends. It probably helped that Pedro decided to save my life when the police chief, a man called Rodriguez, was cheerfully beating me up. But it was more than that. Think about the odds of our ever finding each other, me living in a provincial town in England and him, a street urchin surviving in a city ten thousand miles away. We were drawn together because that was how it was meant to be. We were two of the Five.

Pedro is pure Inca: a descendant of the people who first lived in Peru. More than that, he's somehow connected with Manco Capac, one of the sun gods.

The Incas showed me a picture of Manco—it was actually on a disc made of solid gold—and the two of them looked exactly the same. I'm not sure I completely understand what's going on here. Is Pedro some sort of ancient god? If so, what does that make me?

Like me, Pedro has a special power. His is the ability to heal. The only reason I'm able to walk today is because of him. We were both injured in the Nazca Desert. He broke his leg, but I was cut down and left for dead . . . and I would have died if he hadn't come back and stayed with me for a couple of weeks. It's called radiesthesia, which is probably the longest word I know. I've only managed to spell it right because I've looked it up in the dictionary. It's something to do with the transfer of energy. Basically, it means that I got better thanks to him. And as a result, Pedro is more than a friend. He's almost like a long-lost brother—and if that sounds corny, too bad. That's how I feel.

And then came Scott and Jamie Tyler.

They really were brothers . . . twins, in fact. Formerly the telepathic twins, performing with The Circus of the Mind *at* The Reno Playhouse in Nevada. *While Pedro and I had been fighting (and losing) in the Nazca Desert, they'd been having adventures of their own, chased across America by an organization called the Nightrise Corporation. They'd also managed to get tangled up in the American election and were there when one of the candidates was almost assassinated.*

Scott and Jamie are more or less identical. They're thin to the point of being skinny and you can tell straight away that they have Native American blood—they were descended from the Washoe tribe.

70

They have long, dark hair, dark eyes and a sort of watchful quality. Physically, I would have said that Jamie was the younger of the two, but when they finally reached us—they travelled through a doorway that took them from Lake Tahoe in Nevada to a temple in Cuzco, Peru—he was very much in charge. His brother had been taken prisoner and tortured. We're still not sure what they did to him and Pedro has spent long hours alone with him, trying to repair the damage. But Scott is still suffering. He's withdrawn. He doesn't talk very much. I sometimes wonder if we'll be able to rely on him when the time comes.

It's been more than four months since I faced the Old Ones in the Nazca Desert and I still haven't recovered from my own injuries. I'm in pain a lot of the time. There are no scars but I can feel something wrong inside me. Sometimes I wake up at night and it's as if I've just been stabbed. Even Pedro still has a limp. So between the four of us, I certainly wouldn't bet any money on our taking on unimaginable forces of darkness and saving the world. I'm sorry, but that's how it is.

Jamie is very bright. He seems to see things more clearly than any of us, mainly because he was there at the very start. It's too complicated to explain right now, but somehow he travelled back in time and met us . . . before we were us. Yes. There was a Matt ten thousand years ago who looked like me and sounded like me and who may even have been me. Jamie says that we've all lived twice. I just hope it was more fun the first time.

Four months!

We've all been hanging out in this house near the coast, to the south of Lima. It belongs to a professor

71

called Joanna Chambers who's an expert on pretty much anything to do with Peru. The house is wooden and painted white, constructed a bit like a hacienda, which is a Spanish farmhouse. There's a large central room which opens onto a veranda during the day and a wide staircase that connects the two floors. Everything is very old-fashioned. There are scatter rugs and a big open fireplace and fans turn slowly beneath the ceiling, circulating the air.

We've passed the time reading, watching TV (the house has satellite and we've also shipped in a supply of DVDs) and surfing the net, looking out for any news of the Old Ones. The professor insists that we do three or four hours of lessons, although it's been ages since any of us went to school and Pedro never stepped into one in his life. We've played football in the garden, passing the ball around the llamas that wander onto the grass, and we've gone for hikes in the desert. And, I suppose, we've been gathering strength, slowly recovering from everything we've been through.

But even so, there have been times when it all seems unreal, sitting here, doing nothing in the full knowledge that somewhere in the world the Old Ones must be spreading their power base, preparing to strike at humanity. They'll be making friends in all the right places . . . As far as we know, they could be all over Europe. Their aim is to start a total war, to kill as many people as possible and then to toy with the rest, maiming and torturing until there's nobody left. Why do they want to do this? There is no why. The Old Ones feed on pain in the same way that cancer will attack a healthy organism. It's their nature.

Sometimes, in the evening, the six of us will play Perudo, which is a Peruvian game, a bit like liar dice. Me, Richard, Pedro, Scott, Jamie and the professor. We'll sit there, throwing dice and behaving as if nothing is happening, as if we're just a bunch of friends on an extended holiday. And secretly I want to get up and punch the wall. We're safe and comfortable in Nazca. But every moment we're here, we're losing. Our enemy is gaining the upper hand.

What else can we do? The Old Ones have disappeared. And even if we knew what they were doing, we're not yet strong enough to take them on. Only four of the Gatekeepers have come together. There have to be five.

And now there are. At last we've found Scar.

It's hard to believe that today I actually held a picture of her in my hands. Now she has a name— Scarlett Adams. We know where she lives. We can actually reach out to her and tell her the truth about who she is—or was.

Ten thousand years ago, she was in charge of her own private army. Jamie actually met her and fought with her at the final battle when the King of the Old Ones was banished and the first great gate was constructed. She must have a power—we all do. But he never found out what it was. When he met her, he said she was brave and resourceful. She could ride a horse, fight with a sword, lead an army of men who were at least twice her age. But she never did anything that looked like magic . . . at least, not anything that he noticed.

Very soon, we will leave Nazca. I really want to see England again.

73

And now I'm going to bed.

Richard is worried that Scar turning up is the start of a new phase. The Old Ones have left us alone but now they'll have been alerted. If they were planning a move against us, this is the time when they'll make it.

But I don't care. There are five of us and that means that soon this whole thing will be over. We'll get together and do whatever it takes to bring it all to an end. After that, I'll go back to school. I'll take my GCSEs and my A-levels. I'll have an ordinary life.

That's all I want. I can hardly wait.

LAST NIGHT IN NAZCA

Twenty-four hours after the fax had arrived, Professor Chambers organized a dinner. It was her way of saying goodbye. The following day, Matt, Richard, Pedro, Jamie and Scott would be leaving for England—the professor had arranged passports for all of them—and at last she would have the house to herself.

Joanna Chambers had spent most of her life in Peru, studying the Incas, the ancient Moche and Chimu tribes and, of course, the Nazca Lines. She was an expert on a dozen different subjects, a qualified pilot, a good shot with a rifle or a handgun and a terrible cook. Fortunately, the meal had been prepared by a local help: creole soup, followed by *lomo saltado*—a dish made with grilled beef, onions and rice. There were two jugs of Pisco Sour, a frothing, white drink made from grape brandy, lemon and egg white—it tasted much better than it looked.

74

Richard Cole was sitting at the head of the table. He had changed in the past few months. His hair had been bleached by the sun and he had grown it so that it fell in long strands over his collar. He had a permanent, desert tan and although he didn't quite have a beard, he looked rough and unshaven. Tonight, he had changed into jeans and a white, linen shirt. Normally he slouched around in shorts and sandals and if the house had been nearer the sea, he might easily have been mistaken for a surfer. He started every morning with a five-mile run. He was keeping himself in shape.

Scott and Jamie Tyler were sitting on one side of the table, together as usual. Matt and Pedro were on the other. There was one empty seat and someone had placed the article with the picture of Scarlett Adams on the table in front of it, as if she were there in spirit.

All six of them were in a good mood. The food had been excellent and the drink had helped. Upstairs, their cases were packed and ready in the various rooms. Professor Chambers waited until the food had been cleared away, then tapped a fork against her glass and rose to her feet. Matt had never seen her wearing a dress and tonight was no exception. She had put on a crumpled safari suit and there was a small bunch of flowers in her buttonhole.

'We ought to go to bed,' she began. 'You have a long journey to make tomorrow—but I just want to wish you *bon voyage*. I can't say I'm too sorry that you're finally on your way . . .' There were protests around the table and she held up a hand for silence. 'It's been impossible to get any work done with all your infernal noise, football games out on the front lawn, four boys clumping up and down the stairs, and all the rest of it.

'But I will miss you. I've enjoyed having you here. That's the truth of it. And although it's wonderful that Scar has finally turned up, I can't help wondering what lies ahead of you.' She stopped for a moment. 'I feel a bit like a mother sending my sons off to war. I can only hope that one day I'll see you again. I can only hope that you'll come back safe.'

She lifted her glass.

'Anyway, here's a toast to all five of you. The Five, I should say. Look after yourselves. Beat the Old Ones. Do what you have to do. And now let's get some hot chocolate and have a final game of Perudo. You have an early start.'

Later that night, Richard and Matt found themselves standing on the veranda outside the main room. It was a beautiful night with a full moon, an inky sky and stars everywhere. Matt could hear classical music coming from inside the house. Professor Chambers had an old-fashioned radio that she liked to listen to while she worked. Scott and Jamie were sharing a room on the first floor. Pedro was probably watching TV.

'I can't believe we're going home,' Matt said.

'England.' Richard gazed into the darkness as if he could see it on the horizon. 'Do you have any idea what happens when we get there?'

Matt shook his head. 'I don't know. I've thought about it. I've tried to work out some sort of plan. Maybe it would be easier if we knew what the Old Ones have been doing all this time.' He thought for a moment. 'Maybe we'll know when the five of us get together. Maybe it will all make sense.'

Matt stared into the darkness. The nights in Nazca were always huge. Even without seeing it, he could feel the desert stretching out to the mountains. There seemed to be five times more stars in the southern hemisphere than he'd ever seen in Europe. The sky was bursting with them.

'What you said yesterday . . .' He turned to Richard. 'About the Old Ones . . .'

'They were looking for kids with special powers,' Richard said. 'That's how they found Scott and Jamie. If Scarlett went through the door at St Meredith's, they'll know about it. They'll have read the article too.'

'You think they'll be waiting for us?'

'Scarlett's being watched by the Nexus. Her father's with her. She took a couple of days off school. So far everything seems OK. She doesn't seem to be in any danger.'

Richard had been in constant touch with the Nexus, the strange collection of millionaires, politicians, psychics and churchmen who knew about the Old Ones and had come together in a sort of secret society to fight them. It had to be secret because they were afraid of being ridiculed. How could they admit that they believed in devils and demons? The Nexus had made it their job to look after Matt and the other children. At one stage, they had paid for him to go to a private school. They were still paying for everything while the four of them were out here.

And they were also protecting Scarlett Adams. They had moved in the moment she had been identified in the national press, hiring a team of private detectives to watch over her night and day.

They were lucky that she lived in England. That made things easier. One of the Nexus members was a senior police officer called Tarrant and he had arranged for all her calls to be monitored. Meanwhile, Scarlett had gone back to school. Her father was still with her in London and there was a Scottish helper living in the house. By now, Richard knew a great deal about her. She was in the school play. She had a boyfriend called Aidan and she regularly beat him at tennis. She seemed to have a happy life.

Richard and Matt were about to rip all that up. Somewhere inside him, Matt felt guilty about that—but he knew he couldn't avoid it. She had been born for a purpose. His job was to tell her what that purpose was.

Somewhere, an owl hooted in the darkness. The house was on the outskirts of Nazca but the two of them could make out the lights of the town, twinkling in the distance. Everything was very peaceful but they knew that it was an illusion. Soon the whole world would change.

'I'm not sure you should go,' Richard said, suddenly.

'What do you mean?' Matt was surprised. Everything was ready. The tickets had been bought.

'I've been thinking about it . . . this trip to England. You and Pedro and Scott and Jamie . . . all on the same plane. Suppose the Old Ones have got control of American air space. They could smash you into the side of a mountain. Or a building.'

'They don't want to kill us,' Matt said. He was fairly sure about that. 'If they kill us, we'll all be

78

replaced by our past selves. That's how it works. And what good will that do them? They'll only have to start searching for us all over again. It's easier for them to keep us alive.'

Richard shook his head. 'They could still force the plane down somewhere and capture you.'

Matt considered the possibility. The trouble was that the Old Ones had been silent for months. They seemed to have slipped into the shadows, as if they had never existed at all. Richard had been scouring the Internet, waiting to hear of a news event, some horror happening somewhere in the world that might suggest that the Old Ones were involved. There were plenty of stories. The war in Afghanistan. Ethnic cleansing in Darfur. Misery and starvation in Zimbabwe. But that was just everyday news. That would happen even without the Old Ones. He had been looking for something worse.

'What do you think they're doing?' Matt asked. 'Why do you think they haven't shown themselves?'

Richard shrugged. 'I guess they've been waiting,' he said.

'Waiting for what?'

'Waiting for Scar.'

There was a movement on the veranda and Matt tensed for a moment, then relaxed. He could tell it was Professor Chambers, even without turning round. The smell of her cigar had given her away and sure enough, there it was. She was clutching it in one hand with a glass of Peruvian brandy in the other.

'Are you two going in?' she asked. 'I'm putting on the alarms.'

The house was completely surrounded by a security system that had been installed shortly after Richard, Pedro and Matt had arrived. There were no fences or uniformed guards—the professor had said she couldn't live like that. The system was invisible. But there was a series of infra-red beams at the perimeter, and the garden itself had pressure pads concealed in different places under the lawn. Most sophisticated of all was the radar dish mounted on the roof, sweeping the entire area. It could pick up any movement a hundred metres away. That was how they had been living. It might look as if they were free, but they had all been aware that they were actually in a state of siege.

'We were just talking about tomorrow,' Richard said.

'It'll be here soon.' Chambers blew smoke. 'It's after ten. Shouldn't you be in bed?'

Richard tapped Matt on the shoulder. 'After you.'

The three of them went inside. Matt said goodnight to Richard and climbed the stairs to the small room which he had chosen at the back of the house. He liked it there. When he was lying in bed, his head was directly underneath a slanting roof with a skylight so, lying on his back, he could look up at the stars. His case—a small canvas bag—was already packed and sitting on the floor. He wasn't taking much with him. If he needed anything in London, he could always buy it there.

Matt undressed quickly, washed and slipped between the sheets. For the last few months, he had been searching for Scar in the only way that he could—in his dreams. Time and again he had

80

visited the dreamworld. He had been there so often that he knew the landscape well: the shoreline stretching along a great sea with everything dead and grey, the island where he had once found himself trapped.

The dreamworld baffled him. Was it a dream or was it a real world? That was the first question. And was it there to help him or to throw him off balance? On the one hand it was a frightening place, conjuring up strange, violent images that he couldn't understand: giant swans, walking statues, guns and knives. But at the same time, Matt didn't think he was in any danger there. The more he visited it, the more he felt it was on his side. He wondered if anyone actually lived there—or was it simply there for the Gatekeepers, its only inhabitants?

At any event, he had gone back there almost every night, floating out of the bed, out of the room, out of himself. Then he had begun to travel, searching for Scar. Sometimes he would see a flicker of lightning, an approaching storm. Once, he found footprints. Another time he came upon a grove of trees, which at least proved that the place wasn't entirely dead, that things could grow there.

But there had never been any sign of Scar.

There was no point in searching for her tonight. In just twenty-four hours he would be meeting her anyway. But even so—maybe it was just habit—he found himself back in the dreamworld almost at once. As usual, he was on his own. He was climbing a steep hill, but it took no more effort than if he had been walking on level ground. Far behind him, the wilderness stretched out, wide and empty.

And then he noticed something strange. The ground underneath his feet had changed. He knelt down and examined it, brushing aside the grey dust that covered everything. It was true. He was standing on a path fashioned out of paving stones that had been brought here and laid in place. He could see the joins, the cement gluing everything together. Even though he was asleep, Matt felt a surge of excitement. A man-made path! This was completely new and confirmed what he had always thought. The dreamworld was inhabited. There might be buildings, even whole cities there.

He looked up. The path had to lead somewhere. There could be something on the other side of the hill.

But he wasn't going to find out—not then. Suddenly he was awake. Someone was shaking him, calling his name. The lights were on in his room. He opened his eyes. It was Richard.

'Wake up, Matt,' he was saying. 'There's someone here.'

THE MAN FROM LIMA

Matt heaved himself out of bed, threw on some shorts and a T-shirt and ran downstairs barefoot. The whole house was awake. There were lights on everywhere and the alarm system was buzzing, warning them that somebody was approaching.

It had already occurred to him that this sudden interruption must be connected to the fact that Scarlett had been found. If all five of the Gatekeepers were now out there and known to each other, that made them a greater danger to the Old Ones, and it was no surprise that they'd want to take action. It was exactly what he and Richard had been worrying about. On the other hand, it could be a false alarm. Over the past four months, there had been plenty enough of those. Sometimes the children came out from the town, looking for food or something to steal. Professor Chambers kept llamas for their wool, and one of them might have broken loose. The system was sensitive. Even a bat or a large moth might have been enough to set it off.

Matt hurried into the main room. There was a computer standing on a table in the corner and it had already activated itself, automatically connecting to the radar on the roof. It showed a single blip moving slowly and purposefully towards the front door. It was half past eleven at night. A bit late for a visitor.

Jamie and Scott had come downstairs, fully dressed. Pedro followed them—barefoot like Matt, but then he often preferred to walk without shoes. When the two boys had first met, he had been wearing sandals made out of old car tyres and he still mistrusted proper trainers. He was yawning and pulling on a sweater. Joanna Chambers had arrived ahead of everyone. She was wearing an old dressing gown. Matt watched her open the gun cabinet and take out a rifle. So far, nobody had spoken.

'What's happening?' Jamie asked.

'A single figure moving through the garden.' She nodded at the computer. 'It looks like there's only one of them, but we can't be sure.'

Richard went over and examined the screen. 'I'd

83

say he's trying not to be seen,' he muttered. 'Why don't we take a look at him?'

He leaned over and pressed a switch. This was another part of the security system. The entire garden was instantly lit up by a series of arc lamps so bright that it was as if he had set off a magnesium flare. Matt blinked. It was quite shocking to see the brilliant colours, the wide green lawn, so late at night.

There was a single figure, a man, trapped in the middle of the lawn. He was dressed in a linen jacket, jeans and a polo shirt, buttoned up to the neck. There was a canvas bag across his shoulder. As the lights had come on, he had frozen and stood there with his hands half-covering his eyes, momentarily blinded. He seemed to be on his own. He certainly wasn't carrying any visible weapons. Richard opened the French windows. Professor Chambers stepped outside.

'Stay where you are!' she shouted. 'I have a gun pointing at you.'

'There is no need for that!' the man shouted back in heavily accented English. 'I am a friend.'

'What do you want?'

'I want to speak to the boy. Matthew Freeman. Is he here?'

Richard glanced at Matt who moved forward, stepping through the French windows. He was careful not to go too far. Professor Chambers lifted the gun, covering him. 'What's your name?' he called out.

'Ramon.' The man cupped his hand over his eyes, shielding them, trying to make him out.

'Where have you come from?'

'From Lima.' The man hesitated, unsure what to

do, whether to move forward or not. He seemed to be pinned there by the light. 'Please . . . are you Matthew? I am here because I want to help you.'

Pedro had come over to the window. He was standing next to Matt. 'Why does he come, like a thief, in the middle of the night?' he muttered. Matt nodded. He knew that Pedro was the most suspicious of them all. Maybe it was something to do with the life he'd once led.

Richard agreed. 'We can ask him to come back in the morning,' he muttered.

But Matt wasn't so sure. 'What do you want?' he shouted.

The man hadn't moved. 'I will show you when I am inside,' he said. He looked around him. 'Please . . . it is not safe for me out here.'

Matt knew he had to make a decision. It was something he was finding more and more. Although he was in the professor's house and she and Richard were far older than him, he always seemed to be the one in charge.

Quickly, he turned over the options. They were all supposed to be leaving the house at ten o'clock the next morning, driving up to Lima to catch the flight that would take them to London. This was no time to be meeting with complete strangers. On the other hand, there were six of them and one of him. Professor Chambers had a weapon. And the man seemed genuine enough.

'All right!' Matt called out. 'Come in . . .'

The man began to walk towards the house. At the same time, Richard went over to the cabinet and reached inside. There was another gun there. He wasn't taking any chances.

The man came into the main room, Professor

Chambers following him with the rifle. Now that he was inside, Matt could see that he was a few years older than Richard, with the dark hair and olive skin of a native Peruvian. He had obviously been on the road for a while. He was dusty and unshaven and his clothes were crumpled with sweat patches under the arms. There was a haunted look in his eyes. From the look of him, he didn't seem to be a threat.

The first thing he did was to take a pair of spectacles out of his top pocket and put them on. Now he looked like a school teacher or perhaps an accountant working in a small, local office. He had a cheap watch on his wrist and his shoes were scuffed and down-at-heel. He looked straight at Matt. 'Are you Matthew Freeman?' He blinked. 'I did not think I would find you here.'

'Sit down,' Richard said.

The man sat on the sofa with his back to the French windows. Richard pressed the button that turned off the garden lights and everything outside the room disappeared into blackness again. It had clouded over during the night. The moon and the stars had disappeared. Richard came back over to the sofa and sat down on one of the arms. He hadn't reset the security system. But then the visitor wouldn't be staying very long. Scott and Jamie perched on the edge of the coffee table. Professor Chambers sat in a chair with the rifle between her knees.

'So what do you want?' she demanded.

'I will tell you everything you want to know,' Ramon said. 'But can I first ask you for a drink? I have been travelling all day and I had to wait until night before coming here. Believe me, if I had

86

been seen I would have been killed.'

'I'll get it,' Pedro said. He got up and went into the kitchen, returning a moment later with a glass of water. The man took it in both hands and gulped greedily.

'How do you know about me?' Matt asked.

'I know a great deal about you, Matthew. May I call you that? I know how you came to Peru and I think I know what you have been doing since you arrived here. I was present, also, the night you came to the *hacienda* at Ica, although perhaps you did not see me. I was there because I was hired to work for Diego Salamanda.'

Ramon must have known the effect the name would have on everyone in the room. Salamanda had been the chairman and owner of a huge news corporation in South America. Deliberately deformed as a child—his head had been grotesquely stretched—he had used his power and wealth to bring back the Old Ones. Matt and Pedro had gone to his *hacienda* searching for Richard, and later on Matt and Salamanda had confronted each other in the Nazca Desert. Matt had killed him, turning back the bullets fired from his own gun.

'Please . . . do not think of me as your enemy,' Ramon continued, hastily. 'I swear to you that I was not part of his plans.' He paused. Beads of sweat were standing out on his forehead. 'I am not even in business. I am a lecturer at Lima University and *Señor* Salamanda paid me to help him with a special project. I should explain that my speciality is Ancient History.' He bowed in the direction of Professor Chambers. 'I have heard you speak many times, *Señora*. I was there, for

87

example, last April when you gave the presentation at the Museo Nacional de Antropologia. I thought it was a brilliant talk.'

Professor Chambers thought for a moment. 'It's true that I was there,' she said. 'But anyone could know that.'

'*Señor* Salamanda told me that he was in possession of a diary which he wanted me to interpret on his behalf,' Ramon went on. 'The diary had been written in the sixteenth century by a man called Joseph de Cordoba. This man travelled here to Peru with the Spanish conquistadors. Salamanda told me that he bought the diary from a bookseller in London, a man called William Morton.'

'He didn't buy it,' Matt said. 'He stole it. He killed William Morton to get it.' Matt knew because he had been there at the time. Morton had been demanding two million pounds but all he had got was a knife in the back.

'I did not know these things,' Ramon exclaimed. 'I was innocent. My job was to work only on the text, to unlock its secrets and I spent many, many hours in his office and also at his home in Ica. The diary was never allowed to leave his side. He made it clear to me from the start that it was the most precious thing to him in the world. And as I read it, as I began to study it, I realized why. It told this extraordinary history . . . the Old Ones, a battle many thousands of years ago and a gate that could be unlocked by the stars.'

He lowered his head.

'I know that I am responsible for what happened last June. I did the work that I was paid to do and I helped Salamanda to open the gate. I have allowed a terrible thing to happen and it has been on my conscience ever since.' He twisted on the sofa, urging them to believe him. 'I am not a bad man. I am a Catholic. I go to Church. I believe in heaven and hell. And I have been thinking . . . what can I do to make amends for what I have done? What can I do to undo the damage that I have caused? And I knew, finally, that I must find you. So I came.'

'How did you know where we were?' Jamie asked.

'*Señor* Salamanda often mentioned the name of Professor Chambers. I guessed that you would be with her and I have brought you something. You will not shoot me if I reach into my bag?'

He glanced at the professor, then reached beside him. He took out an old, leather-bound book and laid it on the table. Nobody in the room said anything. But they all knew what it was. It was hard to believe that it was actually there, in front of them. The cover was dark brown with a few faint tracings of gold, tied with a cord. The edges of the pages were rough and uneven. Matt recognized it at once. It contained everything they needed to know about the Old Ones. It might even describe how they could be defeated.

'It is the diary of the mad monk,' Ramon said.

And it was. The small, square book sitting there in the middle of the table was, supposedly, the only copy in the world. There was no limit to how many secrets it might contain, how valuable it might be.

'How did you get it?' Richard demanded.

'I stole it!' Ramon took out a handkerchief and wiped it across his forehead. 'I thought it would be impossible but in fact it was easy. You see, I still had my electronic pass-key to the office of Salamanda News International in Lima. And I had this crazy idea. Maybe the key had not been cancelled. *Señor* Salamanda was dead but surely they had forgotten about me. Two days ago I returned to the office. Nobody saw me, although by now they will know that it is gone. I took it from his desk and hurried away into the night. It is possible that the cameras will have identified me and that they will be searching for me even now.'

Richard was still suspicious. 'What do you want from us?' he asked. 'Do you want us to pay you?'

Ramon shook his head. 'Can you not understand me?' he exclaimed. He clasped his hands in front of him. 'I am twenty-eight years old. Next year I hope to be married. When I was given this work by *Señor* Salamanda, I knew nothing. It was just, for me, a job.'

He pushed the diary away.

'Here! You can have it without payment. It is yours. I brought it to you only because I thought you might make use of it in this great . . .' He searched for the word in English. '. . . *lucha*. Struggle. I want nothing from you. I am sorry that I came.'

There was a pause. Matt knew that he had just been given a fantastic prize. The diary might explain the dreamworld. It might tell them the history of the twenty-five doorways that stood in so many different countries. Who had built them, and when? It might even help them work out what they were supposed to do when the five of them finally met in London. Ramon was right. Salamanda had been prepared to kill to get his hands on the diary and now it had just been handed to them, out of the blue.

Jamie leaned forward and picked it up. He unwound the cord and the diary opened in his hands. He examined the page in front of him. It was covered in handwriting which would have been almost unreadable even if it hadn't been in Spanish. There were tiny diagrams in the margins. Suddenly his eyes lit up. He pointed to a single word.

'Sapling,' he said. 'That was my name when I went back in time. Sapling was killed and I took his place.'

The diary was real. Matt had no doubt of it. But what about the man who had brought it to them? He looked genuine, but Richard had been expecting some sort of trap and this could well be it. Suddenly Matt had an idea. There was an easy way to find out. 'Jamie,' he said. 'Ask him if he's telling the truth.'

Jamie understood at once. But before he could act, Scott stood up. 'I'll do it,' he said.

Scott walked forward and stopped in front of the visitor. He looked Ramon straight in the eyes. 'Are you telling the truth?' he demanded.

'On my mother's grave,' Ramon replied, crossing himself and then kissing his thumb. 'I'm only here because it is the right thing to do. Because I want to help.'

Scott concentrated. This was his power, the ability that had kept audiences entertained for the many months when he was performing in Reno. They had thought it was a trick but in fact it was real. He could read minds.

Unfortunately, it wasn't quite as easy as that sounded. It wasn't like throwing a switch. Scott

91

and Jamie had a connection with each other. When they were in the same room or even a short distance away, they could communicate with each other just by thinking. But when it came to other people, strangers like Ramon, what they saw was confused, chaotic. Nothing was ever black and white.

Perhaps a minute passed. Then Scott nodded. 'He's telling the truth,' he said.

'I promise you . . .' Ramon knew that he had been tested in some way. The words came pouring out. 'I don't care if you don't trust me. I'll leave you with the diary. I'll go. I have no other reason to be here.'

'You said it wasn't safe for you outside,' Richard said. 'Were you followed?'

Ramon shook his head and swallowed nervously. 'I don't think so. After I had taken the diary, I hid in Lima. I wanted to see if the police would come. Then, when nothing happened, I took a tourist bus to Paracas. I thought it was less likely that I would be noticed that way. By now they will know that the diary is missing. They will know that I have taken it. And although Salamanda is gone, there are people in his organization who will still wish to continue what he began.'

'So where will you go now?' Professor Chambers asked. 'Do you have somewhere to hide?'

'I was hoping . . .' Ramon began. There was a strange sound, a whistling that came through the air, then the tearing of fabric. He looked down. There was something sticking out of his shirt. Puzzled, he reached down and touched it, then tried to pull it free. It wouldn't move and when he

92

released it, his hand was wet with blood.

They had all heard it but hadn't realized what it was. A fence post. It had been thrown with impossible force from out of the darkness. It must have travelled more than fifty metres before the pointed end smashed into the back of the sofa penetrating through the leather and padding before impaling the man who was sitting there. Ramon's eyes widened. He tried to speak. Then he slumped forward, pinned into place, unable even to fall.

The alarms hadn't gone off. The radar screen was empty. Professor Chambers sprang to her feet and pressed the button to turn on the outside lights. Nothing happened.

Something was moving in the garden. There were figures, edging forward, dressed in filthy, tattered clothes that hung off them as if they were rotting away. Matt could just make them out in the light spilling from the room. It was suddenly very cold and he knew at once that dark forces were at work and whatever they were, coming towards him, they weren't human.

They had come for the diary.

NIGHT ATTACK

Slowly, determinedly, they closed in on the house.

There were more than a dozen of them: nightmare figures, shuffling across the lawn. Where had they come from? Matt could imagine them climbing out of the local cemetery. There was something corpse-like about them. A gleam of light from the living room caught one of their faces and he saw glistening bone, one empty eye socket, dried blood streaking down the side of the cheek and neck. At that moment he was sure of it. These creatures couldn't be killed. They were already dead.

As if to prove him wrong, Professor Chambers stepped forward and fired a shot at the nearest of them. Matt saw a great gout of blood explode out of the back of its head. It fell face down and lay, shuddering in the grass. So at least they could be stopped! She fired again, hitting another of them in the shoulder. The creature twitched as if shrugging off the bullet. Blood spread across what was left of its shirt. But it kept on coming. It didn't seem to feel pain.

Richard was already on his feet, loading the revolver that he had taken from the gun cabinet. A few weeks before, Matt had smiled when he had stumbled across him, shooting tin cans in the desert. Now he was glad that Richard had decided to practise.

When the attack had begun, Scott and Jamie had snatched up a couple of makeshift weapons— anything they could get their hands on. Jamie had a baseball bat. Scott had found a kitchen knife which he was holding in front of him, the blade slanting up. Pedro had backed away to the other side of the room. He was standing with his back to a full-length window, his eyes darting left and right, waiting for the first attack.

He hadn't looked behind him.

'Pedro . . .! Watch out!' Richard shouted the warning.

One of the creatures was looming out of the

94

shadows on the other side of the glass. Pedro spun round just in time to see a dead, white face, staring eyes, grey lips, hands stretching towards him. The creature didn't stop. It walked straight through the window, smashing the glass which cascaded all around it, and came into the room with blood streaming down its face. Shards of broken glass were sticking out of its flesh, but it didn't seem to notice. Richard lifted his revolver and shot it twice in the head. It crumpled and fell at Pedro's feet. At the same time, Richard twisted round and fired again. Another of the creatures had reached the open French windows and was about to step inside. It threw up its hands and fell back with a bullet between its eyes.

But there were still many more of them moving slowly across the lawn, unafraid of dying, determined only to reach the house. Perhaps Ramon had been a diversion after all. While he had been talking, the night attackers had completely surrounded the house. Matt heard the sound of wood splintering upstairs and knew that some of them must have climbed up to the balcony and broken in that way. Jamie stepped forward and grabbed the diary, which he threw to Scott in a single movement. Scott caught it without even looking and slipped it into his jacket. Neither of them had spoken and Matt knew that the two of them must have communicated telepathically. He had seen them do it often enough. Each one of them knew instantly what the other was going to do. They were almost like reflections of each other.

Richard was reloading. Joanna Chambers fired again. She pulled some more bullets out of her dressing gown pocket but even as she fumbled with the loading mechanism, one of the creatures launched itself at her, grabbing hold of her with one hand, lifting an ancient-looking knife with the other. The blade was black with a broken, serrated edge. It stabbed down.

Matt stopped him.

Six months ago, he wouldn't have been able to do it. But then he had been alone. Now four of the Gatekeepers had come together and Scott, Jamie and Pedro had added their power to his. All he had to do was think about it and the blade snapped in half. The creature screamed in pain and a wisp of smoke rose from the palm of its hand as the hilt of the knife burned into it. By now, Chambers had loaded her rifle. She fired a single shot at point blank range, putting it out of its misery.

'We can't control them!' Jamie shouted.

If these creatures had been fully human, he might have been able to make them turn round and leave the house. He and Scott didn't just read minds. They were also able to control them. All their lives, the two brothers had recognized that they were living under a curse. Always, they had to be careful what they said. One unguarded thought, one word spoken in anger, could turn them into murderers. Once, Scott had almost killed a boy at school. And later, when their foster father committed suicide, Scott had known that he was secretly to blame.

But this time it wasn't going to work. Their attackers didn't seem to have minds that could be controlled. It was as if they had already been programmed to kill with no thoughts of their own. And there were too many of them. Matt glanced into the garden. It was still very dark outside but he could make out a whole crowd of them, moving relentlessly across the lawn. There were more at the back of the house and yet more of them upstairs.

Matt heard a horrible gargling sound and turned just as a man—or the remains of one—stumbled over the sofa and launched himself at him. The man was naked to the waist, sweat and slime dripping off his chest. Matt nodded and the man was flung backwards, crashing into the wall. He slid to the floor and lay still.

'They're on the stairs.'

It was Scott who had seen them. The creatures from the balcony were making their way down, their movements slow, almost robotic. Jamie ran forward with the baseball bat and swung it into the face of the first man that he reached. There was a crunch of breaking bone. The man crumpled.

Matt looked all around him, wondering where the next attack was going to come from. At the same time, he smelled something. His eyes had begun to water and he was aware that it was getting more difficult to breathe. The temperature had risen too. Richard fired again, hitting one creature, then used the revolver as a club, smashing it into a second. 'The house is on fire!' he yelled.

Matt didn't need to be told. Smoke was pouring down the staircase, sucked into the ground floor by the turning fans. He could already hear the crackle of burning wood. Stretched out in the hot Nazca sun—it almost never rained in this part of Peru—the professor's house would be bone dry. There were fire extinguishers in all the rooms, but they

97

weren't going to be given a chance to use them. Left to itself, the fire would consume the whole building in minutes.

Richard fired two more shots but then the gun clicked uselessly in his hand. He rummaged in his pocket, searching for more ammunition. Professor Chambers blasted off another round, but she too had only a few bullets left. And the creatures kept on coming. Kill one and another two or three would take its place. There seemed to be no end to them. Matt saw another one appear on the stairs, holding an iron post similar to the one that had killed Ramon. It had been torn free from the garden fence. He watched as the creature lifted it up to its shoulder, realized too late what it was about to do.

The creature flung the rod like a spear, aiming straight at Pedro. Matt shouted a warning. Pedro twisted round. The missile turned once in the air and then struck him a glancing blow on the side of the head. He cried out and fell to the floor, dazed and bleeding. Another creature—dressed bizarrely in the rags of a dinner suit—closed in on him. Matt couldn't reach him. He was too far away. But Scott was there. He still had the kitchen knife. He was standing between Pedro and his attacker. Matt waited for him to move.

Scott did nothing. He stood where he was, frozen to the spot. He wasn't even blinking. Matt could see his chest heaving and his hands seemed to be locked in place, the fingers bent. His whole body was rigid.

Matt knew what was happening. He had seen it before. Scott wasn't afraid. He wasn't a coward. But he had spent weeks with Nightrise, with the

98

woman called Susan Mortlake and in that time they had got into his mind. It was hard to imagine how much pain they had put him through, trying to turn him against his friends. This was the result. In moments of stress, he simply shut down. Even Pedro had so far been unable to help him. The wounds were too deep.

Pedro was lying still. There was a gash on the side of his head. Jamie was lashing out with the baseball bat, using it like a club or a sword. Matt looked for a weapon but couldn't see one. The man in the dinner jacket had reached Pedro and was standing over him. He had produced a second weapon, an axe which he was holding in both hands. Desperately, Matt searched across the room, saw a jagged piece of broken glass on the floor and—using his power—swept it through the air and into the creature's throat. The creature screamed horribly and fell back in a fountain of its own blood.

'We have to get out of here!' Richard shouted.

The air was full of smoke. It was getting harder to breathe inside, but running out into the fresh air would be suicide. Nobody would be able to see anything in the darkness—and if these creatures had night vision they would be in total command. Matt stood there, cursing himself. There were tears streaming down his cheeks. He knew that this was happening because of Scarlett. He had been expecting it. So why hadn't he been better prepared?

At any event, he knew that Richard was right. They had to get out of the house before they suffocated. The smoke didn't seem to have any effect on the attackers. It was as if their lungs had rotted away and they didn't need to breathe. Jamie threw the baseball bat at one of the creatures on the stairs, then ran over to his brother. Matt reached Pedro and helped him to his feet. At least he didn't seem to be too badly hurt. Professor Chambers blasted away with the rifle, clearing a way to the French windows.

'Look out!'

It was Richard who had shouted the warning. Matt looked up just in time to see part of the ceiling come crashing down in a chaos of orange fire and black smoke. The flames were leaping up at the night. It seemed that most of the roof and part of the second floor had gone. Taking Pedro with him, he threw himself to one side and the falling debris missed him by inches, crashing down onto the sofa where Ramon, the man who had started all this, was sitting. The iron rod that had killed him was slanting out of his chest. He was watching it all like a disinterested spectator.

The six of them staggered out into the garden leaving the burning house and the remaining creatures—nine or ten of them—behind. Professor Chambers fired one last shot. 'No more ammo!' she called out to Richard but there was a strain in her voice and Matt wondered if she had been hurt. He looked at her in alarm. There was a patch of red spreading across the front of her dressing gown. A dark gash showed in the material. But she wasn't going to let the pain slow her down. 'How about you?' she demanded.

'Two more bullets . . .' Richard replied.

Two more bullets and the attackers were everywhere. Matt could see them clearly in the light of the flames, their eyes glowing red, their hands clutching knives, axes, chains and lengths of barbed wire which they flailed like whips. Pedro was leaning against him, blood running down the side of his face. Scott and Jamie were standing together, catching their breath. They had made it outside but they had nowhere to run. Another creature lumbered towards Professor Chambers, who stood where she was, clutching her wound. Richard shot it twice.

Matt was almost ready to give up. He couldn't believe that it was going to end this way, surprised and surrounded in a garden in Nazca. Was this what the fight had all been about? He was a Gatekeeper. He had returned to the world after ten thousand years. Was he really going to allow himself to be beaten so easily?

And then the night exploded a second time, with lights bursting out all around them, slanting in from every direction. Matt and Pedro stood where they were, swaying on their feet. Jamie moved towards his brother. Richard and Professor Chambers swung round with their now useless guns. They were trapped, huddled together in a group with the blazing house behind them, the lights in front, surrounded on all sides. Matt tried to see who it was that had arrived at this late stage. Did he have the power to send them back? He bowed his head, drawing on the last of his strength.

Then, as if from nowhere, a volley of arrows was fired in his direction. But not at him. They had been aimed deliberately over his head. Some of the creatures on the edge of the house cried out and fell back as they were hit. Another volley followed, taking out more of them. The lights were coming from the headlamps of four or five cars that had driven to the edge of the garden and parked in a semicircle. There were men running across the lawn. There were several gun shots. One of the men stopped and reached out for Professor Chambers who more or less collapsed in his arms. The others continued into the house, blasting away with hand guns, searching for any remaining attackers and setting to work, fighting the fire.

And suddenly Matt knew who they were.

They had helped Pedro and him when they had first come to Peru, spiriting them out of Cuzco through a network of underground tunnels. The two boys had stayed with them in their hidden city, Vilcabamba, high up in the mountains. They were Incas, the tribe that had once ruled Peru, but which had been reduced to little more than a handful of survivors, living in secret. They had promised to look after Matt and the other Gatekeepers while they were in Peru. And they had come, true to their word.

They were armed with guns as well as their own traditional weapons and they made short work of the attackers. Machetes swung through the darkness, slicing into rags and flesh. Bullets hammered through the night. It was over very quickly. Matt, Pedro, Scott and Jamie waited on the lawn while the last of the creatures was finished off. Richard was now helping to support Joanna Chambers. All the colour had left her face. She was barely able to stand.

One of the Incas came over to them. He was short with broad shoulders and a dark, serious face. 'Are you OK?' he asked.

'We're all right,' Richard said. 'But Professor Chambers has been hurt.'

'I am Tiso. We came when we heard the first alarm. I am sorry. We arrived too late.'

'We're just glad you're here,' Richard said. 'Can we go back into the house? We need to get her inside . . .'

But it was another half hour before the Incas had put out the flames and they could get back in. The roof and part of the first floor had gone, but there were still two bedrooms that were habitable and, once the debris and the dead bodies had been cleared, the six of them would be able to camp out on the ground floor.

The house would never be the same again. Matt looked at the charred wood and the soiled carpets, the broken windows and debris, and felt a mounting sadness. It had been such a beautiful place. Professor Chambers had lived there for much of her life but then he and the others had come along and ruined it for her. In a few hours, they were supposed to be departing—on their way to London. And this was the mess that they were leaving behind.

Tiso and some of the other Incas helped carry Professor Chambers into her study. Richard went with her and Pedro followed too. His healing powers were going to be needed more than ever, although it looked as if the professor might be too badly injured even for him. She needed medical help, and sure enough a doctor arrived a few minutes later, urgently summoned from the nearby town. Matt, Scott and Jamie stayed outside while she was examined. None of them said anything. They were exhausted. Just a few hours before they had been laughing together, having dinner and playing dice games. And now this!

Matt glanced at Scott. 'Where's the diary?' he asked. At that moment he almost wished they didn't have it. It didn't matter how valuable it was. It had so far brought them nothing but trouble.

Scott took it out of his jacket pocket and handed it over. 'I'm sorry,' he said. His voice was low. 'I didn't help you, back there. I didn't help Pedro. I wanted to. But . . .' His voice trailed off.

'It doesn't matter,' Matt said. 'Everything happened so quickly. Anyway, Pedro's going to be OK.'

'What are they doing in there?' Jamie stared at the closed study door. His voice was angry. He kicked out at the sofa were Ramon had been sitting. The dead man had been carried outside but there was still a great gash in the leather to remind them of what had happened. He turned to his brother. 'You got it wrong,' he said. 'You said he was telling the truth.'

Scott blushed—with embarrassment or perhaps with anger. 'I thought he was telling the truth,' he said.

'You may have been right,' Matt interrupted. The two brothers seldom argued and he was surprised to see them starting now. 'We can't be sure that Ramon was responsible for what happened tonight. He told us he was in danger and he was certainly right about that. They killed him. So maybe the rest of his story was true.'

'Can we use it?' Scott asked.

Matt opened the diary. There was a page covered with diagrams. One of them looked a bit like a motor car, though as if drawn by a child, and he remembered that Joseph of Cordoba—the mad monk—was supposed to have been able to predict the future. He flicked through it. Some of the pages had been marked with a modern pen. Someone had scribbled down words and figures, underlining certain areas of the text. Diego Salamanda? The diary had belonged to him and he could have spent weeks deciphering it. It seemed that he had left some of his handiwork behind.

Matt tried to make sense of some of the words but the monk had written in ancient Spanish and anyway his handwriting was almost illegible. 'I can't read this language,' he said. 'And although Pedro can speak it, he can't read . . .'

'Maybe the professor will be able to work it out,' Jamie suggested.

Professor Chambers. Matt remembered how Richard had looked when he had helped carry her in. The two of them had been inside for a long time.

And then the door of the study opened. Pedro came out. He shook his head briefly and sat down, looking miserable. The doctor followed him. He muttered a few words to Richard, then left the house, doing his best to avoid eye contact. That was when Matt knew that it wasn't going to be good news.

'Matt . . .' Richard called him over to the door. 'She wants to see you,' he said. His voice was hoarse. 'She wants to say goodbye.'

'Is she . . . ?' Matt realized what he'd just been told. 'She can't be dying,' he said. 'What about Pedro? Can't he help her?'

'It's too late for Pedro. There's nothing he can do.' Richard sighed. 'We've called an ambulance for her and it's on its way now. But she's not going to make it. I'm sorry, Matt. I don't know how it happened but she was stabbed. There's been a lot of internal bleeding and . . .' He stopped and took a deep breath. 'She's not in any pain. The doctor's seen to that. But there's nothing more we can do for her. Do you want me to come in with you?'

'No . . .' Matt went into the study.

Joanna Chambers was lying on the day-bed that she liked to use as a place to think when she was working. As usual, her desk was completely covered in papers along with a bottle of brandy and a box of her favourite cigars. The old-fashioned radio that she liked to listen to was next to her computer but it was turned off, silent, and somehow that made Matt sadder than anything else, the thought that she would never listen to it again.

She was still in her dressing gown but someone had drawn a blanket over her legs and chest. There was only one light on and it was burning low, casting a soft glow across the room.

He thought she was asleep but as he closed the door, she looked up. 'Matt . . . ?'

He went over to her. 'The ambulance is on its way,' he muttered. 'The doctor says . . .'

'Don't tell me any stuff and nonsense,' she cut in, and just for a moment she sounded exactly like her old self. 'There's nothing they can do for me and anyway I'm not going into any local hospital. Dreadful place.' She tried to shift her position but she didn't have the strength. 'Come and sit next to me,' she said.

Matt did as he was told. His eyes were stinging and there was an ache in his throat. Why did it have to happen like this? Why couldn't she be all right? He remembered Professor Chambers as he

106

had first seen her, piloting her own plane. She had worked out the secret of the Nazca Lines and she had been with him, in the middle of the desert, when they were attacked by the condors. He knew that without her, he would never have located the second gate. And since then, she had looked after them, never once complaining as her house was invaded and her work interrupted.

Matt had used his power to protect himself. Why hadn't he been able to do the same for her?

'Now you listen to me,' she said. She found his hand and clasped it. 'You mustn't be upset about me. You have a very great responsibility, Matt. I don't think you have any idea yet what is going to be asked of you. And how old are you? Fifteen! It's not fair . . .'

She closed her eyes for a few seconds, fighting for breath.

'The Old Ones will be beaten,' she said. 'Ever since the world began, there's always been good and evil, but somehow we've managed to muddle through. You'll see. It may not be easy. What happened today . . . silly, really. We should have known they would come.'

She let go of his hand. She couldn't manage very much more.

'That's what I wanted to tell you,' she said. Her voice was fading away. 'I'm so glad I met you, really. I'm glad we had our time here. I've always loved this place, always been happy here . . .'

She pointed at the door with one finger, telling him to leave her. Matt did as she said. Richard was waiting for him outside.

The ambulance arrived ten minutes later. But it was too late. Professor Chambers was already dead.

COUNCIL OF WAR

Matt woke up with the smell of burnt wood in his nostrils and the taste of it in his mouth. He had slept for about six hours but he might as well not have bothered. Even before he got out of bed, he knew that he was as tired as he had been when he got into it shortly after two o'clock the night before.

He'd had to share with Pedro. His own room had been destroyed by the fire, along with everything inside it—and it was only as he opened his eyes the following morning that he realized exactly what that meant. He no longer had a passport. He wasn't going to be travelling anywhere today, certainly not on a commercial flight—and that must have been just what the attack had set out to achieve. The Old Ones didn't want him arriving in London. They didn't want him anywhere near Scarlett Adams. And although there were policemen and private detectives looking out for her, she was completely isolated. One in England. Four in Peru. It certainly didn't add up to the Five.

Pedro was sitting, cross-legged on his bed, wearing only a pair of shorts. There was a plaster on the side of his head. Matt guessed that he had been awake for a while. Pedro was always the first to get up, but then, of course, in his old life he would have been begging on the streets of Lima, waiting for the commuter traffic long before dawn.

The two boys had been lying next to each other in twin beds.

'So what do we do now?' Pedro asked.

'I don't know, Pedro.' Matt got out of bed and pulled on a fresh T-shirt. 'We'll have to meet and decide.'

'Will we still go to England?'

'Yes.'

Pedro hadn't spoken very much about the journey and Matt suspected that he was finding it difficult to get his head around it. He had never been out of Peru in his life. Even the notion of getting on a plane was completely alien to him. He had only flown once and that had been in a helicopter which had crashed. The thought of spending fifteen hours in the air and landing in a completely different world unnerved him.

'I am sad that the professor is dead,' he said. 'She was very kind.'

'I know.' Matt wondered if he could have saved her. Was her death his fault? It seemed to him now that she had been doomed from the moment they had arrived, although he knew she would never have seen it that way. Even so . . . It had been two days since they had received the fax with the news about Scar. He wished now that they had all left at once.

There were now just five of them remaining: Matt, Pedro, Scott, Jamie and Richard. They met outside, sitting at a wooden table in the shade of a silk-cotton tree—a kapok, as it was also known. Professor Chambers had liked taking the boys around her garden, showing them all the different plants and talking about them. This one had somehow found its way out of the rainforest, she had said, and she couldn't understand how it was growing here at all. The table had been set up in the shade, the umbrella-shaped canopy and creamy white flowers of the kapok shielding them from the sun.

They might have been safer in the house but they could hardly bear to look at it, the ruin that it had become. Somehow, it didn't seem likely that the Old Ones would return . . . not in the daylight. And anyway, the Incas were somewhere close. There was no danger of a second attack. Richard had brought out a tray of iced lemonade and a plate of *empanadas*, the little cheese pastries that they had often devoured. But nobody was hungry. They were exhausted and unhappy. Nobody knew what they were supposed to do.

One thing was sure. They couldn't stay here much longer. The house still had water and electricity and they might even be able to repair the roof. But there was no alarm system. The Incas couldn't protect them indefinitely. And—more to the point—none of them wanted to be here. The moment Professor Chambers had been taken from the *hacienda*, all of its life seemed to have gone with her.

'OK . . .' It was Richard who was the first to speak and Matt was grateful to him for breaking the silence, for taking control. He was wearing a clean polo shirt and jeans, but he looked completely worn out, as if he hadn't slept at all.

'This is a council of war,' he said. 'Because it looks as if the war has finally arrived. We have to talk about last night. We have to deal with it and put it behind us. And I might as well start by saying that it was mainly my fault.' He held up a hand before anyone could interrupt him. 'When Ramon came to the house, I turned off the security system. But I never put it back on again. Not the radar, anyway. Maybe that was the idea. Maybe that was why he was sent to us. A diversion . . .'

'It was my fault too,' Scott cut in. 'Matt wanted me to look into his mind and I did. But somehow he managed to fool me. I thought he was telling the truth.'

'Maybe he *was* telling the truth,' Matt said. 'He brought us the diary . . . and do you really think he would have just sat there and allowed himself to be killed? Maybe they followed him from Lima. The whole point of last night could have been simply that they wanted the diary back.'

'The question we've got to ask ourselves is— what are we going to do next?' Richard said. 'It's been more than forty-eight hours since Scarlett Adams appeared in the newspapers. The Nexus are still watching her but we can't leave her on her own much longer. On the other hand . . .' He nodded at Matt. 'Matt has lost his passport so he's not flying anywhere.'

'We can use the door,' Jamie said. 'The same one that Scott and me came through. All we have to do is get to the Temple of Coricancha in Cuzco. We walk in . . . we walk out in London. We don't need a plane.'

It seemed obvious. It was exactly the reason why the doors had been built in the first place. But Richard shook his head. 'We can't use the doors,' he said. 'Think about it, Jamie. Salamanda had the diary and he obviously studied it carefully. If the Old Ones are looking for us—and it seems pretty likely that they are—that's exactly how they'll expect us to travel.'

'Maybe they never saw the diary,' Pedro said. 'It was in the office of *Señor* Salamanda. He could never have shown it to them.'

Richard was still unhappy. 'It's too much of a risk. Anyway, they know about the door in St Meredith's. Scarlett went through it. That's probably what started all this. They could be waiting for us there. I know it's boring, but I reckon we're much safer taking planes.'

'But Matt doesn't have a passport,' Scott said.

'The Nexus can get us into America,' Richard replied. 'I spoke to Nathalie Johnson this morning and she's sending a private plane. It's already on its way. And she's been in touch with John Trelawney. The two of them have enough clout to get us through immigration. They can also get Matt a new passport. After all, they didn't have any difficulty getting Pedro his. It'll take a couple of days but we could be in England by Tuesday.'

Scott and Jamie had met Nathalie Johnson before they came to Peru. She was an American businesswoman who had made a fortune out of computers before she had been drawn into the Nexus. John Trelawney was the senator who had been fighting in the presidential election. The result was going to be announced in just one day and he was still the favourite to win. The two of them were powerful friends.

Jamie considered what Richard had said. 'All right, then.' He shrugged. 'Let's go.'

'Not all of us,' Matt said.

There was a sudden silence around the table. All eyes were turned on him.

'I think we should separate,' he said.

'Are you crazy . . . ?' Scott began.

'Why?'

'What do you mean, Matt?'

Everyone was talking at once. Matt wasn't surprised. Even as he had decided what he was going to do, he had known that the rest of them would be against it. They were supposed to stick together. Finding each other, coming together . . . it was what their lives were all about. Five Gatekeepers. So far, against all the odds, four of them had managed to do exactly that. They were hours away from finding the fifth. It seemed completely mad to split up now.

'We've just got to be careful,' Matt explained. 'Richard and I were talking about it last night, before we were attacked. If all four of us get onto one plane and the Old Ones somehow manage to get control of it, they'll have us at their mercy. They'll be able to do anything with us. All four of us at once.'

'So what are you saying?' Jamie asked.

'We can't stay here,' Pedro added.

'I'm going to London with Richard,' Matt said. 'We'll meet the Nexus as soon as we can and we'll meet Scarlett as soon as we know it's safe.' He turned to Jamie. 'I'd like you to come with us.'

Jamie opened his mouth but said nothing. He understood the implications of what Matt had just suggested.

'You're leaving me behind,' Scott muttered. His voice was low and sullen.

'It's just for a few days. A week, no longer.'

'Is this because I screwed up last night?'

'You didn't screw up.' Matt had to choose his words carefully. In a way, Scott was right. He

113

might not be to blame, but he still couldn't be completely trusted. Matt looked at him, slumped back from the table with his hands in his pockets, and saw the cold anger in his face. And there was something else. A sort of cruelty. When Scott had lived ten thousand years ago, his name had been Flint and it suited him. Sitting in the garden, his eyes were as hard as stone.

'Scott and I don't like being apart,' Jamie said.

'I know that and I'm sorry,' Matt said. 'It's true that we're stronger together. That's why I want to stay in pairs. Two and two. If anything goes wrong in London, I'll need someone to back us up.'

'So why not take Pedro?'

'Because Pedro doesn't know London. He's never been to England.'

'Nor have I.'

Matt sighed. 'Jamie . . . if you really don't like the idea, I'll go on my own. I don't mind doing that. I just don't think we should all go. That's all. I'm trying to do what's best for everyone.'

'And since when did you get to tell everyone what they should do?' Scott demanded. 'I thought we were meant to be equal. Who put you in charge?'

There was another long pause. Richard opened his mouth as if to say something, then changed his mind. The day was getting warmer as the sun climbed over the mountains, but the atmosphere right then was anything but. Matt looked across the lawn to the track that led back to the town of Nazca. He had been there a couple of days ago, kicking a football, waiting for Professor Chambers to get back from the shops. Now she was dead, her house was in ruins and the four of them were at

114

each other's throats. How could things have gone wrong so quickly?

'Scott, I don't think . . .' Jamie began.

'Are you on his side?' Scott directed his anger at his brother.

'We're all on the same side,' Matt cut in. 'And if we turn against each other, we might as well give up.'

'You've never been on my side, Matt. You've never trusted me, not from the day I arrived here. Well, you go without me. You can all go without me. I don't care.'

Scott got up angrily, knocking his chair over behind him. He didn't even notice. He walked away in the direction of the house and disappeared through the front door. Nobody spoke. Then Jamie stood up. 'I'm sorry, Matt,' he said. 'I'll go and talk to him. He'll be all right.'

Jamie followed his brother. That just left Richard, Pedro and Matt. Richard poured out a glass of the lemonade. He offered it to Matt who shook his head. Richard drank it himself.

'Where do you want me to go?' Pedro asked. 'I do not think it is good for us to stay here.'

Matt sighed. 'I thought you'd go back to Vilcabamba with Tiso and the other Incas,' he said. 'I was hoping you could spend a bit more time with Scott . . .' Pedro understood. Scott still needed help after his experiences as a prisoner of Nightrise.

'I do what I can,' he said. 'But Scott has a lot of pain. There are things happening here . . .' He tapped the side of his head. 'I do not understand.'

'You were nearly killed last night. He didn't help you.'

115

'Yes. But he and Jamie are very close. Twins. Maybe it is not such a great idea to split them up.'

There didn't seem anything more to say. Pedro collected the jug and the glasses and carried them in. Richard and Matt were left on their own.

'That went well,' Matt said, gloomily.

Richard finished his lemonade and set the glass down. 'Don't be too hard on yourself,' he said. 'We're all feeling bad about last night, the death of Joanna. Jamie will talk to Scott. He knows you're doing the best you can. They'll work it out.'

'I hope so.'

'In just a week, you'll be in Vilcabamba. All of you. You've got the diary now. And despite what happened last night, you all came out of it OK. None of you was badly hurt. I'm sure you've made the right decision, Matt. It's all going to work out.'

But Matt wasn't so sure. He twisted round and looked at the house, at the scorched wood, what was left of the roof, and suddenly he was aware that something was wrong, that it didn't quite add up.

If Ramon had been able to find them so easily, why had it taken the Old Ones so long? And if they had wanted the diary back so badly, why hadn't they sent a larger force? Matt had seen the sort of creatures the Old Ones had at their disposal. They had crawled out of the floor of the Nazca Desert . . . the armed soldiers, the giant animals, the hoards of shape-changers. But they hadn't been there last night.

Was he making the right decision, splitting them up? Or was this what he was meant to do? Was he reacting to decisions that had already been made?

Later that afternoon, two cars came to the

house. One would take Pedro and Scott to Arequipa, the famous 'White City' in the south of Peru. They would have to stay there overnight before flying to Cuzco. Because of the thin air high up in the Andes, planes were only able to take off and land in the morning. Two of the Incas would go with them and then escort them up through the cloud forest to Vilcabamba.

Jamie, Richard and Matt had a shorter drive to Nazca airport where a private plane was already waiting to fly them up to Miami. They would wait in Miami until Matt's new passport arrived and then they would cross the Atlantic to England. If things went well, they would only be apart for a few days.

Matt took one last look at the professor's house. The town children would probably raid it in the next few days, stripping it of anything of value. He had been there for a long time. He had almost begun to think of it as his home but now it was nothing. Burned out. Broken. Empty.

Richard loaded their bags into the boot.

'Vilcabamba,' Matt said.

'Vilcabamba,' Pedro agreed.

The two of them shook hands. Scott and Jamie said nothing—but Matt knew that they were communicating even so.

It was all over very quickly. The four boys climbed into their different cars and went their separate ways.

THE HAPPY GARDEN

In London, Scarlett Adams was trying to get back to her old life.

The doctors had decided there was nothing wrong with her. The police had asked more questions but had finally given up. Maybe she had suffered from amnesia. Maybe the whole thing about her disappearance had been a schoolgirl prank—but either way they had better things to do. Even the press had decided to leave her alone. A new president, a man called Charles Baker, had just been elected in the USA, and according to all the reports, there had been something strange about the way the votes had been counted. It was turning into a huge scandal and that left no room in the papers for a girl who had been missing for less than a day.

Just forty-eight hours after he had flown all the way to England, Paul Adams went back to Hong Kong.

Scarlett understood why he couldn't stay with her. He had only recently started his new job, working in the legal department of a huge company involved, amongst other things, in the manufacture of computer equipment and software. It hadn't made a good impression, shooting off to London at such short notice. He had to get back again.

Back to Nightrise.

Paul Adams took Scarlett out to dinner on his last night at home. The two of them went to a little Italian restaurant that he liked in Dulwich. He ordered half a bottle of wine for himself and a lemonade for her and the two of them sat facing each other trying to think of things to say. Paul was wearing expensive jeans and a jersey that didn't really suit him. The truth was that he was only really comfortable in a jacket and tie. It was like a second skin to him. Maybe it was his age. He was forty-nine years old and he had been a lawyer for more than half that time, devoting his life to contracts, complicated reports and charts. It was hard to imagine what he had been like as a teenager.

'Are you going to be all right, Scarly?' he asked.

'Yes.' Scarlett nodded.

Neither of them had spoken very much about St Meredith's. Paul Adams seemed to have accepted her story. She had fallen ill. She had forgotten whatever had happened. Scarlett wondered why she hadn't confided in him. He had always been kind to her. Why was she lying to him now?

'I'm sorry, Dad,' she said.

'There's nothing to be sorry about.' Paul Adams paused and sipped his wine. 'Do you really have no idea what happened to you?'

'I wish I did.'

'You could tell me, you know. I wouldn't be cross with you. I mean, if there's some sort of secret or something you're afraid of . . .'

Scarlett shook her head. 'I told the police everything.'

Paul Adams nodded. Then the waiter arrived with spaghetti carbonara for him, a pizza for Scarlett. There was the usual business with the oversized pepper grinder, the sprinkle of parmesan cheese. At last they were on their own again.

119

'How's the job going?' Scarlett asked. She had deliberately changed the subject.

'Oh. It's not too bad.' Paul Adams twirled his fork in the spaghetti. 'Do you want to come to Hong Kong for the Christmas holidays? I've spoken to your mother and she's happy for me to have you this year. I'll get a few days off and we can travel together.'

'I'd like that,' Scarlett said, although she wondered what it would be like, travelling, just the two of them. They seemed to have grown apart so quickly.

They ate in silence. Paul Adams didn't seem to be enjoying his food. He left half of it, then took off his glasses and began to rub them with his napkin. Looking at him just then, Scarlett thought how old he had become. It wasn't just his hair that was going grey. It was all of him.

'I'm sorry, Scarly,' he said. 'I'm afraid I've rather let you down, haven't I? If I'd known that Vanessa and I weren't going to stay together . . . maybe we should have thought twice about adopting a child, although of course I'm glad we did. I think the world of you. But it hasn't been fair. Leaving you on your own with Mrs Murdoch.'

'It was my decision,' Scarlett reminded him.

'Well, yes. I suppose it was.'

'Why do you have to work in Hong Kong?' Scarlett asked.

'It's a wonderful opportunity. Not just the money. Nightrise has offices all over the world and if I can work my way up the ladder . . .' His voice trailed off. 'I'll only be there a couple of years. I've told them already. Then I want them to transfer me to the London office and we'll be together

120

again.'

'Don't worry about me, Dad. I'll be all right.'

'Will you, Scarly? I hope so.'

He left on the early flight the next day.

Scarlett had already gone back to school—and that hadn't been easy either. The headmistress, a grey-haired woman who looked more severe than she actually was, had made a speech in assembly, telling everyone to leave her alone, but of course they had been all over her, bombarding her with questions, desperate to know where she had really been. Scarlett had been on TV. She was a minor celebrity. Some of the younger girls had even asked her for an autograph. On the other hand, some of the teachers had been less than happy to see her—Joan Chaplin in particular. The art teacher had taken some of the responsibility for Scarlett's disappearance and she in turn blamed Scarlett for that.

The next couple of days passed with the usual routine of lessons and games. There were piles of homework and rehearsals for the Christmas play. Everything had returned to normal—at least, that was what Scarlett told herself. But in her heart, she knew that nothing was really normal at all. Maybe it never would be again.

She had already decided that there was only one person she could talk to and tell the truth about her disappearance. Not her father. Not Mrs Murdoch. It had to be Aidan. He was her closest friend. He wouldn't laugh at her. She had already texted him and the two of them met after school and walked home together, taking their time, allowing the other school kids to stream ahead.

She told him everything: the door, the

monastery, Father Gregory, the escape. She was still talking as they turned into Dulwich Park, opposite the art gallery, taking the long way round past the playground and across the grass.

'Do you think I'm mad?' she asked, when she had finished. There had been times when she had begun to wonder herself. Could it be that the official version of events was actually true? Had she somehow hit her head against a wall and dreamed the whole thing?

'I always thought you were pretty strange,' Aidan said.

'But to dream something like that . . .'

'You don't make it sound like a dream.' His eyes brightened. 'Hey—maybe we could go back to the church. We could go through the door a second time and see what happened.'

Scarlett shuddered. 'I couldn't do that.'

'Why not? If you went with me, at least it would prove it was true.'

'I couldn't go back. They might be waiting for me. They'd grab me and the whole thing would just start again.'

'I'd protect you!'

'They'd kill you. They'd kill both of us.'

They had reached the other side of the park and were coming out of the Court Lane Gate on the north side. From here the road cut down to the lights where, two years before, Scarlett had almost been killed.

Scarlett had just turned the corner when she saw the car.

It was a silver Mercedes with tinted windows so that although she could make out two people inside it, she couldn't see their faces. It was parked on the opposite side of the road and she might not even have noticed it . . . except that it was the fourth time she had seen it. It had been in the street that morning, parked outside The Crown and Greyhound when she was on her way to school. Once again, there had been two people sitting inside. It had overtaken her when she was walking to the Italian restaurant with her father. And she had seen it from her bedroom, cruising down the street where she lived. She had made a note of the registration number. It contained the letters GEN which just happened to be the first three letters of St Genevieve's. That was why she remembered it now.

She stopped.

'What is it?' Aidan asked.

'Those two men.' She pointed at the car. 'They're watching me.'

'Scarl . . .'

'I mean it. I've seen them before.'

Aidan looked in their direction. 'Maybe they're journalists,' he said. 'You're still a mystery. They could be after an interview.'

'They've been following me.'

'I'll ask them, if you like.'

They must have seen him coming or guessed what he had in mind. As Aidan stepped off the pavement, the driver started the engine up and tore away, disappearing round the corner with a screech of tyres.

Scarlett didn't see the Mercedes again but that wasn't the end of it. Quite the opposite. It told her something that she had been feeling all along.

She was being watched. She was sure of it. It had crept up on her over the past few days, before

Paul Adams had left, a sense that she was trapped, like a specimen in a laboratory glass slide. She had found herself gazing at complete strangers in the street, convinced that they were spying on her. When she walked past a security camera outside a shop or an office it almost seemed to swivel round, its single, glass eye focusing on her—and she could imagine someone in a secret room far away, staring at her on a television monitor, picking her out from the crowd.

Even when she was on her own in her room she had got the sense of someone eavesdropping, and after a while, just the flapping of a curtain would be enough to unnerve her. When she made phone calls—it didn't matter if it was her mobile or a landline—she was sure she could hear something in the background. Breathing. A faint echo. Someone listening.

She wasn't imagining it. It was there.

Scarlett had tried to tell herself that none of this was possible. She knew that there was a word for what she was experiencing. Paranoia. Why would anyone bother to watch her? Nobody was watching her. She was just freaked out by what had happened before.

'There were five children. They came to be known as the Gatekeepers. Four boys and a girl. You are the girl.'

It was when she saw the Mercedes with Aidan that Scarlett understood that what had started at St Meredith's wasn't over yet. It had only just begun.

The next day—Friday—was miserable. Scarlett hadn't slept properly. She was snappy with Mrs Murdoch and managed to make a spectacular

124

mess of a maths test at school. She didn't want to be in class. She just wanted to go back to her room and close the door—to shut 'them' out, even though she didn't have any idea who 'they' might be.

That evening, she got a phone call. It was Aidan.

'Hi, Scarlett,' he said. 'I was wondering . . . do you want to come to a movie tomorrow?'

Just that one sentence and she knew that something was wrong. Scarlett didn't reply immediately. She cradled her mobile in the palm of her hand, playing back what she had just heard. First of all, Aidan never called her Scarlett. He called her Scarl. And there had been something weird about his tone of voice. He hadn't asked her out as if he really meant it. He sounded fake, as if he was reading from a script.

As if he knew he was being overheard.

She lifted the mobile again. 'What do you want to see?'

'I don't know. The new Batman or something. We can go into the West End . . .'

And that was odd too. Why travel all the way into town? Dulwich had a perfectly good cinema.

'OK,' she said. 'What time do you want to meet?'

'Twelve?'

'I'll see you here . . .'

Aidan arrived at exactly midday, dressed in his trademark hoodie and jeans. As they walked over to the Tube station together, Scarlett wondered if she hadn't read too much into the conversation the night before. He seemed completely relaxed and cheerful. The two of them chatted about school, football, fast food and the American election which was still in the news. Aidan was interested in politics even if it left Scarlett completely cold.

'Charles Baker is a creep,' he said. 'I can't believe anyone voted for him as President. The other guy, Trelawney, should have walked it.'

'So why didn't he?'

'I don't know. Some people are saying they screwed up the voting slips. But I'm telling you, Scarl, the wrong guy won.'

They reached the cinema, the Empire in Leicester Square, but as they approached the box office, Aidan suddenly grabbed Scarlett and dragged her to one side. In an instant, his whole mood had changed. He made sure there was no one else around, then hurriedly began to speak.

'Scarl, I've got to tell you. Something really weird has happened.'

'What is it?' Scarlett was completely thrown.

'I didn't know whether to tell you or not. But yesterday, when I called you, I was told to do it! This guy came up to me when I was coming out of school.'

'What guy?'

'I'd never seen him before. At first I thought he was trying to sell me something. He was Chinese. A young guy. He asked me to get a message to you.'

'Why didn't he tell me himself?'

'I'm only telling you what he told me.' Aidan ran a hand through his long, shaggy hair. There was still no one in this part of the foyer. A short distance away, a family of four was just going in to the film. 'He just came up to me and asked if he could talk to me. He knew my name. And he knew

126

I was your friend.'

'What did he want?'

'Listen . . . I don't want to freak you out but he told me that he couldn't approach you himself because your phone was bugged and you were being watched. He said you were in danger.' Aidan paused. 'Has this got something to do with what happened in the church?'

'I don't know, Aidan,' Scarlett said. All her fears had just been confirmed. She didn't know if that made her feel better or worse. She looked around her. 'So where is this mysterious Chinese man? Are we meeting him here?'

'No. He's round the corner . . . in a restaurant. The Happy Garden. It's in Wardour Street, about five minutes away.'

'So why are we here?'

'That was my idea. I had to tell you what was going on, but I couldn't do it on the Tube in case someone was listening. I'm sorry, Scarl. I didn't want to lie to you but this guy sounded really serious. And it was only yesterday we saw that car at the park.' Aidan drew a breath. 'You don't have to go,' he said. 'Maybe you shouldn't go.'

'Why not?'

'Maybe you should go to the police.'

Scarlett had to admit that he had a point. Everyone knew that when a strange adult approached a kid outside school, it was time to dial 999. But she had already made up her mind. If she didn't go to this restaurant, she might never find out who the man was or what he wanted.

'The Happy Garden,' she muttered. 'What sort of name is that?'

'It's a Chinese restaurant,' Aidan said.

'Oh yes,' she nodded. 'I suppose it would be.'
She thought for a moment. 'Did the man say
anything else?'

'Yes. He said that the two of you had met
before. On Dulwich Grove, two years ago. He
must have been talking about the accident . . .'

If Scarlett had had any doubts, that decided it.
The man who had saved her, who hadn't waited to
be thanked, had been Chinese. It had to be the
same person. But what was he doing back in her
life?

'What time am I meant to be there?' she asked.

'Half past one.'

She looked at her watch. It was just after one
o'clock. 'We're going to be early.'

'So you're going?'

'I've got to, Aidan. I don't think anything too
bad can happen in the middle of a Chinese
restaurant. And anyway, you'll be with me.' She
paused. 'Won't you?'

'Sure.' Aidan nodded. 'I wouldn't leave you on
your own. Anyway, I can't wait to find out what
this is all about.'

They left the cinema the way they'd come,
slipping quietly into the crowds in Leicester
Square. It was unlikely that anyone had followed
them all the way from Dulwich but Scarlett wasn't
taking any chances. They turned up an alleyway
that led into Chinatown, an area that was packed
with Chinese restaurants and supermarkets. From
here, they crossed over Shaftesbury Avenue,
heading for the address that Aidan had been given.

The afternoon was surprisingly warm. It was
lunch-time, there were lots of people around. The
smell of fried noodles hung in the air.

The explosion happened just as they were about to turn the corner into Wardour Street. They didn't just hear it. They felt it too. The pavement actually shuddered under their feet and a gust of warm air punched into them, carrying with it a cloud of dust and soot. If they had been just ten seconds earlier, they might have been hit by the full impact. A bomb had gone off. A large one. It had happened somewhere near.

'Stop . . . !' Aidan began.

He was too late. Scarlett had already run forward and turned the corner.

A scene of devastation greeted her on the other side. A building about half-way up the road had been blown to pieces. It was as if someone had punched a giant fist into it. There was glass and debris all over the pavement, and tongues of flame were licking out of the shattered brickwork. A taxi must have been passing at the moment the bomb went off. All its windows were broken and the driver had tumbled out, blind, blood pouring down his face. A woman was standing nearby, screaming and screaming, her clothes in tatters, covered in blood and broken glass. There was smoke everywhere but Scarlett could make out several bodies, lying still, some of them in rags. She had seen images like this on TV, in Baghdad and Jerusalem. But this was Soho, the centre of London. And she knew that she'd almost been part of it. It might have been Aidan and her, lying in the rubble.

Aidan had caught up with her. 'We should go,' he said.

'But the restaurant . . .'

'That *is* the restaurant.'

Scarlett couldn't move. She stared at the gaping hole, the smoke billowing out, the smashed furniture and the bodies. It was a restaurant. He was right.

'Come on . . . !' Aidan pleaded.

Scarlett could already hear the sirens of the police cars and ambulances moving in from some other part of the city. It was amazing how quickly they had been alerted. She allowed Aidan to lead her away. She didn't want to be found there. Part of her even wondered if she might somehow have been to blame.

It was the first story on the news that night. A restaurant called The Happy Garden had been the target of a lethal attack. Three people had been killed and a dozen more injured by a bomb that had been concealed under one of the tables. According to the police, this wasn't a terrorist incident. They put the blame on Chinese gangs which had been operating in the West End.

'Police today are speculating that the attack is the result of rising tension within the Chinese community,' the newscaster said.

Scarlett watched the broadcast with Mrs Murdoch. The housekeeper was knitting. 'Weren't you in Soho today, Scarlett?' she asked.

'No,' Scarlett lied. 'I was on the other side of the town. I was nowhere near.'

'This is the most serious attack so far,' the report went on. 'It follows other incidents involving gangs in Peckham and Mile End. Any witnesses are urged to come forward and Scotland Yard has set up a special phone line for anyone with any information that might help.'

Scarlett texted Aidan that night before she went

to bed and he texted back. They both agreed that it was just a coincidence. Despite what they had thought earlier, it would be absurd to suggest that a restaurant in the middle of London had been blown up just to stop them meeting someone there.

But as she turned out the lights and tried to get to sleep, Scarlett knew that it wasn't. The newscaster had been lying. The police were lying. There were no gangs . . . just an enemy who was still playing with her and who wouldn't stop until she was completely in their control.

MATT'S DIARY (2)

Sunday
A bomb has gone off in London. I've just been watching it on the television news and I wonder if it might have something to do with Scarlett. Richard thinks it's unlikely. According to the reports, the bomb had been hidden in a restaurant in Chinatown. It was something to do with Chinese gang warfare. Three people have been killed.

I saw the images on the big plasma screen TV in my hotel room. Dead people, ambulances, screaming relatives, smoke and broken glass . . . it was hard to believe that it was all happening in the middle of Soho. You just don't expect it there. It made me feel even further away than I actually was.

Miami. I've never been here before and I certainly never dreamed that I'd wind up in a five-star hotel overlooking the beach, surrounded by Cadillacs, Cuban music and palm trees. The Nexus has certainly put us up in style while we wait for my new passport to arrive. The only trouble is, it's taking longer than we had hoped. We're now booked onto a flight leaving on Monday evening and we'll have to kick our heels until then. Scarlett will just have to manage without us for a couple more days. We'll be with her soon enough.

It feels strange, being back in a big city after spending so much time in a backwater like Nazca. Miami is full of rich people and expensive houses. It's too cold to swim at this time of the year, but a lot of life still seems to be happening in the street. We didn't do much today. I bought myself some new clothes, replacing the stuff that got lost in the fire. We walked. And tonight we ate on Ocean Drive, a long strip of fancy cafés and bars with bright pink neon lights, cocktails and live bands. It was good to be able to enjoy ourselves, sitting there, watching the crowds go past.

Nobody noticed us. For a few hours we could pretend we were normal.

Monday afternoon

This morning, the passport finally arrived, delivered in a brown, sealed envelope by a motorbike rider who didn't say a word. Terrible photograph. The Nexus have sent Jamie a new passport too, and they've decided that we should both travel under false names, for extra security. So now I'm Martin Hopkins. He is Nicholas Helsey. Richard is going to stay as himself but then, as far as we know, nobody is trying to kill him.

We have economy tickets. The Nexus could have flown us first class but they didn't want us to stand out.

132

We had our final meal on Ocean Drive. A huge plate of nachos and two Cokes. Richard had a beer. I wondered what the waiter must have made of us: Richard in a gaudy, Hawaiian shirt, sitting between two teenagers, the two of us wearing sunglasses even though there wasn't a lot of sun. We'd bought them the day before and hadn't got round to taking them off. We liked them because they kept us anonymous. If anyone had asked, we were going to say that he was a teacher and that we were on a school exchange. It was a pretty unlikely story—but nothing compared to the truth.

I've spoken to Pedro via satellite phone a couple of times while we've been here. He and Scott reached Vilcabamba without any problem. We've agreed to contact each other every day while we are apart. If there's silence, we'll know something is wrong. Pedro told me that Scott was OK. But Scott didn't come on the line.

Jamie asked me something today. It took me by surprise. 'Why did you really leave Scott behind? You didn't think you could rely on him, did you?'

'I never said that.'

'But you thought it.' He lowered his voice. 'You have no idea what he went through with Mrs Mortlake. It was worse than anything you can imagine.'

'Has he talked to you about it?'

Jamie shook his head. 'He's put up barriers. He won't go there. He's not the same any more. I know that. But you have no idea how he looked after me all those years. When Uncle Don was beating me around or when I was in trouble at school, Scott was always there for me. The only reason he got caught was that he was helping me get away.' He suddenly

133

took off his sunglasses and laid them on the table. 'Don't underestimate him, Matt. I know he's not himself right now, but he'll never let you down.'

I hope Jamie is right. But I'm not sure.

I looked across the road. There were some little kids throwing a ball on a lawn beside the beach. A couple of rollerbladers swung by. A pale green convertible drove past with music blaring. And just a few metres away, we were talking about torture and thinking about a war that we might not be able to win. Two different worlds. I know which one I'd have preferred to be in.

We finished eating and went back to the hotel. Our car was already there. The concierge carried out our cases and then it was a twenty-minute drive across the causeway. The water, stretching out on both sides, looked blue and inviting. We reached Miami International Airport and went in, joining the crowds at the check-in desks. Thousands of people travelling all over the world. And this is what I was thinking . . .

Suppose the Old Ones are already here. Suppose they control this airport. We are allowing ourselves to be swallowed up by a system . . . tickets, passports, security. How do we know we can trust it, that it will take us where we want to go, or even let us out again?

We got to the baggage check. Richard took one look at the X-ray machines and stopped. 'I'm an idiot,' he said.

'What is it?'

He was carrying a backpack on his shoulder, cradling it under one arm. He'd had it with him at the restaurant too and I knew that among other things, the monk's diary was inside. But now he was watching as people took out their computers and removed their belts and I could see that he was

134

furious with himself. 'The tumi,*' he said. 'I meant to transfer it to my main luggage. They'll never let it through.'*

The tumi *is a sacrificial knife. It was given to him by the prince of the Inca tribe just before we left Vilcabamba. I could understand Richard wanting to keep it close to him. It was made of solid gold, with semi-precious stones in the hilt, and it must have been worth a small fortune. But this was a mistake. He might try to argue that the* tumi *was an antique, an ornament or just a souvenir, but given that the airlines wouldn't even allow you to carry a teaspoon unless it was made of plastic, there was no way it was going to be allowed on the plane.*

It was too late to do anything now. There was a long line of people behind us and we wouldn't have been allowed to turn back. Richard dumped the bag on the moving belt and grimaced as it disappeared inside the X-ray machine. I suppose he was hoping that the security people might glance away at the right moment and miss it. But that wasn't going to happen. The bag came out again. It was grabbed by an unsmiling woman with her name—Monica Smith—on a badge on her blue, short-sleeved shirt.

'Is this yours?' she asked.

'Yes.' Richard prepared for the worst.

'Can you unzip this, please?'

'I can explain . . .' Richard began.

'Just open it, please.'

The tumi *was right on the top. I could see the golden figure of the Inca god that squatted above the blade. I watched as the woman, wearing latex gloves, began to rifle through Richard's clothes. Briefly, she picked up the diary, then put it back again. She examined a magnifying glass that Richard had* bought in Miami, trying to decipher the monk's handwriting. But she didn't even seem to notice that the tumi was there. She closed the bag again.

'Thank you,' she said.

Richard looked at me. Neither of us said anything. We snatched up our belongings and hurried forward. It was only afterwards that we understood what had happened.

The tumi has another name. It's also known as the invisible blade. When the prince of the Incas gave it to Richard, he said that no one would ever find it, that he would be able to carry it with him at any time. He also warned Richard that one day he would regret having it—something neither of us really like to think about.

But now we both realized what we had just seen. It was a bit of ancient magic. And it was all the more amazing because it happened in the setting of a modern, international airport.

Monday night

We took off exactly on time and once the seat belt signs had been turned off, I sat back in my seat and began to write this. In the seat next to me, Jamie had plugged himself straight into the TV console, watching a film. Richard was across the aisle, working with a Spanish dictionary, trying to unravel the diary.

A bit later, I fell asleep.

And that was when I went back. I had wanted to visit the dreamworld again, ever since I had discovered the path set into the side of the hill. Was it really possible that a civilization of some sort had once lived there? Might they be living there still? The dreamworld was a sort of in-between place, connecting where we were now with the world that Jamie had visited and where he had fought his battle, ten thousand years ago. It was there to help us. The more we knew about it, the better prepared we would be.

*   *   *

I was right where I wanted to be, back on the hillside, half-way up the path. But that was how the dreamworld worked. Every time I fell asleep, I picked up exactly where I had left off. So if I woke up throwing a stone into the air, when I went back to sleep I would immediately catch it again. And I was wearing the same clothes that I had on the plane. That was how it worked too.

The hill became steeper and the path turned into a series of steps. They had definitely been made by human hand. As I continued climbing up, they became ever more defined and when I finally reached the summit I found myself on a square platform with some sort of design—it looked like a series of Arabic letters—cut into it. The letters made no sense to me, but then I lifted my head and what I saw was so amazing that I'm surprised I didn't wake up at once and find myself back on the plane.

I was looking at a city, sprawling out in all directions, as far as the eye could see. More than that. From where I was standing, high up on the hill, I could see thousands of rooftops stretching all the way to the horizon, perhaps ten miles away, but I got the impression that if I managed to walk all the way to the other side, it would continue to the next horizon and maybe to the one after that.

It was impossible to say if the city was ancient or

modern. It somehow managed to be both at the same time. Some of the buildings were huge, cathedral-like with arched windows and domes covered in tiles that could have been silver or zinc. Others were steel and glass structures that reminded me of an airport terminal and then I realized that there were actually dozens of them and they were all identical, radiating out of central courtyards like the spokes of a wheel. Towers rose up at intervals, again with silver turrets. Everything was connected, either by spiral staircases or covered walkways.

There were no parks and no trees. There weren't any cars or people. In fact, I wasn't looking at a city at all. This vast construction was one single building: a massive cathedral, a massive museum, a massive . . . something. It was a mishmash of styles, some parts must have been added hundreds or even thousands of years after others—but it was all locked together. It was one. I couldn't work out where the centre was. I couldn't see where it had originally begun. Nor could I imagine how it had come into being. It was as if someone had taken a single seed— one brick—and dropped it into a bubbling swamp. And this, after thousands of years of growth, was the result.

* * *

Leaving the platform behind me, I walked down the other side of the hill and made my way towards the outer wall. I was now following a road with a marble-like surface and it was taking me directly towards a great big arch and, on the other side of it, an open door. The air was very still. I could actually hear my heart beating as I approached. I didn't think

I was in danger, but there was something so weird about this place, so far removed from my experience, that I admit I was afraid. I didn't hesitate though. I passed through the arch and suddenly I was inside, in a long corridor with a tiled, very polished floor and a high, vaulted ceiling held up by stone pillars: not quite a church, not quite a museum, but something similar to both.

'Can I help you?'

Another shock. I wasn't on my own. And the question was so normal, so polite that it just didn't seem to belong to this extraordinary place.

There was a man standing behind a lectern, the sort of things lecturers have in front of them when they talk. He was quite small, a couple of inches shorter than me, and he had one of those faces . . . I won't say it was carved out of stone (it was too warm and human for that) but it somehow seemed ages old, gnarled by time and experience.

From the look of him, I would have said he was an Arab, a desert tribesman, but without any of the trappings such as a headdress, white robes or a dagger. Instead, he was dressed in a long, silk jacket—faded mauve and silver—with a large pocket on each side and baggy, white trousers. A beard would have suited him but he didn't have one. His hair was steel grey. His eyes were the same colour. They were regarding me with polite amusement.

'What is this place?' I asked.

'This place?' The man seemed surprised that I had asked. 'This is the great library. And it's very good to see you again.'

A library. I remembered something Jamie had told me. When he met Scarlett at Scathack Hill, she had mentioned visiting a library to him.

139

'We've never met.'

'I think we have.' The man smiled at me. I wasn't sure what language he was speaking. In the dreamworld, all languages are one and the same and people can understand each other no matter where they've come from. 'You're Matthew Freeman. At least, that's the name you call yourself. You're one of the Gatekeepers. The first of them, in fact.'

'Do you have a name?'

'No. I'm just the Librarian.'

'I'm looking for Scarlett,' I said. 'Scarlett Adams. Has she been here?'

'Scarlett Adams? Scarlett Adams? You mean . . . Scar! Yes, she most certainly has been here. But not for a long time. And she's not here now.'

'Do you know where I can find her?'

'I'm afraid not.'

We were walking down the corridor together, which was strange because I couldn't remember starting. And we had passed into a second room, part of the library . . . it was obvious now. I had never seen so many books. There were books on both sides of me, standing like soldiers, shoulder to shoulder, packed into wooden shelves that stretched on and on into the distance, finally—a trick of perspective— seeming to come together at a point. The shelves began at floor level and rose all the way to the ceiling, maybe a hundred rows in each block. The air was dry and smelled of paper. There must have been a million books in this room alone and each one of them was as thick as an encyclopaedia.

'You must like reading,' I said.

'I never have time to read the books. I'm too busy looking after them.'

'How many of you are there?'

'Just me.'

'Who built the library?'

'I couldn't tell you, Matt. It was already here before I arrived.'

'So what are these books? Do you have a crime section? And romance?'

'No, Matt.' The Librarian smiled at the thought. 'Although you will find plenty of crime, and plenty of romance for that matter, among their pages. But all the books in the library are biographies.'

'Who of?'

'Of all the people who have ever lived and quite a few who are still to be born. We keep their entire lives here. Their beginnings, their marriages, their good days and their bad days, their deaths—of course. Everything they ever did.'

We stopped in front of a door. There was a sign on it, delicately carved into the wood. A five-pointed star.

'I know this,' I said.

'Of course you do.'

'Where does this door go?'

'It goes anywhere you want it to.'

'It's like the door at St Meredith's!' I said.

'It works the same way . . . but there you have only twenty-four possible destinations. In your world, there are twenty-five doors, all connecting with each other—although none of them will bring you back here. This library, on the other hand, has a door in every room and I have absolutely no idea how many rooms there are and wouldn't even know how to count them.' The Librarian gestured with one hand. 'After you.'

'Where are we going?'

'Well, since you're here, why don't we have a look

141

at your life? Aren't you curious?'
   'Not really.'
   'Let's see . . .'

                    *   *   *

We went through the door and for all I knew at that
moment we crossed twenty miles to the other side of
the city. We found ourselves in a chamber that was
certainly very different from the one we had left, with
plate-glass windows all around us, held in place by a
lattice-work of steel supports. Maybe this was one of
the airport terminals I had seen. The books here were
on metal shelves, each one with a narrow walkway
and a circular platform that moved up and down like
a lift but with no cables, no pistons, no obvious
means of support.
   We went up six levels and shuffled along the ledge
with a railing on one side, the books on the other.
   'Matt Freeman . . . Matt Freeman . . .' The
Librarian muttered my name as we went.
   'Are they in alphabetical order?' I asked. All the
volumes looked the same except that some were
thicker than others. I couldn't see any names or titles.
   'No. It's more complicated than that.'
   I looked back at the door that we'd come through.
It was now below and behind us. 'How do the doors
work?' I asked.
   'How do you mean?'
   'How do you know where they'll take you?'
   He stopped and turned to look at me. 'If you just
wander through them, they'll take you anywhere,' he
said. 'But if you know exactly where you want to go,
that's where they'll take you.'
   'Can anyone use them?'

'The doors in your world were built just for the five of you.'

'What about Richard?'

'You can each take a companion with you, if you're so minded. Just remember to decide where you're going before you step through or you could end up scattered all over the planet.'

We continued on our way but after another couple of minutes, the Librarian suddenly stopped, reached up and took out a book. 'Here you are,' he said. 'This is you.'

I looked at the book suspiciously. Like all the others it was oversized, bound in some grey fabric, old but perhaps never read. It looked more like a school book than a novel or a biography. I noticed that it had fewer pages than many of the others.

'Is that it?' I asked.

'Absolutely.' The Librarian seemed disappointed that I wasn't more impressed.

'That's my whole life?'

'Yes.'

'My whole life up to now . . .'

'Up to now and all the way to the end.'

The thought of that made my head swim. 'Does it say when I die?'

'The book is all about you, Matt,' the Librarian explained patiently. 'Inside its pages you will find everything you have ever done and everything you will do. Do you want to know when you next meet the Old Ones? You can read it here. And yes, it will tell you exactly when you will die and in what manner.'

'Are you telling me that someone has written down everything that happens to me before it happens?' I know that was exactly what he had just said but I had to get my head around it.

'Yes.' He nodded.

'Then that means that I've got no choice. Everything I do has already been decided.'

'Yes, Matt. But you have to remember, it was decided by you.'

'But my decisions don't mean anything!' I pointed at the book and suddenly I was beginning to hate the sight of it. 'Whatever I do in my life, the end is still going to be the same. It's already been written.'

'Do you want to read it?' the Librarian asked.

'No!' I shook my head. 'Put it away. I don't want to see it.'

'That's your choice,' the Librarian said with a sly smile. He slid the book back into the space it had come from. But I had one last question.

'Who wrote the book?' I asked.

'There is no author listed. All the books in the library are anonymous. That's one of the reasons why it makes them so hard to catalogue.'

I was beginning to feel miserable. The dreamworld seemed to exist to help us, but every time we came here it was simply confusing. Jamie and Pedro had both found this too. 'You call yourself a librarian,' I snapped at the man. 'So why can't you be more helpful? Why don't you have any answers?'

He tapped the spine of the book. 'All the answers are here,' he said. 'But you just refused to look at them.'

'Then answer me this one question. Am I going to win or lose?'

'Win or lose?'

'Against the Old Ones.' I swallowed. 'Am I going to get killed?'

'We are experiencing some turbulence . . .'

The Librarian was still looking at me, but he

144

hadn't spoken those words. With a sense of frustration, I felt myself being sucked away. There was someone leaning over me. A member of the cabin crew.

'I'm sorry I've had to wake you up,' she said. 'The captain has put on the seat belt sign.'

I looked at my watch. We still had four more hours in the air. Richard and Jamie were asleep but I knew I wouldn't be able to join them. I took out my notepad and started writing again.

Four hours until London.

Soon we will be home.

CROSSING PATHS

Scarlett thought she'd be safe, back at school. She'd slip back into the crowd and nobody would notice her. After all, nothing exciting ever happened at school. Wasn't that the whole point? So, for the first time in her life, she found herself looking forward to the next Monday morning. There would be no bombs, no strange men in cars, no cryptic messages. She would be swallowed up by double maths and physics and everything would be all right.

But it didn't happen that way.

Shortly before lunch, she was called into the headmistress's office. There was no explanation, just a brief: 'Mrs Ridgewell would like to see you at twelve fifteen.' Scarlett was nervous as she climbed the stairs. In a way, she'd been expecting trouble ever since the trip to St Meredith's. She had been the centre of attention for far too long and for all the wrong reasons. Her work had gone rapidly downhill. She'd been told off twice for daydreaming in class. And then there had been that terrible maths test. The teachers had already decided that all the publicity had gone to her head and Scarlett fully expected Mrs Ridgewell to read her the riot act. Get your head down. Pull your socks up. That sort of thing.

But what the headmistress said came right out of the blue.

'Scarlett, I'm afraid you're going to be leaving us for a few weeks. I've just had a phone call from your father. It seems that some sort of crisis has arisen . . .'

'What crisis?' Scarlett asked.

'He didn't say. He was very mysterious, if you want the truth. But he wants you to join him immediately in Hong Kong. In fact, he's already arranged the flight.'

There was a moment's silence while Scarlett took this in. There were all sorts of questions that she wanted to ask, but she began with the most obvious. 'Has this got something to do with what happened to me?'

'I don't think so.'

'Then what?'

'He didn't say.' Mrs Ridgewell sighed. She had taught at St Genevieve's for more than twenty years and it showed. Her office was cluttered and a little shabby, with antique furniture and books everywhere. A Siamese cat—it was called Chaucer—lay asleep in a basket in a corner. 'You haven't had a very good term, have you Scarlett?'

'No.' Scarlett shook her head miserably. 'I'm sorry, Mrs Ridgewell. I don't know what's going

146

on, really. Everything seems to have gone wrong.'

'Well, maybe we should look on the bright side. A complete break for a few weeks might do you good. I'll ask your teachers to prepare some work for while you're out there—and, of course, we're going to have to recast the Christmas play. I have to say that it is all very inconvenient.'

'Didn't he say anything?'

'I've told you everything I know, I'm afraid. I thought he would have discussed it with you.'

'No. I haven't heard from him.'

'Well, I'm sure there's nothing to worry about. He told me he'd ring you tonight. So you've just got time to say goodbye to your friends.'

'When am I leaving?'

'Your flight is tomorrow.'

Tomorrow! Scarlett couldn't believe what she was hearing. Tomorrow was only a few hours away. How could her dad have done this to her? He hadn't mentioned anything when they were in the Italian restaurant. What crisis could possibly have arisen in less than a week?

Scarlett spent the rest of the day in a complete daze. Her friends were equally surprised, although the truth was that she was beginning to get a bit of a reputation. She was weird. First the church and now this. She didn't even get to see Aidan. She looked for him on the way home and tried texting him, but he didn't reply. Mrs Murdoch had already heard the news. She had started packing by the time Scarlett got home. And she didn't seem pleased.

'Not a word of warning,' she muttered. 'And no explanation. What do you suppose I'm meant to do, sitting here on my own?'

147

Paul Adams rang that night as he had promised, but he didn't tell Scarlett anything she wanted to know.

'I'm really sorry, Scarly . . .' His voice on the line was thin and very distant. 'I didn't want to do this to you. But things have happened . . . I don't want to explain until I see you.'

'But you've got to tell me!' Scarlett protested. 'Is Mum all right? Is it you?'

'We're both fine. There's nothing for you to worry about. It's just that there are times when a family has to be together and this is one of them.'

'How long am I staying with you?'

'A couple of weeks. Maybe longer.'

'Why?' There was silence at the other end of the line. 'Can't you tell me anything?' Scarlett went on. 'It's not fair. It's the middle of term and I'm going to miss the school play and all the parties and everything!'

'Look, I'm just going to have to ask you to trust me. You'll be here in twenty-four hours and I want to explain everything to you face to face, not over the phone. Can you do that for me, Scarly? Just wait until you get out here . . . and try not to think too badly of me until you arrive.'

'All right.' What else could she say?

'I've booked you into business class, so at least you'll be comfortable. Make sure you bring lots of books. It's a long flight.'

He rang off. Scarlett stood there, holding the receiver. She was feeling resentful and she couldn't stop herself. This wasn't fair. She was being bundled onto a plane and flown to Hong Kong as if she were a parcel being sent by Fed-Ex. She was fifteen years old. Surely she should have some control over her own life?

The taxi came at midday. Scarlett's flight was leaving Heathrow at half past three. Mrs Murdoch helped carry the cases out and load them into the back and the two of them got in together. The housekeeper was coming with her as far as the airport and would then return to the house alone. It was a grey, overcast day and the weather reflected Scarlett's mood. She twisted round as they pulled away and watched the house disappear behind her. She knew she was only going to be abroad for a couple of weeks but even so she couldn't escape a strange feeling. She wondered if she would ever see it again.

They reached the bottom of the street and were turning left into Half Moon Lane. And that was when it happened. A car crash. Scarlett only saw part of it and it was only later that she was able to piece together what had happened. A car had been driving towards them—it had just come from the main road—and a second car, a BMW, had suddenly pulled out in front of it. Scarlett heard the screech of tyres and the smash of impact and looked up in time to see the two cars ricocheting off each other, out of control. One of them had been forced off the road and was sliding down a private driveway. She could make out at least three people inside.

'London traffic!' The taxi driver sniffed. He completed the turn and they picked up speed.

Scarlett twisted round and looked out of the back—at the crumpled bonnet of one of the cars, steam rising into the air, glass scattered on the road. A bus had been forced to stop and the driver was climbing down, perhaps to see if he could help. The accident was already disappearing into the distance behind them and she supposed it was just a coincidence. It couldn't mean anything.

But even so it made her uneasy. It reminded her of the moment—two years ago, and just a short distance away—when she had almost been killed. And that made her think of the man who had contacted Aidan, wanting to meet her at the restaurant that had been blown to pieces before she could arrive. Scarlett sank back into her seat, feeling anxious, unable to control what was happening to her. Mrs Murdoch gazed out of the window with no expression on her face.

They parted company at the airport. Scarlett was flying as an unaccompanied minor—what the airline called a Skyflyer Solo. She had to suffer the indignity of a plastic label around her neck before she was led away. She said goodbye to Mrs Murdoch, hugging her awkwardly. Then she picked up her hand luggage and headed for the departure gate.

*   *   *

It had been so close. None of them would ever believe just how close it had actually been.

Matt Freeman had landed at the same airport earlier that morning. There had been a uniformed chauffeur waiting for him and the others, and soon they were sitting in the air-conditioned comfort of a new Jaguar, being driven to their hotel. Richard was dozing in the front seat. He had spent much of the flight working on the diary and had barely slept at all. Jamie was looking out for his first sight of the city. Matt could see that so far he was

150

disappointed. They were driving through a wasteland of blank, modern warehouses and unwelcoming hotels—the sort of places that always surround airports—and Matt wanted to tell him that this wasn't London at all.

But then, twenty minutes later, they turned off the motorway and suddenly they were in the city itself, passing the Natural History Museum in Kensington—it was still closed for repairs following Matt's last visit there—then the Victoria and Albert Museum, Harrods and Hyde Park Corner. Jamie stared, open-mouthed. He had spent much of his life in the desert landscape of Nevada and he wasn't used to seeing anything that was actually old. For him, London with its monuments and palaces was another world. He saw red buses, pigeons, policemen in blue uniforms, taxis . . . It was like falling into a pile of picture postcards. His one disappointment was that Scott wasn't with him. The two brothers had never been so far apart.

The driver took them to a hotel in Farringdon, a quiet part of London with narrow streets and a meat market that had been around when the animals were driven there in herds rather than delivered from Europe, pre-packed in boxes. The Tannery, as it was called, was small and anonymous—Richard and Matt had stayed there before. It was just a few minutes away from the private house where the Nexus met. By the time they arrived, it was eleven o'clock. A meeting had been arranged for half past seven that evening, giving them the rest of the day to relax and unwind from the long flight.

They made their way into a reception area

151

which was like the front room of someone's house, with thick carpets, flowers and the comforting tick of a grandfather clock. The receptionist was a tight-lipped woman who took care not to give too much away. She glanced disapprovingly at Richard—still in his Hawaiian shirt, looking more like a beach bum than ever—and the two boys who were with him, then asked for their passports and slid forward some forms for them to sign.

'How many nights?' she asked.

'We're not sure,' Richard said.

'Two rooms. I see they've been prepaid . . .'

The telephone rang. The receptionist plucked the receiver as if it were an overripe fruit and held it to her ear. 'The Tannery Hotel,' she said. A moment's silence. Her eyes fluttered and she handed the phone to Richard. 'It's for you, Mr Cole.'

Richard took the phone. Whatever he was hearing, it wasn't good news. He muttered a few words, then put the phone down.

'What is it?' Matt asked.

'Scarlett Adams . . . She's leaving London.'

'What?' Matt couldn't believe what he had just said. 'Where's she going?'

'We can still catch her.' Richard looked at his watch. 'She's going to Hong Kong. She's booked on the three thirty flight . . .'

'Not back to Heathrow!' Jamie groaned.

'No.' Richard weighed up the options. He was finding it hard to concentrate. He needed a shave more than ever and his eyes were red with jet lag. 'We can't intercept her at Heathrow,' he said. 'It's too public. She's never met us. She might not even want to talk to us. But her taxi isn't collecting her

152

until midday. We can reach her before she leaves.'

The decision had been made. The three of them dumped their luggage with the receptionist, turned round and walked out again. Fortunately, the driver was still waiting. Richard went up to him and told him where they wanted to go. The driver didn't argue. Matt and Jamie got back in again.

They hadn't even seen their rooms. The next moment they were off again, threading their way through Farringdon and down to Blackfriars Bridge. But it was now approaching the lunch hour and London had changed. Although they had made good progress from the airport, the traffic had snarled up. Every traffic light was red. It felt as if the entire city had turned against them.

'Who was it on the phone?' Matt asked.

'Susan Ashwood. She's already in London.'

Miss Ashwood was a medium who also happened to be blind. Matt had first met her in Yorkshire and it had been she who had introduced him to the Nexus.

'How did she know?' Matt asked.

'The Nexus are still bugging Scarlett's phone. They had two people following her too . . .'

It didn't look as if they were going to make it. The whole of South London had become one long traffic jam. The car crossed Tower Bridge—giving Jamie a quick glimpse of the River Thames and St Paul's—but after that, the city just felt drab and overcrowded with an endless stretch of cheap shops and restaurants punctuated by new office developments that would have looked out-of-date the moment they were built. Bermondsey, Walworth, Camberwell . . . they crawled from one district to the next without ever noticing where one

153

ended and the next began and all the time they were aware of time ticking away. Half past eleven, twenty to twelve . . . they didn't seem to be getting any nearer.

'This is hopeless,' Richard said. 'Maybe we'd better go to Heathrow after all.'

The driver shook his head. 'We're nearly there,' he said.

They dropped down a steep hill—Dog Kennel Hill, it was called—and, looking out of the window, Matt began to feel something very strange. He had never visited this part of London . . . he was sure of it. And yet, at the same time, he knew where he was. He glimpsed a radio mast in the distance, a road sign pointing to King's College Hospital. They meant something to him. He had been here before.

And then it hit him. Of course he knew this part of the city. He had lived here—from the time when he was a baby to when he had been about eight years old.

He should have remembered it. It hadn't been that long ago. But perhaps he had blocked it out. It wouldn't have been surprising after everything he had been through. Now it all came flooding back. The mast belonged to Crystal Palace. He had often played football there. He had gone into the hospital on his seventh birthday with suspected food poisoning. He remembered sitting miserably in reception—short trousers—with a plastic bowl balanced on his knees. They drove past a very ordinary house but Matt knew at once who lived there. It was a boy called Graham Fleming who had been his best friend at school. The two of them had always thought they would be

154

inseparable. Matt wondered if he was still living there. What would he say if the two of them met now?

And there was something else he remembered. If he went past Graham's house, turned the corner and walked past the old scout hut, he would come to a small, terraced house in a leafy street where all the houses were small and terraced. Number 32. It would have a green door and—unless they'd finally mended it—a cracked front step. It was his home. That was where he had once lived.

'How much further?' Richard asked.

The driver glanced at his sat nav. 'We're a minute away,' he said.

*   *   *

They went through a traffic light at a busy junction, then drove up towards North Dulwich station, turning into Half Moon Lane which was just opposite. Matt felt dazed. It was extraordinary to think that for half their lives, he and Scarlett had almost been neighbours. They might have passed each other a dozen times without even knowing it. She lived in Ardbeg Road, which was the next on the left, and just for a moment the way ahead was clear. The driver accelerated, glad finally to be able to use the Jaguar's power.

'Look out!' Richard shouted out the warning too late.

A car shot out from a private drive and smashed right into them.

Matt saw everything. He heard the roar of an engine and that made him turn his head. The car was coming straight at them. The driver was

155

staring at them, his hands clenched on the wheel, not even trying to avoid them. He was middle-aged, clean-shaven—and there was no emotion in his face. He should have been scared. He should have been showing some sort of reaction, knowing what was about to happen. But there was nothing at all.

Half a second later, there was a huge crash of metal against metal as he smashed into them.

The other car was a four-by-four, a BMW, and it was like being hit by a tank. The Jaguar was swept off the road, the world tilting away as it was hurled towards a wide, modern house with a short driveway sloping steeply down to the front door. There was a second collision as it hit the door, more crumpling metal. The house alarms went off. Jamie cried out as he was thrown sideways, his head hitting Matt's shoulder. Matt tasted blood and realized that he had bitten his tongue. The Jaguar was lying at an angle, almost underneath the front wheels of the BMW which was still on the road above them. Both the windows on the driver's side had shattered. The engine had cut out.

For a moment, nobody moved. Then Richard swore—which at least meant he was alive. He twisted round in the front seat. 'Are you two all right?' he asked.

'What happened?' Jamie groaned.

'An accident . . .' Richard said. 'Idiot . . . wasn't looking where he was going.'

He was wrong. Matt knew that already. He had seen what had happened. The BMW driver had been waiting for them, knowing they would come this way. Why else would he have shot out like that, slamming straight into them? Matt had seen him, gripping the wheel. He had known exactly what he was doing.

Richard was already out of the car.

'Wait . . .' Matt said.

*   *   *

But Richard hadn't heard. He staggered up onto the road, only now becoming aware that he was in pain. There were no cuts or bruises but, like all of them, he had suffered from whiplash. 'What the hell do you think you were doing?' he demanded.

The driver of the BMW had got out and was standing in the road. He was a middle-aged man, well-built, wearing a long, black coat and leather gloves. His mouth was soft and flabby, with small teeth, like a child. His skin was very pink. He had curly hair. His head was almost perfectly round, like a football.

'I'm so terribly sorry,' he said. 'I didn't see you. I was in a hurry. I hope none of you are hurt.'

Richard was still angry but he suddenly knew something was wrong. 'You did it on purpose,' he said. His voice had faltered. 'You tried to kill us.'

'Not at all. I just pulled out without looking. I can't tell you how sorry I am. Thank goodness you don't seem to be seriously hurt.'

By now, Matt and Jamie had joined him. There was nothing they could do for their driver and they left him, unconscious in the front seat. Jamie stared at the man and the colour drained out of his face. He knew at once what he was looking at. It was the last thing he had expected to find here.

'Matt . . .' he whispered. 'He's a shape-changer.'

Matt didn't doubt him. Jamie had met shape-

157

changers when he had gone back in time. Shape-changers were able to take on human form but it didn't suit them. It didn't quite fit. One of them, an old man who had suddenly become a giant scorpion, had almost killed him at the fortress at Scathack Hill. He knew what he was talking about. And Matt could see it for himself. Everything about the BMW driver was fake, even the way he stood there, stiff and unnatural, like a dummy in a shop window. The words he was saying could have been written out for him, on a script.

'I'm insured,' he continued. 'There's absolutely nothing to worry about. It was my fault. No doubt about it.'

Richard stared. None of them knew quite what to do. Barely a minute had passed since the collision but already other people were arriving on the scene. A bus, on its way to Brixton, had pulled up and the driver was climbing out of his cabin, coming over to help. Two more cars had stopped further up the road. Matt had seen a taxi pull out of Ardbeg Road and thought it might be coming their way, but it had already turned off and driven away.

They couldn't risk a fight. They were in the middle of a suburban, South London street. If they challenged the shape-changer, if he decided to drop his human form, all hell would break loose. And already the police had arrived. A squad car turned the corner and pulled over. Two officers got out.

'Good afternoon, officers.' The BMW driver was pretending that he was pleased to see them. 'Glad you're here. We're in a bit of a pickle.'

His language was as fake as the rest of him and

158

for just a few seconds, Matt was tempted to take him on, to show the entire crowd what was really happening here. He could use his own power. Without so much as moving, he could tear a strip of metal off the shattered car and send it flying into him. There were a dozen witnesses on the scene. How would they react when the blushing, curly-haired BMW driver turned into a half-snake or a half-crocodile and bled green blood? Maybe it was time to show the world the war that was about to engulf it.

It was Richard who stopped him.

'No, Matt.'

He must have seen what Matt was thinking because he muttered the two words under his breath, never taking his eyes off the man who was standing in front of them. Matt understood. For some reason, the shape-changer was playing with them. It was pretending that this was just an ordinary accident. If he took it on, if he began a fight here in the street, innocent people might get hurt. And he was in England with a fake passport and a false name. This was the wrong time to be answering questions. Right now he had everything to lose.

'I'm so very sorry,' the shape-changer said.

'I saw what happened!' the bus driver exclaimed. He nodded at the BMW driver, his face filled with outrage. 'He pulled out at fifty miles an hour. He didn't look. He didn't signal. It was all his fault.'

'Is anyone hurt?' one of the policeman asked.

'Our driver,' Richard said.

The right-hand side of the Jaguar had taken the full force of the impact and it looked as if the driver had suffered a broken arm. He was only

159

semi-conscious and in pain. One of the policemen helped him out and laid him on the pavement and they waited about fifteen minutes for an ambulance to arrive. Meanwhile the other officer began questioning the BMW driver—'Mr Smith'. He had no ID.

'I was on my way to Chislehurst. I'm a piano teacher. I pulled out without looking. I can't tell you how dreadful I feel . . .'

Matt watched as they breathalysed him and it almost made him smile, seeing him blow into the machine. His breath wasn't human and if he'd drunk a crate of whisky it was unlikely that it would register. Meanwhile, their driver was loaded into an ambulance and driven off to hospital. Thirty minutes or more had gone by and Richard was desperate to be on his way, but the police weren't having any of it. They would have to take a statement. Will you come with us to the station, sir? There was no way out. Richard, Matt and Jamie were driven away.

It was almost four o'clock by the time the police finished with them. Even if they had wanted to go to Heathrow, it would have been too late. Scarlett would already be in the air, on her way to Hong Kong.

They left the police station and dropped into a local café but Matt refused the offer of a drink. He was angry and depressed. The Old Ones were out-manoeuvring him at every turn. They seemed to know exactly what he was going to do and the trap they had set had been childishly simple. He didn't mention the taxi that he had seen pulling out of Ardbeg Road, but it had already occurred to him that Scarlett might well have been inside it.

Their paths had finally crossed . . . but seconds too late.

'Let's go to her house,' Matt suggested.

'Why?' Richard didn't even look up from his tea.

'I don't know. She could still be there. But even if she isn't, now that we've come this far . . .'

Neither Richard nor Jamie spoke.

'I'd just like to see where she lives,' Matt said.

The three of them walked back to Ardbeg Road. It reminded Matt a little of the street where he had once lived. All the houses were terraced with bay windows, neat front gardens and shrubs to hide the wheelie bins. Scarlett's was about half-way down.

They rang the bell, not expecting it to be answered, but after about half a minute the door opened and they found themselves being examined by a short, stern-looking woman with black hair tied back and eyes that seemed to be expecting trouble.

'Yes?' she said. She had a Scottish accent.

'We're looking for Scarlett Adams,' Matt said.

'I'm afraid you've missed her. She left this morning.'

Richard moved forward. 'Do you live here?' he asked.

'Yes. I'm the housekeeper. Are you friends of Scarlett's?'

'Not exactly,' Matt said. 'We've just arrived from America. We were hoping to see her.'

'That's not going to be possible. She's going to be out of the country for a while.'

'Do you know when she'll be back?'

'It could be a week or two. I'm very sorry, if

161

you'd been here just a few hours ago, you'd have caught her. Do you want to leave a message?'

'No, thank you.'

'Right.'

The woman closed the door.

And that was it. There was nothing more to be done. For a moment, nobody spoke. Then Richard sighed. 'Anyone fancy a trip to Hong Kong?' he said.

PUERTO FRAGRANTE

Originally, there had been twelve members of the Nexus—the organization that existed only to fight the Old Ones. Professor Sanjay Dravid had been the first to be killed, stabbed at the Natural History Museum the same night that he had met Matt. Later on, a man called Fabian had also died. That just left ten—powerful people who lived in America, Australia, Europe . . . all over the world.

They had all flown in to meet Matt and Jamie and at half past seven that evening they came together in the secluded, wood-panelled room which was their London base.

The building, which the Nexus owned, stood between two shops and there was nothing, no name or other marking, to suggest that it was anything but a private house. The room itself, up on the first floor, was equally plain. It could have been the meeting place of some small business, perhaps a firm of expensive solicitors. There didn't seem to be much there—just a long table with thirteen antique chairs, a handful of telephones

162

and a computer and a lot of clocks showing the time all over the world. But the glass door that slid open automatically and then hissed shut, sealing itself as the ten men and women came in, suggested that there might be more to the place than met the eye. A sophisticated camera blinked quietly in the corridor. And the Nexus arrived one at a time, each one entering a different six-digit code before they were allowed in.

Matt wasn't looking forward to seeing them again. He knew that they were supposed to be on his side, but even so he felt a certain dread entering the room. It was like facing ten head teachers at the same time, knowing he was about to be expelled. There were only two people there who he felt he knew. He had met Susan Ashwood, the medium, at her home near Manchester, and although he had thought she was completely mad, at least he was fairly sure that her heart was in the right place. And he had got to know Nathalie Johnson in the past few months. She was the American computer billionaire who had helped Scott and Jamie and she had travelled down to Nazca a couple of times to make sure they were all right.

But that still left eight strangers. There was an Australian, broad and bullish with a round face and close-cropped hair. His name was Harry Foster and he owned a newspaper empire. Next to him, there was a bishop who dressed like a bishop and talked like a bishop but who hadn't actually told Matt his name. He was about sixty years old. Tarrant, the senior policeman who had helped put taps on Scarlett's phone, was at the head of the table, dressed in a smart blue and silver uniform.

163

Among the others, Matt had noted a Frenchman in an expensive suit, a small Chinese man who was continually rubbing his hands, a German who was something big in politics and two others who had made no impression on him at all. They might all be world leaders. But tonight they just looked tired and scared.

Richard, Jamie and Matt had taken their places at the table, bunched together at one end. The three of them were in a gloomy mood. Scarlett Adams, the fifth Gatekeeper, had turned up in London and they had flown thousands of miles to see her. But she had slipped through their fingers and even as they sat there, she would be thirty thousand feet up in the air. Every word that they spoke, every second that passed, only carried her further away.

'We made a mistake.' Nathalie Johnson came straight to the point. 'We knew who she was. We knew where she lived. We should have approached her ourselves.'

'It was my fault,' Susan Ashwood said. 'I didn't want to frighten her. I thought it would be easier for her if she heard it all from you.' She turned to Matt. 'I hoped you'd be here sooner. I didn't realize we'd have to wait for the new passports.'

'I thought you had people watching her,' Matt cut in. 'Weren't there two private detectives or something?'

'They were ex-policemen,' Tarrant said. 'Duncan and McKnight. Good men, both of them. I'd worked with them before.' He paused. 'Scarlett may have caught sight of them. They were parked in a car outside a park in Dulwich and they had to be more careful after that. They kept their distance. But they were still on top of the case. Until last night . . .'

'What happened' Richard asked.

'They've both disappeared. Vanished without a trace. I've tried to contact them but with no luck. I have a feeling they may have been killed.'

There was a brief silence while the rest of the room took this in. It was obvious to all of them that they had underestimated the Old Ones. From the moment Scarlett had been identified, they had been running rings around the Nexus.

'So why has she gone to Hong Kong?' Matt asked.

'Her father is there,' Tarrant replied. 'He's a lawyer. He works for the Nightrise Corporation.'

'Nightrise?' Jamie spoke for the first time. Jet lag had hit him badly and he was exhausted. He'd only managed to keep himself awake with a black coffee and a can of Red Bull. 'They're the people who came after Scott and me. Are you saying her dad is one of them?'

'Nightrise is a legitimate business,' Nathalie Johnson reminded him. 'They have offices all over the world. They employ hundreds of people. The vast majority of them probably have no idea who— or what they're working for.'

'Even so . . .'

'We don't know, Jamie. His name is Paul Adams. He's divorced. He and his wife adopted Scarlett fifteen years ago and as far as we can tell, he doesn't know anything about the Old Ones.'

'So what do we do now?' Richard asked. 'Scott and Pedro are still in Peru. Matt and Jamie are here. And Scarlett will soon be in Hong Kong. The one thing we know is that we have to get the five

Gatekeepers together. How are we going to do that?'

'You may have to follow her there.'

It was the bishop who had spoken and the other members of the Nexus nodded. But for his part, Matt wasn't so sure. He knew nothing about the city except that some of the toys he'd played with when he was younger had been manufactured there. MADE IN HONG KONG: it had always been a sign that they would probably break five minutes after they came out of the packaging. Certainly, he had no desire to go there. He had flown enough for one week.

'If I may . . .' The Chinese man had a soft, very cultivated voice. He hadn't spoken until now. He was small, with heavy, plastic glasses and an off-the-peg suit. Perhaps he adopted this sort of appearance on purpose. It was as if he didn't want to be noticed. 'My name is Mr Lee,' he said, bowing his head towards Matt. 'If you are thinking of making the journey to Hong Kong, I may be able to help you. I have connections throughout Asia and especially in that area. However, I would like to make one observation if I may.'

He waited for someone to speak against him, as if he was nervous that there might be someone at the table who didn't want to hear what he had to say. When nobody protested, he went on.

'There is something very strange happening in Hong Kong,' he began. 'I know the place well. In fact, I was there—passing through—just a week ago. On the face of it, there is nothing I can put my finger on. Life continues as normal. Business is done. Tourists arrive and leave. But there is something in the city that makes no sense. How

166

can I put it? There is an atmosphere there that is not pleasant. Friends of mine who live there, people I have known for many years, seem to be in a hurry to leave and when I ask them why, they are afraid to say. And those who remain are nervous.'

'The Old Ones are there,' Susan Ashwood said, as if she had known all along. She worked as a medium, talking to ghosts. Matt wondered if they had told her.

'That is what I believe, Miss Ashwood,' Mr Lee agreed. 'It is hardly a coincidence. Nightrise is based in Hong Kong. It is quite possible that much of the city is now in the control of the Old Ones. And if that is the case, then the moment this girl, Scarlett Adams, arrives there, it will be as if she is in prison and none of us will be able to reach her.'

'We have to reach her,' Richard said. 'If we don't, we might as well all pack up. There have to be five Gatekeepers.'

'Then we have to get her out of there—and that means following her. We have failed here in London. Maybe Matthew and Jamie will have more success over there.'

'You want to send the two of them to Hong Kong?'

'They have certain powers, Mr Cole, which may be of use to them.' Mr Lee nodded. 'Yes. In my opinion they must find a way to enter the city, but without the Old Ones knowing they are on their way.'

'The two of them travelled here with false names and false ID,' Tarrant said. He sounded disapproving. 'They can use them again.'

'Absolutely.' The Australian, Harry Foster banged a fist on the table. 'They could be on the next flight out of here. There must be fifty thousand people a day flying in and out of Hong Kong. Who's going to notice a couple of kids in a crowd like that?'

'I don't agree.' Susan Ashwood shook her head. 'If Mr Lee is correct and the Old Ones are there, it would be complete madness to attempt to go in by air. Matt and Jamie would be seized the moment they stepped off the plane . . . and I don't care how many people there are at the airport.'

'I have an office in Hong Kong,' Harry Foster said. 'I could look in there on my way back to Australia. Why don't you let me try and find her? I can explain what's going on and she—and her father, for that matter—can leave with me. I'll take them down to Sydney and you can pick them up there.'

'I think it's too dangerous,' Mr Lee said.

'Well, at least I can get a message to her. Let her know the score.' The Australian took out a pad and scribbled a note to himself. 'A letter to warn her that she's in danger. I can get someone in my Hong Kong office to deliver it by hand.'

'I think we have to be very careful,' Susan Ashwood said. 'We all know what happened today. The Old Ones were waiting outside her house in Dulwich. They knew Matt was on his way and they were determined to stop him.' She glanced at Tarrant. 'You had two men watching Scarlett and now you say they may have been killed. How many more mistakes do we have to make before we realize what we're up against?'

'Then maybe it's time to use one of the doors,' Richard said.

He had the diary and he slid it onto the table in

168

front of him. All ten members of the Nexus stared at it. Only a few months before, they had been prepared to spend two million pounds to get their hands on it and here it was, right in front of them. They wanted to reach out and touch it. And yet at the same time they were afraid of it, as if it was a snake that might bite.

'I've been trying to work this out ever since Ramon brought it to us,' Richard went on. 'I've read bits of it, though I won't pretend I've understood very much . . . even with a Spanish dictionary and a magnifying glass. But there is one thing we do know. Twenty-five doors were built around the world for the Gatekeepers to use. They all connect with each other and they can all be found in sacred places. One of them is in St Meredith's. When Matt went through it, it took him directly to the Abbey of San Galgano in Tuscany.'

'Scott and me found one of the doors in a cave at Lake Tahoe,' Jamie added. 'It took us to the Temple of Coricancha in Cuzco, Peru.'

'That's four of them,' Richard said. 'But there are twenty-one more and our friend, the mad monk, may have helped us. He's made a list . . .'

He unfastened the diary and opened it, laying it flat so that everyone could see. Everyone leaned forward. There was a very detailed map covering two pages, drawn in different colours of ink. It was just about recognizable as the world, although a world seen by a child with only a basic knowledge of geography. America was the wrong shape and it was too close to Europe. Australia was upside-down.

Joseph of Cordoba had used more care

decorating his work. He had sketched in little ships, crossing the various oceans with their sails unfurled. Insect-sized animals poked out of the different land masses, helping to identify them. There was a tiger in India, a dragon in China and, at the North Pole, what could have been a polar bear.

'I don't know how much you know about old maps,' Richard said, 'but for what it's worth, I studied them a bit at university. I did politics and geography. This one is fairly typical of the sixteenth century. That was a time when maps were becoming more important. Henry VIII was one of the first monarchs to realize how much they could give away about a country's defences. And everyone was using them to steal everyone else's trade routes. You see these little bags here?' He took out a pencil and pointed. 'They're probably bags of spice. Joseph may have drawn them to represent the Spice Islands because that was what everyone wanted.'

'There are stars,' Jamie said.

They were scattered all over the pages; the five-pointed stars that he and Matt knew so well.

'That's right. There are twenty-five of them—one for each door. The only trouble is, like a lot of the maps being drawn at the time, this one isn't very accurate. As far as I can make out, there seem to be doors in London, Cairo, Istanbul, Delhi, Mecca, Buenos Aires and somewhere in the outback of Southern Australia. There's one here, close to the South Pole. But the world's changed quite a lot in five hundred years and trying to identify the exact locations isn't going to be easy.'

'You mentioned a list,' Tarrant said.

'Yes . . .' Richard turned a page and sure enough there was a long row of names, all of them in tiny handwriting. 'The problem we've got here is that the names don't quite match up with the modern places and half of them are in Spanish. Here's one, for example. Muerto de Maria. It took me half the night to work that one out.'

'The death of Mary,' the bishop translated.

'Or Mary's death,' Richard said. 'Do you get it? Marydeath. Or the church of St Meredith in London. It's like a crossword clue although I don't suppose Joseph was doing it on purpose to confuse us. Coricancha isn't named at all. It's just represented by a flaming sun—but then, of course, the sun was sacred to the Incas.'

'Is there a door in Hong Kong?' Matt asked.

'There's certainly a door somewhere nearby,' Richard said. He turned the page back to the map. 'You can see it here . . . and if you look at the list, there's a reference to a place called Puerto Fragrante and a little dragon symbol. But that could be anywhere.'

'May I see?' Mr Lee reached out and took the diary in both hands, holding it as if he was afraid it was about to crumble away. He looked at the map, then the list, then turned another page. 'Someone has written in pencil,' he said. 'The words *Tai Shan*".' He glanced at Richard. 'Was that you?'

Richard shook his head. 'That must have been Ramon,' he said. 'He made notes all over it when he was trying to decipher it for Salamanda, but as far as I can see, he didn't have time to work out too much. Anyway, he was mainly focusing on the Nazca Lines.'

'There is a door in Hong Kong!' Mr Lee

171

exclaimed. 'I can tell you that for certain. And I can even tell you exactly where it is.' He laid the diary down. 'Puerto Fragrante—the Spanish for Fragrant Harbour, I think—is another clue,' he said. 'In Cantonese, Fragrant Harbour translates as Heung Gong. Or in other words, Hong Kong. The city was originally given that name because of the smell of sandalwood that drifted across the sea. Whoever studied the diary has been good enough to confirm it for us. *Tai Shan* means "the mountain of the East". It is where the sun begins its daily journey. It is also the place where human souls go when they die. There is a very old and very sacred temple with that name in Hong Kong, in a part of the city called Wan Chai . . .'

There was a sense of relief in the room. It was as if they had all made their minds up. Even Susan Ashwood nodded her head in agreement and seemed to relax. Only Matt didn't look so sure.

'You could leave tonight,' Harry Foster said. 'If things went your way, you could actually be there to meet her at the airport. You could pull her out before the Old Ones even knew you'd arrived.'

'Wait a minute,' Matt said. 'We flew here from Miami because we didn't think the doors were safe. Why has anything changed?' Nobody answered so he went on. 'Salamanda had the diary. He'll have found out about the temple . . .'

'Not necessarily,' Foster insisted. 'This guy, Ramon, was working on it. But he may not have passed on everything he knew. Anyway, Salamanda's dead.'

'Maybe there is an element of risk . . .' Susan Ashwood began.

'It's more than a risk. It's a trap.'

172

Matt hadn't sat down and worked it out. It was just that all the doubts that had been in his mind had somehow come together and he could suddenly see everything very clearly.

'The whole thing is a trap,' he said. 'And it always has been, right from the start. Why were we attacked in Nazca? Why was Professor Chambers killed? It's because the Old Ones wanted to get us on the move. They wanted us to do exactly what we've done.

'Think about it. Scarlett Adams goes through the door at St Meredith's and suddenly the whole world knows about her. She's in all the newspapers and the Old Ones find out who she is. And then, the very next day, a university lecturer called Ramon turns up in Nazca. Somehow he's managed to track us down. He tells us that he's managed to steal the one thing we most want and he hands it across without even asking for money. Why? Because he goes to Church! Because he's planning to get married! His whole story was ridiculous. And it wasn't true. The Old Ones *wanted* us to have the diary.'

'They killed him to get it back,' Nathalie said.

'Did they? I think Ramon was as surprised to get that fence post through his chest as we were to see it happen. He must have been programmed— either drugged or hypnotized—to stop Scott and Jamie seeing into his mind. And then they killed him to make us believe that he had been telling the truth. Otherwise, it would have all seemed too easy.'

Matt took a breath. Normally, he didn't like being the centre of attention but this time he knew he was right.

173

'All along, there was something that bothered me about that night in Nazca,' he went on. 'If they really wanted the diary back so badly, why did they send such a small force? What happened to the giant spider, the fly-soldiers, the shape- changers, the death-riders?' He turned to Jamie. 'You've seen them. You've fought them. Nazca was peanuts compared to what you went through.'

Jamie nodded but said nothing.

'They want me to come to Hong Kong. That's what this has all been about.' Matt was getting tired. He had no idea what time it was according to his body clock. He just wanted to crawl into bed and forget everything for ten hours. 'First of all they got us out of Nazca. They managed to split us up. And now they've given us a nice invitation to walk straight into their hands. The moment I go through that door, I'll be finished. They're using Scarlett to get at me. I hurt them. I wounded their leader, Chaos—the King of the Old Ones, or whatever he calls himself. They want to make me pay.'

There was a long silence.

'What do you want to do, Matt?' Susan Ashwood asked. And that made a change. Normally the Nexus told him what they wanted him to do.

'I still have to go to Hong Kong,' Matt said.

'Matt . . .' Richard began.

Matt stopped him. 'What Miss Ashwood said was right. They're not going to let any of you get anywhere near Scarlett. It has to be the two of us, Jamie and me. And you too, Richard, if you want to come. But maybe we can use this situation to our advantage. The Old Ones expect us to turn up

174

in the Temple of Tai Shan. That's how they've arranged the trap. But suppose we arrive another way? We could still take them by surprise.'

'You could go in by sea,' Foster said. 'There are cruise ships going in and out of Hong Kong all the time.'

'May I suggest something?' Mr Lee interrupted, asking permission again. 'The best way to enter Hong Kong might be through Macau. It is part of China, a small stub of land on the South China Sea—and like Hong Kong it is a Special Administrative Region, which is to say, it is—at least in part—independent. You can fly from one to the other in a very short time. Helicopters make the journey several times a day.'

'And how do we get to Macau?' Richard asked.

'You cannot fly there direct. I believe you will have to go via Singapore. But it is, if you like, a back door into Hong Kong—and one that the Old Ones may have overlooked.' He took out a handkerchief and polished the lenses of his glasses. 'More than that, I have a connection in Macau who may agree to help you. He has many resources. In fact, if anyone knows the truth about what is going on in that part of the world, it will be him.'

'Wait a minute . . .' Richard was worried and he didn't try to hide it. He was wishing he'd never mentioned the diary in the first place. 'Matt . . . are you really sure you have to go there?' he asked. 'You've already said that it's you that they want. You say it's a trap. Now you're walking straight into it.'

'We need Scarlett,' Matt replied, simply. 'They have her. We can't win without her.' He looked round. 'Jamie, will you come with me?'

Jamie shrugged. 'I've always wanted to see Hong Kong.'

'Then it's agreed.' Matt turned back to Mr Lee. 'How quickly can you get in touch with your friend?' he asked.

'His name is Han Shan-tung,' Lee replied. 'He is a man with great influence. He has many friends inside Hong Kong. But it may not be easy to find him. He travels a great deal. You may have to wait.'

'We can't wait.'

'It will just be a few days. But trust me. It would be foolish to enter the city without his support.'

A few days. More waiting. Matt thought about Scarlett. In a few hours' time she would be landing in Hong Kong. What would she find when she got there? How would she manage on her own?

But there was no other way. Somehow she would have to survive until he got there. He just hoped it wouldn't be too long.

WISDOM COURT

The nightmare started almost from the moment Scarlett arrived at Hong Kong Airport.

She was still a Skyflyer Solo and the airline had arranged for an escort to meet her at the plane and to take her through immigration and customs. His name was Justin and he was dark-haired, in his early twenties, dressed like a member of the cabin crew.

'Did you have a good flight?' He spoke with an

Australian accent and seemed friendly enough.

'It was OK.'

'You must be tired. Never mind. I'll see you through to the other side. Is this your first time in Hong Kong?'

'Yes.'

'You're going to love it here!'

He prattled on as Scarlett followed him to passport control. It would have been easy to find her own way—there were signs written in English as well as Chinese—but she was glad to have company after eleven hours sitting on her own in what had felt like outer space. The worst thing about the flight hadn't been the length or the boredom. It had been the sense of disconnection. She was going somewhere she didn't want to go, not even knowing why she was going there. What could be so urgent that her father had made her travel all this way? And why hadn't he been able to tell her on the phone?

The airport was surprisingly quiet, but then it was only six o'clock in the morning and perhaps there hadn't been that many international flights. Even so, Scarlett felt uneasy. She examined the people around her as they stood on the travelator, being carried down the wide, silver and grey corridors. The other passengers looked more dead than alive, bleary-eyed and pale. Nobody was talking. Nobody seemed happy to be there.

And there was something else that struck her. Everyone was heading the same way. They were all pouring into the main building. People might be arriving in Hong Kong but, this morning at any rate, no one seemed to be leaving.

They arrived at immigration, joining a queue

that snaked back and forth up to a line of low, glass booths with officials in black and silver uniforms, seated on low stools. They all looked very much the same to Scarlett—small, with brown eyes and black, spiky hair. She put the thought out of her head. She was probably being racist.

And then it was her turn. The official who took her passport and arrivals card was young, polite. He opened the passport and examined her details and as he did so, she noticed a surveillance camera just above him swivel round to examine her too. It was quite unnerving, the way it moved, without making any sound, somehow picking her out from the rest of the crowd.

'Scarlett Adams.' The official spoke her name and smiled. He wasn't asking her to confirm it. He was just reading it off the page as if he didn't quite understand what it meant. Then he reached out for his stamp, inked it and brought it down on the passport with a bang.

And at that exact moment, he changed. Did it really happen or was her mind playing tricks with her after the long flight? It was his eyes. As the stamp hit the page, they seemed to flicker as if someone had blown smoke over them and suddenly they were yellow. The pupils, which had been brown a second ago were now black and diamond-shaped. The passport official glanced up at her and smiled and right then she was afraid that he was going to leap out of his booth and tear into her. His eyes were no longer human. They were more like a crocodile's eyes.

Scarlett gasped out loud. She couldn't help herself. She was paralysed, staring at the thing in front of her. The escort, standing next to her, hadn't noticed anything wrong. Nobody else had reacted. There was a stamp as another visa was issued in the booth next door and Scarlett glanced in that direction as a student with a backpack was allowed through. When she looked back, it was over. The official was normal again. He was holding out her passport, waiting for her to take it. She hesitated, then snatched it from him, not wanting to come into contact even with the tips of his fingers as if she was half expecting them to turn into claws.

'We need to pick up your bags,' Justin said.

'Right . . .'

He looked at her curiously. 'Is something the matter, Scarlett?'

'No.' She shook her head. 'Everything's fine.'

The cases took about ten minutes to arrive. Scarlett's was one of the first off the plane. Justin picked it up for her and the two of them went through the customs area, which was empty. Presumably nobody bothered smuggling anything into Hong Kong. The arrivals gate was directly ahead of them and Scarlett hurried forward. Despite everything, she was looking forward to seeing her father again.

He wasn't there.

There were about a hundred people waiting on the other side of the barriers, quite a few of them dressed in chauffeur uniforms, some of them holding names on placards. She saw her own name almost at once. It was being held by a black man in a suit. He was tall and bald with a face that could have been carved—it showed no emotion. Somehow, he didn't seem to belong in Hong Kong. It wasn't just his colour. It was his size. He towered over everyone else, staring over the crowd with empty eyes as if he didn't want to be there.

There was a woman standing next to him and Scarlett took a dislike to her at first sight. Was she even a woman? She was certainly dressed in women's clothes, with a grey dress, anorak and fur-lined boots that came up to her knees. But she had the face and the physique of a man. Her shoulders were broad and square. Her neck was thick-set. She wore no make-up although she was badly in need of it. She had skin like very old leather. She was Chinese and half the height of the chauffeur, with black hair hanging lifelessly down and thick, plastic glasses that wouldn't have flattered her face even if there had been something to flatter. She reminded Scarlett of a prison warden. It was impossible to guess her age. Forty? Fifty? She didn't look as if she had ever been young.

Scarlett went over to her.

'Good morning, Scarlett,' the woman said. 'Welcome to Hong Kong. I hope you had a good flight.'

'Who are you?' Scarlett asked. She wasn't in any mood to be polite.

The woman didn't take offence. 'My name is Mrs Cheng,' she said. 'But you can call me Audrey. This is Karl.' The man in the suit lowered his head briefly. 'Shall we go to the car?'

'Where's my dad?' Scarlett asked.

'I'm afraid he couldn't come.'

'Where is he?'

'I will explain in the car.'

The escort—Justin—had listened to all this with growing concern. It was his job to hand Scarlett over to the right person and that clearly didn't seem to be the case. 'Excuse me a minute,' he interrupted. He turned to Scarlett. 'Do you know these people?'

'No,' Scarlett said.

'Well, I'm not sure you should go with them.' He turned back to the woman. 'Forgive me, Mrs Cheng,' he went on. 'I was told I was delivering this girl to her father. And I'm not sure . . .'

'You're being ridiculous,' Mrs Cheng interrupted. 'You can see quite clearly that we were waiting for her. We are both employed by the Nightrise Corporation and were sent here by her father.'

'I'm sorry. She doesn't know you and right now I'm responsible for her. I think you'd better come over to the desk and talk to my supervisor.'

Scarlett was beginning to feel embarrassed with two adults quarrelling over her, especially in the middle of such a public place. But Justin and Mrs Cheng had reached an impasse. The Chinese woman was breathing heavily and two dark spots had appeared in her cheeks. She was struggling to keep her temper. Suddenly she snapped out a command, her voice so low that it could barely be heard. The chauffeur, Karl, lumbered forward.

'Now hold on a minute . . .' Justin began.

It looked as if Karl was going to punch him. But instead he simply reached out and laid a hand on Justin's shoulder, his long, black fingers curving around the escort's neck. There was no violence at all. Then he leant down so that his eyes were level with the other man.

And Justin caved in.

'You're making a fuss about nothing,' Mrs

181

Cheng said.

'Yes . . .' He could barely get the word out.

'Why don't you phone the Nightrise offices when they open? They'll tell you everything you want to know.'

'There's no need. Of course the girl can go with you.'

'Let him go, Karl.'

Karl released him. Justin swayed on his feet, then abruptly walked away. It was as if he had forgotten about Scarlett. He wanted nothing more to do with her.

'Let's be on our way, Scarlett. We've wasted enough time here.'

Scarlett picked up her case and followed Karl and Mrs Cheng down an escalator. A sliding door led to a private road with a number of smart executive saloons and limousines waiting for their pick-ups. Karl took the case and hoisted it into the boot. Meanwhile, Mrs Cheng had opened the door, ushering Scarlett into the back.

'Where are we going?' Scarlett asked.

'We will take you to your father's apartment.'

'Is he there?'

'No.' Audrey Cheng spoke English like many Chinese people, cutting the words short as if she were attacking them with a pair of scissors. 'Your father had to go away on business.'

'But that's not possible. He just got me out of school. He made me come all this way.'

'He has written a note for you. It will explain.'

They had left the airport. Karl drove them across a bridge that looked brand new with steel cables sweeping down like tendrils in a web. The airport had been built on an island, one of several

182

that surrounded Hong Kong. Everything here was cut into by the sea.

They reached the outskirts of the city and Scarlett saw the first tower blocks, five of them in a row. They warned her just how different this world was going to be, how alien to everything she knew. All five tower blocks were exactly the same. They had almost no character. And they were huge. Each one of them must have had a thousand windows, stacked up forty or fifty floors in straight lines, one on top of another. From the road, the windows looked the size of postage stamps and anyone looking out of them would have been no bigger than the Queen's head in the corner. It was impossible to say how many people lived there or what it would be like, coming home at night to your identical flat in your identical tower, identified only by a number on the door. This was a city that was far bigger than the people who lived in it. Hong Kong would treat its inhabitants in the same way that an ant hill looks after its ants.

The motorway had turned into an ugly, concrete flyover that twisted through more office and apartment blocks. It was only seven o'clock in the morning but already the traffic was building up. Soon it would start to jam. Looking down, Scarlett saw what looked suspiciously like a London bus, trundling along with far too many passengers crammed on board. But it was painted the wrong colours, with Chinese symbols covering one side. Hong Kong had once belonged to the British, of course. It had been handed back at the end of the Nineties and although it was now owned by China, it more or less looked after itself.

They passed a market where the stalls were still

being set up and made their way down a narrow street with dozens of advertisements, all in Chinese, hanging overhead. Finally, they turned into a driveway that curved up to a set of glass doors in a smaller tower block. Scarlett saw a sign: WISDOM COURT. The car stopped. They had arrived.

Wisdom Court stood to the east of the city in what had to be an expensive area, as it had the one thing that mattered in a place like this: open space. The building was old-fashioned—with brickwork rather than steel or glass. It was only fifteen storeys high and stood in its own grounds. There was a forecourt with half a dozen neat flower-beds and a white, marble fountain, water trickling out of a lion's head. There were two more lions with gaping mouths, one on each side of the door. Inside, the reception area could have belonged to a smart hotel. There were palm trees in pots and a man in a uniform sitting behind a marble counter. Two lifts stood side by side at the end of the corridor.

They went up to the twelfth floor, Karl carrying the luggage. Audrey Cheng had barely looked at Scarlett since they had left the airport, but now she fished in her handbag and took out a key which she dangled in front of her as if to demonstrate that she really did have a right to be here. They reached a door marked 1213. Mrs Cheng turned the key in the lock and they went in.

Was this really where her father lived? The flat was clean and modern, with a long living room, floor-to-ceiling windows and three steps down to a sunken kitchen and dining room. There were two bedrooms, each with their own bathroom. But at first sight there was nothing that connected it with him. The paintings on the wall were abstract blobs of colour that could have hung in any hotel. The furniture looked new . . . a glass table, leather chairs, pale wooden cupboards. Had Paul Adams really gone out and chosen it or had it been there when he arrived? Everything was very tidy, not a bit like the warm and cosy clutter of their home in Dulwich.

But looking around, Scarlett did find a few clues that told her he had been there. There were some books about the Second World War on the shelves. He always had been interested in history. The fridge had some of his favourite food—a packet of smoked salmon, Greek yoghurt, his usual brand of butter—and there was a bottle of malt whisky, the one he always drank, on the counter. Some of his clothes were hanging in the wardrobe in the main bedroom and there was a bottle of his aftershave beside the bath.

And there was the note.

It was printed, not written, in an envelope addressed to Scarlett and it wasn't signed. Scarlett wondered if he had asked his secretary to type it. He only used two fingers and usually made lots of mistakes. The note was very short.

Dear Scarly,
Really sorry to do this to you but something came up and I've got to be out of Hong Kong for a few days. I'll try to call but if not, enjoy yourself and I'll see you soon. No need to worry about anything. I'll explain all when we meet.
Dad

Scarlett lowered the note. 'It doesn't say when he'll be back,' she said.

'Maybe your father doesn't know.'

'But he's the only reason I'm here!'

Mrs Cheng spread her hands as if to apologize but there was no sign of any regret in her face. 'This afternoon I will take you into the place where your father works,' she promised. 'We will go to Nightrise and you will see the chairman. He will tell you more.'

Karl had carried Scarlett's suitcase into the spare bedroom. So far he hadn't said a word. He was waiting at the front door.

'I'm sure you're tired,' Mrs Cheng said. 'Why don't you have a rest and we can explore the city later. Maybe you would like to do some shopping? We have many shops.'

Scarlett didn't want to go shopping with Audrey Cheng. It seemed that the two of them were going to be together until Paul Adams returned. It wasn't fair. Had she really swapped Mrs Murdoch for her? But she was certainly tired. She had barely slept on the plane. Right now, in London, it would be about midnight.

'I would like a rest,' she said.

'That's a good idea. I will be here. Call if there is anything you need.'

Scarlett went into her room. She undressed and had a shower, then lay on the bed. She fell asleep instantly, darkness coming down like a falling shutter.

And once again she returned to the dreamworld, to the desert and the sea. She could sense the water behind her but she was careful not to turn round. She remembered the creature that

186

had begun to emerge—the dragon or whatever it was—and didn't want to see it again.

Everything was very still. Her head was throbbing. There was something strange in the air. She looked for the four boys that she had once known so well and was disappointed to find that they were nowhere near.

Something glowed red.

She looked up and saw the sign, the neon letters hanging in their steel frame. They were flashing on and off, casting a glow across the sand around them. But the words were different. The last time she had seen them, they had read: SIGNAL ONE. She was sure of it.

Now they had changed. SIGNAL THREE. That was what they read. And the symbol beside them, the letter T, had swung upside-down.

SIGNAL THREE
SIGNAL THREE

What did it mean? Scarlett didn't know. But behind her, far away in the sea, the dragon saw it and understood. She heard it howling and knew that once again it was rushing towards her, getting closer and closer, but still she refused to turn round.

And then it fell on her. It was huge, as big as the entire world. Scarlett screamed and after that she remembered nothing more.

THE CHAIRMAN

The view was amazing. Scarlett had to admit it despite herself. She had never seen anything quite

187

like it.

It was the middle of the afternoon, her first day in Hong Kong, and she was standing in front of a huge, plate glass window, sixty-six floors up in the headquarters of the Nightrise Corporation. The building was called The Nail and looked like one too, a silver shaft that could have been hammered into its position on Queen Street. She was in the chairman's office, a room so big that she could have played hockey in it, although the ball would probably have got lost in the thick-pile carpet. Paintings by Picasso and Van Gogh hung on the wall. They were almost certainly original.

From her vantage point, Scarlett could see that the city was divided in two. She was staying on Hong Kong Island, surrounded by the most expensive shops and hotels. But she was looking across the harbour to Kowloon, the grubbier, more down-at-heels neighbour. The two parts were separated by what had to be one of the busiest stretches of water in the world, with ships of every shape and size somehow criss-crossing around each other without colliding. There were cruise ships, big enough to hold a small army, tied up at the jetty with little *sampans*, Chinese rowing boats, darting around them. Tugs, cargo boats and container ships moved slowly left and right while nimbler passenger ferries cut in front of them, carrying passengers over to the other side and back. There were even a couple of junks, old Chinese sailing ships that seemed to have floated in from another age.

The Hong Kong skyscrapers were in a world of their own, each one competing to be the tallest, the sleekest, the most spectacular, the most bizarre. And there was something extraordinary about the way they were packed together, so many billions of tons of steel and glass, so many people living and working on top of one another . . . It had already reminded Scarlett of an ant nest but now she saw it was for the richest ants in the world. There weren't many pavements in Hong Kong. An intricate maze of covered walkways connected the different buildings, going from shopping centre to shopping centre, through whole cities of Armani and Gucci and Prada and Cartier and every other million-dollar designer name.

There was very little colour anywhere. If there were any trees or parks, they had been swallowed up in the spread of the city and even the water was like slate. Although it was late in the day, the light hadn't changed much since the morning. Everything was wrapped in a strange, silver mist that made the offices in Kowloon look distant and out of focus.

While she was being driven there, Scarlett had noticed quite a few people in the street had covered their mouths and noses with a square of white material, like surgeons, so that only their eyes showed. Was the air really that bad? She sniffed a couple of times but could detect nothing wrong. On the other hand, the air in the car was almost certainly being filtered. The same was true of the office. The windows here were several centimetres thick, cutting out all the noise and the smells of outside.

'It's quite a sight, isn't it?'

Scarlett turned round. A man had crept up on her without making any sound. He was a European, about sixty, with white hair and thin, silver glasses and although he was smiling, trying to be friendly, she found herself recoiling from him . . . . as if he were a spider or a poisonous snake. There was something very unnatural about the man. He had clearly had a lot of work done to his face—Botox or plastic surgery—but there was a dead quality to his flesh. His eyes were a very pale blue, so pale that they had almost no colour at all.

This was the chairman of the Nightrise Corporation. It had to be. He was wearing an expensive suit, white shirt and red tie. Very successful people have a way of walking, pushing forward as if they expect the world to get out of the way, and that was how he was walking now. He had a deep, throaty voice—he could have been a heavy smoker—and spoke with a faint American accent. There was a silver band on the middle finger of his left hand. Not the wedding finger. Scarlett somehow doubted that he would be married. Who in their right mind would choose to live with such a man?

'It's all right,' Scarlett said.

The chairman seemed disappointed by her reaction. 'There is no greater city on the planet,' he muttered. He pointed out of the window. 'That's Kowloon. Some people say that the best reason to go there is to admire the views back again but there are many museums and temples to enjoy too. You can take the Star Ferry over the water. The crossing is quite an experience, although it is one I have never enjoyed.'

'Do you get seasick?'

'No.' He shook his head. 'When I was twelve years old, a fortune-teller predicted that I would be killed in an incident involving a boat. I'm sure you will think me foolish, but I am very superstitious. It is something I have in common with the Chinese. They believe in luck as a force, almost like a spirit. This building, for example, had to be built in a certain way, with the main door slanting at an angle and mirrors placed at crucial points, according to the principals of *feng shui*. Otherwise, it would be considered unlucky. And you see over there?' He pointed to a factory complex on the other side of the water, in Kowloon. 'How many chimneys does it have?' he asked.

Scarlett counted. 'Five.'

'It has four real chimneys. The extra one is fake. It is there because 'four' is the Chinese word for death but on the other hand they believe that five brings good luck. Do you see? They take these things very seriously and so do I. As a result I have never been close to the water and I have certainly never stepped on a boat.'

He gestured at a low, leather sofa opposite his desk. 'Please. Come and sit down.'

Scarlett did as she was told. He came over and joined her.

'It's a great pleasure to meet you, Scarlett,' he said. 'Your father told me a lot about you.'

'Where is my father?'

'I'm afraid I owe you an apology. I'm sure you were disappointed that he wasn't here to meet you. The fact is that we had a sudden crisis in Nanjing.'

'Is that in China?'

'Yes. There was a legal problem that needed our immediate attention. Obviously, we didn't want to send him. But your father is very good at his job and there was no one else.'

'When will he be back?'

'It shouldn't be more than a week.'

'A week?' Scarlett was shocked. 'Can I talk to him?' she asked.

The chairman sighed. 'That may not be very easy. There are some parts of China that have very bad communications. The landlines are down because of recent flooding and there are whole areas where there's no reception for mobile phones. I'm sure he will try to call you. But it may take some time.'

'So what am I meant to do?' Scarlett asked. She didn't even try to keep the annoyance out of her voice.

'I want you to enjoy yourself,' the chairman said. 'Mrs Cheng will be staying with you until your father returns and Karl will drive you wherever you want to go. There are plenty of things to do in Hong Kong. Shopping, of course. Mrs Cheng has the necessary funds. There's a Disneyland out on Lantau. We have all sorts of fascinating markets for you to explore. And you must go up to The Peak. Also, I have something for you.'

He went over to the desk and opened a drawer. When he came back, he was holding a white cardboard box. 'It's a small gift for you,' he explained. 'By way of an apology.'

He handed the box over and she opened it. Inside, on a bed of cotton wool, lay a pendant made out of some green stone, shaped like a disc and threaded with a leather cord. Looking more closely, Scarlett saw that there was a small animal carved into the centre; a locust or a lizard or a cross between the two, lying on its side with its legs drawn up, as if in the womb. It was very intricate.

If the work hadn't been so finely done, it might have been ugly.

'It's jade,' he explained. 'And it's quite old. Yuan Dynasty. That's thirteenth century. Can I put it on you?'

He reached forward and lifted it out of the box. Compared to the delicacy of the piece, his fingers looked thick and clumsy. Scarlett allowed him to lower it over her head although she didn't like having his hands so close to her throat.

'It looks beautiful on you, Scarlett,' he said. 'I hope you'll look after it. It's very valuable, so you don't want to leave it lying around.' He got to his feet. 'But now I'm afraid I will have to abandon you. I have a board meeting. I'd much rather not go. But even though I'm the chairman, they still won't accept my cry for mercy. So I'll have to say goodbye, Scarlett. It was a pleasure meeting you.'

My cry for mercy . . .

Why had he said that? Cry for Mercy was the name of the monastery where Scarlett had been kept prisoner, on the other side of the door. Of course, he couldn't possibly have known that but nonetheless he had chosen the words quite deliberately. Was he taunting her? The chairman was already moving back to the desk, but even as he had turned Scarlett thought she had detected something in his eyes, behind his silver-framed glasses. Was she imagining it? He had just given her an expensive gift. And yet, for all his seeming kindness and concern, she could have sworn she had seen something else. A brief flash of cruelty.

Scarlett spent the rest of the afternoon shopping—or window shopping anyway. She didn't actually buy anything, which was unlike her. Back in England, Aidan had often teased her that she'd lash out money on a diving suit if it had the right designer label. But she wasn't in the mood. She wondered if she'd caught a cold. It was still very damp, with a thin drizzle that hung suspended in the air without ever hitting the ground. She was also more aware of the silver-grey mist that stretched across the entire city, even following her into the arcades. The skyscrapers disappeared into it, the top floors fading out like a badly developed photograph. There was no sense of distance in Hong Kong. The mist enclosed everything so that roads went nowhere and people and cars seemed to appear as if out of nothing.

She asked Audrey Cheng about it.

'It's pollution,' she replied, in a matter-of-fact sort of voice. 'Its not ours. It blows in from mainland China. There's nothing we can do.' She looked at her watch. 'It's time for supper, Scarlett. Would you like to go home?'

Scarlett nodded.

And then a man appeared, a little way ahead of them. Scarlett noticed him because he had stopped, forcing the crowd to separate and pass by him on both sides. They were in Queen Street, one of the busiest stretches in Hong Kong, surrounded by glimmering shop windows filled with furs, gold watches, fancy cameras and diamond rings. The man was young, Chinese, dressed in a suit with a white shirt and a striped tie. He was holding an envelope.

'Scarlett . . .' he began.

He disappeared. The moment he spoke her name, the crowd closed in on him. It was one of the most extraordinary things Scarlett had ever seen. One moment, the people had been moving along the pavement—hundreds of them, complete strangers. But it was as if someone, somewhere had thrown a switch and suddenly they were acting as one. Scarlett tried to look past the seething mass but it was impossible. She thought she heard a scream. Then the crowd parted. The man had gone.

Only the envelope remained. It was crumpled, lying on the pavement. Scarlett moved forward to pick it up but someone got there ahead of her . . . a pedestrian walking past. It was just a man going home. She didn't even get a chance to look at his face. He snatched up the envelope and took it with him, continuing on his way.

'What was that?' Scarlett demanded.

'What?' Audrey Cheng looked at her with empty eyes.

'That man . . .'

'What man?'

'He called out my name. Then everyone closed in on him.' She still couldn't take in what she had just seen. 'He had a letter. He wanted to give it to me.'

'I didn't see him,' Mrs Cheng said.

'But I did. He was right there.'

'You still have jet lag.' Audrey Cheng signalled and Karl drew up in the car. 'It's easy to imagine things when you're tired.'

Scarlett was glad to get back to Wisdom Court even though she wished her father had been there to greet her. She was going to sleep in his room. Audrey Cheng had taken the guest bedroom. Karl, it seemed, would spend the night elsewhere. She had been completely shaken by what she had seen.

How could a whole crowd behave like that? She remembered the way they had suddenly turned. They could have been controlled by some inner voice that she alone had been unable to hear.

She ate dinner, said goodnight to Mrs Cheng and went to her room. She hadn't finished unpacking and it was as she took out the last of her clothes that she made a discovery. Someone had placed a guidebook for Hong Kong at the bottom of her suitcase. She assumed it must have been Mrs Murdoch and if so, it was a kind gesture—although it was odd that she hadn't mentioned it. She flicked through it. 'The World Traveller's Guide to Hong Kong and Macau. Fully illustrated with thirty colour plates and comprehensive maps.' It was new.

But that wasn't the only thing she found that night.

Scarlett had brought a little jewellery with her—a couple of necklaces and a bracelet Aidan had given her on her last birthday. She decided to keep them safe by putting them into one of the drawers in the dressing table. As she pulled, the drawer stuck. That was probably why nobody had noticed that it wasn't completely empty. She pulled harder and it came free.

There was a small, red document at the very back. It took Scarlett a few seconds to recognize what it was, but then she took it out and opened it.

It was her father's passport.

Paul Edward Adams. There was his photograph. Blank face, glasses, neat hair. It was full of stamps from all over the world and it hadn't yet expired.

The chairman had lied to her.

If her father had left his passport in the flat, he

196

couldn't possibly have travelled to China. And now that she thought about it, there had been something strange about the note he had left her. Why had he typed it? It hadn't even been signed. It could have been written by anyone.

It was eleven o'clock in Hong Kong. Four in the afternoon in England. Scarlett got into bed but she couldn't sleep. She lay there for a long time, thinking of the passport, the passport official with the crocodile eyes, the chairman joking about the cry for mercy, the man who had tried to give her a letter.

She had only been in Hong Kong for one day. Already she was wishing she hadn't come.

CONTACT

Over the next few days, Scarlett tried to forget what had happened and put all her energies into being a tourist. There had to be another explanation for her father's passport. He might have a second copy. Or maybe his company had been able to arrange other travel documents for his visit to China. It was, after all, just the other side of the border. She made a conscious decision not to think about it. He would be back soon—and until then she would treat this as an extended holiday. Surely it had to be better than being at school!

So she took the Star Ferry to Kowloon and back again and had tea at the old-fashioned Peninsula Hotel—tiny sandwiches and palm trees and a string quartet in black tie playing classical music.

She went to Disneyland which was small and didn't have enough fast rides, but which was otherwise all right if you didn't mind hearing Mickey Mouse talking in Cantonese. She went up to The Peak, a mountain standing behind the city which offered panoramic views as if from a low-flying plane. There had been a time when you could see all the way to China from there, but pollution had put an end to that.

She visited temples and markets and went shopping and did everything she could to persuade herself that she was having a good time. But it didn't work. She was miserable. She wanted to go home.

For a start, she was missing her friends at school, particularly Aidan. She had tried texting him but the atmosphere seemed to be interfering with the signal and she got nothing back. She tried to call her mother in Australia but Vanessa Adams was away on a trip. Her secretary said that she would call Scarlett back but she never did.

And it was worse than that. Scarlett didn't like to admit it. It was so unlike her. But she was scared.

It was hard to put her finger on what exactly was wrong, but her sense of unease, the fear that something was going to jump out at her from around the next corner, just grew and grew. It was like walking through a haunted house. You don't see anything. Nothing actually happens. But you're nervous anyway because you know the house is haunted. That was how it was for Scarlett. But in her case it wasn't a house—it was a whole city.

First of all, there were the crowds, the people in the street. Scarlett knew that everyone was in a hurry—to get to work, to get to meetings, to get home again. In that respect, all cities were the same. But the people in Hong Kong looked completely dead. Nobody showed any expression. They walked like robots, all of them moving at the same pace, avoiding each other's eyes. She realized now that what she had seen in Queen Street hadn't been an isolated incident. It was as if the city somehow controlled them. How long would it be, Scarlett wondered, before it began to control her too?

The strange, grey mist was still everywhere. Worse than that, it seemed to be getting thicker, darker, changing colour. Mrs Cheng had said it was pollution but it seemed to have a life of its own, lingering around the corners, hanging over everything. It drained the colour from the streets and even transformed the skyscrapers: the higher storeys looked dark and threatening and it was easy to imagine that they were citadels from a thousand years ago. They didn't seem to belong to the modern world.

And then there was Wisdom Court. From the moment she had arrived there, Scarlett had been aware that something was wrong. It was just too quiet. But after two days there, going up and down in the elevator, in and out of the front door, she suddenly realized. *She hadn't seen anybody*. There were no sounds coming from the other flats, no doors slamming or babies crying. No cars ever pulled up. No smells of cooking or cleaning ever wafted up from the other floors. Apart from Mrs Cheng, she seemed to be living there entirely on her own.

Of course, there was the receptionist. She had

barely registered him to begin with. He was always sitting in the same place, in front of a telephone that never rang, staring at a front door that hardly ever opened. He wore a black jacket and a white shirt. His face was pale. And he never changed. Nobody ever replaced him.

How was that possible? Scarlett found herself examining him more closely. The same man in the same place, morning, noon and night. Didn't he ever eat? Didn't he need toilet breaks? It could have been a corpse sitting there and once that thought had entered her head, she found herself hurrying through the reception area, doing her best to avoid him. Not that it would have made any difference. He never spoke to her once.

On the third evening, after their visit to Disneyland, she challenged Mrs Cheng. The Chinese woman was making dinner, tossing prawns and bean shoots in a wok.

'Where is everybody?'

'What do you mean, Scarlett?'

'We're on our own, aren't we? There's nobody else in this building.'

'Of course there are other people here.' Mrs Cheng turned up the flame. 'They're just busy. People in Hong Kong have very busy lives.'

'But I haven't seen anybody. There's nobody else on this floor.'

'Some of the flats are being redecorated.'

Scarlett gave up. She knew when she was being lied to. It was just another mystery to add to all the others.

The next day, Mrs Cheng took her to a market in an area known as Wan Chai. As usual, Karl drove them. By now, Scarlett had got used to the fact that he accompanied them everywhere and never spoke. She even wondered if he was able to. His role seemed to be to act as a bodyguard. He was always just a few paces behind.

Scarlett had always liked markets and in Hong Kong there was a vibrant street life, sitting side by side with the expensive Western shops and soaring offices. She had been keen to explore the Chinese streets, the stalls piled high with strange herbs and vegetables, soup noodles bubbling away in the open air and the signs and advertisements, all in Chinese, filling the sky like the flags and banners of an invading army.

And yet these markets were full of horrible things. She saw dozens of live chickens trapped in tiny cages and—next to them—dead ones, beaten utterly flat and piled up like deformed pancakes. On the stand next door there was an eel cut into two pieces, surrounded by a puddle of blood. A goat's head hung on a hook, its eyes staring lifelessly, severed arteries spilling out of its neck. It was surrounded by the other pieces of what had once been its body. And finally there was a whole fish, split lengthways, the two bloody halves lying side by side. That was in many ways the most disgusting sight of all. The wretched creature was still alive. She could see its internal organs beating.

Mrs Cheng took one look at it and smiled. 'Fresh!' she said.

Scarlett wondered how long she could stay in Hong Kong without becoming a vegetarian.

They continued on their way, walking past a row of meat shops. Mrs Cheng was going to cook in the flat again that night and she was looking for ingredients. As they paused for a moment, Scarlett noticed one of the butchers staring at her. He was completely bald with a large, round head and a strange, childlike face. He seemed fascinated by her, as if she were a film star or visiting royalty. And he wasn't concentrating on what he was doing.

He was chopping up a joint of meat with a small axe. Scarlett watched the blade come down once, twice . . .

On the third blow, the butcher missed the meat and hit his own left hand. She actually saw the metal cut diagonally into the flesh, almost completely severing his thumb. Blood spouted. But that wasn't the real horror.

The butcher didn't notice.

He raised the axe again, unaware that his hand was lying flat on the chopping board, the thumb twitching, the pool of blood widening. He was so interested in Scarlett that he hadn't noticed what he'd done. Scarlett stared at him in total shock and that must have warned him because then he looked down and backed away immediately, cradling the injured hand, disappearing into the dark interior of the shop.

What sort of man could just about cut off his own hand without any sort of reaction? On the chopping board, human blood mingled with animal blood. It was no longer possible to tell which was which.

Scarlett didn't eat meat that night. And as soon as she had finished dinner, she went back to her room. The flat had cable TV and she watched a rerun of an old British comedy. It didn't make her laugh but at least it reminded her of home. She was thinking more and more about leaving. If her father didn't arrive soon, she would insist on it. How could this have happened to her? How had she found herself on the wrong side of the world, on her own?

She went over to the window and looked out.

Hong Kong by night was even more stunning than it was by day. The windows were ablaze—thousands of them—and all the skyscrapers used light in different ways. Some seemed to be cut into strange shapes by great slices of white neon. Others changed colour, going from green to blue to mauve as if by some sort of electronic magic. And quite a few of them carried television screens so huge that they could be read all the way across the harbour, advertisements and weather information glowing in the night, reflecting in the dark water below.

One such building was directly opposite her. As she gazed out, thinking about the butcher, thinking about the still-living fish that had been cut in half, she found herself being drawn almost hypnotically towards it. It must have belonged to some sort of bank or financial centre—the screen was displaying the performance of stocks and shares. But even as Scarlett watched, the long lists of numbers were wiped from left to right and replaced by four letters in burning gold.

SCAR

It was her own name, or at least half of it. She smiled, wondering what the letters actually stood for. South China Associated Railways? Steamed Chicken And Rice? But then four more letters appeared, tracking from the other side.

203

And that was no abbreviation. It *was* her. Scarlett. The two blocks had formed her name and now they were flashing at her as if trying to attract her attention. She stood at the window, not quite believing what she was seeing. Was someone really trying to send her a message, using an electric sign on the side of a building to get it across?

A few seconds later, the screen changed. Now it had turned white and the message it was displaying read:

PG 70

Scarlett was taken aback. Maybe she was mistaken after all. What did it mean? PG Tips was a type of tea, wasn't it? It was also a type of certificate, before a film. And what about the figure 70?

Scarlett waited, hoping that the sign would change a third time and tell her something more— but nothing happened. It seemed to have frozen. Then, abruptly, it went black, as if someone had deliberately turned it off. At the same moment she heard police sirens, a lot of them, racing through the streets on the other side of the harbour in Kowloon.

There was a knock at the door.

Scarlett went over to the bed and sat down, then quickly picked up a magazine and opened it. Although she wasn't quite sure why, she had decided that she didn't want to be found at the window. 'Come in,' she called.

204

The door opened and Audrey Cheng came in. She was wearing a tight jersey that showed off the shape of her body—round and lumpy. Her black hair was tied back in a bun. Her eyes, magnified by the cheap spectacles, were full of suspicion. 'I just wanted to check you were all right, Scarlett,' she said.

'I'm fine, thank you very much,' Scarlett replied.

'Are you going to bed?'

'In a few minutes.'

'Sleep well.' She seemed pleasant enough, but Scarlett saw her eyes slide over to the window and knew exactly why she had come in. It was the message. She wanted to know if Scarlett had seen it.

And it *was* a message. She was sure of it now. Someone was trying to reach her and had decided that this was the only way. There was some sort of sense in that. A man had tried to hand her an envelope and he had been dragged off the pavement. Mrs Cheng and Karl were watching her all the time. Perhaps this was the only way.

But what did it mean? Scarlett had never been any good at puzzles. Aidan had always laughed at her attempts to do a crossword and she had come bottom in the school quiz. PG 70. It obviously had nothing to do with tea. Could it be an address, a map reference, the registration of a car? She went back over to the window and looked out again but the screen was still dark. Somehow, she doubted it would come back on again.

Eventually she stopped thinking about it and tried to go to sleep—and that was when the answer suddenly arrived. Maybe not thinking about it had helped. PG. Wasn't that an abbreviation for page?

Could it be that someone was trying to make her look at page seventy? But in what? There were about forty or fifty books in the bedroom, most of them old history books that could have nothing to do with Hong Kong.

She got out of bed and picked one off the shelf at random. Sure enough, page seventy took her to a fascinating description of the way Paris had been laid out in the nineteenth century. She tried a dictionary that had been lying on the table. Page seventy began with 'Bandicoot . . . a type of rat' and continued with a whole lot of words beginning with B. How about a page in the telephone book? That would make sense if someone was trying to get in touch.

And then she remembered. There had been one book which she hadn't packed but which had turned up mysteriously in her luggage. A guide to Hong Kong and Macau.

She went back to her case. She hadn't even taken it out—but then she hadn't needed a guide, not with Karl and Mrs Cheng ferrying her every step of the way. She carried it over to the light, flicking through to page seventy and found herself reading a description of somewhere called Yau Ma Tei—'a very interesting area in Kowloon,' the text said. 'Yau Ma Tei means "hemp oil ground" in Cantonese, although you are unlikely to see any around now.' There was a photograph opposite of a market selling jade, which reminded her of the amulet that the chairman had given her. She was wearing it now and wondered if he had bought it there.

She was about to throw the book down—another false lead—when she noticed something.

There was a pencil line against the text. It was so faint that she had almost missed it—but perhaps that was deliberate. The line drew her attention to a single paragraph.

Tin Hau Temple. You shouldn't miss this fascinating temple in a quiet square just north of the jade market. Tin Hau is the goddess of the sea, but the temple is also dedicated to Shing Wong, the city god and Tou Tei, the earth god. Admission is free. And watch out for the fortune-tellers who practise their trade in the streets outside. If you're superstitious, you can have your palm read or your future foretold by a 'bird of fortune'.

And at the very end of the paragraph, also in pencil, was a message: *5.00 p.m.*

Scarlett didn't get very much sleep that night. Someone was trying to reach her—and the risk was so great that they'd had to take huge precautions. First, they'd slipped a book into her case. Maybe they'd bribed someone at the airport. Then they'd somehow taken over a whole office block to draw her attention to it. The message had been clever too. PG 70. Anyone whose first language was Chinese would have had difficulty working out what it meant. It had taken her long enough herself.

She had to visit the temple and she had to be there at five o'clock. Maybe someone who knew her father would be there. Maybe they'd be able to tell her where he really was.

There was a fire in Hong Kong that night. The

office building with the giant screen burned to the ground and when Scarlett woke up, the air was even greyer and hazier than ever, the smoke mixing in with the pollution. She looked out of the window but she couldn't see the other side of Victoria Harbour. The whole of Kowloon was covered in fog.

Mrs Cheng was more chatty than usual at breakfast. She mentioned that nine people had been killed and insisted on turning on the television to see what had happened. And, sure enough, there it was on a local news channel. The image was a little grainy and the announcer was speaking in Chinese but Scarlett recognized the building, directly opposite Wisdom Court, right on the harbour front. The images had been taken the night before and there were flames exploding all around it, the reflections dancing in the black water. Half a dozen fire engines had been called to the scene.

But the firemen weren't doing anything. The camera panned over them. None of them moved. None of them even unwound their hoses.

They just stood there and let the building burn.

BIRDS OF FORTUNE

The Tin Hau Temple was a low, narrow building, crouching behind a wall and surrounded by trees, almost as if it didn't want to be found. There were tower blocks on every side, the dirty brick walls crowding out the sky, but in the middle of it all there was a space, a wide square with trees that

208

seemed to sprout out of the very concrete itself. Some benches and tables had been set out and there were groups of old men playing a Chinese version of chess. A few tourists were milling around, taking photographs of each other against the green, sloping roofs of the temple. The air smelled faintly of incense.

It hadn't been easy getting Mrs Cheng to bring her here.

From the very start, Scarlett knew she had to be careful. Mrs Cheng had shown her the news report for a reason. She hadn't been fooled by Scarlett's act of the night before and she was letting her know it. If Scarlett asked straight out to go to the Tin Hau Temple at five o'clock, she would be more suspicious than ever.

'Is there any news from my dad?' As they cleared the breakfast plates away, Scarlett asked the same question she asked every morning.

'I'm sure he'll call you soon, Scarlett. He's very busy.'

'Why can't I call him?'

'It's not possible. China is very difficult.' She flicked on the dishwasher. 'So where would you like to go today?'

This was the moment Scarlett had been waiting for. She shrugged her shoulders. 'I don't know,' she said.

'We could go out to Stanley Village. It is on the beach and there are some nice stalls.'

Scarlett pretended to consider. 'Actually,' she said, 'I wanted to buy some jade for my friend, Amanda.'

Mrs Cheng nodded. 'You can find jade in the Hollywood Road. But it's expensive.'

'Can't we go to a market?'

'There's a jade market in Kowloon . . .'

It was exactly what Scarlett wanted her to say. She had read the entire chapter in the guidebook and knew that the most famous jade market in Hong Kong was just round the corner from the temple. If they visited one, they'd be sure to walk over to the other. And that way she would arrive at Tin Hau without even having mentioned it.

She still had to make sure that they got there at the right time, so after they had finished clearing up she announced that she had some school work to do and they didn't leave Wisdom Court until two o'clock. Scarlett would have preferred to have taken the subway that went all the way there but as usual, Mrs Cheng insisted that Karl should drive them. And that meant he would be with them all afternoon. They were certainly keeping her close.

The jade market was in a run-down corner of Kowloon, just off the Nathan Road, which was a long, wide tourist strip known as the 'Golden Mile'. Not that there was much gold amongst the rather tacky shops which specialized in cheap electronics, fake designer watches and cut-price suits. The market was located in a low-ceilinged warehouse, sheltering under one of the huge flyovers that seemed to be knotted into the city.

The pollution was even worse today. The weather was cold and damp and the mist was thicker than ever. Scarlett could actually feel it clinging to her skin and wondered how the people of Hong Kong put up with it. She noticed that increasing numbers of them had resorted to the white masks on their faces and wondered how long it would be before she joined them.

There were about fifty stalls in the jade market, selling necklaces, bracelets and little figurines. Keeping one eye on her watch, Scarlett made a big deal out of choosing something, haggling with the stallholders, asking Mrs Cheng for advice, before finally settling on a bracelet which cost her all of three pounds. As she handed over the money, it occurred to her that Amanda would actually quite like it—she just hoped that she would be able to give it to her some time soon.

'Do you want to go back down to the Peninsula?' Mrs Cheng suggested as they came back out into the street. Karl was waiting for them, leaning against the car. He never seemed to have any trouble parking in Hong Kong. For some reason, the traffic wardens—if there were any—never came close.

'Not really . . .' Scarlett looked around her. And she was in luck. There was a signpost pointing to the Tin Hau Temple. They were standing right in front of it. 'Can we go there?' she said, trying to make the suggestion sound casual.

'We've already visited a lot of temples.'

'Yes. But I'd quite like to see another.'

It was true. They'd already been to the Man Mo in Central Hong Kong and to the Kuan Yin only the day before. They were strange places. Chinese temples seemed to mix religion and superstition—with fortune sticks and palm readers sitting comfortably among the altars and the incense. The people who went there didn't pray like an English congregation. They bowed repeatedly, muttering to themselves. They left offerings of food and silk on the tables. They burned sacks of paper in furnaces that were kept going for precisely that

211

purpose. Hong Kong had been Westernized in many ways, but the temples could only belong to the East and provided glimpses of another age.

Tin Hau was just like the others. As Scarlett stepped inside, she found herself facing not one but several altars, surrounded by a collection of life-size statues that could have come out of a bizarre comic book: a cross-legged old man with a beard that was made of real hair, two devil monsters, one bright red, the other blue, both of them more childish than frightening. One of them was crying, wiping its eyes and grimacing at its neighbour. The other stood with a raised hand, trying to calm his friend down. There was a china-doll woman carrying a gift and, in a long row, more than fifty smaller figures, each one a different god, perched on a shelf. The temple was a riot of violent colours, richly patterned curtains, lamps and flowers. The smoke from the incense was so thick that they'd had to install a powerful ventilation system which droned continuously, trying to clear the air.

Scarlett had arrived on time but she had no idea what she was looking for. There were about a dozen people in the temple, but they were all busy with their devotions and nobody so much as turned her way. Was it possible that she had misunderstood the passage in the guidebook? It had definitely told her to be there at five o'clock and it was already a few minutes past. She waited for someone to approach her, to slip another message into her hand—one of the worshippers, or a tourist perhaps. She even wondered if her father might be there.

Nothing happened. Nobody came close. Scarlett

knew that she could only pretend to be interested in the place for so long. Mrs Cheng was watching her with growing suspicion. She certainly hadn't shown much interest in temples the day before—so what was so special about this one?

'Have you had enough, Scarlett?' she demanded.

'Who is that?' Scarlett asked desperately, pointing at one of the statues.

'His name is Kuan Kung, the god of war.' Something flickered deep in her eyes. 'Maybe you should pray to him.'

'Why do you say that, Mrs Cheng?'

'You never know when another war will begin.'

In the end, Scarlett had to leave. She had lingered for as long as she could but it seemed clear that nobody was going to come. She was hugely disappointed. Of course, the note had only given her a time. It hadn't told her what day to be there. On the other hand, it was unlikely that she would be able to find an excuse to return, and slipping out of Wisdom Court on her own was out of the question. Nine people had died when the office on the waterfront had burned down. Maybe whoever had sent the message had been among them.

It was beginning to get dark when they emerged into the square. Karl was sitting on a bench with his arms folded, looking about as animated as the statues that they had just seen. A number of stalls were being set up all around. They didn't look particularly interesting—selling socks, hats, reading glasses and useless bits of bric-à-brac—but they were attracting quite a crowd.

'Can we look at them?' Scarlett asked.

It had only struck her there and then. The passage in the guidebook had described the Tin Hau Temple. But it had also gone on about the square outside. Maybe her secret messenger would be waiting there. Mrs Cheng scowled briefly but Scarlett had already set off. She followed.

Scarlett pretended to browse in front of a stand selling cheap alarm clocks and watches. She was determined to spend as much time here as possible. She noticed that the next stall wasn't selling anything. There was a woman with a pack of tarot cards. In fact now that she looked around her she saw that at least half the market was devoted to different methods of fortune-telling.

She walked over to a very old man, a palm reader who was sitting on a plastic stool, close to the ground. His stall was decorated with a banner showing the human hand divided into different segments, each one with a Chinese character. He was examining the palm of a boy of about thirteen, his nose and eyes millimetres away from the skin as if he really could read something there. Scarlett moved on. There was a woman a little further along, also telling the future. But in a very different way.

The woman was small and round with long, grey hair. She was wearing a red silk jacket, sitting behind a table, arranging half a dozen packets of envelopes which were stacked up in front of her. On one side, there were three cages, each one containing a little yellow bird—a canary or something like it. On the other, she had a mat with a range of different symbols and a jar of seeds. The woman seemed to be completely focused on what she was doing but as Scarlett approached, she

214

suddenly reached out with a single, gnarled finger and, without looking up, tapped one of the symbols on the mat.

It was a five-pointed star.

Scarlett had seen exactly the same thing on the door that had led her to the monastery of the Cry for Mercy. She was careful not to give anything away—Mrs Cheng was standing right next to her—but she felt a rush of excitement. According to Father Gregory, the doors had been built centuries ago to help the Gatekeepers. They were there to help her. Had the woman sent a deliberate signal? Scarlett examined her more closely. She still didn't look up, busying herself with the envelopes and occasionally muttering at the birds.

Scarlett turned to Mrs Cheng. 'What's this all about?' she asked.

'She uses the birds to tell fortunes,' Mrs Cheng explained.

The old woman had heard the English voices and seemed to notice Scarlett for the first time. She squinted at her and muttered something in Chinese.

'She's offering to tell your fortune,' Mrs Cheng translated. 'But it will cost you thirty Hong Kong dollars.'

'That's about two pounds.'

'It's a complete waste of money.'

'I don't care.' Scarlett dug in her pocket and took out the right amount. She set it down on the mat and then took her place on the plastic seat on her side of the table. The fortune-teller folded the money and transferred it to a little purse that she wore around her neck. Then she reached for a white card and laid it in front of Scarlett. She said

215

something to Mrs Cheng.

'She wants you to make a choice,' Mrs Cheng explained.

There were a number of categories set out on the card, written in both Chinese and English. Scarlett could choose which part of her life she wanted to know about: family, love and marriage, health, work, business and wealth or study.

'Maybe I should choose family,' she said. 'She may be able to tell me what's happened to my dad.'

'Your father will be home very soon, Scarlett.'

'All right, then. Love and marriage.' Scarlett tapped the words on the card and thought briefly of Aidan. She wondered what he was doing right then.

The fortune-teller took the card away and selected one of the piles of envelopes which she had spread out in front of the three cages. Each one had a door in the front and she opened one of them. The little yellow bird hopped out as it had been trained to do, perched on the line of envelopes, then pulled one out with its beak. The old woman rewarded it with a couple of seeds and the bird obediently hopped back in again. It was all over very quickly.

The woman opened the envelope and handed Scarlett the slip of paper which had been inside.

'Do you want me to translate it for you?' Mrs Cheng asked.

Scarlett glanced at the sheet. 'No, it's OK,' she replied. 'It's in English.'

'Tell me what it says.'

'Good news from Fortune Bird Two.' Scarlett read out the words. 'You will find your true love in the month of April. Your marriage will be long and happy and you will travel to many countries. When you are old, you will make a great sum of money. Spend it wisely.' She folded the page in half. 'That's it.'

'The note only tells you what you want to hear,' Mrs Cheng remarked.

'The bird chose it for me.' She held out the page so that Mrs Cheng could see it. 'There you are. You can see for yourself. I'm going to be rich.'

Mrs Cheng nodded but said nothing. The two of them and Karl walked back to the car. And all the time, Scarlett's heart was racing and she kept the piece of paper close to her. She had folded it quite deliberately. She had only shown Mrs Cheng half of what had been written.

For underneath the printed fortune, there had been another message, written by hand:

Scarlett.

You are in great danger. Do not let the woman read this. Come to The Peak tomorrow afternoon. Follow the path from Lugard Road. We will be waiting.

We are your friends. Trust us if you want to leave Hong Kong alive.

THE PEAK

Scarlett knew something was wrong, the moment she opened her eyes.

A glance at her bedside clock told her that it was eight o'clock in the morning but for some

217

reason the sun wasn't reaching her bedroom. It wasn't just cloudy. It was actually dark. What was going on? She turned over and looked at the window. At first she thought that someone had drawn a black curtain across the glass, but then she realized that it wasn't on the inside. It was outside. How was that possible, twelve storeys up? She propped herself on one elbow, still half-asleep, trying to work it out.

And then the curtain moved. It seemed to fold in on itself and at the same time she heard the beating of tiny wings and understood what she was looking at. It was a great swarm of insects, black flies. They had attached themselves to the window like some single living organism.

She lay where she was, staring at them with complete disgust. She had never seen so many flies, not even in the heat of the summer. And this was a cold day in November! What had brought them here? How had they managed to fly across an entire city to come together on a single pane of glass? She could hear their buzzing and the soft tapping as they threw their bodies against the window. She could make out their legs, thousands of them, sticking to the glass. Their wings were blurring as they held themselves in place. Scarlett felt sick. She was suddenly terrified that they would find their way in. She could imagine them swirling around her head, a great black mass, crawling into her nostrils and mouth. On an impulse, she scooped up her pillow and threw it at the window. It worked. As one, the flies peeled away. For a moment they looked like a long silk scarf, hanging in the breeze. Then they were gone.

For about twenty minutes, Scarlett stayed where

she was, almost afraid to get up. She didn't like insects at the best of times but this was something else again. She knew that what she had seen was completely impossible . . . just like the door in the church of St Meredith's. And that told her what should have been obvious all along.

She had thought that, at the very least, her sudden departure to Hong Kong would be an escape from what had been happening in London—the monastery, the sense of being followed, the restaurant that had blown up. But of course it wasn't. It was a continuation, part of the same thing. The events that had closed in on her in London had followed her here. She was caught in the same trap. But here it was even worse. She was far from her friends and family, alone in a city that seemed to be hostile in every way.

This was all happening because she was a Gatekeeper. She remembered what Father Gregory had told her. He had talked about an ancient evil . . . the Old Ones. Scarlett didn't know exactly what they were but she could imagine the worst. They were here, in Hong Kong. That would explain everything. The Old Ones were toying with her. They were the ones who were controlling the crowd.

What was she going to do?

She could march into the kitchen and tell Mrs Cheng that she didn't want to wait for her father, that she was taking the next flight back to London. She could telephone her mother in Australia or the headmistress at St Genevieve's. They would get her out of here. She could even contact the police.

But she knew that none of it would work. The

forces ranged against her were too powerful. She could see it every time she went outside. Hong Kong was sick. There was a sort of cancer that had spread through every alleyway and every street and which had infected everyone who walked there. Did she seriously think that they were just going to let her walk out of here? So far, they hadn't threatened her directly. That hadn't been part of their plan. But if she challenged them, if she tried to assert herself, they would close in on her and she would only make her situation worse.

She had just one hope. The people who were trying to reach her: they had to be on her side. *We are your friends*. That was what they had told her. She just had to behave normally until she reached them. Then, once she knew what was really happening, she would be able to act.

She got up and got dressed. The fortune-teller's note was beside the bed, but now she tucked it away beneath the mattress. Whoever her friends were, they were being very careful. They were contacting her in four separate stages: the guidebook hidden in her luggage, the illuminated sign across the harbour, the bird of fortune at Tin Hau and finally a meeting this afternoon. The question was, how was she going to persuade Mrs Cheng to take her back to The Peak?

They had already been there once. Victoria Peak was the mountain that rose up behind Hong Kong, a must-see for every tourist. Scarlett had gone there on the second day, taking the old wooden tram—it was actually a funicular railway— up the slope to the top, five hundred metres above the city. The views were meant to be spectacular but they hadn't seen very much on account of the pollution. Maybe that was the answer. If the weather cheered up, it would give her an excuse to go back.

Mrs Cheng was in the kitchen, cooking an omelette for Scarlett's breakfast.

'Good morning, Scarlett.'

'Good morning, Mrs Cheng.'

'Did you sleep well?'

'Very well, thank you.'

As Scarlett sat down, it occurred to her that she had never seen the woman eat—not so much as a mouthful. Even when they went to restaurants together, Mrs Cheng only ordered food for Scarlett. In fact she had only ever shown hunger once. That had been at the market when they examined the hideous, sliced-in-half but still-living fish.

'So where would you like to go today, Scarlett?' They were exactly the same words she had used the day before. And she spoke without any real enthusiasm, as if it was simply what she had been programmed to say.

'Why don't we go back to The Peak?' Scarlett suggested. 'We didn't see anything very much last time. Maybe we'll get a better view.'

Mrs Cheng looked out of the window. 'There's a lot of cloud,' she remarked.

'But it's going to cheer up this afternoon,' Scarlett said. 'I saw the forecast on TV.' It was grim outside with a non-stop drizzle sweeping across the sky. And the forecast had said it would stay the same for the rest of the week. But somehow Scarlett knew she was right.

'I don't think so.' Mrs Cheng shook her head. 'Maybe you would like to go to the cinema?'

'Let's see what it's like this afternoon,' Scarlett pleaded. 'I'm sure it will clear up.'

And against all the odds, it did. At around two o'clock, the clouds finally parted and the sun came out, still weak against the ever-present pollution, but definitely there. Even Mrs Cheng had to agree that it was too nice an afternoon to stay indoors and so the two of them set out.

The receptionist was in his usual place as they left Wisdom Court, sitting stiffly behind the desk and wearing the same dark suit and white shirt, watching them with no expression at all. As they went past, Scarlett noticed something. The man had a black spot, a mole, on the side of his face. At least, that was what she thought. Then the spot moved. It crawled over his cheek and began to climb up and she realized that it was actually a fly, one of the fat, black insects that had come to her window that morning. The receptionist didn't move. He didn't try to swat it. He didn't even seem to have noticed it and did nothing as the creature reached the corner of his eye and began to feed.

Scarlett couldn't get out of the building fast enough. Wisdom Court was only a few minutes from the tram station and they could have walked but Karl drove them anyway. But at least he had decided not to come to the top. Mrs Cheng bought tickets for the two of them and she and Scarlett got onto the tram.

Although the station looked new, the tram itself had been built more than a hundred years before. Climbing on board was like stepping back in history. They took their places on the polished, wooden seats and a short while later, with no warning, they set off, trundling up the tracks through thick vegetation with occasional glimpses of the city, ever smaller and more distant as they went. There were about twenty tourists sharing the ride, some of them small children, laughing and pointing. Watching them, Scarlett wished that she could be like them, part of an ordinary family, out here on holiday. She was only a few seats away from them but they could have been inhabiting a different world. Had they really got no inkling about what was happening in Hong Kong? Was she the only one to feel the all-pervading sense of evil?

We will be waiting.

She focused her mind on what lay ahead. Who would be there and why had they chosen The Peak of all places? Maybe it was because it was outside the city, away from the buildings. At the summit there would be no crowds, no surveillance cameras. It was somewhere with room to breathe.

The tram arrived and the passengers poured out, straight into a complex that seemed to have been specially built to make as much money from as many tourists as possible. From the outside it looked like a bizarre observation tower, like something out of *Star Wars*. Inside, it was full of tacky shops and restaurants with a Madame Tussaud's and a Ripley's Believe-it-or-Not with signs inviting visitors to 'come and see the world's fattest man'. Scarlett couldn't wait to get out.

'Let's go for a walk,' she suggested. She was careful to sound as innocent as possible.

Mrs Cheng looked doubtful. She wasn't dressed for a walk—in a short, grey skirt, black stockings and high-heeled shoes. 'Maybe a short way . . .' she muttered.

There was a distinct chill in the air as the two of

223

them made their way down a slope, passing a man who was sweeping leaves. Scarlett knew what she was looking for. A path that led off from the Lugard Road. That was what the fortune-teller's note had said. She saw the sign almost at once. Without even waiting for Mrs Cheng to catch up, she set off.

The path was three miles long, snaking all the way round the mountain, paved all the way. On one side there was The Peak itself, with a tangle of exotic trees and bushes hanging overhead. On the other was an iron railing, to prevent anyone falling down the hill. There weren't many other people around. The changing weather must have dissuaded them, and the other tourists who had come up in the tram had all stayed inside. Soon Scarlett found that she and Mrs Cheng were entirely on their own.

There was a strange atmosphere on The Peak. The mist had returned, hanging in the air, almost blotting out the sun. Everything was washed out, dark green and pale white. There were birds whistling, squawking and rattling in the undergrowth, but none of them could be seen. The path was lost in the clouds and it was impossible to see more than twenty metres ahead. As she made her way forward, Scarlett found it easy to imagine that she had somehow travelled back in time, that this was some Eastern version of *Jurassic Park* and that a dinosaur might be waiting for her round the next corner.

But then she arrived at an observation point where the vegetation had been cut back and Hong Kong appeared, sprawled out below. It was incredible to see so many skyscrapers packed together on both sides of the water. There were hundreds of them, every shape and size, made small and insignificant by the distance—with thousands or even millions of people invisible among them.

Mrs Cheng plodded along behind, saying nothing. Her face was sullen, her hands—loosely curled into fists—hung by her side. Scarlett was quietly amused. Her guardian clearly wasn't enjoying the visit. She wasn't even bothering to glance at the view.

A couple of people walked past them . . . a woman pushing an old-fashioned pram and a man, jogging. The man was wearing a blue tracksuit and his face was covered by an anti-pollution mask, with only his eyes showing above the white square. Scarlett tensed as each one of them approached. She was waiting for someone to make contact. But neither of them so much as noticed her, both continuing on their way.

They walked for another five minutes, still following the path which curved round the side of The Peak.

'I think we should go back, Scarlett,' Mrs Cheng said.

'But it's a circular walk,' Scarlett protested. 'If we keep going, we'll find ourselves back anyway.'

Three more walkers appeared ahead of them: two men and a woman, all Chinese. They were dressed in much the same way with jeans, zip-up jackets and walking shoes. One of the men had a walking stick although he looked young and fit and surely didn't need it. The other man carried a backpack. He was in his thirties, with glasses and a pock-marked face. The two of them were chatting.

225

The woman—she was slim and athletic, her long hair tied back with a pink band—was listening to an iPod. As they drew nearer, they showed no interest in Scarlett at all.

The three of them drew level.

'Scarlett . . .' Mrs Cheng began.

She never finished the sentence. The man with the backpack reached behind him and drew out something that was flat and silver. It was a move that he must have rehearsed many times. To Scarlett's eyes, it was as if he had suddenly produced an oversized kitchen knife. Then she realized what it was. A machete. The blade was about half a metre long and razor-sharp. At the same time, the other man twisted the handle of his walking stick, revealing the sword that had been concealed inside. Scarlett saw the glint of metal and heard it slice the air as he pulled it free. The woman wasn't armed. She was looking behind her, checking the path was clear.

Both men plunged their weapons into Audrey Cheng. The Chinese woman screamed—but there was nothing remotely human about the sound. It was a high-pitched howl, almost deafening. Scarlett stared in horror. Her face was unrecognizable, her mouth stretched open in a terrible grimace. Blood was pouring in a torrent over her lower lip. Her eyes had clouded over. She hadn't had time to defend herself or react in any way. Scarlett saw her neck open as if it was hinged and she looked away. She heard the thud as Mrs Cheng's severed head hit the ground. She knew that it was a sound that she would never forget.

The woman ran forward and put an arm around her, comforting her. Some of Mrs Cheng's blood

226

had splattered onto her. There were flecks of it on her jacket. The very air had gone a hazy red.

'I'm sorry you had to see that, Scarlett,' she said, in perfect English. 'Don't look round. We had to do it. There was no other way.'

'You killed her!' Scarlett was in shock. She had never liked Mrs Cheng but she couldn't believe what she had just seen. These people hadn't given her a chance to defend herself. They had murdered her in cold blood.

'Not her. It.'

Scarlett stared. 'What do you mean?'

'Show her!' one of the men snarled.

'We're your friends,' the woman said. 'We sent you the message with the fortune-teller. We've come to help you and, believe me, there was no other way.' She placed her hands on Scarlett's shoulder. 'Turn round and have a look for yourself,' she went on. 'The woman isn't what you think. She's a shape-changer. We'll show you, but then you have to come with us. They'll know what's happened. They'll have heard her. We don't have much time . . .'

Scarlett turned round. The man with the sword-stick was already sheathing it. The other was wiping his machete on a piece of cloth. She swallowed hard, not wanting to do this. There was a lot of blood, spreading across the path.

Mrs Cheng was lying on her back, the legs in their black stockings lying straight out in front of her. There was a dreadful wound in her chest where one of the blades had stabbed her through the heart. The other had decapitated her. Scarlett forced herself to examine the rest of the body. She saw something thick and green coming out of the

227

jacket where Mrs Cheng's neck should have been. It had been severed half way up. But it didn't belong to a human body. It looked like part of a snake.

And the head, lying on the path, wasn't human either. It was the head of an oversized lizard, with yellow and black diamond eyes, scales, a lolling forked tongue. Scarlett glanced back at the body. Mrs Cheng had thrown out one of her arms as she fell. It was also covered in scales.

A shape-changer.

That was what they had said. And in the shock of the moment, all Scarlett could think was—was this the creature she had been living with since she had come to Hong Kong? Audrey Cheng had cooked for her. She had been sleeping in the same flat. And all the time . . .

She thought she was going to be sick. She couldn't get the hideous images out of her head. But then she heard the sound of an approaching engine, coming down the path towards her. Had they been discovered? The woman and the two men weren't moving. They didn't look alarmed. Scarlett relaxed. Whoever was coming was part of the plan.

A motorbike appeared, speeding round the corner. It was a silver-grey Honda, being ridden by a figure in black leather, gloves and boots. Scarlett guessed that it was a man, but it was hard to be sure as his head was concealed by a helmet with a strip of mirrored plastic across his face. He stopped right in front of them, the wheels tilting underneath him, one leg stretching out to keep the bike upright.

The woman grabbed hold of Scarlett once

again. 'We need to get you out of here fast,' she said. 'We don't have time to explain.'

'Where are you taking me?'

'Somewhere safe.'

They had produced a second helmet. Scarlett hesitated, but only for a few seconds. Audrey Cheng's dead body told her everything she needed to know. She had been living in a nightmare and these people, whoever they were, were rescuing her from it. She grabbed the helmet and put it on, then climbed onto the bike, putting her arms around the driver. At once they were away. She felt the engine roar underneath her as they shot down the path and she tightened her grip, afraid that she would be blown over backwards by the rush of wind.

They shot past a man walking a dog and then a family of local people who had been posing for a photograph but who scattered to get out of the way. They turned another corner. If they went much further, they would surely arrive back at the tram station where Scarlett had begun. On one side there was a small park, on the other a driveway leading up to a house, for there were a few private homes scattered along the upper reaches of The Peak. But that wasn't where they were heading. Scarlett saw a parked car with two more men waiting. They skidded to a halt.

She got off, quickly removing her helmet. The two men were young, in their twenties, both wearing jeans and sweatshirts. One was Chinese but the other was a foreigner, maybe from Japan or Korea. They both hurried over to her, their faces filled with a mixture of determination and fear.

'You have to come with us,' the first one said. He had a thin face and his nose and cheekbones were so sharp-edged that they could almost have been folded out of paper. 'We must leave at once.'

'Where are we going?'

'Somewhere safe.' That was exactly what the woman had said. 'Not far. Maybe twenty minutes.'

'Wait a minute . . .'

'No time.' He spoke in fractured English, spitting out the words. 'You want to die, you stay here. You ask your questions. You want to live, get in the car. Now! They will be coming very soon.'

'Who will be coming?'

'Shape-changers. Or worse.'

The other man had gone over to the car. But he hadn't opened the door. He had opened the boot.

'You don't expect me to get in there!' Scarlett said.

'It must be this way,' the thin-faced man insisted. 'You can't be seen. But you'll be all right. We make air-holes . . .'

'No . . .' It was too much to ask. Scarlett didn't care how many shape-changers there might be, making their way up The Peak. She wasn't going to be locked in the boot of a car by two people she had never met before and driven off to God knows where. 'You can forget it . . .' she began.

The man had whipped something out of his pocket and he grabbed her before she knew what he was doing. She felt a handkerchief being pressed against her face. She kicked out, trying to knock him off balance, but he was too strong. The fumes of some sort of chemical, sweet and pungent, crept into her nose and mouth. Almost at once, all the strength drained out of her. She felt

230

her legs fold and the world spun. And then she was falling, being guided into the boot, which had become a huge black hole waiting to swallow her up.

The end came very quickly. Darkness. Terror. And then the welcome emptiness of sleep.

LOHAN

She was in a cage, not lying down but standing. And there was something strange. The wall was moving. It seemed to be scrolling downwards in front of her. Or was it she who was moving up?

As consciousness returned, Scarlett realized what was happening. She was in a lift, one of the old-fashioned sort with a folding iron gate instead of a door. What she was looking at was the brickwork between floors in what must be a very tall building. She was pinned between the Japanese man and the one she had decided to call Paper Face. They were supporting her. She could still taste the drug—chloroform or whatever it was—that had knocked her out.

Scarlett groaned and the two men immediately tightened their grip. There was no chance she was going to start a fight in such a confined space, but she had already struggled at the car and they weren't taking any chances.

'You are safe now,' Paper Face said.

'Where am I?'

'You will see . . . very soon.'

The lift slowed down and stopped and the Japanese man jerked the cage door open. They

231

stepped out into a long, dimly lit corridor with walls that were either grimy or had been deliberately painted the colour of grime. There were doors every few metres. The whole place looked like a cheap hotel.

There was a Chinese man guarding the corridor with a machine gun cradled across his chest. The sight of the weapon struck Scarlett as completely bizarre. It was like something out of a gangster film. But the man didn't look anything like her idea of a gangster. He was dressed in jeans and a loose-hanging shirt. He was skinny, with a wispy beard, a tattoo on his neck and a gold tooth prominent at the front of his mouth. A drug dealer perhaps? Looking at him, it was hard to believe that he was on her side.

The two men took her to the fourth room along the corridor. Paper Face knocked and the door was unlocked from inside. They entered. Machine Gun stayed where he was, opposite the lift.

Scarlett found herself in a large, almost empty flat that looked as if someone had recently moved out . . . or in. There were a few pieces of furniture, some of them covered in dust sheets, and no decoration: no carpet, no lampshades, no pictures on the walls. The windows had been blanked out with sheets of papers. Scarlett wondered why. They had to be fairly high up so surely there was no chance of anyone looking in. An archway led into a small kitchen and there was a corridor on the other side, presumably with a bedroom and bathroom at the end.

Another man had been waiting for her to arrive. He was Chinese, more smartly dressed than the others—in a grey suit and grey T-shirt—and everything about him radiated confidence and control. Was he the one in charge? He examined Scarlett briefly. His eyes were very dark, almost black, and gave nothing away. There was a thin scar starting high up on his left cheek and then slanting diagonally across his lips so that the two halves of his face didn't quite meet, like a reflection in a broken mirror. But he was handsome even so. Scarlett guessed that he was barely more than twenty years old.

'How are you?' he said. 'You must have been very frightened by your ordeal. I'm sorry that there was no other way.'

'Who are you?' Scarlett demanded. 'Where am I and who are these people? What do you want with me? And what was that with Mrs Cheng? They said she was a shape-changer. What does that mean?' Once the questions had started, they wouldn't stop.

The man held up a hand. He had long, elegant fingers, like a piano player. 'We have a great deal to say to each other,' he said. 'Would you like a drink?'

'No, thank you.'

'But I would.' He nodded and Paper Face hurried into the kitchen. He was obviously used to being obeyed. He turned back to Scarlett. 'Please, come and sit down.'

Scarlett went over to the sofa. She was surprised how quickly the drug had worn off. She sat down. The man followed her and sat opposite. He moved slowly, taking his time. Everything about him was very deliberate.

'My name is Lohan,' he said. 'Does that answer your first question? I doubt if my colleagues will have very much to say to you but I will tell you their names too. The man in the kitchen is called Draco. And this here . . .' he nodded in the direction of the Japanese man, '. . . is Red. Not their real names, you understand. Just the names they use.

'Your next question—what do we want with you? Very simply, we want to get you out of Hong Kong as quickly as possible. Quite frankly, it would have been better for everyone if you had never arrived, but never mind. We couldn't stop you coming, although we tried. It's remarkable how many people you've already managed to get killed.'

He certainly wasn't sparing her feelings. But Scarlett wasn't going to let him intimidate her. 'I want to see my father,' she said. 'Do you know where he is?'

'I'm afraid not,' Lohan replied. 'I have never even met him. For what it's worth, I would imagine that he is dead. A very great many people have died in Hong Kong in the last weeks. He was probably one of them.'

'You're telling me my father's dead! Don't you care?'

Lohan shrugged. 'I've told you. I've never met him. Why should it matter to me whether he is alive or dead?'

Draco came back in from the kitchen, carrying a tray with a small porcelain bowl and a jar of some sort of spirit—vodka or sake. He set the whole thing down in front of Lohan, bowed and then took his place on a seat beside the front door. Lohan poured himself a drink. He held it briefly between his index finger and his thumb, then threw it back and swallowed. He set the bowl back down.

'You want to know where you are,' he continued. 'This apartment is in Mong Kok, a couple of blocks north of the Tin Hau Temple, where you had your fortune told. The entire building belongs to us and with a bit of luck, nobody will come up here. While you remain in this room, you are safe. Every minute you spend outside it, you are in more danger than you can possibly imagine.'

'You mean shape-changers.'

Lohan ignored her. For a moment he gazed past her, as if focusing on something outside the room. Then he began.

'You have to understand the nature of a city,' he said. 'You live in London and so maybe what I'm about to say will be obvious to you. All cities are the same. They have an atmosphere. More than that. You might call it a flow. The traffic moves in a certain way. The trains pull in and out of the stations. People go to work, they have their lunch, they go shopping, they go home again. Postmen deliver the post. Policemen patrol the streets. Sweepers and refuse collectors come out in the evening. The night bus arrives at the right time and picks up the people who are waiting at the stop and takes them where they expect to go. Everyone is obeying the flow, even if they don't realize it, because if they didn't life would descend into chaos.

'Now . . . consider Hong Kong. It is one of the most densely populated cities in the world. There are more than seven million people living here. That works out at around 6,500 people per square kilometre. A few of them are rich. Most of them

235

are very poor. And then there are the millions in between—the doctors and dentists, the shopkeepers, builders, plumbers, teachers . . .'

'I think I get the point,' Scarlett interrupted.

'No, Scarlett. I don't think you do.' Lohan hadn't raised his voice. His face was as impassive as ever. But Scarlett realized that she shouldn't have spoken. He wasn't used to being interrupted. 'This is the point,' he went on. 'How many of those people could die, do you think, before you noticed? How many of them could be shot or knifed while they lay in bed before the city seemed any different? Fifty of them? Or five hundred? Or how about five hundred thousand? Can you describe to me, accurately, the man who sold you the ticket when you boarded the tram this morning? Or the driver who took you to The Peak? Or the man who was sweeping the leaves away when you began your walk? Suppose they had all been taken away and replaced with people who looked a little like them but who were not the same? Would you notice? If they and their entire families had been murdered, would you care? We see only what we want to see because that is the way of the city. In a village, in the country, people notice things. But on the streets, we are wilfully blind.'

'Are you saying that's what's happened?' Scarlett asked. 'Ever since I've been here, I've been seeing weird things. And there's nobody living at Wisdom Court. The whole place is empty. Are you saying they were all killed?'

'In the last three months, Hong Kong has been taken over,' Lohan replied. 'It happened very quickly, like a virus. It is impossible to know how many people have been killed. Anyone who has noticed what has been going on or who has tried to fight it has been removed. What has happened has been so huge, so terrible that it is almost impossible to understand.

'Of course, some people have guessed, or half-guessed, and they have managed to get out, taking their money and their families with them. Ask them why they have gone and they will lie to you. They will say they wanted a change or they had new business opportunities. But in truth they have gone because they were afraid. Other people are aware that Hong Kong has changed. They have stayed here because they have no choice, because they have nowhere else to go. They are frightened too. But they keep their heads down and they go about their daily business in the hope that, if they ask no questions, they will be left alone. If you are poor, Scarlett, if you run a tiny stall in the street, what does it matter who controls the city? All you care about is your next meal. The city can take care of itself.'

'Who has taken over Hong Kong?' Scarlett asked, although she already knew the answer.

'They are called the Old Ones,' Lohan said. 'At least, that is what you call them. In the East, we talk of *gwei*, evil spirits. We have many names for them.'

'I know about all this,' Scarlett said. 'It's what Father Gregory told me.'

'Who is Father Gregory?'

'He's a monk. I went through a door in a wall and I met him . . .'

'This was at the Church of St Meredith's.' Lohan knew the name. Perhaps he had read about it in the newspapers when Scarlett disappeared, but she doubted it. He seemed to know a lot about a lot of things. She wondered how. She still wasn't sure how he fitted in. 'You have to understand that we have been interested in you for a long time, Scarlett,' Lohan said. It was as if he had been reading her thoughts.

'We?'

'I am referring to the organization to which I have the great honour to belong. In fact, we have been watching you since the day that you were born.' He allowed this to sink in, then went on. 'Have you ever wondered how you came to find yourself in the Pancoran Kasih Orphanage in Jakarta? Well, I can tell you. We arranged it. Why were you taken to live in Great Britain, thousands of miles away from your true home? We wanted it.'

'Why?'

'To keep you safe. To hide you from the enemies that we knew would one day search for you.'

'There was an accident in Dulwich. A white van ...' Scarlett didn't know why it had come into her mind right then, but she was suddenly sure that it was connected. She had a sense of everything coming together.

Lohan nodded. 'It happened when you were thirteen years old,' he said. 'It was not enough simply to send you far away. My organization had a sacred pledge to protect you, even from your own carelessness. When you stepped in front of the van which was speeding towards you, one of our people was there to push you out of the way. He was able to save you once. Unfortunately, he was less successful a second time.'

238

'He tried to contact me. In London . . .'

'His task was to give you a message. Under no circumstances were you to come here to Hong Kong. We had hoped to intercept you before you even left for the airport. But by then it was too late. The Old Ones had discovered who you were. They killed him.'

'He was waiting for me at the restaurant—the Happy Garden.'

Lohan nodded and there was a tiny spark of anger in his eyes. Perhaps part of him blamed her for the death. 'Three people died in the explosion,' he said. 'And the British authorities didn't even bother to investigate. They just blamed it on us . . . Chinese gangs fighting each other. What did it matter to them? A few dead *fei jais*.' He used the Cantonese slang for petty criminals. 'To the police, it just meant more paperwork.'

'This all happened because of the church, didn't it.'

It was all making sense. Father Gregory had told her he was going to hand her over to the Old Ones. Scarlett had managed to escape—but not before she had given him her name and address. That had been all he needed. From that moment on she had been in a trap from which there was no escape.

'As soon as you returned, the Old Ones closed in on you,' Lohan said. 'They knew that they had found one of the Gatekeepers and they weren't going to let you go. From that moment on, they never let you out of their sight.'

Scarlett thought back. She had felt all along that she had been under surveillance but it was only now that she realized how true that had been. Every movement she had made had been watched.

She had been pushed around like a piece on a board game and the last roll of the dice had brought her here.

'They used my dad to bring me to Hong Kong,' she said, and felt a sudden ache of sadness. Lohan had said Paul Adams might be dead. He could well be right.

'We never wanted you to come to this city,' Lohan said. 'Once you were here, you would be utterly in their power, and you have no idea to what extent that has been true. All day, every day, you have been surrounded by them. Nobody has been allowed to come anywhere near you. Haven't you noticed? Since you have been here, nobody has approached you. Nobody has come near.'

'There was a man with a letter . . .' Scarlett began. 'In Queen Street.'

Lohan shook his head. 'We didn't send him. We knew that it would never have worked.' He paused. 'The Old Ones control the police, the government and the civil service. They have made deals with the Chinese authorities and anyone who has stood in their way, they have killed. The hospitals, the fire service, the newspapers, the television and radio stations all serve them now. They keep constant watch on us through the surveillance cameras in the streets and know what we buy every time we use a credit card. They have taken over the mobile phone network and the Internet and every call is monitored, every one of the millions of e-mails that are sent every day is read by them. Criticize the government . . . you die. Even try to tell people what you know . . . you die. We're back where we started, Scarlett. How many thousands of people can you kill in a city like this without

240

anyone noticing? Only the Old Ones know the answer.

'And they are everywhere. The woman and the driver who pretended to work for your father were both shape-changers. We don't know where they came from or what exactly they are. Many of the crowds that surrounded you were the same. Why do you think Wisdom Court is empty? They wanted to keep you in isolation and every man, woman or child who might come into contact with you was either taken away, killed or replaced.'

'Replaced with what?' Scarlett asked.

'With creatures that belong to the Old Ones.' Lohan filled the bowl a second time and drank it. The alcohol had no effect on him at all. 'The whole city is against you, Scarlett. If you stepped outside now, you would be seen and identified in seconds. That was why you couldn't travel here, sitting in a car. It was also why we had to be so careful reaching you. One of my people added the guidebook to your luggage at the airport. Then we bribed the supervisor of an office building and transmitted a message on the screen. The fortune-teller is part of our organization and she sent you to The Peak. Four different approaches and each time we had to be certain that you alone knew our intentions.'

'So what am I going to do?' Scarlett couldn't keep the helplessness out of her voice. This is what it came down to. She was stuck in a room in a dirty block of flats. And outside a whole city was searching for her. She remembered how the day had begun when she had woken up. Even the flies were on their side.

'You must not be weak!' For a moment, Lohan

didn't even try to hide his contempt. He spat out the words and his mouth, cut in half by the scar, was twisted into a sneer. 'It will not be easy,' he said. 'The Old Ones chose this city very carefully. You are on an island with only four possible ways out. First, of course, there is the airport, where you arrived. But that is out of the question. Every flight will be watched and even if we disguise you and give you a false passport, the danger is too great.

'The second possibility would be to travel by jet-foil to the island of Macau, which is only an hour away. From there you would be able to fly to Singapore or Taiwan. But again there is too much risk. I don't think that you would even get on board before you were spotted. There is a passport control at the terminal and remember—every single official will be looking for you.'

'Can't I go into China?' Scarlett asked.

'It is possible to cross into China at Shenzhen. Many tourists go there to shop because the prices are cheap. But there are police everywhere. The border is well patrolled. And once the Old Ones know you are missing, they will be looking carefully at everyone who crosses.'

'So what's the fourth way?'

But she wasn't going to find out. Not then. She hadn't even noticed the telephone in the room but suddenly it rang. The three men froze and she saw at once that it wasn't good news. Lohan didn't answer it himself. He gestured at the Japanese man, Red, who snatched up the phone and listened for a moment in silence. He put it down and muttered a few words in Chinese. Scarlett didn't understand what he'd said but nor did she need to. The call was a warning. The Old Ones were here.

242

Lohan turned to her, examining her as if for the first time. Even now he seemed undisturbed, refusing to panic.

'Have they found us?' Scarlett blurted out the question.

Lohan nodded slowly. 'They're outside. The building is surrounded.'

'But how . . . ?'

'We seem to have missed a trick.' Lohan's eyes were still fixed on her. For a few seconds, he didn't speak. Then he worked it out. 'You have something with you,' he said. 'The woman—Mrs Cheng or someone at Nightrise—gave you something to wear.'

'No . . .' Scarlett began. But then she remembered. Her hands went to her throat. 'The chairman gave me this . . .'

She was still wearing the jade pendant. Now, with trembling fingers, she unhooked it and took it off. The little green stone with the carved insect hung at the end of the chain. She handed it over. 'It can't be bugged,' she said, weakly. 'It can't . . .'

Lohan examined it with cold anger. Then he turned it round and dangled it in front of her face.

Scarlett gasped. The creature inside the pendant—the lizard or the locust or whatever it was—was moving. She saw it blink and shift position. Its legs curled up underneath it. One of its wings fluttered. Scarlett cried out in revulsion. The thing was alive. And all this time it had been around her neck . . .

Lohan laughed briefly and without humour, then closed his fist over the pendant, winding the chain around his wrist.

'What are we going to do?' Scarlett asked.

243

Before anyone could reply, there was an explosion in the street. It sounded soft and far away but it was followed at once by screaming and the sound of falling glass. There was the wail of police sirens—not one car but any number of them, closing in from all sides.

Lohan produced an automatic pistol, drawing it out of his back pocket. It was sleek and black and he handled it expertly, loading it with a clip of ammunition, releasing the safety catch and briefly checking the firing mechanism. 'You must do whatever we tell you,' he said. 'No questions. No hesitation. Do you understand?'

Scarlett nodded.

From somewhere in the building came the first burst of machine-gun fire. Lohan threw the door open, signalled and together they began to move.

ACROSS THE ROOF

Lohan was the first out into the corridor, then Draco and Scarlett with Red behind. They were all armed apart from her. The man outside the lift had unhooked his machine gun and was cradling it in his arms. He didn't look scared. In fact, he was completely relaxed, as if this was all in a day's work.

Scarlett was feeling sick with anger. This was her fault. The jade pendant that she had been given was bugged in every sense of the word—and it had told the chairman exactly where she was. Why had she even worn it? She should have left it beside the bed. But it was too late to think about it now. The Hong Kong police had arrived. They were already on their way up.

Her every instinct would have been to get out of there as quickly as they could but they were moving slowly, taking it one step at a time. Lohan was listening out for any sound, his head tilted sideways, his gun level with his shoulder. Scarlett saw him signal to the man at the lift, pointing with two fingers, ordering him to stay where he was, and she knew that it was probably a death sentence. These people had some sort of code among themselves. They did exactly what they were told no matter what it might cost.

For a brief moment, everything was silent. The police cars had turned off their sirens and the gunfire had stopped. The corridor was empty. But then, with a surge of alarm, Scarlett saw a blinking light. There were two arrows next to the lift doors, one pointing up, the other down. One of them was flashing. The lift was on its way up.

Lohan gestured with the gun. 'You follow me. This way . . .'

They set off down the corridor but it seemed to Scarlett that he was leading them the wrong way. It would obviously have been crazy to have tried taking the lift, but wouldn't the emergency stairs be somewhere near by? Lohan was taking them ever further into the building and away from what was surely the only way out.

But nobody argued. Scarlett still had no idea who Lohan was or what authority he had over the others. He had said that he belonged to an organization and one that had been looking out for her from the day she had been born, but he hadn't told her what it was called, who ran it or anything like that. It seemed that he and his people were some sort of resistance, fighting against the Old Ones, the last survivors in a city that had been attacked from within. But they weren't the police. They weren't the army. What did that leave?

It was too late for any more questions now. Lohan was moving a little faster but still on tiptoe, making no noise, as if he expected one of the many doors to spring open and someone to jump out. How high up were they? How long did they have before the lift arrived? The end of the corridor was about thirty metres away with ten doors on either side. A row of light bulbs hanging from the ceiling on wires lit the way ahead. Scarlett heard a loud, metallic click and risked a glance back. The man with the machine gun had released the safety catch. Lohan muttered something under his breath.

There was the ping of a bell.

The lift had arrived.

Scarlett was still watching as the lift doors opened and yellow light flooded out. The man with the machine gun had positioned himself directly opposite with his shoulders planted against the wall. Without any warning, he opened fire, sending a firestorm of bullets into the lift. The noise in the confined space was shocking. She could actually feel it, hammering into her ears. But she couldn't see what the man was shooting at. The entire corridor blazed white and red and she heard a high-pitched scream like nothing she had ever heard before, as whatever was inside the lift was pulverized.

Then something appeared, stretching out of the open doorway. It was impossible to make it out clearly between the gloom of the corridor and the brilliance of the gunfire, the two of them strobing—black, white, black, white—turning everything into slow motion chaos. Some sort of tentacles, extending themselves into the corridor. They reached the man. One slammed into his face. Another curled around his throat. But it was the third that killed him, punching right through his stomach and dragging him up the wall, a great streak of blood following up behind him. The man was screaming, his legs writhing in agony. But his finger was clenched around the trigger and he was still firing. His last bullets went wild, tearing into the ceiling and floor.

Something spilled out of the lift. It seemed to be partly human, but there was smoke everywhere now, adding to the confusion. A second creature followed it. The two had come up together. A huge pincer snapped open and shut. Black eyes on stalks. Straight out of a nightmare. It saw Scarlett and the others and began to move with frightening speed.

'Hurry!'

It was the first time that Lohan had raised his voice. He broke into a run. Scarlett followed him, convinced that they didn't have a chance. There was no emergency exit, nowhere for them to go and the things from the lift must already be closing in on them. Red turned round and fired twice. The bullets had no effect. Then Draco dragged something out of his pocket, brought it to his mouth and threw it. A hand grenade! The pin was still between his teeth. A door to one of the other flats opened and Lohan threw himself in, pulling Scarlett with him, just as there was a deafening explosion and an orange ball of flame in the corridor behind.

Scarlett leant against the wall on the other side of the door. She was choking and there were tears streaming down her face. She wasn't crying. It was the dust and the plaster which had cascaded down, almost blinding her. She wiped a sleeve across her eyes. Red slammed the door shut. It had about half a dozen locks, chains and bolts which he fastened, one after another. Lohan snapped out another command. Draco muttered something in reply.

The flat they were in was very similar to the one they had left but more run down, with even less furniture. There was a woman living here. She had opened the door to let them in and Scarlett recognized her. It took her a moment to work out where they had met but then she realized—it was the fortune-teller from the temple. She was standing by the door, blinking nervously. Her three birds were in their cages on a table, hopping up and down, frightened by all the noise.

Lohan hadn't stopped moving. He was heading towards a second door and the kitchen beyond. 'This way, Scarlett,' he called out.

Scarlett followed him into a room with a fridge and a cooker and little else. A large hole had been knocked through the wall. The sides were jagged, with old bits of wire and pipework sticking out, but this was the way out. They climbed through the brickwork and into the next-door flat and then into the one after. Each one had been smashed through to provide a passageway that couldn't be seen from the corridor. The last two flats were completely abandoned, with dust and rubble all over the floor. They came to a window with a steel structure on the other side. A fire escape. Lohan jerked the window open. They climbed out.

Scarlett found herself standing on a small, square platform with a series of metal ladders zigzagging all the way down to street level, about twenty floors below. It was very cold up there, the air currents rushing between the buildings, carrying with them a driving rain. She looked down onto the sort of scene she would normally have associated with a major accident. There must have been at least a dozen police cars parked at different angles in the street. They might have turned their sirens off but their lights were flashing, brilliant even in the daylight. Barricades were still being erected around the building and all the traffic had been stopped. Men in black and silver uniforms were holding the crowds back.

They couldn't go down. The fire escape led into the middle of all the chaos and the moment they reached the bottom, they would be seized. Worse still one of the policemen had seen them. He shouted out a warning and pointed. At once a group of armed officers ran forward and began to climb up.

Lohan didn't seem worried. 'We don't go down,' he muttered. 'We go up.'

There were just three flights of stairs from the platform to the roof and, aware of the policemen getting nearer all the time, Scarlett made her way up as quickly as she could, keeping close to the wall in case any shots were fired. Draco and Red followed up behind and a minute later they had all reached the roof and were squatting there, catching their breath in the shelter of a rusty water tank. The rain was slicing down. Scarlett was already drenched, her hair clinging to her eyes.

Lohan had taken out a mobile phone. He pressed a direct dial button and spoke urgently into it, then folded it away. The other men hadn't said a word but they seemed to understand what had been agreed. Then Red muttered something and pointed. Scarlett looked up, wondering what he had seen. And shuddered. She had thought their situation couldn't get any worse . . . but it just had.

There was a cloud of what looked like black smoke in the distance, high above the tower blocks of Kowloon. It was travelling towards them, against the wind. Scarlett knew at once that it couldn't be smoke. It was the swarm of flies. They had come back again. They were heading directly for her.

'Move!'

Lohan set off at once, running across the roof, no longer caring if he was seen or not. He had hung the jade pendant around his neck and Scarlett realized that as long as he was wearing it, the flies would know where he was. But that was his plan. It was the reason he had taken it from her. He was protecting her, making himself the target in her place. He leapt over stacks of cable, moving towards the back of the building. Scarlett followed. She still had no idea where they were heading, how they were going to get down.

They reached the other side and came to a breathless halt. Once again, Scarlett was completely thrown. There was no fire escape, no ladder, no window cleaner's lift. The next apartment block was about twenty metres away and there was no possible means of crossing.

250

Lohan was standing at the very edge of the building. For a moment he looked like a ghost or maybe a scarecrow with his pale skin and his dark clothes, drenched by the falling rain. His black hair had fallen across his face. The scar seemed more prominent than ever.

'Follow me,' he instructed. 'Don't look down.'

And then he stepped into space.

Scarlett waited for him to fall, to be killed twenty storeys below. Instead, impossibly, he seemed to be standing in mid-air, as if he had learned to levitate. More magic? That was her first thought—but then she looked more closely and saw that it was just an incredible trick. There was a bridge constructed between the two buildings, a strip of almost invisible glass or Perspex . . . some see-through material strong enough to take his weight. Nobody would have been able to see it from the street or from the air, and even now she might not have been able to make it out but for the rain hitting it and the faint coating of grime that covered the surface. It still looked as if Lohan was suspended between the two buildings. He had walked some distance from the edge of the roof and was standing over the road, the toy cars and people far below.

It would be Scarlett's turn next.

A door burst open on the roof behind her. A staircase led up inside and their pursuers had finally reached them, pouring out onto the roof, nine of them, human from the look of them but with dead eyes and pale, empty faces that might have spent years out of the light. Their hair was ragged, their clothes mouldering away and they wore no shoes. Some of them carried long, jagged knives. Others had lengths of chain hanging down to the ground and wooden clubs spiked with nails. Slowly, they began to fan out.

'You—go!' Red pushed Scarlett forward, propelling her towards the glass bridge. 'Draco . . .' He finished the sentence in Chinese.

There was no time to argue. The creatures were already getting closer. Red moved towards them, away from the safety of the bridge, his own gun raised in front of him. Scarlett looked down. The bridge had no sides, no safety rails. The surface was wet and slippery. Worse still, because it was transparent, it felt completely insubstantial. She could imagine herself falling through it or losing her balance and plunging over the side. And she could see where she would land. The road was there, waiting for her far below.

Red fired a shot and the sound of it propelled her forward. She couldn't look back. She couldn't see what was happening behind her. All her concentration was focused on what she had to do. She took one step, then another. Now she was in mid-air with the wind buffeting her. She felt Draco behind her, urging her on, but fear was paralysing her. Lohan had told her not to look down, but if she didn't, how could she be sure that her foot was coming down in the right place? The rain sliced into her face, half-blinding her. She could feel it running down her cheeks.

There were two more shots but then they stopped and she heard screaming and knew that Red had been caught, that terrible things were being done to him. Scarlett hated herself for doing nothing to help him. He had stayed behind for her, to give her the time to cross, and she was literally walking out on him. All these people were risking their lives for her. The whole apartment block with its knocked-through walls and this incredible glass bridge had been prepared for the time she might need it. And the crazy thing was that she still didn't know who they were or why they had decided to help.

Somehow, she got to the other side, taking the last step with a surge of relief. At that exact moment, Red's screams ended and she turned round to see him being held in the air by a group of the creatures who were standing at the edge of the building she had just left. His body was limp. Blood was pouring from a dozen stab wounds in his arms and chest. Then they let him go. He seemed to glide rather than fall through the air, as if he weighed nothing. Finally, he smashed into one of the parked cars, crumpling the roof and shattering the front windscreen. An alarm went off. With a screech of triumph, the creatures who had killed him lurched themselves onto the bridge.

Lohan was standing, watching them. He let them get about half-way across before he stretched out a hand and closed it around a lever set in a wall. He smiled briefly, malevolently, and pulled. At once, the bridge collapsed. It was like one of those magic wands used by conjurors at children's parties. The different sections folded, then plunged downwards. Five of the creatures went with it, hitting the road in an explosion of bone and blood. The rest were left on the other side, jabbering and shaking their fists, unable to cross.

Behind them, something vague and dark rose up over the side of the rooftop. The swarm of flies had arrived. Lohan signalled and set off across the second apartment block, making for a door on the far side. If he was going to mourn the man who had died, it would have to wait. He went through, waited for Scarlett and Draco, then slammed it shut. There was a flight of stairs on the other side. It led down into a room humming with pipes and banks of machinery. There was a service lift on the other side. Lohan hit the button and the doors opened at once. The three of them piled in. He pressed two buttons: the ground floor and the basement.

Scarlett stood inside the confined space, panting. Her heart was racing at a hundred miles an hour. It felt unnatural to be suddenly standing still, knowing that there was danger all around but there was nothing she could do and nowhere she could go as the lift carried them down. She just hoped there wouldn't be anyone waiting for them at the bottom.

But Lohan was completely relaxed, leaning against the back wall, the pendant hanging around his neck. Water was dripping down his forehead, over his eyes. 'You are to go with Draco,' he said. 'I have made arrangements. There are people waiting. You will be safe with them.'

'What about you?' Scarlett asked.

'I will lead them away.' He lifted the pendant, glanced at it, let it fall again.

'They'll kill you . . .'

'If they find me, they will kill me. But my life is not in question here. You are all that matters. You must get away.'

'This is my fault.' Scarlett felt miserable. She had led the creatures to the apartment. They were only here because of her. 'I'm sorry . . .'

'You are one of the Five!' Lohan stared at her as if he couldn't believe what she had just said. 'Do not be sorry. Do not be a little girl. You have the power to destroy them. Use it.'

The lift doors opened. They had arrived at the ground floor. Lohan stepped forward and looked outside. Scarlett could hear the wail of police cars, but there was nobody around and she guessed that the police hadn't yet worked out that they had crossed from one building to another. But the jade pendant would bring them soon enough. Lohan gave a last instruction in Chinese to Draco and then he was gone. The doors slid shut behind him.

'You stay with me now,' Draco muttered.

Red had been killed. The man with the machine gun was dead. Lohan was probably next. But he didn't seem to care.

The lift continued down to the basement. It opened into an underground car park. There was a shiny black car waiting for them and at first Scarlett couldn't believe what had been arranged for her, what was waiting there beneath the building. But at the same time, she knew it made complete sense. She remembered what Lohan had told her. The entire city was against her. Every policeman, every surveillance camera, every official was looking out for her. How was she meant to get past them all?

The car was a hearse. There was an open coffin in the back, the inside of it lined with cream-coloured satin with a pillow at one end. Two men were waiting for her. They were dressed in dark suits, like undertakers, but she recognized them from The Peak. They were the ones who had killed Mrs Cheng. One of them made a gesture. Scarlett knew what she had to do.

This time she didn't argue. Without even hesitating, she climbed into the back of the hearse and lay down. It occurred to her that only a few hours ago, when they had tried to lock her in the boot of a car, she had thought it would be like being buried alive. And here it was, happening for real.

She laid her head on the pillow. The two men moved towards her. And then once again darkness claimed her as the lid was bolted into place.

OCEAN TERMINAL

Nobody noticed the hearse as it swung out of the underground car park and began to make its way south towards Victoria Harbour. Everyone's attention was on the building where Lohan and his friends had been found. The hearse emerged on the other side, turned left at a set of traffic lights and set off down the Golden Mile.

It never did more than ten miles an hour. If anyone had been watching it, the fact that it was moving so slowly would only have made it all the more unlikely that it was being used as an escape vehicle. But very soon it had left the crowds and the police cars behind. In the front, the driver and his assistant gazed straight ahead, their grim faces hiding their joint sense of relief.

For Scarlett, it was less easy.

She couldn't see anything. She couldn't do anything. She couldn't even move. She was lying on her back, trapped in a black, airless space with the lid bolted into place only inches above her head. She was completely at the mercy of her own imagination. Every time the car slowed down or stopped, she wondered if they had been discovered. Worse than that, she imagined a nightmare scenario where something had gone horribly wrong and she really was taken to a cemetery and buried alive. Every nerve in her body was screaming. She could hardly breathe.

After what seemed like an hour, she felt the car stop. She heard the doors open and slam shut. A long pause. And then suddenly a crack of daylight appeared, widening as the coffin lid was lifted off. A hand reached out to help her and gratefully she grabbed hold of it. Gently, she was pulled out like a corpse returning to life. She found herself trembling. After all she had been through, she wasn't surprised.

Where was she? The hearse had been parked next to a fork-lift truck in a warehouse, filled with pallets and crates. There were skylights in the ceiling but it was also lit by neon strips, hanging down in glass cages. One of the men had hit a switch that brought a sliding door rumbling down on castors, but before it reached the floor Scarlett glimpsed water and knew that they were near the harbour. The smell of gunpowder hung in the air. Normally, she might not have recognized it—but there had been plenty of it around in the building she had just left.

The driver was already stripping off his jacket and black tie. The last time Scarlett had seen him, he had been wiping a bloody machete on a cloth up on The Peak. He had been the one with the backpack—long hair and glasses—and he was younger than she had first thought, in his mid-twenties. He was wearing a short-sleeved shirt under the jacket and she noticed a tattoo on his upper arm, a red triangle with a Chinese character inside.

'My name is Jet,' he said. Like all the others, he wasn't bothering with surnames. He spoke hesitant English but with a polished accent. 'I will be looking after you now. This is Sing.'

The other man came over from the door and nodded.

'Where are we?' Scarlett asked.

'Still in Kowloon. This is our warehouse.' Jet walked over to one of the crates and pulled off the tarpaulin that half covered it so that she could read the words stencilled underneath. They were written in Chinese and English.

KUNG HING TAO FIREWORK MANUFACTURERS

'Fireworks . . . ?'

'It's good business,' Jet explained. 'In China, we let off fireworks if someone marries and again when they die. The Bun Festival, the Dragon Boat Festival, the Hungry Ghost Festival and New Year. Everyone wants fireworks! There are one hundred thousand dollars' worth in this warehouse. I suggest you don't smoke.'

'You want Coke?' the man called Sing asked. He still had his walking stick with the sword concealed inside. It had been inside the hearse, but he had yanked it out and carried it with him.

'We have a small kitchen and a toilet,' Jet said.

'We have to stay here for a while.'

'How long?'

'Twenty-four hours. But nobody will find you here . . .'

'What about Lohan?' Scarlett had been worrying about him. She knew that it was her fault that he was in danger.

'He will come. You do not need to be afraid. Very soon you will be on your way out of Hong Kong.'

Lohan had spoken of four ways to get out of the city and he had dismissed three of them: the airport, the jet-foil to Macau, the Chinese border. What did that leave? Scarlett had seen the harbour. Perhaps they were going to smuggle her out on a container ship. First a car boot, then a coffin. These people wouldn't think twice about packing her into a crate of fireworks and sending her somewhere in time for Bonfire Night.

Sing had gone into the kitchen but now he came back with three bottles of water and sandwiches on plastic plates. He was still wearing his undertaker's suit but he had taken off the tie. The three of them ate, sitting cross-legged in a circle on the floor. It was only when she took her first bite that Scarlett realized how hungry she was. She'd had little breakfast, no lunch and it was now six o'clock.

'It is not possible to take you out on a container ship.' Jet had seen her sizing up the crates and must have guessed what was on her mind. 'There's too much security. The ports are all watched day and night, and anyway, it will be the first thing that they expect. We will take you out in public, in front of their eyes.'

'How?'

He glanced at the other man who nodded, as if giving him permission to go on.

'Tomorrow morning, a cruise ship arrives in Kowloon. It will dock at the Ocean Terminal on the other side of Harbour City, just ten minutes from here. It spends a day in Hong Kong on its way from Tokyo to the Philippines and then Singapore. That is where it will take you. The ship is called the *Jade Emperor* and it will be full of wealthy tourists. You will be one of them.'

'How do I get on board?'

'For their own reasons, the Old Ones do not want the world to know that they have taken over this city. That is good. When the *Jade Emperor* ties up, they will have to be careful. There will be security but it will have to be invisible. They will not want to frighten the tourists. Everything will have to seem normal and that gives us the advantage. We will smuggle you onto the ship with the other passengers. And once you are there, you will be safe.'

'What happens when I get to Singapore?'

Jet shrugged. Sing muttered something in Chinese and laughed. 'That is the least of your worries,' Jet said. 'First of all, you have to survive tomorrow. And remember—there are a hundred thousand people who are looking for you. This is a trap and you walked straight into it. Now that you're here, it's not going to be so easy to get you out.'

He wasn't being fair. Scarlett hadn't walked into Hong Kong. She had been deliberately drawn in and there had been nothing she could have done to avoid it. But she didn't argue. There was no point.

'We will disguise you,' he went on. 'We will cut your hair and change its colour and we will dress you as a boy. You must learn to walk in a certain way. We will show you. There is a family joining the boat. Their names are Mr and Mrs Soong and they are part of our organization. Right now, they are travelling with their twelve-year-old son, Eric. You will change places with him and travel on his passport. By midnight tomorrow, you will be in international water and out of danger. Do you understand?'

'How will you make the change?' Scarlett asked.

'We have arranged to meet in a shop in Harbour City. The shop is also owned by us. It pretends to sell tea and Chinese medicine.'

'What does it really sell?'

Jet thought for a moment. He was reluctant to answer the question but for some reason he decided to. 'Do you really want to know?' He smiled. 'Normally it sells opium.'

*   *   *

Scarlett spent the night on a mattress behind a row of crates that the two men had arranged to form a private 'room'. She barely slept at all. It was cold in the warehouse—there wasn't any form of heating—and she had only been given a couple of thin blankets. Every night is trapped between the day before and the day after and she had never been so torn between the two.

She thought about the creatures she had seen coming out of the lift, the flies approaching the tower block and the people—were they actually living people?—who had followed her onto the

261

roof. How could things like that be happening in a modern city—monsters and shape-changers and all the rest of it?

Then she turned her mind to the people she was with. Despite everything that had happened, she still knew almost nothing about them. There were lots of them and they were well organized. Lohan had spoken about them with reverence, almost as if they were a holy order. And yet she had just been told that they sold opium! Opium was a drug that came from the same source as heroin. Could it be that they were some sort of gangsters after all? They carried machine guns and hand grenades. And although they were helping her, none of them was exactly friendly.

Finally, she thought about the next day and the dangers it would bring, walking onto a cruise ship disguised as a boy. Would it really work and what would happen to her if it didn't? As far as she could see, the Old Ones didn't want to kill her. Father Gregory could have done that, and he'd made it clear he had other plans. For some reason, they needed her alive.

Lying on her back, gazing at the skylight, she watched night crawl towards day. In the end, she did manage to sleep—but only fitfully. When she woke up, her neck was aching and she felt even more tired than she had been when she began. Her two bodyguards were already awake. Sing had made breakfast, a plate of noodles, but she hardly ate. Today was her last chance. She knew that if she didn't get out today, she never would.

Nothing happened for the next three hours. Jet and Sing sat silently, waiting, and for some reason Scarlett found herself trying to remember her lines in the school play. She had lost track of the date but guessed that it would be performed—without her—in a couple of weeks' time. All the parents would be there along with some of the boys from The Hall. She thought of Aidan. And as she sat there, trapped in a warehouse full of fireworks, Dulwich seemed a very long way away and she wondered when, if ever, she would see it again.

And then Jet's mobile phone rang. He snapped it open and muttered a few words into it, then nodded at Sing who went and unlocked the door. They opened it just a little bit, enough for Scarlett to see that it had stopped raining outside. Bright sunlight streamed in through the crack, lighting up the dust that hung in the air. Two more people came into the warehouse.

The first of them was Lohan. He went straight over to Scarlett. 'Are you OK?' he asked.

Scarlett was relieved to see him. 'How about you?' she asked. 'What did you do with the pendant?'

'The pendant is on a flight to Australia. Hopefully the Old Ones will follow it there.'

'I'm glad you're OK.'

'And I will be glad when you have gone.'

He gestured at the man who had come with him. He hurried forward, carrying a canvas suitcase about the size of a weekend bag. This man was quite a bit older than the others, wearing a crumpled cardigan and glasses. He placed the suitcase on the floor and opened it to reveal scissors, hair brushes, lots of bottles, pads of cotton wool. There were clothes packed underneath.

It was time for Scarlett to change.

Jet dragged one of the crates over and Scarlett sat down. The older man examined her for a moment, using his fingers to brush her hair back from her face. He nodded as if satisfied, then reached for the scissors.

Scarlett would never forget the way he cut her hair. She wouldn't have said she was particularly vain, but she had always taken care of how she looked. There was something brutal about the way he attacked her, chopping away as if she had no more feelings than a tree. She looked down and saw great locks of her hair hitting the ground. Although she knew that it was necessary and that anyway it would all grow back soon enough, she still felt like a victim, as if she were being assaulted. But the man didn't notice her distress— or if he did, he didn't care.

He kept cutting and soon she felt something she had never felt before: the cold touch of the breeze against her scalp. He finished her hair with a scoop of Brylcreem, then set to work on her face, turning it first one way, then the other, his fingers pressing against her chin. There was absolutely nothing in his eyes. He had done this many times before. It was his business and he did it well. He just wanted to get it over with as quickly as possible.

He painted her skin with a liquid that smelled of vinegar and stung very slightly, then added a few splodges with a thin brush. After that, he set to work on her eyes. Just when Scarlett thought he had finished, he muttered something to Lohan, the first time he had spoken. His voice was completely flat.

'He wants to put in contact lenses,' Lohan explained. 'They're going to sting.'

They did more than that. The man had to clamp Scarlett's head while he pressed them in, the lens balanced on the end of his finger, and when he backed away the entire room was out of focus, hidden behind a blur of tears.

'Now you must get dressed,' Lohan said.

They didn't allow her any privacy. The four men stood watching as she stripped down to her underwear and then the man in the cardigan dug a white, padded thing out of his case. Scarlett understood what it was. The boy whose place she was taking must have been quite a bit fatter than her. She slipped the pads over her shoulders and saw at once that she had a completely new body shape and that the slight curve of her breasts had gone. The man handed her a shirt, linen trousers, a blazer and a pair of black leather shoes that added about three centimetres to her height. Finally he gave her a pair of glasses. The disguise was complete.

'Look in the mirror,' Lohan said.

They had brought a full length mirror out of the kitchen. Scarlett stood in front of it. She had to admit that the transformation was incredible. She barely recognized herself.

Her hair was now short and spiky, held rigidly in place by the Brylcreem. Her eyes, which were normally green, were now dark brown, the colour magnified by the spectacles which were clumsy and old-fashioned, in plastic frames. There was a touch of acne around her nose. She had become one hundred percent Chinese; a slightly pudgy thirteen-year-old who probably went to an expensive private school and dressed like his dad. She even smelled like a boy. Maybe they had put

265

something in all the chemicals they had used.

'Now you must practise walking,' Lohan said. 'Walk like a boy, not like a girl.'

For the next two hours, Lohan kept her pacing up and down with slouching shoulders, hands in her pockets. Scarlett had never really thought that teenage boys were so different in the way they walked, but she was sensible enough not to argue. Finally, Lohan was satisfied. He crouched next to her. 'It is time for you to leave,' he said. 'But there is something I must tell you before you go.'

'What?'

She was alarmed, but he held up a hand, reassuring her. 'There is a boy who is coming to meet you,' he said. 'He is on his way already, travelling from England.'

Her first thought was that it was Aidan—but that was ridiculous. Aidan knew nothing about what was happening.

'His name is Matt.'

The boy out of her dream! The boy who had led her through the door at the church of St Meredith's. Scarlett felt a surge of hope and excitement. She didn't know why, but if Matt was on his way then she was sure that everything would be all right.

'He is not coming to Hong Kong,' Lohan went on. 'It is too dangerous here. But he will be in Macau. He is being protected by the Master of the Mountain. He will remain there until he knows that we have been successful and that you have escaped. Then he will follow you and our work will be done.'

'Who is the Master of the Mountain?' Scarlett asked.

'He is a very powerful man.' That was all Lohan was prepared to say. He straightened up. 'Don't speak until you are on the boat. If anyone tries to talk to you, ignore them. When you are with your new parents, hold your mother's hand. She alone will talk to you and you'll smile at her and pretend that you understand. When you are on the *Jade Emperor*, she will take you straight to her cabin. You will remain there until the ship leaves.'

'Thank you,' Scarlett said. 'Thank you for helping me.'

Lohan glanced at her and just for a moment she saw the hardness in his eyes and knew that whatever else he was, he would never be her friend. 'You do not need to thank us,' he said. 'Do not imagine that we are helping you because we want to. We are obeying orders from the Master of the Mountain. You are important to him. That is all that matters. Do not let us down.'

They opened the warehouse door and, remembering her new walk, Scarlett went out. She found herself in a concrete-lined alleyway. It was after five o'clock and the light was already turning grey. As she stood there, a car drove past and she flinched, afraid of being seen. But she was a boy now: the son of Chinese parents. Nobody was going to look at her twice. Jet and Sing had joined her. The three of them set off together, making their way towards the main road.

The alleyway came out at the very tip of Kowloon, where the Salisbury Road curved round on its way to the ferry terminals. The harbour was in front of them. Scarlett could see all of Hong Kong on the other side of the water with The Nail, the headquarters of Nightrise, slanting diagonally out of the very centre where it seemed to have been smashed in.

'Walk slowly,' Jet whispered. 'If you see anyone looking at you, just ignore them. Don't stop . . .'

They walked down the Salisbury Road, passing the Hong Kong Cultural Centre, a huge, white-tiled building that looked a little bit like a ski slope. The weather had changed again. The sky was clear and the evening sun was dipping down, the water shimmering silver and blood-red. Despite the horror of the last thirty-six hours, everything looked very ordinary. There were several groups of tourists on the promenade, enjoying the view. Crowds of people were pouring out of the terminal for the Star Ferry, on their way home. Young couples holding hands walked together. Newspaper and food sellers stood behind their stalls, waiting for business. A fleet of ships, all different shapes and sizes, were chugging back and forth.

And all the time Scarlett was thinking—what is real and what isn't? Which of these people are shape-changers? How many of them are looking for me? She walked on between Jet and Sing, trying to behave normally but knowing all the time that there were a thousand eyes searching for her. She was already beginning to sweat with all the padding pressing down on her. It made it difficult to breathe.

They passed the Peninsula Hotel. Just a few days before, Scarlett had gone there with Audrey Cheng. They had sat down for tea and sandwiches. It felt like a lifetime ago. They turned into a wide avenue and she found herself walking past a police station. Two men came out, chatting together in dark blue and silver uniforms. Both of them carried guns. Scarlett remembered what Lohan had told her. The Old Ones controlled the police as well as the government and the civil service. These two men would have her description. If they recognized her it would all be over before they got anywhere near the ship.

But they didn't. They continued past and it was only when they had gone that Scarlett realized she had stopped breathing. She felt completely defenceless, waiting for someone to shout her name and for the crowd to close in. A few inches of padding and a handful of make-up was all that stood between her and capture. She was terrified that it wouldn't be enough.

Harbour City lay ahead of them. It was just another shopping centre, though much bigger than any she had visited with Mrs Cheng. They strolled in as if that was what they had always intended to do, as if they were just three friends out for an evening's shopping. The interior was very ugly. It was brightly lit with small, box-like shops standing next to each other in corridors that seemed to go on for ever. They were selling the usual goods: jeans and T-shirts and sunglasses and souvenirs, with fewer famous names than could be found in Hong Kong Central and presumably lower prices.

They continued past a luggage store and there, ahead of them, Scarlett saw a neon sign that read TSIM CHAI KEE HERBAL REMEDIES and knew that they had reached the place where the exchange would happen. The shop was directly in front of them. It was filled with cardboard boxes and glass bottles. Three people were standing with their backs to the front door. A man, a woman and, between them, a boy.

The woman was plump with grey hair, dressed in black. The man was smaller than her, laden down with shopping bags, with a camera around his neck. Their son was dressed exactly the same as Scarlett. They were waiting while the shop assistant wrapped up a packet of tea.

Scarlett walked in. Jet and Sing didn't follow her but continued on their way. At the same time, the boy walked forward, further into the shop and disappeared. The man and the woman stayed exactly where they were so that as Scarlett entered, there was a space between them. And that was it. A moment later she was standing between them. The woman paid for the tea. The shopkeeper handed over some change. The three of them left together.

A mother, a father and a son had gone into the shop. A mother, a father and a son walked out of it. As they left, Scarlett glanced up and noticed a TV camera in the passageway trained down on them and wondered if there was anybody watching and, if so, whether they could possibly have seen anything that might have aroused their suspicions. But for the first time, she was feeling confident. She was no longer on her own. She was part of a family now. She would be joining hundreds or even thousands of tourists returning to the *Jade Emperor*. Even the Old Ones with all their agents would be unable to spot her.

The family left Harbour City through a set of huge glass doors that brought them straight out onto Ocean Terminal. And there was the ship, tied to the quay by ropes as thick as trees. The *Jade Emperor* was massive, with at least a dozen decks, each one laid out on top of the other with two smoking funnels at the very top. The lower part of the ship was punctuated by a long line of tiny-looking portholes, but further up there were full-sized sliding windows that probably opened onto state rooms for the multi-millionaires on board. The *Jade Emperor* was entirely white, apart from the funnels which were bright green. Crew members, also in spotless white, were hurrying along the corridors, mopping the decks and polishing the brass railings as if it were vital for the ship to look its best before it was allowed to leave.

Scarlett examined her surroundings. The ship was on her left, blocking out the view over to Hong Kong, with a single gangplank, slanting down at its centre. On the right, running the full length of the quay, was a two-storey building lined with flags. This was the back of Harbour City, the shopping centre she had just visited. Between them was a strip of concrete about ten metres across, which they would all have to walk along if they wanted to go on board.

The way was blocked by a series of metal fences that forced passengers to snake round to a control point where half a dozen men in uniforms were checking passports and embarkation slips. The sun was beginning to set now, and although it still sparkled on the water and glinted off the ship's railings, the actual walkway was in shadow. So this was it. Five minutes and maybe fifty paces separated Scarlett from freedom. Once she was on board the *Jade Emperor*, it would be over. Matt was waiting for her. Help had finally arrived. She would set sail and she would never see Hong Kong again.

271

The woman acting as Scarlett's mother, Mrs Soong, said something and reached out for her hand. Scarlett took it and they began to walk towards the barrier. Nobody stopped them. Nobody even seemed to glance their way. They passed a restaurant with floor-to-ceiling plate glass windows and tables and gas umbrellas outside. It was too late for lunch and too early for dinner so there was hardly anyone there, but as they continued forward Scarlett noticed a man with grey hair and glasses, sipping a glass of beer. He was partly obscured by the window but there was something familiar about him, the way he sat, even the way he held his glass. She stopped dead.

It was Paul Adams.

Maybe if she hadn't stopped so abruptly, he wouldn't have noticed her. But now he looked up and stared at her. Even then he might not have recognized her. But they had made eye contact. That was what did it. Even with the spectacles and the contact lenses, the strange clothes and the short hair, the two of them had made the link.

And Scarlett was glad to see him. For the past week she had been worrying about him, wondering if he was dead or alive. She had hated the thought of skulking out of Hong Kong without letting him know and if there had been any way to warn him what was happening, she would have done so. This was her opportunity. She couldn't just leave him behind.

A second later, he burst out of the restaurant and onto the quay. He still couldn't decide if it was really her. The disguise was that good. But then she smiled at him and he came over to her, his face a mixture of bafflement and relief.

'Scarly . . . Is that you?'

Scarlett felt Mrs Soong stiffen beside her. Mr Soong stopped, his face filled with alarm. None of the guards at the passport control had noticed them. Tourists were streaming past on both sides, taking out their documents as they approached the fence. Scarlett knew she would have to be quick. She was risking everything even by talking to him but she didn't care. She felt a huge sense of relief. Her father was alive.

'Scarly . . . ?' Paul Adams spoke her name again, peering at her, trying to see through the disguise.

'Dad . . .' Scarlett whispered. 'We can't talk. You have to leave Hong Kong. We're in terrible . . .'

She didn't finish the sentence.

To her horror, Paul Adams grabbed hold of her, dragging her hand up as if to show her off. His face was flushed with excitement—and something else. He looked demented. There was a sort of terror in his eyes. He was like a man who had just committed murder.

'It's her!' he shouted. 'I've got her! She's here!'

'No, Dad . . .'

But it was already too late. The uniformed policemen had heard. They were already heading towards them. The tourists had stopped moving and in an instant Scarlett saw that half of them weren't tourists at all. They began to close in, their faces blank, their eyes shining with triumph. More people appeared, pouring out of the shopping centre. Matted hair. Dead, white skin. Their mouths hanging open. Dozens of them. And the flies. They burst into the air like a dark geyser and spread out, swarming overhead.

'Dad . . . what have you done?'

273

He clung onto her, one hand on her wrist, the other around her neck, strangling her. Mr and Mrs Soong stood there, paralysed, then tried to run. The woman was the first to be brought down. One of the tourists grabbed her. A few seconds earlier he had looked like a grandfather, an Englishman enjoying his retirement. But the mask had slipped. He was grinning and his eyes were ablaze. He was holding her with terrible strength, his hooked fingers gouging into her face, forcing her down to her knees. Then they were all onto her. Mrs Soong disappeared in a crowd that was moving now like a single creature. Mr Soong had taken out a gun. He pointed it at one of the approaching policemen and fired. The bullet hit the policeman in the face, tearing a huge hole in his cheek, but he didn't even flinch. He kept on coming. Mr Soong fired a second time, this time straight into the man's chest. Blood spouted but still the policeman came. Mr Soong was trapped. He had nowhere to run. Scarlett saw him push the barrel of the gun into his own mouth. She closed her eyes a moment before he fired.

It was easy to tell who were the real tourists now. They were screaming, in hysterics, dropping their new purchases and scattering across the quay, unsure what was going on, not wanting to be part of it. A woman in a fur coat slipped and fell. She was immediately trampled underfoot by the rest of the crowd, trying to get past. Two men were knocked over the side into the narrow space between the ship and the quay. Scarlett heard them hit the water and doubted that either of them would ever climb out again.

Her father was still holding her. She couldn't

believe what he had done. He had deliberately told them she was there. He had been waiting for her all along. And she had helped him. There had been one final trap and she had fallen into it.

'I'm sorry, Scarly,' he was saying. 'I had to do it. It was the only way. They've promised that they won't hurt you, and my reward, the reward for both of us—we're going to be rich! You have no idea how much power they have. And we're going to be part of it . . . their new world.'

Of course he had been in it all along. He worked for Nightrise. He had invited her here, made her leave school early with no explanation. He had been skulking somewhere nearby, leaving her in their clutches. And finally he had been positioned here, just in case she tried to get onto the ship . . .

Scarlett thought of all the people who had tried to help her, all the people who had died because of her. Mr and Mrs Soong had spent just a few minutes with her but it had been enough. She had killed them.

She listened to this pathetic man—he was still jabbering at her—and she spat in his face.

Then someone grabbed her from behind. It was Karl. She didn't know where he had come from, but the chauffeur was unbelievably strong. He lifted her into the air, then dashed her down. Her head hit the concrete so hard that she thought her skull must have cracked. A bolt of sheer pain ripped across her vision.

In the final moments of consciousness, she saw a whole series of images, flickering across her vision like an out-of-control slide show. There was Matt, the boy she had never met in the real world, on his way to Macau. There were the other three—Scott,

Jamie and Pedro—gazing at her helplessly. There was the beach where she had found herself night after night. And there, once again, was the neon sign with a symbol that was shaped like a triangle and two words:

SIGNAL EIGHT

The letters flared in the darkness and looking through them she saw the chairman, Audrey Cheng, Father Gregory and, for one last brief moment, her father.

'It's coming,' she managed to whisper to them.

Then the darkness rushed in, slamming into her like an express train and at that moment she felt something unlock inside her. It was like a window being shattered and she knew that she would never be the same again.

And five hundred miles away, in a place called the Strait of Luzon, between Thailand and the Philippines, the dragon heard her. It was there because she had summoned it. The dragon had been sleeping in the very depths of the ocean but it slowly opened one eye.

SIGNAL NINE

The letters burned in brilliant neon light. There was a symbol beside it, an hour glass and Scarlett almost wanted to laugh because she knew what it was saying. Time's up. The countdown has begun.

The dragon began to move. Nothing could get in its way.

It was heading for Hong Kong.

MATT'S DIARY (3)

I don't think I'm going to be able to write much more of this diary. I don't find it easy, putting all these words together, and anyway, what's the point? Who will ever read it? Richard thought it was a good idea but really it just fills in time.

I can't believe we've finally made it to Macau. Jamie is asleep, worn out with jet lag after another flight across the world, and Richard is in a room next door. In an hour's time, we're going to meet a man called Han Shan-tung who can help us get into Hong Kong. We've waited almost a week for him to turn up and I just hope that we haven't been wasting our time. We have no idea at all what's been happening to Scarlett, whether she is even alive or dead. Harry Foster, the Australian newspaper man who was at the meeting of the Nexus, sent someone to meet her—an assistant from his office. Maybe he managed to track her down but we never heard. The assistant went missing . . . presumed dead.

The Old Ones are there, waiting for me to arrive. In a way, it's extraordinary that they've managed to keep themselves hidden, but that has always been their way. When I was in Yorkshire, they worked through Jayne Deverill and the villagers who lived at Lesser Malling. In Peru, it was Diego Salamanda. Now it's Nightrise. They like people to do their dirty work for them and when war finally breaks out, as I know it must, my guess is that they won't reveal themselves until the end. And by then it will be too late. They will have won.

Maybe the five days we had in London were worth

277

it after all. Jamie enjoyed himself, seeing all the sights, and in the end I enjoyed being with him. Buckingham Palace, the London Eye, Harrods, the London Dungeon. Richard kept us busy, maybe because he wanted to keep our minds off what lay ahead. We also spoke to Pedro and Scott in Vilcabamba, talking on the satellite phone. Pedro is worried about Scott. He still seems far away, as if he isn't even on our side. I know he's angry that I separated him from Jamie, but I still think it was a good idea. He isn't ready yet.

And then the flight. London to Singapore, followed by Singapore to Macau. I'm too tired to sleep. When I've finished this, I'll have another shower. A cold one, this time. Maybe it will wake me up.

I don't know what to make of Macau. If anyone had asked me about it six months ago, I wouldn't even have been able to point to it on a map. I hadn't heard of it. As it turns out, it's a chunk of land, just ten miles from one end to the other. And it's packed with some of the weirdest buildings I've ever seen. Take the ferry terminal. If you're coming in from Hong Kong on the jet-foil, it's the first building you'll see and you'd have thought they could have made it a bit welcoming. It's not. It's a slab of white concrete, surrounded by flyovers. It's drab and ugly.

But then you come to the casinos and you think you must have landed on another planet. Macau makes its money out of gambling . . . horse racing, greyhound racing, blackjack and roulette. The casinos look like nothing I've ever seen before. One of them is all gold, like a piece of metal bent in the middle. There's another one like a sort of crazy birthday cake. The biggest and the most spectacular reminded me of a giant flower. It was five times taller than anything else in the city. I got a crick in my neck trying to see the top.

The old part of Macau was better. Richard told me that it had once belonged to the Portuguese and he pointed out their influence in some of the palaces with their pillars, arcades and balconies jutting out over the street. But it was still a bit of a dog's dinner. The traffic and the crowds were Chinese. The older buildings seemed to be in better condition than the new ones, which were all dirty and falling down. The Portuguese had built pretty squares and fountains. Then the Chinese had come along and added casinos, shops and blocks of flats, forty or fifty floors high. And now they were all stuck next to each other, like quarrelling neighbours.

Jamie was disappointed too. 'I once read a book about China,' he told me. 'It was in the house when we were in Salt Lake City. I never read very much, but it had dragons and magicians and I thought it must be a really cool place. I guess the book was wrong . . .'

We were met at the airport by a young Chinese guy who was carrying a big bunch of white flowers. That was a bit weird, but it was the signal we had been given so we would recognize him. He dumped them straight away. There was a Rolls Royce parked outside, numberplate HST 1. I noticed that it had been parked in a NO WAITING zone but nobody had given it a ticket. So that told me something about Han Shan-tung. He likes to show off.

The journey from the airport took about half an hour. It was pouring with rain, which certainly didn't make Macau look any better. Fortunately, it eased off a little by the time we arrived here.

279

And where are we now?

The driver stopped in front of a wide flight of stairs which climbed up between two old-looking walls that had been painted yellow. The steps were decorated with a black and white mosaic and there were miniature palms growing in neat beds along the side. There were clumps of trees behind the walls. They were still in leaf, filling the sky and blocking out any sight of the shops and apartments. It was like walking through a park. The driver got out of the car and signalled for us to follow him. We grabbed our bags and went about half-way up the stairs until we came to a metal gate that swung open as we approached.

It wasn't a park on the other side. It was a private garden with a courtyard, a marble fountain that had been switched off and, beyond, a really amazing house built in a Spanish style. The house was painted yellow, like the wall, with green shutters on the windows and a balcony on the first floor. It looked a bit like an embassy, somewhere you weren't normally allowed. The house seemed to belong to its own world. It was right in the middle of Macau and yet somehow it was outside it.

'Quite a place,' Richard said.

The driver gestured and we went in.

The front door also opened as we walked towards it. A woman was waiting for us on the other side. She was some sort of servant, dressed in a long, black dress with a grey shirt buttoned up to the neck. She bowed and smiled.

'Welcome to the home of Mr Shan-tung. I hope you had a good journey. Please, will you come this way? I will take you to your rooms. Mr Shan-tung invites you to join him for dinner at eight o'clock.'

It was one of the most beautiful houses I had ever

seen. Everything was very simple but somehow arranged for maximum effect so that a single vase on a shelf, sitting under a spotlight, somehow let you know that it was Ming or something and probably worth a million pounds. The floors were polished wood, the ceilings double height, the walls clean and white. As we went upstairs, we passed paintings by Chinese artists. They were very simple and clean and they probably cost a fortune too.

We all had bedrooms looking out over the garden, on the same floor; Jamie and me sharing, Richard on his own. The beds had already been turned down with sheets that looked brand new. There was a TV and a fridge filled with Coke and fruit juice. It was like being in a five star hotel, but (as Richard said) hopefully without the bill.

We were all dirty and tired after so much travelling and Jamie and I tossed a coin to see who got to shower first. I won and stood naked in a cubicle that would have been big enough to sleep in, with steaming water jetting at me from nine directions. There were towelling robes to put on when we came out. Jamie went next. He was asleep before he was even dry.

I would have liked to have slept.

I've been thinking a lot about the library that I visited. Did I make the right decision? I didn't read the book and I'm beginning to wish I had. Right now I'm just a forty-five minute journey away from Hong Kong and I have no idea what I will find there. The book would have told me. It might have warned me not to go.

But it might also have told me when and how my life will end—and who would want to read that?

It makes me think of a computer game that I used

to play when I was living in Ipswich. It was an adventure, a series of puzzles that took you through a whole set of different worlds. Shortly after I met Kelvin, he showed me how to download a cheat. It gave me all the answers. It took away the mystery. Suddenly I knew everything I wanted—but here's the strange thing. I never played the game again. I just wasn't interested.

Why did the Librarian show it to me? What was the point he was trying to make? And for that matter, who was he? He never even told me his name. When I think about it, the dreamworld really annoys me. It's supposed to help us but all it ever gives us is puzzles and clues. I know that it's important to what's going to happen, that it's there for a reason. One day, perhaps, I'll find out what that reason is.

I've written enough. It's twenty to eight. Time to wake Jamie and to meet our host. Han Shan-tung.

Hong Kong is waiting for us. It's out there in the darkness, but I can feel it calling.

Very soon now, I will arrive.

MASTER OF THE MOUNTAIN

Han Shan-tung was one of the most impressive men Matt had ever seen. He was like a bronze Buddha in a Chinese temple. He had the same presence, the same sense of power. He wasn't exactly fat but he was very solid, built like a Sumo wrestler. You could imagine him breaking every one of your fingers when you shook hands.

His hair was black. His face was round, with thick lips and hard, watchful eyes. He was

282

elegantly dressed in a suit that was obviously expensive, possibly silk. His fingers, resting on the table in front of him, were manicured and he wore a slim, silver wedding ring. There was a packet of cigarettes and a gold lighter on the table next to him . . . his one vice perhaps. But none of his guests was ever going to give him a lecture on smoking. Everything about the man, even the way he sat there—still and silent—suggested that he wasn't someone to be argued with. He was someone who was used to being obeyed.

And yet his manner was pleasant enough. 'Good evening,' he said. 'Please come and sit down.' His English was perfect. Every word was well-modulated and precise.

He was sitting in the dining room, at the head of a long table that could have seated ten people but which had been laid for only four. The room was as elegant as the rest of the house, with floor-to-ceiling windows looking out onto a wooden terrace and views of the garden beyond. Richard, Matt and Jamie took their places. At once, a door at the side slid open and two women appeared, pouring water and shaking out the napkins.

The man waited until they had gone. 'My name is Han Shan-tung,' he announced.

'I'm Richard Cole.' Richard introduced himself, then the boys. He had already decided he was going to use the names that were on their passports. 'This is Martin Hopkins. And Nicholas Helsey.'

'I would have said that this was Matthew Freeman and Jamie Tyler,' Shan-tung muttered. 'And I would add that it is discourteous to lie to a man in his own home—but I will overlook it as I can understand that you are nervous. Let me assure you, Mr Cole. I know everything about all three of you. More, in fact, than you perhaps know about yourselves. Otherwise you would not be here.'

'And we know nothing about you,' Richard replied. 'That's why we have to be careful.'

'Very wise. Well, it will be my pleasure to enlighten you. But first we should eat.'

As if on cue, the two women returned, carrying plates of food. Silently, they laid out a Chinese dinner. It was a world apart from the sweet and sour, deep-fried grease balls that Matt had once purchased at his local takeaway in Ipswich. The dinner came in about a dozen china bowls—fish, meat, rice, noodles—and it had obviously been cooked by a world-class chef. Matt was glad to see that he had been provided with a spoon and fork. Han Shan-tung ate with chopsticks.

'I must apologize to you,' he began. There was no small talk. He didn't ask them about their journey or what they thought of their rooms. 'Urgent business took me to America. It was badly timed because it delayed your arrival here. And I'm afraid I have bad news. I had hoped that the object of your journey would have been sitting here with us tonight. I am referring to the girl, Lin Mo.' He continued quickly, before Richard could interrupt. 'You call her Scarlett Adams. But I refer to her by the name she was given before she was adopted and taken to the West.'

'How do you know about Scarlett?' Richard asked.

Shan-tung leaned forward and plucked a prawn off one of the dishes. Despite his large hands, he

284

used the chopsticks very delicately, like a scientist handling a specimen. 'I know a great deal about the girl,' he replied. 'The fact of the matter is that she was with my agents in Hong Kong only yesterday. I have spent a great deal of time and money—not to mention human life—trying to remove her from the city.'

Matt played back what Shan-tung had just said and realized that it confirmed exactly what he had thought. 'The Old Ones are in Hong Kong,' he said.

'The Old Ones have taken over Hong Kong,' Shan-tung replied. 'They control almost every aspect of the city. From the government and the police to the street cleaners. I do not know how many people they have killed, but the number must run into thousands. My people have been fighting them on your behalf. We are the only remaining resistance.'

'Who are your people?' Richard asked.

Shan-tung sighed. 'It is unnecessary to keep asking me these things. I am about to tell you anyway.'

'I'm sorry.' Richard realized his error. 'I suppose it's a habit. I used to be a journalist.'

'I do not like journalists. It is nothing personal—but they have caused me trouble in the past. I suggest you continue eating. I will tell you everything you need to know.'

Han Shan-tung had barely eaten anything. But he laid down his chopsticks and began to speak.

'I have the very considerable honour to be a member of an organization called the Pah Lien. This translates as the White Lotus Society. You might have remarked upon a clue that I sent you at the airport. The man who met you was carrying a bunch of lilies. The lily is part of the lotus family. My society is a very old one. It was founded in the fourth century to resist the foreign invaders known as the Mongols who then ruled over China. The aim of White Lotus remained the same over the next four centuries. It was to help the Chinese people fight against tyranny and oppression.

'But over the years, something very interesting happened. The White Lotus Society changed. It will be difficult for you to understand the nature of this change, so let me explain it to you by referring to a character from your own history. You will, I am sure, know Robin Hood. He stole from the rich and gave to the poor. He was a hero to the peasants in Sherwood Forest. But to the authorities, he was an outlaw, a criminal. They would have hanged him if they could.

'In the early days, the White Lotus Society operated in much the same way. Indeed, it might interest you to know that the society had a motto: *Ta fu—chih p'in*. This translates as "strike the rich and help the poor". But here was the crucial difference. As the years passed, White Lotus found that it was enjoying and benefiting from the criminal nature of its activities. It was also remarkably successful in the world of organized crime. It continued to steal from the rich but, as its members became richer themselves, it found itself giving rather less to the poor. It also changed its name. It became known as the Three United Society. There was a reason for this. White Lotus believed that the world was made up of three different parts: heaven, earth and mankind. Its members therefore had a triangle tattooed onto their body. The triangle also appeared on their flags. And in the end, they became known simply as the Triads.'

There was a long silence. Matt had heard of the Triads, the criminal gangs that were active all over Asia. They were drug dealers. They were involved in people smuggling, prostitution, extortion and murder. They would torture or kill anyone who got in their way. They were as brutal as they were powerful. And this man was calmly admitting that he was one of them! He glanced at Jamie. The American boy was listening politely. He didn't seem shocked by what he had just heard. Richard, on the other hand, was staring open-mouthed.

'I can see that you are dismayed,' Shan-tung remarked. 'And before you ask me one of your inane questions, Mr Cole, I will answer you. Yes. I am a criminal. More than that, I am what is known as *Shan Chu*, the Master of the Mountain. This means that I am the supreme leader of my own Triad. I cannot tell you how many people I have murdered to get to where I am today, but at a conservative guess I would say about twenty-five. I do know that I am wanted in exactly nine countries, including the United Kingdom and the United States—and I would have been arrested a long time ago if I hadn't paid the right people a great deal of money to leave me alone.

'You are now wondering if you should be sitting at my table, eating my food. You are asking yourself why I should wish to help you in your struggle against the Old Ones. You are thinking, perhaps, that it would be more natural for me to be on their side. But you would be wrong.

'Until very recently, I controlled all crime in

Hong Kong. I have, for example, heroin laboratories in Kowloon and the New Territories. I have illegal casinos and betting shops throughout the island. Immigrants from China were paying $5,000 a time for me to help them cross the border illegally. The arrival of the Old Ones has changed everything. They have no interest in profit. They do not want to do business. They want only to destroy everything around them—and that includes the Triads. They are as much my enemy as anyone's, the only difference being that I have the means to fight back. And that is what I have been doing. There is a certain irony, don't you think? I am undoubtedly a bad man. But a greater evil has come my way and now I am forced to do good.

'And so I have used all my resources within Hong Kong to set up a resistance. I have buildings. I have people. I have weapons ... not that they are of much use against creatures that can form themselves out of flies. Above all, I have determination. I will not be defeated by the Old Ones. They can destroy the world. But they will not destroy me.'

'I'm surprised they didn't ask you to work for them,' Richard said.

'As it happens, they did indeed ask me to serve them. The Nightrise Corporation approached me exactly a year ago. But the Master of the Mountain does not serve anyone. I mentioned twenty-five victims. The man who put that question to me would have been the twenty-fifth.'

'May I ask a question?' Matt asked.

'You have my permission,' Han Shan-tung replied. 'But I should warn you that soon I have a

288

question to put to you and I very much hope you will be able to provide me with the right answer.'

Matt didn't like the sound of that, but he went on anyway. 'How do you know about Scarlett?' he asked. 'And why did you call her Lin Mo?'

'The White Lotus Society has always known about the Gatekeepers. You must remember that in our early days, almost two thousand years ago, we were to all intents and purposes a religious order. We still are. That means we are the keepers of many secrets . . . sacred texts and ancient beliefs. Even when we began to devote ourselves exclusively to crime, we stayed true to ourselves. The secrets were passed on from generation to generation. And I think we always knew that one day we would be called upon to return to our origins, to take up the sword once again.

'As to the second part of your question regarding Lin Mo, that I am not yet prepared to tell you. I need to be persuaded that I can trust you and that is still not the case.

'However, I can say that she was born in a place called Meizhou. We always knew that the Old Ones would return and look for her . . . that she was one of the Gatekeepers. We therefore arranged for her to be adopted and taken to the West. We wanted her to be as far away from here as possible. We hoped that she would be safe.'

'It didn't work.'

Shan-tung shrugged. 'We did everything we could to protect her. It was not our fault that the Old Ones found her. In fact, if anyone is to blame, it is her. Nonetheless, you are right. The Old Ones found her and brought her back.'

'You tried to get her out of Hong Kong,' Jamie

said. He hadn't eaten very much, absorbed in what he was being told.

'Scarlett was kept under guard from the moment she arrived,' Shan-tung explained. 'With great difficulty, we managed to get a message to her. My most trusted agent in Hong Kong, a man called Lohan, contacted her and arranged for the shape-changer who had been guarding her to be killed. He took her to a safe place where we hoped to keep her hidden, but unfortunately—and again through no fault of our own—she was found again. As I mentioned to you, several of my people died. However, Lohan managed to move her to one of our warehouses and had planned to smuggle her out on a cruise liner. That was yesterday. The plan failed for reasons that are not yet clear. She is now their prisoner.'

'So what do we do now?' Jamie asked. 'How do we get her back again?'

The Master of the Mountain poured himself a glass of water from a crystal jug and drank it.

'Jamie and I can go into Hong Kong,' Matt said. 'We can find her . . .'

'If you go into Hong Kong, you will be doing exactly what they want you to do. They will be waiting for you and although they will not kill you—that is not part of their plan—they will keep you in so much pain that you will wish constantly for death.'

'We can't just leave her.'

'You may have no choice.'

'No, Mr Shan-tung,' Matt said. 'You don't believe that. Otherwise, why would you have invited me here?' Matt looked him straight in the eyes. 'You're going to help us get into Hong Kong,' he said. 'You've already told us. You've got people over there. You can smuggle us in. We can find Scarlett. And we can be out of there before the Old Ones know what's happened.'

Han Shan-tung set his glass down. 'I might help you,' he said. 'But as I mentioned to you earlier, there is still a question you have to answer for me.'

'And what is that?'

'I am, by nature, a very careful man. I have told you that I have killed twenty-five times. What I should have added is that there have been as many attempts on my own life. You are here in my house on the recommendation of my friend, Mr Lee. I trust him. He has been useful to me in the past, and he definitely believes that you and the American boy are who you say you are.'

'Is that your question?'

'It is exactly that. How can I be sure that you are one of the Five?'

Matt thought for a moment. Then he pointed at the crystal jug. He didn't even need to think about it any more. The jug was swept, instantly, off the table. It fell to the floor and smashed. Shan-tung blinked. It was his only reaction. But then he slowly smiled. 'An amusing conjuring trick. But it is still not enough. I do not question your abilities. It is your identity I wish to know.'

'I'll read your mind,' Jamie said. 'You say you know everything about us. In ten seconds I can tell you even more about you.'

'I would recommend that you stay out of my mind,' Han Shan-tung said. He turned to Matt. 'There is a test, a trial you might say, that will prove to me beyond any doubt that you are who you say you are. Only one of you needs to take part in it. But I should warn you though that to fail will cause you great pain and perhaps even death. What do you say?'

Matt shrugged. 'We need your help,' he said. 'We've flown a long way to get it. If there is no other way . . .'

'There isn't.'

'Matt . . .' Richard muttered.

'Then let's go ahead,' Matt said. 'What test do you have in mind?'

Han Shan-tung got to his feet. 'It is called the sword ladder,' he said. He gestured towards a door at the back of the room. 'Please . . . will you come this way.'

THE SWORD LADDER

Matt stood up and followed Han Shan-tung. Richard and Jamie came behind. They went through the door into a long corridor, all polished wood but otherwise undecorated. There was a second door at the far end.

It opened into a large, square room that didn't seem to belong to the rest of the house. It reminded Matt of a chapel or perhaps a concert hall that might comfortably seat fifty or sixty people. The walls were plain and wood-panelled, matching the corridor outside, and there were pews arranged around three of the sides. The fourth was concealed by a dark red curtain that had been pulled across, perhaps concealing a stage. There was a gallery above the curtain, but it was high up, arranged in such a way that it was impossible to tell from floor level what it might contain.

'You are inside a Triad lodge,' Mr Shan-tung explained. 'And you should consider yourselves very privileged. Only Triad members and initiates are allowed in here and normally any outsiders would be instantly killed. We meet in this place on the twenty-fifth day of each Chinese month. There is a separate entrance from the street. You might be interested to know that an initiation ceremony lasts six hours. A new recruit is expected to answer three hundred and thirty-three questions about the society. He learns secret handshakes and recognition signals. A lock of his hair is taken and he signs his name in blood.'

'Actually, I wasn't thinking of joining,' Richard muttered.

Fortunately, Shan-tung didn't appear to have heard. 'I speak of our rituals to remind you that the White Lotus Society is very old,' he went on. 'Things have, of course, changed with modern times. Nine hundred years ago, initiates would have drunk each other's blood, mixed with wine. And there is another part of the ceremony that has fallen out of use. When China was enslaved by Kublai Khan, it is said, the society searched for a leader, the one man who might liberate them. That man would be known as the Buddhist Messiah and he would show himself by a sign . . .'

He crossed the room and pulled on a cord that drew back the curtain. Jamie gasped. Matt stepped forward. At first he thought he was looking at a strange ladder leading up to the balcony above but then he realized that it was actually made up of antique swords, each one polished until it shone, lashed together in a wire frame with the edges of the blades facing upwards. Theoretically, it might be possible to climb. But he doubted it. As soon as you rested your body weight on one sword, you would cut your foot in half. Even if you were light enough, the climb to the top would be agony. It was a long way to the balcony. Matt counted nineteen steps. Nineteen chances to slice yourself apart.

'In my time as Master of the Mountain, three initiates have claimed to be the Buddhist Messiah,' Shan-tung explained. 'They asked my permission to be allowed to climb the ladder and I was glad to give it. Watching their attempts was a fascinating experience. One of them almost made it to the top before he fainted. Sadly, he broke his neck in the fall.'

'What about the other two?' Matt asked.

'One cut off the fingers of his left hand on the first step and chose not to continue. The other bled to death.'

'This is insane!' Richard couldn't restrain himself any more. 'Matt isn't claiming to be your Buddhist Messiah or whatever you want to call it.'

'He is claiming to be one of the Gatekeepers. If he is who he says he is, he has nothing to fear.'

'And if we say no? If we refuse to perform your little party trick?'

'Then I will not help you. You will leave Macau. And the girl will die, slowly, on her own.'

Richard swore under his breath. Jamie came forward and stood next to Matt. 'I don't mind giving it a try,' he said, quietly.

'Thanks, Jamie,' Matt replied. 'But I brought us here. I think this one's down to me . . .'

He took a step closer but Richard held out a hand. 'Forget it, Matt!' he said. 'You don't need to do this. There are plenty of ways we can get into Hong Kong without this maniac's help.'

'We can't go in on our own,' Matt said. 'One of us has to try . . .'

'You're going to cut yourself to pieces.'

'After the first finger, I promise I'll stop.'

He went over to the ladder. Any hope that it might not be as dangerous as it looked vanished at once. The swords were fixed rigidly in place by the wires. The blades were pointing towards each other so that as he climbed up, the hilts and the points would be on alternate sides. The swords had been sharpened until they were razor-thin. He rested a finger on one and almost cut through the skin just doing that. If he had dropped an envelope onto it, he would have sliced it in two.

Could he do it? Every instinct told him that he couldn't, that it was impossible, that he was being asked to mutilate himself. He closed his eyes. Was there any way out of this? Did they really need this man's help? Hong Kong was only fifty miles away. They could get on a jet-foil and take their chances. Why would they want to involve themselves with gangsters anyway?

But he knew he was fooling himself. Scarlett was in trouble. If he'd wanted to go into Hong Kong on his own, he could have done it a week ago. There was no other way. He opened his eyes. 'All right,' he said.

'Remove your shoes,' Shan-tung commanded.

'Sure,' he muttered. 'Shame to waste good leather.' Right then, he was wondering if he would ever wear shoes again. He took them off, and his socks as well, for good measure. He could feel the wooden floor, cool against the soles of his feet. He flexed his toes.

'Matt . . .' Richard tried one last time.

'It's OK, Richard.'

Matt didn't look at him. He didn't look at any of them. He knew there was only one way this was going to work. He had to focus completely on the task ahead of him. Nineteen steps. He had once seen people walking on hot coals on television. And in India, fakirs did incredible things with their bodies. Matt remembered what he had done in the Nazca Desert. He had taken a bullet in full flight and turned it back on the person who had fired it. Mind control. That was what this was all about.

He reached out and gently took hold of one of the swords. He felt the blade cut through his skin. It hurt. Blood welled out of the palm of his hand.

'That's enough!' Richard exclaimed. 'You can't do this.'

'Yes. I can.'

Matt gritted his teeth. He knew the mistake he had made. He had been thinking too much about the impossibility of what he was supposed to do. When he moved things without touching them, it never occurred to him that he couldn't do it. That was how the power worked. It was part of him and he could use it any time. This task might seem different but the principle was just the same. Nineteen steps. He wasn't going to hurt himself a second time. He was a Gatekeeper. He had nothing to fear.

He forgot Richard. He forgot where he was. The balcony above him . . . that was all that mattered. He let the swords blur in front of him.

They were no longer there. He reached out with one hand. At the same time, he lifted his left foot and rested his bare sole on the first blade. There was no going back now.

Richard had seen many unforgettable things in his time with Matt, but this was the most incredible of all. He watched Matt begin to climb, one sword at a time, resting his entire weight on edges that were clearly razor sharp. He seemed to be in a self-induced trance, moving steadily upwards as if he were levitating. Already he was half-way up and he hadn't cut himself at all. Next to him, Jamie stared in wonderment. Even Han Shan-tung looked quietly impressed.

He reached the top. He climbed off the ladder and stood on the balcony. Nobody spoke. Shantung hurried to the side of the room and took a staircase that also led up. Matt waited for him. There was a single wound on his right palm, the result of his false start, but otherwise he was unharmed.

The Master of the Mountain reached him. He was holding a bandage. He bowed low, then handed it over. 'I apologize for questioning you, Matthew,' he said—and he sounded completely sincere. 'You are indeed one of the Five and it is my honour to be able to help you.'

Matt took the bandage and wrapped it round his hand. At the same time, he noticed an altar on the far side of the balcony, hidden from the room below. There were several gold bowls, incense sticks, two crouching Buddhas and, between them, a jade figure of a young girl, slim with long hair falling in waves around her shoulders.

'That is Lin Mo,' Han Shan-tung said. 'It is the

answer to the question that you asked me earlier. Lin Mo is the name of a young girl in Chinese legend. She was born in Meizhou, in the eastern Guangdong province. She had the power to forecast the weather. And she grew up to become the goddess of the sea, very important to the sailors who explored these uncharted waters. She is still worshipped in Macau.'

He moved over to the altar and bowed in front of it.

'This figure is very precious to me,' he continued. 'It is Ming dynasty. From the seventeenth century. It is said to be a true representation of Lin Mo, copied from an earlier work.'

Matt recognized the face. He remembered the picture he had seen in the newspaper. 'It's Scarlett, isn't it,' he said.

'The girl that you know as Scarlett was also born in Meizhou. It was always our belief that she was the reincarnation of Lin Mo. And it is true, yes, that in appearance the two are identical.'

'So you're going to help us.'

Shan-tung nodded. 'You must leave very soon,' he said. 'Come now with me to my study and we will make the final preparations.'

He led Matt over to the staircase and the two of them made their way down. Richard and Jamie were waiting for him.

'That was quite a trick,' Richard muttered through clenched teeth.

Jamie said nothing. He rested a hand briefly on Matt's shoulder. He was glad that it hadn't been him.

They followed Shan-tung back down the

298

corridor and into a study that also overlooked the garden. It was an austere room with a large desk, a few shelves of books and little else. His whole manner had changed. He was still in command, a man who was used to being obeyed instantly, but he was being a little quieter about it. Had he really expected Matt to climb the sword ladder? He seemed shaken by what he had seen.

He took out a map and laid it on his desk. Matt glanced at his watch, wondering how long this would take. It was already ten o'clock.

'The Old Ones may control the city,' Shan-tung said. 'But if they have underestimated the size and extent of the Triads, then they have made a fatal mistake. I have a thousand foot-soldiers that I can place at your service. If called to do so, they will not hesitate to lay down their lives for you. That is our way. The man who commands them is called Lohan. His rank is 438 which we also call Incense Master. He will meet you when you arrive in Hong Kong.'

'How do we know we can trust him?' Richard growled.

'Very simply, Mr Cole. He is my eldest son. You will recognize him because his face is scarred.' Shan-tung drew a line with his finger, starting on his left cheek and crossing his mouth. 'A man was sent to kill me with a *jian*, a Chinese sword. Lohan got in his way. If it were not for him, I would be dead. This is where you will meet . . .'

His finger stabbed down on the map, at a point close to the waterside.

'I have a legitimate business delivering fireworks to Kowloon. There is a warehouse next to the Salisbury Road and it is there you will be taken.

Scarlett was also there before she was captured. You don't need to worry. The location is still secure.

'We are trying to discover where Scarlett is being held prisoner but so far we've had no luck. It is possible that she is here . . .' He pointed again, this time to a street on the other side of the water. 'This is The Nail. It is in Queen Street and it is the headquarters of the Nightrise Corporation. If the girl is there, Lohan will lead an assault on the building. You will be with him.

'The Tai Shan Temple with the door that you were seeking is also in Queen Street.' He pointed to a crossroads close to a patch of green with what might be a lake in the middle. 'You would be wise not to go there as it is almost certainly being watched. But once you have the girl, the rules will change. It is less than a quarter of a mile away, close to Hong Kong Park. Lohan will help you enter the compound. He will kill anyone who gets in your way. You will enter the temple and the door will take you wherever you want to go.'

'But what if Scarlett isn't at The Nail?' Richard asked.

'Then you will have to search for her. Perhaps her father will be able to help you.' The finger slid across the page. 'Paul Adams has returned to Wisdom Court, the apartment block where he lives. It is here, on Harcourt Road. Be warned. He was with her when she was captured and may have had a hand in what took place. We can't trust him. Even so, he may know where she is.'

'And you think he'll tell?'

'We will make him tell us.' Han Shan-tung muttered the words casually but there was something about the way he spoke that made the skin crawl.

He seemed to have finished. Matt was exhausted. He was looking forward to getting to bed. But then Han Shan-tung went over to the desk and took a mobile phone out of one of the drawers. He handed it to Richard. 'You can use this to contact me at any time of the day or night,' he explained. 'The speed dial is already set. Just press one and it will connect you directly.'

'So when are we leaving?' Jamie asked.

Shan-tung turned and looked at him. There was no expression on his face. 'The boat is already waiting for you,' he said. 'You must enter Hong Kong under cover of darkness. You leave tonight.'

INTO HONG KONG

The boat was tied up at Porto Exterior, the outer port of Macau. Han Shan-tung had said a brief goodbye in the hallway of his home and now Matt, Jamie and Richard were being driven across the city through half-empty streets. It was raining again and the pavements, black and glistening, had been deserted by the crowds, many of them sheltering in the casinos, throwing their money after dice and cards in the artificial glare of the chandeliers.

They were all tired. Jamie was half asleep, his head resting on the window, his long hair falling across his face. Richard was sitting next to him. Matt could tell that he was angry—with Shan-tung for arranging the ordeal of the sword ladder and

301

with himself for allowing it. Matt was in the front, beside the driver. The speed of events had taken him by surprise. He had only just arrived in Macau and already he was leaving. He thought about what might lie ahead of him in Hong Kong and wondered if he was doing the right thing. It was obvious now that the whole place was a trap, set up by the Old Ones. And yet, he was walking straight into it.

But they wouldn't be expecting him . . . not like this. That was what he told himself. And there was no other way. He couldn't leave Scarlett on her own any longer. It had already been too long. It was his responsibility to find her and bring her out. He was a Gatekeeper. It was time to take control.

The ferry terminal was ahead but they didn't drive into it. Instead, the driver took them down a narrow road that led to the water's edge and stopped. They got out, bracing themselves against the cold night air.

For a moment, Matt and Richard found themselves standing next to each other. 'Do you really think we should trust these people?' the journalist muttered, putting into words what he had been thinking all along. 'They're Triads. Do you know what that means? Drugs and guns. Gambling. Prostitution. They'll chop up anyone who gets in their way—including you and me. Between them and the Old Ones, I wouldn't have said there was a lot to choose.'

A few hours ago, Matt might have agreed. But he remembered how Han Shan-tung had looked at the statue of Scarlett, or Lin Mo as he preferred to call her. 'I think they're on our side,' he said.

'Maybe.' Richard reached out for Matt's injured

hand and turned it over. There was a dark stain seeping through the bandage. 'But he still shouldn't have done that to you.'

'I did it to myself,' Matt said. 'I wasn't concentrating.'

Jamie came over to them. 'I think he wants us to go with him,' he said, glancing at the driver. He yawned. 'I just hope this boat has got a decent bed.'

There wasn't much to the port: a stretch of white concrete, a couple of gantries and arc lamps spreading a hard, electric glow that only made everything look more unwelcoming. Once again the rain had eased off but a thin drizzle hung in the air. The driver led them over to a boat, moored along the quayside. This was going to take them across.

It was an old, hard-working cargo boat with just two decks. The lower of them had a cargo hold that was open to the elements and looking into it, Matt saw that it was filled with wooden crates, each one marked with a name that had been stencilled in black letters: KUNG HING TAO. The cabin was on the upper deck. It was shaped like a greenhouse and not much bigger, with windows all the way round. There were two radio masts jutting into the air, a radar dish and a funnel that was already belching black smoke. The boat was completely ringed with car tyres to stop it colliding with the quay and this, along with the flaking paint and patches of rust, made it look as if it had been rescued from a junkyard. Matt just hoped the sea would be calm.

'We've got company,' Richard said.

A man had appeared, climbing down from the

303

cabin, his feet—in wellington boots—clanging against the metal rungs. As he stepped into the light, it became clear that he wasn't Chinese. He was a European, a big man with a beard, dark eyes and curly, black hair. His whole face looked beaten about—cracked lips, broken nose, veins showing through the skin. Either the weather had done it, too many years at sea, or he had once been a boxer ... and an unsuccessful one. He was wearing jeans, a thick knitted jersey and a donkey jacket, dark blue, with the rain sparkling on his shoulders. His hands were huge and covered in oil.

'Good evening, my friends,' the man said. 'You are welcome to *Moon Moth*.' He had introduced his ship but not himself. He had a deep voice and a Spanish accent. The words came from somewhere in his chest. 'Mr Shan-tung has asked me to look after you. Are you ready to come on board?'

'How long will the journey take us?' Richard asked. He sounded doubtful.

'Three hours ... maybe longer. We don't have the power of a jet-foil and the weather's strange. All this rain! It may hold us up, so the sooner we get started, the better.' The man took out a pipe and tapped it against his teeth as if checking them for cavities. 'I often make the journey at night, if that's what's worrying you,' he went on. 'Nobody's going to take any notice of us. So let's get out of this weather and be on our way.'

He turned and climbed back onto the boat. Richard glanced at Matt. Matt shrugged. The captain hadn't been exactly friendly, but why should they have expected otherwise? These people were criminals. They were only obeying orders. They had no interest in the Gatekeepers or

304

anybody else, so it was pointless to expect first class comfort and smiles.

Richard had brought his backpack with them— it was their only luggage. He picked it up and they followed the man on board. They reached the ladder and Matt was grateful that this one had ordinary rungs instead of swords. As he began to climb, he noticed a Chinese man in filthy jeans and an oil-skin jacket, drawing a tarpaulin over the crates. For a moment their eyes met and Matt found himself being studied with undisguised hostility. The man spat, then went back to work. He seemed to be the only crew.

There wasn't much room in the cabin which looked even older than the ship, with equipment that wouldn't have been out of place in a Second World War film. The captain was sitting on a stool in front of a steering wheel, surrounded by switches and gauges with markings that had largely faded away. The rain had picked up. It was streaming down the windows and the world outside was almost invisible, broken up into beads of water that clung in place, reflecting everything but showing very little. The engines were throbbing sullenly below. The whole cabin was vibrating. It smelled of salt water, diesel fuel and stale tobacco.

There was a low sofa and a couple of chairs for the three passengers. All the furniture was sagging and stained. Richard, Matt and Jamie took their places. The captain sat at the wheel, flicking on a pair of ancient windscreen wipers which began to swing from left to right, clearing the way in front of them. The Chinese crewman cast off and the boat slipped away, unseen, into the night.

A single row of lights shone ahead. There was a road bridge, at least half a mile long, snaking across the entire length of the harbour. But once they had passed underneath it there was nothing. *Moon Moth* had its own spotlights mounted on the bow and the cabin roof, but they barely penetrated the driving rain and showed nothing more than a circle of black water a few metres ahead.

The captain switched on the screens and the cabin glowed green with a soft beeping sound that divided up the silence like commas in a sentence. For about ten minutes nobody said anything but then the crewman appeared, carrying a battered tray with four tin mugs of hot chocolate which he had brought up from a galley somewhere below.

'You haven't told me your names,' the captain said. He lit his pipe and blew smoke into the air, making the cabin feel closer and snugger than ever. It was very warm inside, presumably from the heat of the engines below.

Richard introduced them. 'I'm Richard. This is Matt and Jamie.' They were being smuggled into Hong Kong illegally, and anyway Han Shan-tung already knew who they were. There was no need for false names.

'And I am Hector Machado. But you can call me Captain. That is what everyone calls me—even when I am not on the ship.'

'Are you Spanish?' Richard asked.

'Portuguese. I was born in Lisbon. Have you been there?'

Richard shook his head.

'I'm told that it's a beautiful city. I left there when I was three. My father came to Hong Kong to fight against the communists. This was his boat.'

306

Machado sucked on his pipe which glowed red. He blew out smoke. 'He was shot dead in the very seat where I am sitting now. And the boat is mine.'

'How many crew do you have?' Matt was thinking of the man he had seen. Why had he appeared so unfriendly?

'Just Billy. No need for anyone else.'

'What's in the crates?'

Machado hesitated, as if afraid of giving too much away. Then he shrugged. 'Fireworks. A lot of fireworks. Mr Shan-tung has a business selling them to mainland Hong Kong.'

'And what do you carry when you're not delivering fireworks?' Richard asked. His voice was hostile. It clearly bothered him, being with these people.

'I've carried all sorts of things, Richard. Stuff that maybe it would be better you didn't know about. I've smuggled people in, if that's what you want to know. And maybe you should be grateful. I know the ins and outs. *Moon Moth* may not be much to look at but she'll outrun the Hong Kong harbour patrols any time . . . not that they'll bother themselves about us. Everyone knows me in these parts. And they leave me alone.'

'So how long have you worked for the Triads?'

'You think this is an interview? You want to write about me?' Machado gestured with the pipe. 'I'd get some rest if I were you. It could be a long night.' He slipped the pipe between his teeth and said no more.

They cruised on into the darkness, guided by the strange, green light of the radar system. The night was so huge that it swallowed them completely. There was no moon or stars. It was impossible to

307

tell if it was still raining as the windows were being lashed by sea spray. Machado sat where he was, smoking in silence. Richard, Matt and Jamie sat at the back of the cabin, out of his way. All three of them were tense and nervous. They hadn't discussed what they might find in Hong Kong, but now that they were finally on the way, they could imagine what they might be up against. A whole city, millions of people . . . and the Old Ones infesting everything. They had to be mad to be going in there. But there seemed to be no other way to get Scar out.

Jamie finished his hot chocolate and dozed off. Richard opened his backpack and began to go through his things: he had brought maps, money, a change of clothes. The precious diary—written by Joseph of Cordoba—was also there, sealed in plastic to keep it protected. Matt noticed a glimmer of gold and realized that he was carrying the *tumi*—the Inca knife.

Richard glanced up. 'You never know when it may come in handy,' he said. 'Anyway, I didn't like leaving it behind with that bunch of crooks.' He zipped the backpack shut, then lowered his voice. 'What do you think?' he asked.

He was referring to Hector Machado, although he didn't need to whisper as the captain would never had heard him above the noise of the engines.

'Shan-tung trusts him,' Matt said.

'He doesn't seem to be exactly friendly.'

'He doesn't have to be friendly. He just has to get us there.'

'Let's hope he does.'

The two of them fell silent and soon they were

both asleep. But then—it felt like seconds later— Matt found himself being woken by something. It was the boat's engine which had changed tempo, slowing down. He opened his eyes. It was still dark, still raining. But there were lights ahead.

'You can wake up your friends,' Captain Machado said. 'We're here.'

Matt stood up and went over to the window.

And there it was. It was two o'clock in the morning but a city like Hong Kong never really slept. Matt could make out the skyscrapers by the lights that burned all around them, picking out their shapes in brilliant green, blue and pink neon. It was as if someone had drawn the city onto the darkness with a vast, fluorescent crayon. There were advertisements—PHILIPS, SAMSUNG, HITACHI—burning themselves onto the night sky, the colours breaking up in the water, being thrown around by the choppy waves. There were signs in Chinese too, and they reminded him how very different this city would be from London or Miami. This was another world.

It was very misty. Maybe it was an illusion caused by all the neon, but the mist was a strange colour, an ugly, poisonous yellow. It was rolling across the harbour towards them, reaching out to surround them as if it were a living thing and knew who they were. As they continued forward, it pressed itself against the glass of the cabin and the sound of the engines became even more distant.

Richard had joined the captain at the steering wheel. 'Why are we going so slowly?' he asked. It was a good question. They were barely moving at all.

'We don't want to draw attention to ourselves,'

309

Machado replied.

'I thought you said nobody cared about you anyway.'

'There's still no reason to make too much noise.'

Another minute passed.

'I thought we were going to Kowloon,' Richard said.

'We are.'

'But isn't Kowloon on the other side?'

Machado grinned in the half light. He had put the pipe away. 'The current will carry us over,' he said and at that moment Matt knew that he wasn't telling the truth and felt the familiar tingle of imminent danger. For what seemed like an age, nothing happened. They weren't moving. Machado was standing there, almost daring them to challenge him—to do anything. But there was nothing they could do. They were trapped on board his boat, completely in his power.

And then a searchlight cut through the darkness, pinning *Moon Moth* in its glare. The entire cabin seemed to explode with dazzling light. A second beam swung across. Two boats. They were still some distance away but they were rapidly closing in. They must have been waiting there all the time.

At the same moment, Machado swung his hand, crashing it into the side of Richard's head and then bringing it around on Matt. He was holding a gun. Richard fell. Machado's lips curled in an unpleasant smile. 'If you move, I will kill you,' he said.

He had betrayed them. He had known the boats were coming. He had led them straight to them.

'The Triads will kill you for this . . .' Richard muttered. He had pulled himself onto one knee and was cradling his head in his hand. Blood was trickling from a wound just above his eye.

'The Triads are finished,' Machado replied. 'They're nothing any more.'

'So who's paying you?' Matt asked.

'There's a big reward out for you, boy. Two million Hong Kong dollars. More than I've earned with Shan-tung and his friends in ten years. They want you very badly. And they warned me about you. If you even blink, I'll shoot you.'

Matt looked out of the window. The boats were getting closer and they had been joined by three more, making five in all, moving in from every side. They were police launches—grey, solid steel with identifying numbers printed on the side. They were coming out of the night like miniature battleships, with bullet-proof windows and bows shaped like knives.

Richard pulled himself to his feet. Machado aimed the gun at him. 'Nightrise doesn't want you,' he said. 'So I hope you don't mind a burial at sea.' He was about to fire at point blank range. He licked his lips, enjoying himself. Richard stared at him helplessly.

'Put the gun down,' Jamie said.

Machado didn't hesitate. He laid the gun on the floor although his face was filled with puzzlement. He had no idea why he'd done it. But Matt did. In his moment of triumph, the captain had forgotten Jamie. He'd thought he was still asleep . . . but he'd been wrong. Jamie had seen what was happening and had used his power. If he'd told Machado to stop breathing, the man would have stood there until he died. And, Matt reflected, maybe that was what he deserved.

'This is the Hong Kong police. Heave to . . .'

The voice echoed out of the water, amplified through a megaphone. There was a man standing on the bow of the nearest boat—except he looked far too tall to be human. He was black and was dressed in the uniform of a senior officer in the Hong Kong police. But it was obvious he was no policeman. He was like something out of a nightmare with his bald head and empty, staring eyes. It was freezing cold out on the water but he wasn't shivering. He showed no feeling or emotion at all.

Richard lunged forward, grabbed hold of the steering wheel and slammed down the throttle. Matt felt the floor tilt beneath him as the cargo boat surged forward. Captain Machado had been standing there, dazed, as if unsure what to do, but now he seized hold of Richard and the two of them began to grapple for the steering wheel.

'Get rid of him, Jamie,' Matt said.

'Jump overboard,' Jamie commanded.

Machado let go of Richard and lurched out of the cabin, moving as if in a trance. There was shouting, a shot, then a splash as Machado was gunned down even as he hit the sea. The Hong Kong police had assumed he was trying to escape. Or maybe they knew who he was but had decided to kill him anyway. Machado floated face down in the water. He didn't move.

Richard had control of the cargo boat. He spun it round, taking the police by surprise. Seconds later, he burst through them, weaving round one of their boats, heading for the Central side of Hong

Kong.

'The gun!' Richard shouted.

Matt snatched it up and handed it to him. Then Jamie shouted and pointed. 'Watch out!'

A face had appeared at the window, glaring at them with furious eyes. For a moment Matt thought one of the policemen had somehow boarded *Moon Moth*. Then he remembered the single crewman—Billy—who had sailed with them from Macau. He was holding a gun, bringing it round to aim at the cabin. Richard shot him through the window, a single bullet between the eyes. The boat lurched crazily. The wheel spun. The crewman disappeared.

Then the nearest police launch opened fire. The noise was deafening as the bullets smashed into the metal plates of the cargo boat, cutting a line along the bow and ricocheting back into the water. One of the windows shattered and Richard ducked as tiny fragments of glass showered down onto his shoulders and back. The cold night air rushed into the cabin, carrying with it the spray of water and the foul, decaying smell of the pollution. *Moon Moth* surged forward. Richard was fighting with the wheel, trying not to be shot. Matt looked back. The police launches were regrouping, preparing to come after them. The man at the front suddenly opened his mouth and howled, a sound that split the night, louder than all the boats put together. Matt knew at that moment that he wasn't a man at all.

'We're going to have to jump!' Richard shouted above the roar of the engines and the raging wind. 'Jamie, can you swim?'

Jamie nodded.

'I'm going to take us in as close as I can.' He turned to Matt. 'If we get separated, meet at . . .'

But Matt didn't hear the rest of the sentence. There was another burst of gunfire, this time strafing the stern and the cargo hold where the fireworks were packed.

'Now!'

Richard abandoned the wheel and the boat began to zigzag. Matt needed to ask him what he had just said, but everything was happening too quickly. Richard snatched up his backpack and forced it over his shoulders. Jamie was right next to him. The five police boats were getting closer, only a few metres behind.

'Go!' Richard shouted.

Jamie hurried out to the deck and without stopping disappeared over the side of the boat. But Richard hadn't followed. He had climbed down from the cabin and was balancing himself, clinging to a handrail as *Moon Moth*, its engines screaming on full power, swerved drunkenly through the sea. Blood and water streamed down his face and his eyes were wild. Matt had never seen him like this before. Gritting his teeth, he brought the gun up and fired into the crates of fireworks, again and again, emptying the chamber into the same spot.

Nothing happened until the final shot. Then there was a flare of magnesium, burning through the tarpaulin. Richard noticed that Matt was still there, that he hadn't jumped overboard. 'Jump!' he pleaded.

Matt jumped.

Even as his feet left the deck, the fireworks went off. There were thousands of pounds worth in the hold. A tonne of gunpowder. But there was nothing beautiful about the explosion. It was just a blinding, burning wheel of fire that seemed to take Richard and hurl him into the air. That was the last thing Matt saw before he hit the water. For a moment everything was panic. The sea was black and freezing. He was still wearing his clothes and trainers. He was being sucked down. He had to fight with all his strength just to get back to the surface.

He emerged, gasping for air, into a brilliant, blazing nightmare. It was as if the whole night was on fire. *Moon Moth* was alight. The fire was burning so intensely that the metal plates would surely melt away. With no one to steer it, the boat had turned a full circle and was ploughing into the police launches, which had been too slow to get out of the way. It was right in the middle of them and Matt could just make out figures in helmets and full riot gear staring at the destruction, knowing that they were too close, that they were part of it. One of their boats was already on fire. The tall man was still howling—but this time in agony. Every part of him was on fire. His suit and the skin beneath it were peeling away. At the very end, his head split open and something began to snake out of it—a second head, but not a human one. Then there was a great rush of white flame as more of the fireworks exploded and he was blown out of sight.

Individual fireworks were going off, one after another and Matt saw cascades of red, blue, white, green and yellow as blazing missiles were shot into the air, reflecting in the water below. About fifty rockets screamed out at once, some of them twisting into the sky, others slamming into the

315

police boats. One of them spluttered across the water and plunged down in front of him, missing his head by inches. He saw a policeman on fire, jumping into the water to save himself. Another was less lucky. He seemed to be holding a spinning Catherine wheel, unable to let go of it even though it was burning into his chest. Fireworks were cracking and buzzing and whining all around him. He didn't make it into the sea. He died where he stood.

Matt was treading water, forcing himself to breathe. He was so cold that his lungs had shut down. He knew that he couldn't stay out here much longer. Two of the police boats were undamaged. Very soon they would be looking for him. But where was Richard? Where was Jamie? The surface of the water was like a black mirror, reflecting the light, but he couldn't see them anywhere. He wanted to shout out for them but he didn't dare. The policemen would have heard him.

There was only one thing he could do. The edge of the water was about a hundred metres away. He had to get to dry land and hope to find them there. He took one last look and then turned round and began to swim, slowed down by his clothes. The glow from the flames spread out over his shoulders, helping to light the way, and there were more bangs and fizzes as the last fireworks went off. He heard someone shouting an order in Chinese but doubted that they'd seen him. He was wearing dark clothes. His hair was dark. The currents were carrying him away.

He reached land without even realizing it. Suddenly there was a slimy concrete slope under his knees. He crawled onto it and pulled himself out. He was on a building site. That was what it looked like. It was hard to tell as he squatted in the darkness, shivering, filthy water dripping out of his hair.

'Richard? Jamie?'

He didn't dare call too loudly. The whole city—anyone who was awake—must have seen the firework display. The Old Ones knew he was there. They would already be searching.

'Richard? Jamie?'

There was no reply.

He waited ten minutes before he made a decision and set off, moving while he still could. If he stayed still much longer, he would freeze.

It was three o'clock in the morning. He had entered the enemy city. He had no idea where he was going. He was dripping wet. He was unarmed.

And he was alone.

NECROPOLIS

Leaving the water behind him, Matt made for the wall of light that defined the edge of Hong Kong. He came to a main road, empty at this time of the night, with a block of luxury hotels and shopping centres on the far side. The smog was worse than ever. The entire city reeked of it, like a chemical swamp. He had only been there for a few minutes but he already had a nagging headache and his eyes were smarting.

Where were Richard and Jamie? He had to find them. He was lost without them. Jamie had been the first off the boat and although Matt hadn't

317

seen Richard jump, he must surely have followed moments later. Like him, the two of them must have swum ashore—unless the police had managed to find them first. The thought of his friends in captivity sickened him.

He tried to shake off the sense of hopelessness. He had to work out what to do. Get in touch with the Triads. There were a thousand of them, waiting to help him, but the way things had turned out, it wasn't going to be so easy after all. Han Shan-tung had given them a mobile with a direct dial. Richard had been carrying it. But it would have been made useless the moment it hit the water. And then there was Shan-tung's son, Lohan. He would already know that something had gone wrong. Presumably his men would be searching for them all over the city.

But Matt had no way of contacting them. He remembered the address of the place where they were supposed to be going, a warehouse on the Salisbury Road. But that was on the other side of the harbour, in Kowloon. Matt had no map and no money. He was soaking wet. It was the middle of the night. How was he supposed to get there?

He was already finding it hard to walk. Every time his foot came down, his shoes squelched and he felt the water rise over his foot. His shirt and trousers were clinging to him, digging in under his arms and between his legs. As he crossed the road and passed between the first of the buildings, he wondered if it wasn't a little warmer here than it had been in the harbour. But it was only a matter of degrees. He was soaked and shivering and if he didn't want to catch pneumonia he was going to have to find a change of clothes.

He stopped. A man had appeared, coming towards him from round the corner of a building. At first Matt assumed he was drunk, on his way home from a late-night party. The man was wearing a crumpled suit with a tie hanging loosely from his neck, dragged round one side, and he was staggering. Matt thought about hiding but the man obviously had no interest in him. And he wasn't drunk. He was ill. As he drew nearer, Matt saw that his suit was stained with huge sweat patches, and his face was a sickly white. He almost fell, propped himself against a lamppost, then threw up. Matt turned away, but not before he saw that whatever was coming out of his mouth was mixed with blood. The man was dying. He surely wouldn't last the night.

Slowly, the city began to reveal itself. Matt wasn't completely on his own after all. There were street cleaners out, sweeping the pavements, their faces covered by white cloth masks. He saw security men sitting on their own in the neon glare behind the windows, only half awake as they counted the long minutes until dawn. He passed the entrance of a subway station, closed for the night, but there was a woman sitting on the steps, a vagrant, her whole body completely wrapped in old plastic bags. She saw him and laughed, her eyes staring, as if she knew something he didn't. Then she began to cough, a dreadful racking sound. Matt hurried on.

An ambulance raced past, its siren off but its lights flashing, throwing livid blue shadows across the shop windows. It pulled in ahead of him and he saw that a small crowd had gathered round a man lying unconscious on the pavement. The ambulance doors were thrown open and two men climbed out, also wearing white masks. Nobody spoke. The man on the ground wasn't moving. The ambulance men scooped him up like a sack of meat and threw him into the back. He was either dead or dying and they didn't care. There were other bodies in the back, lots of them, piled up on top of one another. The ambulance men slammed the doors then got back in. A moment later, they drove away.

The city was huge, silent, threatening. It seemed to be entirely in the grip of the night, as if the morning would never come. Bald-headed mannequins in furs and diamonds stared out of the shop windows as Matt hurried past. Hundreds of gold and silver watches lay ticking quietly behind armour-plated glass. In the day, in the sunshine, Hong Kong might be a shopper's paradise. But at three o'clock in the morning with the pollution rolling in and the inhabitants sick and dying in the streets, it was something close to hell.

They were looking for him.

He heard the sound of a car approaching and the very speed of it, the angry roar of the engine at this time of the night, told Matt that its journey was urgent and that he should get out of its way. Sure enough, just as he threw himself into a doorway, a police car shot past, immediately followed by a second, both of them heading the way he had just come. He knew that he had to get out of sight before any more arrived. He crossed another wide avenue and began climbing uphill.

And then he heard something coming through the darkness. It was the last thing he would have expected in a modern city and at first he thought he must be mistaken. The clatter of metal against concrete. Horse's hooves . . .

A man appeared, riding a horse through a set of red traffic lights. The hooves were striking the surface of the road with that strange, unmistakable rhythm, and the echo was being trapped, thrown back and forth between shop windows. The horse paused under a street lamp and in the yellow glare, Matt saw that it was even more horrible than he had imagined. It was skeleton-thin and in an act of dreadful cruelty someone had driven a knife into its head, the blade pointing outwards, so that it looked like a grotesque version of a unicorn.

Matt saw it and remembered Jamie telling him about the fire riders who had taken part in the battle ten thousand years before. Was this one of them? As the man and the beast went past, he ducked behind a parked car, watching them in the wing mirror until they had disappeared from sight.

He was about to stand up, then froze as something huge fluttered through the darkness, high above the skyscrapers. Matt didn't see what it was but guessed that it was some sort of giant bird, maybe even the condor that had been part of the Nazca Lines. It was there, a sweeping shadow, and then it had gone. He knew now that the whole city was possessed: the roads, the water, the very air. It could only be a matter of time before he was seen and captured. Every moment he was on the street he was in terrible danger.

He waited until he was sure there was no one around, then straightened up and hurried on his way, keeping close to the buildings so that he could throw himself into the shadows if anyone approached. He came to a junction. A car had swerved and crashed into a bollard. It was completely smashed up, its horn blaring. Matt could see the driver, half hanging out of the front door, pinned in place by his seat belt, his head and chest covered in blood. No one was coming to help.

A street sign. Matt looked up and read two words directly above him. Harcourt Road. The name meant something.

Paul Adams has returned to Wisdom Court . . . It is here, on Harcourt Road.

He remembered Han Shan-tung, talking to him in the study, pointing it out on the map. Suddenly he knew what he had to do. Somehow he had stumbled onto the right road. If Paul Adams was at the flat, maybe he would let him in. At the very least he would have somewhere to stay until the break of day.

'Help me . . .'

The man in the car wasn't dead. His eyes, very white, had flicked open. He seemed to be crying, but the tears were blood. There was nothing Matt could do for him. He turned away and began to run.

The road seemed to go on for ever. Matt went past more shopping malls, a hospital, a huge conference centre. He didn't see any more police cars but he heard them in the distance, their sirens slicing through the air. At one point, a taxi rushed past, zigzagging crazily, on the wrong side of the road. He turned a corner and came upon a tram, parked in front of an office building. It was an old-fashioned thing. Apart from the Chinese symbols, it was like something that might have driven through London during the Second World War.

322

And it was full of people. They were just sitting there, slumped in their seats, unmoving. Matt didn't know if they were alive or dead and he didn't hang around to find out. He guessed they were a mix of both.

Somehow he found his way to Wisdom Court. He had only glanced at the map when he was in Macau and he'd got no more than an overview of the city. But there it was, suddenly in front of him, the name on a block of stone and behind it a driveway leading up to a fountain, a wide entrance and, on each side, a statue of a snarling lion. The building was very ordinary, shrouded in darkness, but there was one light burning on the twelfth floor—Matt counted the windows—and he thought he saw a curtain flicker as somebody moved behind.

The driveway hadn't been swept. It was strewn with dead leaves and scraps of paper. The fountain had been turned off. As he walked up to the door, Matt got the feeling that the whole place, apart from that one room on the twelfth floor, might be deserted. There were no cars parked outside. He put his face against the glass door and looked into the reception area. It was empty. The door was locked but there was a panel of buttons next to it, more than a hundred of them, numbered but with no names.

Was this really a good idea? He stood there for a few seconds, cold and wet, and tried to work out his options. Han Shan-tung had suggested that Paul Adams might have been working with the Old Ones. He had been there when Scarlett was taken prisoner. But could he really have sentenced his own daughter to death? Surely not.

323

At the end of the day it didn't make any difference if Matt trusted him or not. He was freezing. He had to get inside, off the street. He had nowhere else to go.

He began to ring the bells, one after another, beginning with 1200 and moving along, waiting briefly for each one to reply. There was silence until he reached 1213, then a crackle as a voice came over the intercom.

'Yes?'

'Mr Adams?'

'Who is this?'

'I know it's very late, but I'm a friend of Scarlett's. I wonder if I could talk to you.'

'Now?'

'Yes. Could you let me in?'

A pause. Then a buzz and the door opened.

As Matt walked into the reception area, he became aware of a stench—raw sewage. A pipe had burst. He could hear it dripping and the floor was wet underfoot. There was just enough light to make out a staircase leading up, but once he began to climb he had to feel his way in total darkness. He counted twelve floors, sliding his hand along the banister, pressing his shoulder against the wall as he turned each corner. It really was like being blind and he felt smothered, afraid that at any moment something would jump out and grab hold of him. But at last he arrived at a swing door, pushed it open and found himself at the beginning of a long corridor. Light spilled out from an open door about half-way down. Scarlett's father was waiting for him, but Matt couldn't make him out because the light was behind him and he was in silhouette.

324

'Who are you?' Paul Adams called out.

'My name is Matt.'

'You're a friend of Scarly's?'

'I want to help her.'

'You can't help her. You're too late.'

Matt walked down the corridor, afraid that Paul Adams would go back in and close the door before he could reach him. But Adams waited for him. He reached the door and saw a small, unhappy man with grey hair and glasses. Scarlett's father hadn't shaved for a couple of days, nor had he washed. He was wearing a blue jersey which might have been expensive when he had bought it but now hung off him awkwardly, as if he had been sleeping in it. And he had been drinking. Matt could smell the alcohol on his breath and saw it in the eyes behind the glasses. They were red with exhaustion and self-pity.

'Mr Adams . . .' Matt began.

'I don't know you.' Paul Adams looked at him blankly.

'I told you. My name is Matt.'

'You're soaking wet.'

'Can I come in?'

Matt didn't wait for an answer. He pushed his way past and entered the flat. The place was a mess. There were dirty plates stacked in the sink and on the kitchen counter. Everything smelled stale and airless with the sewage creeping up from below. It was as if someone had died there . . . or maybe it was the place itself that had died. Once it had been luxurious. Now it was sordid and sad.

Paul Adams closed the door. 'Do you want something to eat?' he asked.

'I'd like some tea,' Matt said. The man didn't

move so he went into the kitchen and began to make it himself. He looked in the fridge for some food. There were only leftovers but he helped himself anyway. It was only now that he realized how hungry he was. A clock on the oven showed twenty past four. Six hours had passed since he had left Macau.

Paul Adams sat down. He had a glass of whisky and he drank it in one swallow, then refilled it. 'You're English . . .' he said.

'I was at your home in Dulwich,' Matt said. He was rummaging through a cupboard for a tea-bag. 'I tried to find Scarlett there. But she'd gone.'

'They've taken her.'

'Do you know where she is?'

'No.' He drank again. 'I know who you are!' he exclaimed. He had only just worked it out. 'You're the boy they're all looking for. You're the reason why they wanted Scarlett.'

Matt didn't say anything. The kettle boiled and he made himself the tea, adding two spoons of sugar.

'Matt Freeman. That's who it was. Matt Freeman!' He got up and went over to the kitchen, weaving his way across the carpet. Matt didn't know whether to be saddened or disgusted. He had never seen anyone so utterly lost. Paul Adams leant heavily against the side of the counter and suddenly there were tears in his eyes. 'They lied to me,' he said. 'They told me she'd be all right if I helped them. I was the one who caught her! She'd have got away if it hadn't been for me. But I only did it to protect her. They said they'd kill her if I didn't help them.'

'Did they take her to The Nail?' Matt asked.

326

'She's not there.' Paul Adams shook his head.

'Is she still in Hong Kong?'

'Somewhere. They won't tell me.' He paused and looked at the window. The first streaks of morning were beginning to bleed through the night sky. 'I thought they'd be grateful for what I did, but they said I'd never see her again. They were mocking me. I'd helped them and it was all for nothing. They wanted me to know that.' He took off his glasses and wiped his eyes with the back of his hand. 'I don't understand what they want, Matt. I don't understand anything any more. This whole city...' His voice trailed away.

'Mr Adams, I can help you,' Matt said. 'I can find her and get her out of here.'

'How? You're just a kid.'

'I need to have a shower and get changed.' Matt was still dripping water onto the expensive carpet. 'Do you have spare clothes?'

'I don't know . . .' He waved vaguely in the direction of the bedroom.

Matt drew on the last of his strength, forcing his mind into gear. He had to find Scarlett. That was the reason he was here. But that wasn't going to be possible, not if she had been taken to some secret location. Was she even still in Hong Kong? He guessed that she would have to be. The Old Ones were using her to get at him. Surely they would keep her there until he arrived.

How to find her? Matt's eyes were desperately heavy. All he wanted to do was go to bed. But somehow he knew that this was his last chance. He had to bring all the pieces together, here in this room. First there was Paul Adams, destroying himself, wracked with guilt and misery. Then there was the man called Lohan, somewhere in Hong Kong with his thousand foot-soldiers. Richard and Jamie. Maybe they had found their way over to them. And the fireworks. What was the name he had seen, stencilled on the crates?

And suddenly he had it.

'Listen to me,' he said. 'I may be able to find Scarlett, but you're going to have to help me. Will you do that?'

'I'll do anything.'

'Does your telephone work here? And do you have a phone book?'

Paul Adams had been expecting something more. How would a simple phone call save his daughter? 'It's over there . . .' He gestured with the hand that was still holding the whisky glass.

Matt went over to the telephone. It was a desperate plan. But he could think of no other way.

He picked it up and began to dial.

*   *   *

They came for him just after seven o'clock.

Matt was asleep on the sofa, dressed in jeans and a sweater that didn't really fit but were a lot better than the ones he had dumped in the bathroom. He had taken a hot shower, washing the smell of the harbour off his skin and out of his hair. And then he had fallen into a deep, dreamless sleep.

He hadn't heard the police arrive. They had driven down Harcourt Road and turned into Wisdom Court without sirens. He was woken by the sound of the door being smashed open and the shouts of a dozen men as they poured into the flat. Some of them were carrying guns. It was hard to say who was in charge. Suddenly they were everywhere and Matt was surrounded.

He started to get up but something hit him in the chest. It was a dart, fired from what looked like a toy gun, trailing wires behind it. But the next thing he knew, there was an explosion of pain and he was literally thrown off his feet as a bolt of electricity seared through him. He had been hit with a Tasar, a weapon used by police forces all over the world. Despite its appearance, it had fired an electrical charge that had resulted in the total loss of his neuromuscular control. Matt had never felt pain like it. It seemed to shatter every bone in his body. He heard an animal whimper and realized it was him.

Matt collapsed to the ground, unable to move. The policemen weren't taking any chances. They had deliberately neutralized him before he could use his power against them.

A moment later, two of them fell on him. They twisted his arms behind his back and he felt cold steel against his wrists as a pair of handcuffs were locked into place. One of the policemen grabbed him by the hair and twisted him round so that he was in a kneeling position.

Another man appeared at the door.

'So this is Matthew Freeman,' he said.

The chairman of the Nightrise Corporation had wanted to make sure that everything was safe before he came in. Now he strutted forward and stood over Matt, looking down at him with a smile on his face. Although he had been hastily summoned out of bed, he was as smartly dressed as always, in a new suit and polished shoes. 'What a great pleasure to meet you,' he added.

Matt ignored him. He twisted round so that he was facing Paul Adams. His eyes were filled with anger. 'What have you done?' he yelled.

'I called them while you were in the shower.' Adams went over to the chairman. It was clear he was afraid of him. He stood there, wringing his hands together as if trying to wash them clean. 'This is the boy, Mr Chairman,' he muttered. 'He came to the flat in the middle of the night. I called you the moment I could.'

'You've done very well,' the chairman muttered. He was still gazing at Matt. 'I never thought it would be this easy,' he said.

Matt swore at him.

'I knew you were looking for him, Mr Chairman,' Paul Adams went on. 'And now you have him. So you don't need Scarly. Tell me you'll let Scarly go.'

The chairman turned his head slowly and examined Scarlett's father as if he were a doctor about to break bad news. 'I will not let Scarly go,' he said. 'I will never let Scarly go.'

'Then at least let me see her. I've given you the boy. Don't I deserve a reward?'

'You most certainly do,' the chairman said.

He nodded at one of the policemen, who shot Paul Adams in the head. Matt saw the spray of blood as the back of his skull was blown off. He was dead instantly. His knees buckled underneath him and he fell to one side.

'A quick death,' the chairman remarked. He nodded at Matt. 'Soon you'll be wishing you could have had one too.'

He turned and walked out of the room. Two of the policemen reached forward and jerked Matt to his feet. Then they dragged him out, along the corridor and down to the city below.

TAI FUNG

SIGNAL ONE

The dragon was moving towards Hong Kong, closing in with deadly precision, gaining strength as it crossed the water. Scarlett had summoned it and it had heard. Even she couldn't turn it back now.

It had begun its life as nothing more than a front of warm air, rising into the sky. But then, very quickly, a swirl of cloud had formed, spinning faster and faster with a dark, unblinking eye at the centre. By the time the weather satellites had transmitted the first pictures from the Strait of Luzon, it was already too late. The dragon was awake. Its appetite was as big as the ocean where it had been born and it would destroy anything that stood in its path.

The dragon was a typhoon.

Tai fung.

The words mean 'big wind', but they went nowhere near describing the most powerful force of nature; a storm that contained a hundred storms within it. The typhoon would travel at over two hundred miles an hour. Its eye might be thirty miles wide. The hurricane winds around it would generate as much energy in one second as ten nuclear bombs. To the Chinese, typhoons are also known as 'the dragon's breath', as if they come from some terrible monster living deep in the sea.

Since 1884, the Hong Kong Observatory had put out a series of warnings whenever a typhoon had come within five hundred miles and each warning has come with a beacon, or a signal, attached. Signal One was shaped like a letter T and warned the local populace to stand by. Signal Three, an upside down T, was more serious. Now people were told to stay at home, not to travel unless absolutely necessary. Later on came Signal Eight, a triangle, Signal Nine, an hourglass, and finally, most terrifyingly, Signal Ten. Perhaps appropriately, this took the shape of a cross. Signal Ten meant devastation. It would almost certainly bring wholesale loss of life.

And that was what was on its way now.

But there were no warnings. Nobody had been prepared for a typhoon in November, which was months after the storm season should have ended. And anyway, no typhoon could possibly have formed so quickly. It would normally take at least a week. This one had reached its full power in less than a day. The whole thing was impossible.

Nor was there anyone left to send out the signals. Hong Kong Observatory had been abandoned. Many of the scientists had left. The others were too scared to come to work as the city continued its descent into sickness and death.

Unseen, the dragon rushed towards them. The skyscrapers were already in its sight. Suddenly they seemed tiny and insubstantial as, with a great roar, it fell on them. By the time anyone realized what was happening it was already far too late.

SIGNAL TWO

The chairman of the Nightrise Corporation was wondering how many people had died in the last twenty-four hours and how many more would die in the next. He could imagine them, sixty-six floors below, crawling over the pavements, begging for help that would never come, finally losing consciousness in a cloud of misery and pain. He himself would leave Hong Kong very soon. His work here was almost finished. It was time to claim his reward.

The Old Ones were going to give him the whole of Asia to rule over in recognition of what he had achieved. Even Ghengis Khan hadn't been as powerful as that. He would live in a palace, an old-fashioned one with deep, marble baths and banqueting rooms and gardens a mile long. The world leaders who survived would bow in front of him and anyone who had ever offended him, in business or in private life, would die in ingenious ways that he had already designed. He would open a theatre of blood and they would star in it. And anything he wanted he would have. The thought of it made his head spin.

He was behind his desk in his office on the executive floor of The Nail and he was not alone. There was a man sitting on the same leather sofa that Scarlett Adams had occupied just a week before. The man had travelled a very long way and he was still looking crumpled from his flight. He was elderly, dressed in a shabby, brown suit that didn't quite fit him. It was the right size but it hung awkwardly. The man was bald with two small tufts of white hair around his ears and white eyebrows. He looked ill at ease in this smart office. He was out of place and he knew it. But he was glad to be here. It had been a journey he was determined to make.

His name was Gregor Malenkov. For many years he had been known as Father Gregory, but he planned to put that behind him now. He had left the Monastery of the Cry for Mercy for good. He, too, had come for his reward.

'So how do you like Hong Kong?' the chairman asked.

'It's an extraordinary city,' Father Gregory rasped. 'Quite extraordinary. I came here as a young man but it was much smaller then. Half the buildings weren't here and the airport was in a different place. All these lights! All the traffic and the noise! I have to say, I hardly recognized it.'

'A week from now, it will be completely unrecognizable,' the chairman said. 'It will have become a necropolis. I'm sure you will understand what that means, a man of your learning.'

'A city of the dead.'

'Exactly. The entire population has begun to die. In just a matter of days, there will be no one left. The corpses are already piling up in the street. The hospitals are full—not that they would be any use as the doctors and the nurses are dying too. Nobody even bothers to call the cemeteries.

There's no room there. And soon things will get much, much worse. It will be interesting to watch.'

'How are you killing them?' Father Gregory asked. 'Would I be right in thinking it is something to do with the pollution?'

'You would be entirely correct, Father Gregory. Although perhaps I should not call you that, as I understand you are no longer in holy orders.' The chairman stood up and went over to the window, but the view had been almost completely obliterated by the mist which swirled around the building, chasing its own tail. There was going to be a storm. He could just make out the water down in the harbour. The water was choppy, rising into angry waves.

'There has always been pollution, blowing in from China,' he continued. 'And the strange thing is that the people here have tolerated it. Coal-fired power stations. Car exhausts. They have always accepted that it's a price that has to be paid for the comforts of modern life.'

'And you have made it worse?'

'The Old Ones have added a few extra chemicals—some very poisonous ones—to the mix. You've seen the results. The elderly and the weak have been the first to go, but the rest of the city will follow if they are exposed to it for very much longer. Which they will be. An unpleasant death. We are safe, of course, inside The Nail. The air is filtered. We just have to be careful not to spend too long in the street.'

Father Gregory pressed his fingers together. His sty had got much worse. The eyeball was now jammed, no longer able to move. Only his good eye watched the chairman. 'I have to say, I'm disappointed,' he said. 'I was looking forward to meeting—to actually seeing—the Old Ones.'

'The Old Ones have left Hong Kong. They have a great deal of work to do, preparing for a war that will be starting very soon. As soon as they heard that Matthew Freeman had been taken, they went.'

'I don't understand why they don't show themselves to the world,' Father Gregory said. 'You have two of the Gatekeepers. So surely nothing can stop them . . .'

'It's not the way they work. If the Old Ones told the world that they existed, people would unite against them. That would defeat the point. By keeping themselves hidden, they can let humanity tear itself apart. That is what they enjoy.'

There was a moment's silence. Father Gregory licked his lips and something ugly came into his eyes. 'I want to see the girl,' he said. 'I still can't believe that she managed to break free when I had her. I had plans . . .'

'Yes, that was most unfortunate,' the chairman agreed. 'Well, right now they are together. The boy came all this way to find her, so I thought it would be amusing to let them spend one day in each other's company.'

'Is that safe?'

'The two of them are locked up very securely and nobody knows where they are. The boy has certain abilities which make him dangerous. But as for the girl . . .'

'What is her power?'

'It seems that she drew the short straw. I'm afraid Scarlett Adams is not quite the superhero one might have imagined.' The chairman smiled. 'She has the ability to predict the weather. That's all. She can tell if it's going to rain or if the sun is going to shine. As she will never see either of these things again, it will not do her very much good. We are sending her away tonight. To another country.'

'You can't kill her of course.'

'It's vital that both children are kept alive. In pain, but alive. We are going to bury them in separate rooms, many thousands of miles apart. They will be given limited amounts of food and water, but no human contact. The Old Ones have asked me to blind Matt Freeman and that will be done just before Scarlett leaves. We want her to take the horror of it with her. In the end, she will probably go mad. It will be one of the last memories that she has.'

'Excellent. I'd like to be there when it happens.'

'That may not be possible.'

Father Gregory was disappointed. But he continued anyway. 'What about the other boy?' he asked.

'Jamie Tyler?' The chairman was still standing at the window. 'He is somewhere here in Hong Kong. We haven't yet been able to find him.'

'Have you looked for him?'

The chairman blinked slowly. Far below, two Star Ferries were crossing each other's paths, fighting the storm as they made their way across the harbour. Where had the storm come from? It seemed to be getting stronger. He was surprised the ferries were still operating and looked forward to the time when they finally stopped. It had always annoyed him, watching them go back and forth.

A boat will be the death of you. And it will happen in Hong Kong.

A prophecy that had been made by a fortune-teller. Well, soon there would be no more boats. There would be no more Hong Kong.

'Jamie Tyler can't leave the city,' he said. 'Unless, of course, he dies in the street and gets thrown into the sea. Either way, he is of no concern to us.'

There was another silence.

'But now, my dear Father Gregory,' the chairman said. 'It is time for you to go.'

'I am a little tired,' Father Gregory admitted.

'It has been a pleasure meeting you. But—please—let me show you out . . .'

There was a handle on the edge of one of the windows and the chairman seized hold of it and pulled. The entire window slid aside and the wind rushed in, the mist swirling round and round. Papers fluttered off the desk. The stench of the pollution filled the room.

Father Gregory stared. 'I don't understand . . .' he began.

'It's perfectly simple,' the chairman said. 'You said it yourself. You let the girl escape. You let her slip through your hands. You don't really think that the Old Ones would let that go unpunished?'

'But . . . I found her!' Father Gregory was staring at the gap. 'If it hadn't been for me, you would never have known who she was!'

'And that is why they have granted you an easy death.' The chairman had to shout to make himself heard. 'Please don't waste any more of my time, Father Gregory. It's time for you to go!'

Father Gregory stared at the open window, at the clouds rushing past outside. A single tear trickled from his good eye. But he understood.

The chairman was right. He had failed.

'I've enjoyed meeting you,' he said.

'Goodbye, Father Gregory.'

The old man walked across the room and stepped out of the window. The chairman waited a moment, then slid it shut behind him. It was good to be back in the warm again. He wiped some raindrops off his jacket.

The storm was definitely getting worse.

SIGNAL THREE

The Tai Shan Temple was very similar to all the other temples in Hong Kong.

It was perhaps a little larger, with three separate chambers connected by short corridors, but it had the same curving roof made of dark green tiles and it was set back behind a wall, on the edge of a park, in its own private world. Inside, it was filled with smoke, both from the coils of incense that hung from the ceiling and from the oven, which was constantly burning bundles of paper and clothes as sacrifices to the Mountain of the East. There were several altars dedicated to a variety of gods who were represented by standing, sitting and kneeling statues . . . a whole crowd of them, brilliantly coloured, staring out with ferocious eyes.

Despite the bad weather, there were about fifteen people at prayer in the main chamber, bowing with armfuls of incense, muttering quietly to themselves. They were many different ages, men and women, and to all appearances they looked exactly the same as the people who came daily to Man Mo or Tin Hau. And yet there was something about them that suggested that religion was not, in fact, the first thing on their minds. They were too tense, too watchful. Their eyes were fixed on a single entrance at the back of the building—a low, wooden door with a five-pointed star cut into the surface.

The worshippers—who were, in fact, no such thing—had very simple instructions. Any child who passed through that door was to be seized. If they resisted, they could be hurt badly but preferably not killed. The same applied to any young person coming in from the street. They were to be stopped before they got anywhere near the door. The people in the temple were all armed with guns and knives, hidden beneath their clothes. They were in constant touch with The Nail and could call for backup at any time.

This was the ambush that Matt had feared. It was the reason he had refused to take the shortcut to Hong Kong. He had been right from the very start.

The fifteen of them stood there, muttering prayers they didn't believe and bowing to gods they didn't respect. And outside, gusts of wind—growing stronger by the minute—hurled themselves at the temple walls, battering at them as if trying to break through, tearing up the surrounding earth and the grass, whistling around the corners. A tile slid off the roof and smashed on the ground. A shutter came loose and was instantly torn away. The rain, travelling horizontally now, cut into the brickwork. The traffic in the street had completely snarled up. The drivers couldn't see. There was nothing they could do.

The wind rushed in and the flames inside the temple furnace bent, flickered and were suddenly extinguished. Nobody noticed. All their attention was fixed on the doorway. That was what they were there for. Ignoring the storm, they waited for the first of the Gatekeepers to arrive.

SIGNAL FOUR

Scarlett was in a dark place, but someone was nudging her, trying to draw her back into the light. Unwillingly, she opened her eyes to find a boy leaning over her, shaking her awake. She recognized him at once and knew that the fact that he was with her, that he was bruised and dishevelled, could mean only one thing . . . and it was the worst news of all. He was here because of her. The Old Ones must have tricked him into coming to Hong Kong and now the two of them were prisoners. Scarlett felt a sense of great anger and bitterness. She had been drawn into this against her will. And it was already over. She had never been given a chance.

'Matt . . .' she said.

At last the two of them were together. But this wasn't how she had hoped they would meet. She drew herself into a sitting position and rubbed her eyes. They had given her back her own clothes but her hair, cut so short, still felt unfamiliar to her. At least she had lost the contact lenses. She had taken

341

them out the moment she had been left to herself.

'Are you OK?' Matt asked.

'No.' She sounded miserable. 'How long have I been asleep?'

'I don't know. They only brought me here an hour ago.'

'When was that?'

'About eight o'clock.'

'Night or day?'

'Day.'

Matt examined his surroundings. They were in a bare, windowless room with brick walls and a concrete floor. The only light came from a bulb set in a wire mesh cage. From the moment the door—solid steel—had been closed and locked, he'd had to fight a sense of claustrophobia. They were deep underground. The policemen who had brought him here had forced him down four flights of stairs and then along a corridor that was like a tunnel. Ordinary policemen. The same as the ones who had arrested him. It seemed that the shape-changers, the fly-soldiers and all the other creatures of the Old Ones had decided to leave Hong Kong. He wondered why.

Despite everything, he had been relieved to find Scarlett. She looked very different from the photograph he had seen of her. He couldn't imagine what it must have been like for her, being stuck here on her own.

'Why are you here?' Scarlett asked. She still couldn't keep the disappointment out of her voice.

'I came for you,' Matt said. He wanted to tell her more but he didn't dare. There was always a chance that they were being listened to.

'You shouldn't have. I've mucked everything up.

I'd have got away if I hadn't . . .' Scarlett stopped herself. She couldn't bring herself to talk about her last meeting with her father.

Matt sat next to her so that they were shoulder to shoulder with their legs stretched out on the floor. From the way he moved, she could see that he had been hurt. He looked pale and exhausted. 'Why don't you tell me everything that happened to you?' he suggested. 'You could start by telling me where we are. Do you know?'

She nodded. 'The chairman came to see me . . .'

'Who is the chairman?'

'Just some creep in a suit.'

'I think I may have met him.'

'He wanted to gloat over me,' Scarlett continued. 'He told me that you were on your way but I hoped he was lying. This is an old prison. We're right in the middle of Hong Kong. It was left over from Victorian times.'

'So when do they serve breakfast?'

'They don't. It's bread and cold soup and they bring it once a day.'

Matt lowered his voice. 'Hopefully, we won't be here that long,' he said. It was as much as he dared tell her, but even so Scarlett felt a glimmer of hope. 'You know I went to your home in Dulwich,' he said, changing the subject.

'Was that you in the car? There was an accident . . .'

'It was no accident.'

'I knew it had to be you,' Scarlett said. 'They planned it all very carefully, didn't they? Using me to get you here. Are any of the others with you?'

Matt nodded briefly and Scarlett understood. They both had to be careful what they said. She

343

gazed at him as if seeing him for the first and the last time. 'I can't believe you're here. I can't believe I'm really talking to you. Do you know, I've even dreamed about you.'

'Don't worry about it,' Matt said. 'We all dream about each other. It's how it works.'

'There's so much I don't understand.'

'Join the club.'

'It looks like I already have.' She took a deep breath. 'I don't know where my story even begins, but I suppose I'd better start with St Meredith's . . .'

She told him—briefly and without fuss—and as she spoke, Matt knew that he was going to like her. She had been through so much, and in a way her experiences reminded him of his own at Lesser Malling, the way she had been reeled into something so completely beyond her understanding. And yet she had coped with it. She had been brought here. She had been locked in this room for three days. But she hadn't cracked. She was ready to fight back.

She finished talking and it seemed to Matt that just for a moment the building trembled as something, a shockwave, travelled through the walls. Scarlett looked up, alarmed. Part of her knew what was happening and had even been expecting it.

'What . . . ?' Matt began.

'It was nothing.' She said it so hastily that he could see she didn't want to talk about it, didn't even want to imagine what might be happening outside. 'Tell me about yourself,' she went on, quickly. 'Tell me how you got here. Did you go to the temple? They've got people there waiting for

344

you. They thought you'd come through one of the doors.'

'I didn't . . .'

He told her his own story, or part of it, starting in Peru. It would have taken too long to tell her the whole thing and he was still afraid of being overheard. From Nazca to London to Macau . . . It had been a long journey and it was only now that they both saw how closely they had been following each other's paths.

Matt finished by explaining how he had found his way to Wisdom Court. This was the difficult part. He had seen Scarlett's father die and he had been at least in part responsible. How was he going to break the news?

But she was already ahead of him. 'That jersey you're wearing,' she said. She had suddenly realized. 'It's his.'

'Yes,' Matt admitted.

'Where is he now?' Matt didn't answer and she continued. 'They've killed him, haven't they?'

Matt nodded. He didn't want to remember what he had seen in the last moments before he had been taken out of Wisdom Court.

Scarlett's face didn't change but suddenly there were tears in her eyes. 'It was all his fault,' she said. 'He thought he could make a deal with these people—the Old Ones—but they would never have got me if it hadn't been for him.' She paused. 'I don't know, Matt. I suppose that's the way they work. They get ordinary people to do evil things for them. They used him. He really thought he was helping me. And now he's betrayed you too.'

The building shivered a second time. It wasn't as strong as it had been before but they both felt it.

'You know that Hong Kong is dying,' Scarlett said. 'The chairman told me. They're doing it deliberately. They want to turn it into what they call a necropolis. A city of the dead.'

'I saw some of it last night,' Matt said. 'It was horrible.'

'Don't tell me. I lived in it. I can't believe I didn't see what was going on.' She sighed. 'What will happen to us, Matt? Are we going to be killed?'

'They don't want to kill us,' Matt said. 'It's complicated. But killing us doesn't really help.'

'Then what?'

'They think they've beaten us, but they haven't. The others are still out there. And you and me . . .'

'What about us?'

'They put us together because they want to crow over us. But that's their mistake. Because . . .'

He didn't finish the sentence.

There was an explosion. It was loud and immediate—and it came from somewhere inside the building.

'What . . . ?' Scarlett began.

Then the light went out.

SIGNAL FIVE

Lohan had used the storm as cover, closing in on the prison through streets that had quickly emptied as the weather had become more intense. He had only been given one night to prepare the attack, but he had still managed to assemble a small army. He had a hundred men with him, all of them well-armed. The Triads had been smuggling weapons across Asia for many years, supplying anyone from terrorists to mercenaries. Lohan had simply taken what he needed. He had plenty of choice.

Meanwhile, Jet and Sing would be arriving at the Tai Shan Temple. They both had the rank of 426, Red Pole as it was known, making them fighting unit lieutenants. They had another fifty men with them and both operations were to begin at the same moment. There was one door out of Hong Kong. The way there had to be cleared.

Lohan knew where Matt had been taken because he had followed him. This was what Matt had been unable to tell Scarlett. He had played a trick on the chairman. Just for once, he was the one pulling the strings.

Matt had contacted Lohan the night before, the call forwarded through the Kung Hing Tao firework company. The Triad leader already knew what had happened. Richard and Jamie were with him. The two of them had made it out of the water and over to Kowloon. They were standing next to him, worrying desperately about Matt, when the phone rang.

'We have to find Scarlett,' Matt had said. 'And there's only one way to do it. We have to let the Old Ones capture me.'

'How will you do that?'

'Paul Adams—Scarlett's father—will call them and tell them I'm at Wisdom Court. They won't suspect anything. They know that he wants Scarlett back and they'll think he's still trying to help them.'

'And then?'

'You have your men outside. You follow me wherever they take me.'

'How do you know they'll take you to Scarlett?'

'I don't . . . not for sure. But my guess is they'll probably hold us together. I know the way these people think. They'll want to parade us, to boast about how they've beaten us. Having the two of us together will make it more fun for them. Anyway, I haven't got any other ideas so we'll just have to risk it.'

Richard had come onto the phone. He had heard what Matt was suggesting. 'You can't do this,' he pleaded. 'It's too dangerous. Please, Matt, think what could go wrong.'

'We don't know where she is, Richard. There's no other way we'll find her.'

'What about Paul Adams? Once they have no further use for him, you know they'll kill him.'

'He's prepared to risk it. He knows what he's done. And he'll do anything to get Scarlett freed.'

It had worked out just as Matt had hoped. Six police cars had arrived at Wisdom Court just after seven o'clock. Lohan—with Richard and Jamie crouching next to him—had watched the police go in. They had seen the chairman arrive and leave and they were still there when Matt, semi-conscious and in pain, had been dragged out. Jamie had started forward at that moment, wanting to go to him. But Richard had grabbed hold of him, forcing him to remain still. This was Matt's plan. It was all or nothing.

Matt had been driven across the city, never out of sight of Lohan's men. They had seen him disappear into the prison close to Hollywood Road. So now they knew where he was being held.

Hopefully, Scarlett would be there too. As the storm had worsened, Lohan had surrounded the prison, his men closing in from all sides.

The storm.

Lohan was beginning to think that it was getting out of control. In all the years that he had been in Hong Kong, he had never experienced anything like it. When he stood up, he could feel the wind trying to batter him down again. Dust and dead leaves whipped into his face. He could hear the air currents howling as they rushed through the streets. If it got any worse, it would be dangerous out here. But then, of course, it was dangerous anyway. If the storm destroyed the city, it would only be finishing what the Old Ones had already begun.

A crash of thunder. Rain lashing down so hard that he could see it bouncing off the parked cars, turning into miniature rivers that coursed along the side of the road. In seconds, he was soaked. Richard was next to him. 'What's going on?' he muttered.

'We must move now,' Lohan said.

Victoria Prison was a huge, solid building with barred windows and a single, massive door—the only way in. Six armed guards stood outside it in the rain, dressed in uniforms, with their faces partly obscured by their caps. Lohan, Richard and Jamie were watching from the doorway of an antique shop across the road. Lohan's strategy was simple. There was no time to be clever. He knew he had to break in as quickly, as decisively as possible. Once the enemy knew he was there, they would fight back.

He gave the signal.

There was an explosion—the same explosion that Matt had heard—as a rocket launcher, concealed in a parked van, fired a 40mm shell at the main door. The prison hadn't been built to withstand such an attack. The doors were blown apart in a ball of flame. Half the guards were killed instantly. The rest were cut down by a burst of machine-gun fire as the Triad fighters surged forward, pouring out of alleyways and rising up from behind parked cars. Further down the road, two of Lohan's men, disguised as construction workers, cut off the main power supply, isolating the prison and short circuiting the alarms.

'Move!' Richard and Jamie were unarmed but they ran forward with Lohan and in through the shattered doors.

And then they were inside the prison. Lohan's people were spreading in every direction, through the upper floors, smashing open the doors to reveal the empty cells behind them. Some of them were armed with guns and grenades. Others carried swords and chain-sticks. It was pitch black inside the building now that the electricity had been cut, but they had brought electric torches with them, strapped to their shoulders, the beams slicing through the dark and showing the way ahead. Lohan's orders were clear. Kill anyone who gets in your way. Find Matt and Scarlett. We have only minutes to get them out.

There were more guards on the upper levels. Although the building held only two prisoners, the chairman had taken no chances. Now they opened fire on the invaders. Lohan saw the flash of bullets, heard some of the Triad men cry out. A few bodies fell. Then someone threw a grenade. Another fireball, and one of the guards pitched forward as if diving into a swimming pool, disappearing into the darkness below.

Lohan himself led a group of fighters four floors down into the basement, Richard and Jamie close behind him. Only now was Richard beginning to see the hopelessness of the task. There had to be at least two hundred cells in the prison. Were they really going to blow every one of them open? They came to a corridor with more steel doors set at intervals. A guard ran towards them, bringing his machine gun round to aim.

'Drop the gun!' Jamie said. 'Lie on the floor.'

The guard did as he was told. A second guard appeared. He was less fortunate. Lohan shot him down. They had been in the prison for less than three minutes but they knew that re-inforcements would already be on the way. There was another explosion upstairs, a scream, the clatter of bullets hitting metal.

Thirty doors stretched out in front of them. There was no point looking for bolts or keys. Lohan rapped out an order and his men blew them open, one at a time, using balls of plastic explosive. Richard and Jamie continued forward as, one after another, the doors were smashed out of their frames, orange flames briefly flaring up. The corridor stank of cordite. Smoke and brick dust filled the air. But every cell was empty. How much more time did they have?

'They're at the end,' Jamie said suddenly. 'The last door on the left.'

Lohan stared at him. But Richard nodded, relief surging through him. Somehow Jamie had managed to connect with them in his own way . . .

telepathically. Lohan shouted something and his men ran down to the door he had indicated. A final blast. It swung open. Two figures came out into the corridor, choking and covered in dust. It was Matt and Scarlett.

'Matt!' Richard grabbed hold of his friend and embraced him. The night before, when he had pulled himself out of the water, he had been afraid that he would never see him again. 'Are you OK?'

Matt nodded. 'This is Scarlett.'

'I'm delighted to meet you.' Richard didn't know what else to say. He examined the girl with the close-cropped hair. She looked worn out.

Jamie said nothing but he went over to her so that the three Gatekeepers were together.

'We have to get to the Tai Shan Temple,' Matt said.

Lohan was impressed. The boy was only fifteen but already he had assumed command. The experiences of the past twenty-four hours didn't seem to have had any effect on him. But there was still more trouble to come. Quickly, Lohan took out his mobile phone, pressed a button and spoke a few words. He waited until he had heard what he wanted, then he turned to Matt. 'The temple is safe now,' he said. 'But we have another problem and it may be more serious. There is a storm. In fact my people are saying that it may be something worse . . .'

But they had all become aware of it. Above the gunfire and the explosions. Beyond the battle that was taking place inside the prison, the wind was screaming. The whole building was shuddering. The full force of the typhoon had fallen on Hong Kong and its total destruction had begun.

SIGNAL SIX

The sun was setting in Cuzco, the ancient city of the Incas, in Peru. There was a band playing and the sound of pan-pipes and the throb of drums rose up into the evening air. The shadows were stretching out over the foothills. The restaurants and cafés were beginning to fill up at the end of another day.

Pedro knew that they shouldn't be here. This wasn't Matt's plan. He wished that they had been able to speak over the satellite telephone, but for the past forty-eight hours there had been only silence. A whole world separated them. They were thousands of miles apart. But he was about to take the single step that would bring them together. He wondered if it was a good idea.

Not that he had been given any choice.

The night before, Pedro had woken up to find Scott leaning over him. The two boys were sharing a stone house in Vilcabamba, high up in the Andes. This was the lost city where Pedro had gone with Matt when they were hiding from Diego Salamanda. It was hidden above the cloud forest in an extraordinary location, a mountain peak that couldn't be seen by anyone. Getting there had involved a helicopter ride and then a one-day hike from Cuzco. The city itself could only be reached by a stone staircase which could vanish in a single moment.

'Scott . . . ? What is it?'

Scott was deathly pale and his eyes were full of worry. Pedro had never seen him like this before. 'Jamie's in trouble,' he said. 'We have to go to Hong Kong.'

'We can't . . .'

'Pedro. You don't understand. We have to go straight away. I have to go to Jamie. I've had a dream.'

The dreamworld. All of them had been there. They all knew its significance. They had talked about it often enough. Pedro knew that he couldn't argue. If Scott had been sent a message, they couldn't ignore it, particularly if it involved his brother. And yet the doors were supposed to be too dangerous. It was the whole reason Matt and Jamie had flown to Europe and why the two of them had been left behind.

'Are you sure . . . ?' he began.

Scott wasn't in the mood for an argument. 'I'm leaving as soon as it's light,' he said. 'You can come with me or you can stay behind.'

The next morning they left together. One of the Incas escorted them down to the clearing where the helicopter was waiting and then it was a two-hour flight to Cuzco airport. All the time, Scott had been silent and intense. He still hadn't explained what he had seen. He was often reserved but now he seemed miles away, staring ahead with empty eyes. Pedro was trying not to think what they were letting themselves in for. Of all the Gatekeepers, he alone had never been through one of the doors, and the thought of transporting himself half-way round the world filled him with dread.

And here they were now in Cuzco. It was a

beautiful evening with hundreds of tourists milling around the brightly coloured stalls that were spread out in front of them. The cathedral would be closing soon. The last visitors were coming out, surrounded by street children, begging for money and sweets. Taxis, like wind-up toys made out of tin, were buzzing around the main square.

Pedro was hungry but he didn't dare suggest that they stop and eat. He knew what the answer would be.

'There it is . . .' Scott pointed at a great pile of bricks and ornate windows, a Spanish church built on the site of a place of worship that had been there centuries before. The Temple of Coricancha. It was where he and Jamie had found themselves when they first arrived in Peru. Inside was the doorway that had brought them from a cave in Nevada.

Neither of them spoke again. Pedro shook his head and followed as, with grim determination, Scott began to walk across the square.

SIGNAL SEVEN

Matt and Scarlett stood in the shelter of the prison, knowing that they couldn't leave. Hong Kong was being torn apart by a force so devastating it was as if they had arrived at some chapter in the Bible when all the old prophecies happened and Judgement Day finally arrived.

Smashed buildings and debris were being flung along the street as if they weighed nothing. As they looked out of the broken doorway, a huge neon sign spun past like an oversized playing card. It was followed by a table, several crates, a lawn mower, part of a piano . . . They had somehow been sucked out of the shops and sent on their way as if they were prizes in some insane TV game show. Matt could actually see the air currents. Mixed with the rain, they had become a thousand grey needles that raced along the streets, slamming into cars and tipping them over, flattening everything in their path.

He looked up and saw two clouds rushing together, moving faster than he could have believed. They hit and there was a massive burst of thunder. A bolt of electricity so bright that it hurt his eyes crackled down and smashed into a skyscraper half a mile away, cutting it in two. Shards of glass and broken pieces of metal burst outwards as the top seven storeys of the building leaned over and then fell, trailing wires and pipes. Matt didn't see where they landed or how many people were killed but he heard the massive explosion as they hit the street below. Despite the rain, what remained of the building caught fire. The orange flames licked at the falling water, desperately trying to climb into the air.

'We must wait . . .' Lohan was right next to him. Matt understood what he meant. If they took so much as one step forward out of the protection of the walls, they would be whisked away. He was having to shout the words to make himself heard.

'We can't wait!' Matt shouted back. 'We only have this one chance. We must leave Hong Kong now.'

Scarlett was behind him with Richard and

Jamie. Matt turned round and their eyes met—and in that moment they both understood what was happening. They could have no secrets from each other. 'This is you!' he shouted at her. The wind was still howling. A window on the other side of the road was suddenly torn out, the glass leaping away. 'You've done this . . .'

'No!' Scarlett shook her head, trying to deny it.

'We all have powers. All five of us. This is yours.'

And Scarlett knew he was right. In a way, she had known it all along.

Her real name wasn't Scarlett Adams. White Lotus believed that she was a reincarnation of Lin Mo, a figure out of Chinese mythology, a goddess of the sea. And if she had once been a goddess, then she would have a power that went far beyond anything humanly possible. The chairman of Nightrise had made another mistake. He had thought she could only predict the weather. In fact she could control it.

The evidence had always been there. At school in Dulwich, when Scarlett had wanted to go on a history trip, the weather had cleared up against all expectations. The same thing had happened again in Hong Kong when she needed to get to The Peak. Against all the forecasts, the rain had stopped and the sun had suddenly come out.

She had even used the same power at the battle, ten thousand years before. Jamie had once described it to Matt. Just as Pedro had appeared with his reinforcements, a storm had started, the rain coming down so violently that the Old Ones had been unable to see him.

It hadn't been a coincidence.

It had been her.

The chairman had claimed that she was the weakest of the Five. He had been wrong. She was by far the most powerful.

'You can stop it!' Matt shouted.

'I can't!' Scarlett shook her head. She had brought the dragon. She accepted that much. But looking inside herself, after three days in prison, after all she had been through, she knew that she didn't have the strength to turn it back.

'Then you can protect us. You can keep it away.'

Scarlett looked out into the road, at the crashing rain, the buildings being scattered like confetti, cars spinning crazily, broken pieces of wood and metal hurtling past. Had she really done this, brought destruction on an entire city? How many people would she have killed? The thought terrified her more than anything else she had seen. Was she really responsible for this?

'I can't do it, Matt . . .'

'You have to . . . We have to reach the temple.'

Lohan understood. 'It's not so far from here,' he shouted. 'I can show you . . .'

'Scar . . . ?' Matt looked at her.

And maybe it was simply the fact that he had used that name, a name from ten thousand years ago. Maybe that was the trigger. But in that second, something changed. Scarlett took a deep breath. For too long she had been a victim, pushed around by the chairman, by the Old Ones, even by the Triads. It was time to put that behind her. She was a Gatekeeper. That was what had brought her into all this and suddenly she felt a great anger for everything she had lost—her friends, her home,—even her father. And with the anger came the full

358

knowledge of her own strength. She knew what she had to do.

'Follow me,' she said.

They left the prison. First Lohan, then Scarlett and Matt, with Richard and Jamie behind. They stepped outside into the rain, into the wind, into an endless explosion as nature pounded the city with all its strength. They should have been thrown off their feet instantly, or battered senseless to the ground. But the wind spun around them. The rain was lashing everything but they remained dry. They walked into the heart of the typhoon and it swallowed them up without touching them. It was as if they were inside a glass ball that surrounded and protected them. They could barely see. Everything was chaos. But while they stayed together, they were safe.

Lohan led the way but it was Scarlett who made it possible. She seemed to be in a trance, gazing straight ahead, her arms by her side. Matt kept close to her, knowing that his life depended on her protection. All around them, everywhere he looked, brick walls crumbled, buildings fell, windows shattered and, spinning in the rain, lethal shards of broken glass came slashing down. Again and again the thunder sounded. The clouds were a boiling mass.

They didn't hurry. There was no need to. No living thing was going to come out in the typhoon and the five of them were completely invisible. Scarlett was more confident now. She looked almost relaxed. Walking next to her, Matt was amazed by the extent of her power. He could feel it flowing out of her. She was a girl and she was fifteen years old. But she could destroy the entire world.

Another building fell behind them, crumbling in on itself as if it had simply lost the will to live. Bricks showered down, slamming into the pavement, but not near them. The road continued straight ahead. They could see the park. Most of the trees had been uprooted and turned into flying battering rams. The few that remained were bending over, kissing the ground. The Tai Shan Temple was on the other side. Matt was surprised that it was still standing, but perhaps the wall that surrounded it had protected it from the worst of the weather.

Lohan pointed. Scarlett nodded. There was no need for any of them to speak. They had made it. They had crossed Hong Kong in the middle of a Signal Ten typhoon and they had survived.

Moving faster now, they crossed what was left of the park and went in.

SIGNAL EIGHT

The chairman of the Nightrise Corporation was watching the final destruction of his necropolis. He was back in his office on the sixty-sixth floor of The Nail and he could feel the whole building trembling as it was buffeted again and again by the storm. Every now and then there was a grinding sound followed by an explosion of breaking glass as another window burst out of its frame. The lights had long ago flickered and gone out. There was no power in the office. Nor were there any people. The staff had all evacuated, fighting and clawing their way down sixty-six flights of stairs. Some of them might have made it to the basement and would be huddled there now, but he suspected that many more of them would have been killed on the way down—pushed down the stairs or trampled in the general panic. The chairman certainly had no intention of joining them. He was safe here. The Nail could stand up to anything. And it was a spectacular view.

It did trouble him that his plans had somehow gone wrong. The city had been meant to die. That had been the whole idea. But not like this. Indeed, the typhoon might well end up saving many more people than it actually killed because there had been a side-effect. The poisonous gases put in place by the Old Ones had been dispersed. The pollution had been swept away. When the storm finally eased off, the people would be able to breathe again.

He didn't know what had happened at Victoria Prison. All the telephone lines were down and even his mobile didn't work. The whole network must have collapsed. But this devastation couldn't be a coincidence. The girl must have brought it. She was able to predict the weather so at the very least she must have known it was coming. He had put the boy in with her to taunt her, to show her how completely defeated she had been. Perhaps, all in all, it had been a mistake.

He was holding a bottle of Cognac. It had a price tag that made it one of the most expensive in the world and it had always amused him that there were people dying in some countries because they had no water while he could afford to spend five thousand dollars on a drink he didn't even enjoy. Over the years, most of the chairman's taste buds had died. Nothing he ate or drank had any flavour. If he was killed now, it would hardly matter. Most of him was dead anyway.

But he wasn't going to die. Even if Matt and Scarlett had escaped, there was nowhere for them to go. The Tai Shan Temple was protected. They wouldn't be able to reach the door. And soon the typhoon would have passed. He would begin the search through the wreckage immediately, turning it over brick by brick, and next time he would deal with them at once.

He noticed something out of the corner of his eye. It was a speck in the window. At first he thought it was a bird. No. It was extraordinary. As the chairman watched, it grew larger and larger. It was heading towards him.

It was a ship.

Not a huge ship. A wooden *sampan*, one of the Chinese sailing boats that were kept moored up in the harbour, to be photographed by tourists. The wind had grabbed it and torn it free. Even as the chairman watched, it was getting closer, rapidly filling up the window frame. He stood there, transfixed by the sight. He thought about running. Perhaps he could still make it to safety. But what was the point? How could he escape something that had been predicted so many years ago?

He would die in an accident that involved a ship.

He died now.

The *sampan* was thrown at The Nail as if it were a paper dart that had been deliberately aimed. It smashed through the window on the sixty-sixth floor and into the man who stood behind it. At the

362

same time, the wind howled in, scooping up the contents of the room and throwing them out, the files and papers rattling with a sound that was very like applause. The broken body of the chairman went with them, spun once in the air, then plunged down to the pavement below.

Bloodstains on the carpet. A bottle of Cognac with its contents gurgling out. A scattering of broken glass. In the end, that was all that was left.

SIGNAL NINE

There had been a bloody battle inside the Tai Shan Temple. All the bodies had been taken into one of the other chambers, but the evidence was still there in the bullet holes across the walls, rubble and scorch marks from a grenade, a puddle of blood in front of the main altar. One of the porcelain gods was standing with his arms outstretched, but his body now ended at his neck, which was jagged and hollow. His head was in pieces all around him. Another had lost a hand. It was as if they had tried to take part in the fight and had been crippled as a result.

Jet and Sing had been on their own, waiting for Scarlett and the others to arrive. They had no idea how she had managed to cross Hong Kong—it would have been impossible now to leave the building—but they were glad to see her when she walked in. Jet had been wounded. He was holding a dressing against his neck, and his shirt was soaked in blood. Sing was still holding the sword

363

stick that he had used to kill Audrey Cheng. He seemed to be unhurt.

Neither of them had noticed that there was another man in the chamber, hiding underneath the altar. He was one of the chairman's men and he had been shot twice. It was his blood that was pooling out. He knew he didn't have very long. There was a gun inches from his outstretched hand.

Speaking in Chinese, Lohan demanded a report from his two lieutenants. Quickly, they told him what he wanted to know and he translated for Matthew and Richard.

'There were many people waiting here,' he said. 'They would have killed you if you had tried to reach the door. But they have all been dealt with . . .'

'Then let's get out of here,' Richard said. He turned to Matt. 'It's time to go.'

Lohan walked forward and shook Scarlett's hand. 'Good luck,' he said. 'The journey that we made together just now is something that I will never forget.'

'I'm glad I met you, Lohan,' Scarlett said. 'Thank you for helping me.' She had relaxed a little, but Matt could see that she was still concentrating, keeping the typhoon at bay. She had to stay in control. While she was inside the temple the wind and the rain were barely touching its walls.

The door with the five-pointed star was in front of them. It seemed so small and ordinary that it was hard to believe that it would lead them, not outside and into the storm but to anywhere in the world.

'So where are we going, Matt?' Jamie asked.

The dying man had fumbled for the gun. From where he was lying he could only see the two boys and the Chinese man who had arrived with them. The girl was standing right behind and the other man was somewhere out of sight. He could probably take out at least two of them before he was killed himself. He had decided that was what he would do. After all, it was the reason he was here.

Which one first?

The boy who had just asked the question—the one with the long hair and the American accent—was directly in his sight. Slowly, the man took aim. The boy was only a few steps away. The man's hand was sticky with his own blood. The gun was covered in it. But he knew exactly what he was doing. There was no way he was going to miss.

Then the door with the five-pointed star opened.

Scott, with Pedro right behind him, burst into the temple. Jamie opened his mouth to speak. Matt was gazing in surprise. What had seemed impossible for so long had finally happened. The Gatekeepers had come together. They were all here, in the same space.

Scott. Jamie. Matt. Pedro. And Scarlett.

The Five.

But Scott hadn't stopped. He ran forward and threw himself at his brother, knocking him aside.

A second later there was a gun shot.

Lohan acted with lightning speed. His own gun was in his hand instantly and he fired five times, the bullets strafing underneath the altar. The man who had been concealed there was killed before he could fire again.

Richard saw that Jamie was all right. Somehow Scott had known and had arrived in time to save him. But then Matt cried out.

The shot had missed Jamie, but Scarlett had been standing right behind him. She had been hit in the head and the wound was a bad one. Blood was pouring down the side of her neck. She toppled sideways. Richard caught her before she hit the floor.

And as she lost consciousness, the whole world exploded.

The typhoon had been kept at bay for too long. Now, as if recognizing what had happened, it fell on the Tai Shan Temple with all its strength. It was like being hit by a bomb, but in slow motion. As the nine of them stood there—the five Gatekeepers with Richard, Lohan, Jet and Sing— the whole building disintegrated around them. The roof was the first to go, torn off as if by a giant hand. Green tiles came crashing down. The wind roared in. Then one of the walls buckled and collapsed, the huge stones toppling forward. For centuries, the gods inside the temple had never seen daylight. Now they were flooded in it as the outside world burst in.

'The door!' Matt shouted.

It was still standing, but it wouldn't be there for long. Once the walls were destroyed it would all be over. The door would go with them. Even now it might be too late. Jamie had joined his brother. The two of them had already turned towards it. Pedro seemed to be confused, frozen to the spot. Matt reached him and spun him round. Richard was hurrying forward, carrying Scarlett who was in his arms, limp, her eyes closed. Lohan followed. One of the spinning tiles had hit him and he was cradling his arm. There was no sign of his two lieutenants, Jet and Sing. They had disappeared beneath the broken wall.

The door had been built for the Gatekeepers, but each of them could take one companion with them. Richard was with Scarlett. Lohan was with Matt. There was still a chance they could all get out alive.

There was another explosion and a great hole suddenly appeared, punched into the wall. Rain and daylight came shafting through. The whole temple was shaking. Scott was the first to reach the door and threw it open. Behind him, the remaining gods were toppling and smashing to pieces on the hard floor. Pedro was next to him. The others were right behind.

They plunged through just as a last bolt of lightning struck the temple, pulverizing it. The remaining walls were swept away and scattered. Moments later, there was nothing left. Hong Kong Park was empty. And beyond it, Hong Kong itself lay in ruins as the clouds finally parted and the first, small ray of sunlight was allowed through.

SIGNAL TEN

The Necropolis was finished.

Much of it had been destroyed. More than half the skyscrapers had collapsed. Whole streets were buried beneath piles of twisted metal and brickwork that would take years to remove. Scavengers were already hard at work, burrowing into the rubble to find the jewellery—the diamond necklaces and the watches—that must surely lie beneath.

All over the world, people were waking up to the fact that a catastrophe on a massive scale had occurred. Twenty-four hour television news programmes were running the first pictures. There would be thousands dead, but at least the survivors would be able to breathe. The poisonous smog that had been suffocating them for so long had been completely swept aside.

Far away, sitting in the ice palace that he had made his home, the King of the Old Ones saw what had happened. He knew that the chairman had failed him. He knew that the Gatekeepers had escaped.

But it didn't matter.

The Five had entered the door without knowing where they were going, so none of them would have arrived in the same place. They would be as far apart now as they had ever been. Worse than that, the door had been disintegrating even as they had passed through it, and the final blast had played one last trick on them. If the five of them had survived the journey, they would find out very soon.

It would be a very long time before they found each other again.

It was enough.

The King of the Old Ones reached out and gave the order that his disciples had been waiting for. He had made the decision. It was time for the end of the world to begin.